PRAISE FOR *SAL...*

"A fast-paced, sometimes brutal thriller reminiscent of Dan Brown's *The Da Vinci Code.*"

Booklist (starred review)

"A hair-raising thrill ride."

—*Library Journal* (starred review)

"The fascinating historical information combined with a storyline ripped from the headlines will hook conspiracy theorists and action addicts alike."

—*Kirkus Reviews*

"Fans of *The Da Vinci Code* are going to love this book . . . One of my favorite reads of 2016."

—*Crimespree Magazine*

"This suspenseful tale has something for absolutely everyone to enjoy."

—*Suspense Magazine*

PRAISE FOR *MERCY'S CHASE*

"An immersive voice, an intriguing story, a wonderful character—highly recommended!"

—Lee Child, #1 *New York Times* bestselling author

"Both a sweeping adventure and race-against-time thriller, *Mercy's Chase* is fascinating, fierce, and brimming with heart—just like its heroine, Salem Wiley."

—Meg Gardiner, author of *Into the Black Nowhere*

"Action-packed, great writing taut with suspense, an appealing main character to root for—who could ask for anything more?"

—Buried Under Books

PRAISE FOR *THE TAKEN ONES*

"Setting the standard for top-notch thrillers, *The Taken Ones* is smart, compelling, and filled with utterly real characters. Lourey brings her formidable storytelling talent to the game and, on top of that, wows us with a deft stylistic touch. This is a one-sitting read!"

—Jeffery Deaver, author of *The Bone Collector* and *The Watchmaker's Hand*

"*The Taken Ones* has Jess Lourey's trademark of suspense all the way. A damaged and brave heroine, an equally damaged evildoer, and missing girls from long ago all combine to keep the reader rushing through to the explosive ending."

—Charlaine Harris, *New York Times* bestselling author

"Lourey is at the top of her game with *The Taken Ones*. A master of building tension while maintaining a riveting pace, Lourey is a hell of a writer on all fronts, but her greatest talent may be her characters. Evangeline Reed, an agent with the Minnesota Bureau of Criminal Apprehension, is a woman with a devastating past and the haunting ability to know the darkest crimes happening around her. She is also exactly the kind of character I would happily follow through a dozen books or more. In awe of her bravery, I also identified with her pain and wanted desperately to protect her. Along with an incredible cast of support characters, *The Taken Ones* will break your heart wide open and stay with you long after you've turned the final page. This is a 2023 must read."

—Danielle Girard, *USA Today* and Amazon #1 bestselling author of *Up Close*

"Jess Lourey is a master of the coming-of-age thriller, and *The Quarry Girls* may be her best yet—as dark, twisty, and full of secrets as the tunnels that lurk beneath Pantown's deceptively idyllic streets."
—Chris Holm, Anthony Award–winning author of *The Killing Kind*

PRAISE FOR *BLOODLINE*

Winner of the 2022 Anthony Award for Best Paperback Original

Winner of the 2022 ITW Thriller Award for Best Paperback Original

Short-listed for the 2021 Goodreads Choice Awards

"Fans of *Rosemary's Baby* will relish this."
—*Publishers Weekly*

"Based on a true story, this is a sinister, suspenseful thriller full of creeping horror."
—*Kirkus Reviews*

"Lourey ratchets up the fear in a novel that verges on horror."
—*Library Journal*

"In *Bloodline*, Jess Lourey blends elements of mystery, suspense, and horror to stunning effect."
—*BOLO Books*

"Inspired by a true story, it's a creepy page-turner that has me eager to read more of Ms. Lourey's works, especially if they're all as incisive as this thought-provoking novel."

—Criminal Element

"*Bloodline* by Jess Lourey is a psychological thriller that grabbed me from the beginning and didn't let go."

—*Mystery & Suspense Magazine*

"*Bloodline* blends page-turning storytelling with clever homages to such horror classics as *Rosemary's Baby*, *The Stepford Wives*, and *Harvest Home*."

—*Toronto Star*

"*Bloodline* is a terrific, creepy thriller, and Jess Lourey clearly knows how to get under your skin."

—Bookreporter

"[A] tightly coiled domestic thriller that slowly but persuasively builds the suspense."

—*South Florida Sun Sentinel*

"I should know better than to pick up a new Jess Lourey book thinking I'll just peek at the first few pages and then get back to the book I was reading. Six hours later, it's three in the morning and I'm racing through the last few chapters, unable to sleep until I know how it all ends. Set in an idyllic small town rooted in family history and horrific secrets, *Bloodline* is *Pleasantville* meets *Rosemary's Baby*. A deeply unsettling, darkly unnerving, and utterly compelling novel, this book chilled me to the core, and I loved every bit of it."

—Jennifer Hillier, author of *Little Secrets* and the award-winning *Jar of Hearts*

"Jess Lourey writes small-town Minnesota like Stephen King writes small-town Maine. *Bloodline* is a tremendous book with a heart and a hacksaw . . . and I loved every second of it."
—Rachel Howzell Hall, author of the critically acclaimed novels *And Now She's Gone* and *They All Fall Down*

PRAISE FOR *UNSPEAKABLE THINGS*

Winner of the 2021 Anthony Award for Best Paperback Original

Short-listed for the 2021 Edgar Awards and 2020 Goodreads Choice Awards

"The suspense never wavers in this page-turner."
—*Publishers Weekly*

"The atmospheric suspense novel is haunting because it's narrated from the point of view of a thirteen-year-old, an age that should be more innocent but often isn't. Even more chilling, it's based on real-life incidents. Lourey may be known for comic capers (*March of Crimes*), but this tense novel combines the best of a coming-of-age story with suspense and an unforgettable young narrator."
—*Library Journal* (starred review)

"Part suspense, part coming-of-age, Jess Lourey's *Unspeakable Things* is a story of creeping dread, about childhood when you know the monster under your bed is real. A novel that clings to you long after the last page."
—Lori Rader-Day, Edgar Award–nominated author of *Under a Dark Sky*

"A noose of a novel that tightens by inches. The squirming tension comes from every direction—including the ones that are supposed to be safe. I felt complicit as I read, as if at any moment I stopped I would be abandoning Cassie, alone, in the dark, straining to listen and fearing to hear."

—Marcus Sakey, bestselling author of *Brilliance*

"*Unspeakable Things* is an absolutely riveting novel about the poisonous secrets buried deep in towns and families. Jess Lourey has created a story that will chill you to the bone and a main character who will break your heart wide open."

—Lou Berney, Edgar Award–winning author of *November Road*

"Inspired by a true story, *Unspeakable Things* crackles with authenticity, humanity, and humor. The novel reminded me of *To Kill a Mockingbird* and *The Marsh King's Daughter*. Highly recommended."

—Mark Sullivan, bestselling author of *Beneath a Scarlet Sky*

"Jess Lourey does a masterful job building tension and dread, but her greatest asset in *Unspeakable Things* is Cassie—an arresting narrator you identify with, root for, and desperately want to protect. This is a book that will stick with you long after you've torn through it."

—Rob Hart, author of *The Warehouse*

"With *Unspeakable Things*, Jess Lourey has managed the near-impossible, crafting a mystery as harrowing as it is tender, as gut-wrenching as it is lyrical. There is real darkness here, a creeping, inescapable dread that more than once had me looking over my own shoulder. But at its heart beats the irrepressible—and irresistible—spirit of its . . . heroine, a young woman so bright and vital and brave she kept even the fiercest monsters at bay. This is a book that will stay with me for a long time."

—Elizabeth Little, *Los Angeles Times* bestselling author of *Dear Daughter* and *Pretty as a Picture*

PRAISE FOR *THE CATALAIN BOOK OF SECRETS*

"Life-affirming, thought-provoking, heartwarming, it's one of those books which—if you happen to read it exactly when you need to—will heal your wounds as you turn the pages."
—Catriona McPherson, Agatha, Anthony, Macavity, and Bruce Alexander Award–winning author

"Prolific mystery writer Lourey tells of a matriarchal clan of witches joining forces against age-old evil . . . The novel is tightly plotted, and Lourey shines when depicting relationships—romantic ones as well as tangled links between Catalains . . . Lourey emphasizes the ties that bind in spite of secrets and resentment."
—*Kirkus Reviews*

"Lourey expertly concocts a Gothic fusion of long-held secrets, melancholy, and resolve . . . Exquisitely written in naturally flowing, expressive language, the book delves into the special relationships between sisters, and mothers and daughters."
—*Publishers Weekly*

PRAISE FOR *MAY DAY*

"Jess Lourey writes about a small-town assistant librarian, but this is no genteel traditional mystery. Mira James likes guys in a big way, likes booze, and isn't afraid of motorcycles. She flees a dead-end job and a dead-end boyfriend in Minneapolis and ends up in Battle Lake, a little town with plenty of dirty secrets. The first-person narrative in *May Day* is fresh, the characters quirky. Minnesota has many fine crime writers, and Jess Lourey has just entered their ranks!"

—Ellen Hart, award-winning author of the Jane Lawless and Sophie Greenway series

"This trade paperback packed a punch . . . I loved it from the get-go!"

—*Tulsa World*

"What a romp this is! I found myself laughing out loud."

—*Crimespree Magazine*

"Mira digs up a closetful of dirty secrets, including sex parties, cross-dressing, and blackmail, on her way to exposing the killer. Lourey's debut has a likable heroine and surfeit of sass."

—*Kirkus Reviews*

PRAISE FOR *REWRITE YOUR LIFE: DISCOVER YOUR TRUTH THROUGH THE HEALING POWER OF FICTION*

"Interweaving practical advice with stories and insights garnered in her own writing journey, Jessica Lourey offers a step-by-step guide for writers struggling to create fiction from their life experiences. But this book isn't just about writing. It's also about the power of stories to transform those who write them. I know of no other guide that delivers on its promise with such honesty, simplicity, and beauty."

—William Kent Krueger, *New York Times* bestselling author of the Cork O'Connor series and *Ordinary Grace*

SALEM'S CIPHER

YOUNG ADULT

A Whisper of Poison

MURDER BY MONTH MYSTERIES

May Day

June Bug

Knee High by the Fourth of July

August Moon

September Mourn

October Fest

November Hunt

December Dread

January Thaw

February Fever

March of Crimes

April Fools

NONFICTION

Rewrite Your Life: Discover Your Truth Through the Healing Power of Fiction

SALEM'S CIPHER

JESS LOUREY

 THOMAS & MERCER

Text copyright © 2016, 2019, 2024 by Jess Lourey
All rights reserved.

No part of this book may be reproduced, or stored in a retrieval system, or transmitted in any form or by any means, electronic, mechanical, photocopying, recording, or otherwise, without express written permission of the publisher.

Published by Thomas & Mercer, Seattle

www.apub.com

Amazon, the Amazon logo, and Thomas & Mercer are trademarks of Amazon.com, Inc., or its affiliates.

ISBN-13: 9781662519192 (paperback)
ISBN-13: 9781662519185 (digital)

Cover design by Caroline Teagle Johnson
Cover image: © Mehul Patel / Arcangel; © matejmo / Getty Images

Printed in the United States of America

To Jill, my wise, efficient, and kind partner in crime

PROLOGUE

Linden Hills, Minneapolis

Grace Odegaard inserted her key into the top dead bolt and rotated it. The lock slid free with a satisfying *snick*. She repeated the action with the three locks below, humming to herself, a satisfied smile anchoring her face. The date had gone well. Not great—she could have done without the corny jokes—but good enough. He was a high school soccer coach. The conversation had flowed easily. At the end of the night, he'd kissed her. Not too sloppy, exactly the right length of time. He'd even held her face when his lips brushed hers, just like in the movies.

Her smile widened.

"Out late, aren't you?"

Grace jumped, her heart pounding. "Mrs. Gladia." Her neighbor of seven years stood in the shadows of the hallway, hair askew. She wore a quilted robe and slippers.

"Was it a date?" Mrs. Gladia stepped into the light. Her dog, Dante, a ratty puff of yellowish fur, was tucked under her arm.

Grace threw the beast a look. He snarled at her. She'd dog-sat him before, but their relationship had never thawed beyond this stage, primarily because Dante was an asshole. "It was. Our first."

"Did he drive a nice car?"

Grace coughed to mask a laugh. As far as she could tell, Mrs. Gladia hadn't been on a date since the '50s. "I don't know what he drove, but I liked his smile."

Mrs. Gladia tipped her chin and studied Grace. Dante growled, a tiny machine gun of fruitless anger low in his chest. Mrs. Gladia patted his flattened ears. "You're a good girl, Grace. Make sure to lock your doors. This world isn't safe." She shuffled back into the shadows and down the hall.

Grace waited until Mrs. Gladia entered and locked her apartment before crossing into her own two-bedroom, smiling at the glittery jack-o'-lantern cutouts that decorated the door. Tomorrow was Halloween, and she hoped for trick-or-treaters. She tossed her purse onto a chair and stretched before engaging all four locks. Flicking on the TV for background noise, she kicked off her shoes and padded to the bathroom to remove her makeup and brush her teeth.

"The wave of refugees threatens to overwhelm the bordering European nations, with upward of four million people fleeing the conflict. Coming up after the break, this year's presidential election is nine days away and has already broken all campaign . . ."

She hummed as she swiped her eyelids with Vaseline. Forty-nine years old and she was holding up okay, if she did say so herself. Wrinkles around her eyes only when she smiled. She'd been thinking about squirting Botox into those. Her auburn hair had sprouted a few grays, which she plucked the second they appeared. Tummy and thighs had bounced back almost immediately after she birthed Isabel, the welcome result of a one-night stand, twenty-nine years earlier. She'd kept them tight with yoga and weightlifting ever since.

She wiped the last traces of the day from her face, leaving a beige streak on the plush towel. Bel had tried to talk her into wearing less makeup. Made her look older than she was, her daughter argued. Grace had said she'd think about it.

She hadn't.

She glanced at the king-size pillow-top calling her name. Bright and early tomorrow, she was scheduled to show a $2.25 million French

Colonial on the north side of Lake of the Isles. She needed to be on her game.

She clicked the off button on the TV remote at the exact moment a single knock struck her door.

"Mrs. Gladia?" she called out through her door. "It's late."

No answer.

Grace shrugged. Maybe it had been an echo from the TV. She glided across the living room toward her bedroom.

A second knock sounded.

"Mrs. Gladia? I'm going to bed."

Still no answer.

Grace sighed and made her way to the front door. She undid the top lock, then the second, then the third. She had the fourth dead bolt in hand before it occurred to her to peer through the spy hole. Time had made her careless.

What she saw on the other side stopped her breath.

She twisted the fourth lock and whipped the door open. "Vee? What's wrong?"

Her friend spilled through the doorway. Vida's lovely silver and black hair, normally styled in a tight bun, was disheveled. Dark bags packed her eyes. She spun and began locking the door before she was entirely inside the room.

"Have you seen the news?"

Grace stared at the dark television. "I just had it on. Why?"

"We need to leave." Vida turned to face Grace. "Now."

"To where?"

Vida didn't answer. She didn't have to. It was etched in the lines of her face.

Grace's stomach lurched. "It's happened?"

"Another one isn't answering her phone. It's only a matter of time." Vida patted the necklace under her shirt. Grace wore an identical one, half a pink quartz heart, the word *love* etched in it. Bel and Salem had bought them for their moms a decade ago, keeping the other halves for themselves. "We have to tell the girls. In person. The phones aren't safe."

Grace's hand flew to her mouth. "They're not ready," she whispered.

Vida rubbed her eyes. "They're going to have to be. Your suitcase is packed?"

Grace nodded and hurried into her bedroom. She grabbed the duffel from her closet. Of course it was packed. It had been packed since Daniel's murder fourteen years earlier.

"You'll bring it?" Vida stood at the bedroom door, her mouth a tight slice.

Grace's eyes swooped to her nightstand. Daniel, Vida's husband, had built it for one purpose before he died. Grace knelt, pushed four concealed wooden buttons in a prescribed order, and turned the knob on the front panel. A tiny drawer popped open. It held a single item the size of a quarter.

Vida peered over Grace's shoulder. They both stared at the silver locket. The top loop was strung with a platinum chain, nearly unbreakable. A milky seed pearl dripped off the bottom. The locket's hinge was delicate, microscopic.

The inside was smooth except for one engraved word: *mercy*.

"Hide it," Vida commanded. "If we lose that, we lose everything. We *all* lose everything."

Grace stood up too quickly, knocking over the table and the lamp it held. The light crashed to the ground, flashing jerky, macabre shadows across the room. Hands shaking, she righted the lamp and scooped up the locket. It took her three tries to slip the chain over her neck. She tucked the jewelry under her sweater, next to her quartz half heart.

"I'm ready."

Vida nodded curtly, but her face was crumpling. She gathered Grace in an embrace. "I'd hoped it would never come to this."

Grace clung to her for a moment. It felt greedy. They pulled apart and darted toward the front door, their breath matched and quick.

For one sweet second, Grace thought of the future. Of making it out of this alive. Of protecting Salem and Bel, more precious to them than their own lives.

But then she spotted it.

The door handle twisting slowly, a snake in a bush. It took every thing within Grace not to whimper.

Vida grabbed Grace's hand, her finger flying to her lips in warning. Eyes pinned to the doorknob, Vida eased her hand into her jacket and tugged out a wooden box etched with an Om symbol, setting it on the TV stand next to her.

Grace smiled bitterly, recognizing the container for what it was: a fail-safe should they not escape this apartment. She and Vida exchanged a glance pregnant with regret. Beads of sweat erupted on Grace's top lip. She could taste her own salt as she stared at the door, bracing herself.

The door handle stopped moving, replaced by a loud knocking. "Grace! What is all that racket over there? Me and Dante are trying to sleep."

A hot wave of relief washed over Grace. "It's Mrs. Gladia. My neighbor." She attempted to reassure Vida with a smile, but her mouth was too dry and her top lip caught on her teeth. She strode forward to unlock the door.

Vida tried to hold her back, but Grace brushed her off. "You've met her. The Italian widow from next door? If I don't calm her down, she'll never let us leave. Besides, this door is the only way out."

Grace slid open the first dead bolt.

Then the second.

The third.

The fourth.

The air grew syrupy. The heat of it felt impossibly drowsy. She inched the door open.

The apartment shadows shifted as the hallway lights slithered in. Grace's animal brain, her deep instinctual self, screamed at her to run.

She ignored it. She would not lose herself to panic. She would behave normally. That was the only way she and Vida were going to survive this. When your neighbor knocks, you answer.

Only when she landed eyes on Mrs. Gladia on the other side of the door, miserable Dante snarling in the crook of her arm, did she realize she'd been holding her breath. She exhaled in a loud *whoosh*.

Mrs. Gladia was scowling. The sleep-flyaways in her hair made her expression difficult to take seriously. A relieved laugh forced its way out of Grace, but it was shrill, a teakettle giggle. She waved the air as if to erase the sound.

"Sorry, Mrs. Gladia. You remember my friend Vee? We were just going out for a—"

A symphony of tiny pops erupted from the hallway next to Mrs. Gladia, as if a hundred mouse bones were cracking and snapping back into place. Vida's fingertips dug into Grace's shoulder.

What happened next took less than a second.

The blade flashed from the shadows. Dante barked, but it was too late. The knife unzipped Mrs. Gladia's neck, its steel so sharp that for a moment, her flesh was too shocked to bleed. It could only quiver, a deep-red jelly.

Mrs. Gladia turned toward the assailant and gargled. A bloody bubble moistened her lips.

The first spurt erupted from her neck, the counterstroke to her vanishing heartbeat. It sprayed the walls to the right of the apartment door, washed the front of her robe, poured across the floor. Mrs. Gladia dropped Dante. He began yapping in earnest. She toppled backward like a felled tree.

On the floor above, one door opened, and then another. The muffle of voices drifted down. Dante's barks were waking up the building. He licked at his mistress's blood between yelps, an asshole to the end.

Grace would never know any of this.

Vida had grabbed her at the first glint of wicked steel, ripped the duffel bag from her hand, and shoved her toward the window. She'd yanked it open and leaped onto the fire escape, urging Grace to follow.

Grace stuck her head out the window. She hesitated.

Three stories below, a smattering of people walked in the cool fall air. They weren't moving quite right, ambulating a little too slowly, with a little too much precision, like well-crafted robots.

Or puppets.

Grace blinked. The people below shifted, walking normally. It must have been a trick of her eyes. It didn't matter. She had only one option, really.

"Run!" Vida yelled, seizing the collar of Grace's sweater and jerking her out the window.

Behind them, the killer broke Dante's neck with a single smooth twist and stepped over Mrs. Gladia's spouting body and into the apartment. He surveyed the space, eyes darting to the open window.

Grace's white linen curtains danced on the smoke-scented breeze.

He cleaned and then sheathed his blade.

Next, he placed his gloved hands on each side of his skull. The shape of his face began to change—first the brow bones, advancing to the cheeks, and then the nose and mouth.

From long practice, he kept from crying out at the pain.

If he hurried, he could still acquire the women.

MONDAY

OCTOBER 31

CHAPTER 1

Uptown, Minneapolis

"You've been coming home late. I worry."

He stared at her.

Salem planted her hands on her hips. "Strong and beautiful," her mom called her curves, exhorting her to be proud of her half-Persian heritage. The generous hips and thighs came with a head of unruly, dark curls and khaki-green eyes that tipped slightly at the outer edges. From her dad, an Iowa transplant, she'd inherited skin that burned easily, an Irish nose more potato than patrician, and a small chest that did *not* counterbalance her booty. Her best friend, Bel, referred to her as "farm girl on top, phat magic below."

Her mismatched parts had never bothered *him*, though. He'd always been loyal, neither needy nor distant. A perfect balance. That was, until the past two weeks, when his nights out had grown inexplicably late and then later.

"You're tomcatting around, aren't you?"

He held his tongue, watching her coolly.

She sighed, the puff of air pushing a curl out of her eyes. "I deserve better, you know? Have you even seen this?"

She pointed toward the copy of *Minneapolis Magazine*. The cover headline was **Top Twentysomethings to Watch** over a photo of Carl Ivy, a twenty-six-year-old Edina native who'd developed a meme-generating app that simultaneously placed the same image on a dozen different sites, generating a unique, web-vetted, guaranteed-hilarious caption for each of the twelve posts. He'd named the app Looking Glass. Mark Zuckerberg had offered him $3 million for it.

"My face is on page twenty-seven, not that you'd care."

Actually, Salem didn't care, either, unless embarrassment counted. She'd grown up watching her mom, Vida Wiley, deal with the surprising amount of media attention that came with being one of the country's most controversial history professors, and one of the few specializing in women's history. Whenever a politician stuck his foot in his mouth commenting on rape or reproduction or some new international atrocity was committed, Professor Wiley was called on to comment. Behind closed doors, she joked that the media saw her as the "Woman Whisperer." Salem thought it was more likely that they knew her mom could be counted on to contribute jet fuel to any fire.

Professor Wiley's comments always made the news, typically to the chagrin of the Hill College regents who signed her paycheck. The most recent brouhaha had developed when a *New York Post* reporter called Dr. Wiley's office to ask her opinion on the source of the recent virulent media attacks on Democratic senator Gina Hayes, the first viable female presidential candidate in the history of the United States.

Dr. Wiley had offered to send the reporter a mirror and a greased shoehorn to help her remove her head from her own ass.

Professor Wiley's opinions unsurprisingly generated death threats. Buckets of 'em. For a well-armed segment of the population, there was nothing more unnatural, more threatening, more demanding of elimination than a woman with an opinion and an audience.

Salem had learned that young.

Subsequently, she went out of her way to dodge the public eye. Bel teased her that she even avoided having opinions for fear of turning into her mother.

Bel wasn't far off.

Salem's chosen field—a double degree in computer science and mathematics with an emphasis in cryptanalysis as an undergrad, and a fresh master of science in computational analysis and public policy—all from the University of Minnesota—had created a perfect place to hide. At least it had until the news leaked about the breakthrough she'd made two years ago last spring as she was outlining her master's thesis.

It involved two words guaranteed to set the technological community abuzz: quantum computing.

The idea that a computer could run on multidimensional qubits rather than binary digits, processing information a million times faster than the best computer operating today, wasn't new, but the reality of it was fifteen years out. That was, until Salem stumbled across an anomaly while researching Charles Babbage's Difference Engine 2 for her thesis. Babbage, a nineteenth-century polymath famous for his work on computational design, came as close to being a rock star as a mathematician was allowed.

Sure, he'd been a fist-shaking grump, but in addition to conceiving the first computer, he'd established the modern postal system, invented the locomotive cowcatcher and the ophthalmoscope, and cracked Vigenère's autokey cipher, previously believed to be unbreakable.

Salem's Babbage research had been preliminary, really only intended as background for her thesis on cryptanalysis and government security. It was while collating the cipher research with the Difference Engine data that she'd made her unexpected breakthrough. Two seemingly unrelated pages of research had accidentally fallen to the floor. When she reached to pick them up, the link between them shone like a beacon: the modular arithmetic Babbage used to solve Vigenère's cipher could be applied to a binary digit at the atomic level.

Two great tastes that taste great together!

She remembered a cold sweat breaking out. If she was seeing what she thought she was seeing, it would revolutionize the field of computers and computer science.

She'd immediately changed the focus of her research.

The offers to publish her findings began to roll in before she'd even finished her thesis. Every outlet wanted to be the first to announce the quantum computing breakthrough. And indeed, once her thesis was written and published, her discovery turned the security world in particular on its ear. If her innovation played out as hypothesized, it would result in a quantum computer with the power to solve the deepest cryptography and blow through the thickest firewall in less than a second. As a result, the head of the National Security Agency, among others, had been requesting meetings with her for the past two months.

She'd deflected those. Since the day fourteen years earlier when her dad had killed himself, she'd avoided anything that required leaving her familiar path. She was happy teaching North Minneapolis kids how to use Microsoft Office, her job for the past year. The building was familiar. The kids liked her. She didn't correct them when they called her "Salem Whitey" rather than "Salem Wiley," didn't back down when they dared her to dance whatever the latest craze was.

And her thesis adviser had recently offered her a research position at the U of M to supplement her income. She planned on accepting it. The job would mean she'd need to travel to only three places, not counting shopping or doctor's visits: her apartment, the Jordan Neighborhood Community Center, and the University of Minnesota. So what if her adviser had offered the research job as a way to keep her active in computer innovation, a last-ditch effort to save her from "wasting the code-breaking genius" she'd displayed in her thesis?

And anyhow, her idea was only theory at this point.

Enough theory to get her onto page twenty-seven of *Minneapolis Magazine*'s "Top Twentysomethings to Watch," though.

"Meow."

"That's all you have to say for yourself?" Salem asked her cat, who was still largely ignoring her. "You finally talk, and that's all I get?"

She scooped up Beans, nuzzling his head in her neck. She loved the softness of his glossy black fur. A purr rumbled just under the surface.

"Because I expected more from you. A confession, maybe. You've got a lady kitty out there, don't you?"

She leaned over the windowsill he'd been perched on, hugging him tighter. Beans had come with her Uptown apartment. She knew her mom hadn't wanted her to move out of the house, had in fact assumed she never would. While Salem had turned down several scholarships to colleges on either coast because her palms turned clammy at the thought of venturing outside the Twin Cities, she knew she had to get out from beneath her mother's thumb. So, right before she'd first enrolled at the U of M, she'd also upped her Ativan prescription and moved to Uptown, quickly establishing a routine to feel safe.

She inhaled deeply, enjoying the greasy sweetness wafting up from Glam Doll Donuts. She knew it was a leftover smell from yesterday, that the workers wouldn't arrive to begin tomorrow's batch of deep-fried sweetness for a few more hours, but her mouth watered nonetheless. The sour cherry pistachio was her favorite, a fluffy cake donut wrapped around a tart filling.

And they delivered.

Her best friend, Bel, three years older and in her second year on the Chicago police force, would ream Salem inside out if she knew she left her window unlocked on the nights Beans was roaming. Bel—who'd grown up J.Crew beautiful, strawberry-blonde with skin like cream, who felt any teasing of Salem as her own pain, who'd come out in eleventh grade and never looked back—had always looked out for Salem, knuckle-sandwiching the bullies in elementary school and slaying them with scathing words when they reached South High School.

Salem missed Bel so much. They'd grown apart in the last few years, with Bel in Chicago and Salem not willing to leave Minnesota. Salem did like being able to keep her windows open without getting shit for it, though. She lived on the second floor. Who was going to risk the fire escape to get to her?

She glanced at the clock. Almost bar close, so Connor might stop by soon. She didn't confess to Beans that this was really why she was up so late. Connor Sawyer had read the *Minneapolis Magazine* article and called Salem immediately. He'd said he missed her. She knew he didn't. A tall blonde lawyer whom she'd met when she was working at the U of M Law Library and he'd come by to pick up some files, Connor had only ever found time for her when the bars let out. She knew she deserved better. But who did it hurt to let him stop by every now and again? Anyhow, the guy was a wizard in bed.

She set Beans on the couch and shuffled to the mirror to check her makeup for the fifth time. She tousled her hair, touched up her lip gloss. It took a lot of energy to look natural.

Her phone rang, pulling her out of her contemplation.

She sighed. At least he'd bothered to call. Usually he would either show or he wouldn't.

She addressed her cat before she reached for the phone. "What do you think is the excuse this time, Beansy? Too drunk? Respects me too much to sneak around? It's been at least four months since I heard that one. Maybe it'll sound new all over again."

Disappointment heavy on her shoulders, she grabbed the iPhone from the table. A photo of Bel's smiling face, all blue eyes and white teeth, flashed at her. Salem's heart tumbled. Bel never called this late. Salem's hand flew to the scar on her left cheek.

"Isabel?"

"Salem? It's my mom." Bel's voice cracked. "The police are at her apartment. There's blood everywhere."

CHAPTER 2

Five Years Old

"You're the luckiest duck."

Salem sits back on her heels and shoves her night-vision goggles onto the top of her head. They don't work very well, but a movie starring children as spies has recently been released, and the secret agent equipment is being peddled at every toy store. Salem's parents and Bel's mom have pooled their money to buy the girls all the fun gear—the goggles, an invisible ink pen, a lie detector that's really an electronic blood pressure cuff.

The two of them have built a winding pillow-and-quilt fort and are playing "Escape" during what Gracie jokingly calls Spy Night, something they do every Wednesday, with Bel and Salem playing and the three adults drinking wine in the other room.

"Lucky because I got the goggles?" Salem slides them to Bel. "You can have 'em."

"No." Bel shakes her head.

The quilt fort has slipped at the corner, letting in light, so Salem can see Bel's fine, reddish-blonde hair sway toward the static electricity in the blanket like tiny snakes being summoned from a basket.

Salem giggles.

"It's not funny." Bel scowls.

Salem wants to tell her that she's laughing at Bel's hair, not her words, but she isn't sure that would help.

"You're the luckiest duck because your dad is here," Bel says.

Salem sets the goggles on the floor in case Bel really does want them. "Where else would he be?"

"My dad isn't here."

It's true. Salem has never met Bel's dad. Neither has Bel. It's just how things are. Salem has never questioned it. "Do you want him to be?"

Bel licks her palm and runs it through her hair. It makes a crackling noise. "Kids are supposed to have two parents. Everyone knows that."

Salem is three years younger than Bel. She's used to Bel knowing more. She likes hanging out with someone so smart. "I guess."

Bel touches the edge of the goggles. "I'm going to be a police officer. Then I can find my dad." She adds an afterthought: "I can help other people, too."

Salem smiles. "If I were a spy, we could work together!"

Bel holds out her hand. Salem grasps it. It feels warm and soft. They shake.

"Best friends forever," Bel says.

CHAPTER 3

Linden Hills, Minneapolis

Bel stepped out of the Minneapolis terminal, a one-hour red-eye flight having delivered her from Chicago to Minneapolis. She was bleary-eyed, face puffy from crying, still beautiful. Salem wanted to hold her, but there wasn't time. They sped through the disorienting predawn—fog, henna-colored light, air scented with lake and leaves and eggy car exhaust—toward Grace's four-story Linden Hills apartment building. They gripped hands, Salem unsure if it was her hand or Bel's that was corpse-cold.

Still, the words didn't come, not until they took a quiet corner in one of Minneapolis's tonier residential neighborhoods and Grace's apartment loomed into view.

"Holy shit." Salem slapped her hand over her mouth. That was the wrong thing to say.

It's just she hadn't expected there to be so many police cars.

Neighborhood Halloween decorations added a level of surrealism to the scene. A witch collided face-first with a tree in the lawn south of the apartment building. A hanged rubber corpse was strung next to it. Fake gravestones decorated the yard of the house on the north side, strung with orange twinkle lights that pierced the predawn murk.

Bel flew out of the car before it rolled to a complete stop. She bounded past the fleet of police cars toward her mom's apartment building and stopped at the nearest uniform, her badge in her hand.

Salem switched off the car in the middle of the street, snatched her purse, and raced to catch up. She scanned the gathering crowd for Vida. She'd tried her mom as soon as she'd hung up with Bel four hours and a lifetime ago, but Vida had never answered. She must be frantic. Gracie was her best friend. They'd been inseparable as long as Salem could remember, and they'd passed on that loyalty to their daughters.

Salem reached Bel's side, out of breath. Bel was asking questions in her police officer voice, controlled and firm. Her hair was tied in a messy ponytail, her expensive jeans and Salvation Army T-shirt rumpled from the flight, but even so, she commanded respect. Salem saw it in the way the officers stood, their heads cocked, hands relaxed near their guns. It had always been this way for Bel. It wasn't her height, though she was almost six feet, or her looks. She had a *presence*.

Still, Bel seemed to be talking too slowly.

"We're here to see her," Salem blurted. The cool of the morning air turned her breath into white plumes. The sun hadn't yet risen, its promise of light barely agitating the horizon. "To see Grace Odegaard."

The uniform's eyes slid sideways to his partner. Salem suddenly felt like throwing up. "We'll get the officer in charge," he said. "Wait here."

Salem bobbed her head, jittery. She tucked her arm around Bel's waist. Her friend was so stiff she felt corded with steel. The crowd of gawkers kept a respectable distance, milling behind the police tape in their track pants and work suits and dog-walking clothes. Salem counted five women, seven men, two pairs of glasses, one hat.

Behind them, the water of Lake Harriet was as black as a grave. The proximity to water tightened her throat like it always did, but she went through the mantra her therapist had taught her: *I'm safe on land, I'm safe on land.* She inhaled the smoky, earthy smell of a Minnesota fall. She measured her heartbeats. Finally, a man in his early thirties and wearing a well-cut suit stepped out the main door of the yellow brick apartment building.

The other officers stood straighter when he appeared. He was tall, muscled, clean shaven, his skin so dark it reflected a deep purple in the walkway lights. He glanced in Del and Salem's direction as the first officer leaned toward him to speak near his ear. Nodding once, sharply, he began walking toward the two women. Salem's chest grew tighter the closer he came.

"Agent Lucan Stone," he said, extending his hand toward Bel. "FBI."

The elevator slid open onto the third-floor landing.

Salem gasped.

She'd been up here hundreds of times, but the crime had morphed it into a stage set. Grace's open apartment door stood directly across the wide hallway, fifteen feet from the elevator. A deep carmine painted the far wall, a fire hose wash of ghoulish spray. The air smelled strongly of urine and something metallic, like wet pennies. A corpse lay to the right of Grace's door, face up. Salem was reminded of the Resusci Annie doll they'd learned CPR on in high school, except this body wore a slipper on one foot and the other was bare, her upper torso shielded from Salem's view by an examiner wearing white.

A second person was taking instructions from the examiner, snapping photos with a flash camera as she pointed. A man and a woman peered at the wall to the right of Grace's door. Everyone wore white latex gloves and shoe covers. Same with the three uniformed police officers standing to the left of the door, and a fourth officer who crossed in front of Grace's open doorway from inside her apartment. A handful of dark-yellow evidence markers were stacked across the floor. The foyer, the size of a large room, thrummed with the murmurs of quiet, intense activity.

Salem concentrated on these details to calm her jagged heartbeat.

The authorities are here. They'll take care of everything.

Though she'd never been to church in her life, she fought the urge to cross herself.

Agent Stone nodded toward the technician bent over the corpse. "Forensics is still on scene."

Bel stood taller, touching her hip for a gun that wasn't there. "Four hours in?"

Agent Stone glanced at his wristwatch, its silver thickness a bright contrast to his skin. "Four hours and thirty-seven minutes since the initial 911 call. You made good time from Chicago."

"I got in on standby. It's a short flight." Bel hesitated a moment before stepping off the elevator, followed by Agent Stone and then Salem.

Stone lightly touched Salem's arm. "You okay?"

Salem brushed off his concern and stumbled closer to Bel. Her goal was to comfort her, but from this angle, the entire corpse was in view. It was the body of an older woman dressed for bed. Her robe was tied in front. The hem was blue, but the rest of the terry cloth was mottled with blood so thick that it turned black at the shoulders. Her neck housed a four-inch, eye-shaped gash, the meat of it gaping at the ceiling.

A pile of fur lay next to the woman. At first Salem thought it was an article of clothing, but then she caught the beady black eyes staring at her from the dog's face, its body twisted the opposite direction.

She couldn't blink. Her eye muscles had stopped working.

The terror was a lovely sticky web, adhering to her skin and tugging her down.

A tiny sound from Bel mercifully forced Salem's attention away from the horrific sight. Bel was rocking back and forth, the move so slight that Salem would not have noticed if she hadn't reached for Bel's icy hand. She followed her friend's stare, her eyes landing three feet above the corpse. The investigators were scraping something off the wall. Salem kept her eyes moving, to the open doorway that allowed the beginning rays of the chilly Halloween sunshine to filter into the hallway. The furniture inside Gracie's apartment, at least what Salem could see from this angle, was undisturbed.

"We have one body." Agent Stone's voice was a deep rumble directly behind them. "She's been positively ID'd as Carla Marie Gladia."

Bel's hand tightened in Salem's. "Neighbor." Her eyes flicked to the body.

"That's right. And her dog, Dante."

Salem spoke past the pressure at the top of her throat. "Someone murdered a *dog*?"

"Probably to keep the animal quiet." Stone tipped his head toward the two corpses on the floor. "That's exactly as the police discovered them."

One of the uniformed officers walked over to Agent Stone, whispered something to him, and then stepped onto the elevator. The mechanical door closed behind them as Stone continued. "We have the security tapes from the lobby for the past twenty-four hours. You know this is a women's-only building?"

Both Salem and Bel nodded, their eyes locked on apartment 307 as if love and wishes could coax Grace to walk out of it.

"We'll review the tape, but for now, it appears that no men have been in or out of the building in the past twenty-four hours. Not even a repairman or deliveryman. Yet from the blood pattern, we know at least one of the killers, if there was more than one, entered through the front door. That narrows our suspects to women." Stone cocked his head, his eyes unreadable. "Ms. Odegaard, did your mother have any enemies that you know of?"

Bel shook her head, the movement slow.

Salem's heartbeat picked up as she connected two dots. "Wait, you have a body. Two, with Dante. Maybe all this blood is from them!" She turned to Agent Stone, realizing too late how excited she sounded about this grotesque reality. She swallowed past the spongy lump lodged between her chest and mouth.

Stone's eyes remained trained on Bel. "I'm afraid that's unlikely. There's a secondary crime scene inside. If you'll follow me?"

He handed them shoe covers before walking along the carefully marked trail skirting the blood, indicating that Bel and Salem should follow. "Everything in the apartment appears to be in order—all major appliances accounted for, dishes done, bed made. We haven't located a safe."

"Mom doesn't own one." Bel crossed the threshold and surveyed the apartment, her visual assessment snagged by drops of what looked like dried blood under the far window, two more examiners and a uniformed officer busy with the area. She paled. "You're treating this as a murder-kidnapping?"

Stone followed her gaze. "For now."

She indicated the activity at the window. "The secondary crime scene?"

"Yes, extending outside onto the fire escape."

"Can I check the bedrooms?"

When Stone nodded his assent, Bel marched toward the open doorway.

"Stay here and touch nothing," Stone commanded Salem, before following Bel.

Stay was all Salem could do. Stay and stare at *anything* but all the blood in the hallway behind her, suffocating her, threatening to drown her like an encroaching crimson ocean, thick and salty, Mrs. Gladia's screams echoing through its depths like whale song. She reached out to the TV stand to steady herself, the glass edge a sharp return to reality. That's when she spotted the wooden jewelry box her father had helped her craft for her mother when Salem was a seventh grader.

What the hell?

She'd sawed the balsa wood herself, loaded the secret spring that would open the box, glued it all together, heat-etched the Om symbol on the top, and lined the interior with purple felt. She hadn't laid eyes on it since she'd gifted it to her mom. She reached out a trembling hand, surprised at how light the container was. Her finger traced the black, looping groove of the Om. When she was twelve, before her dad's suicide, she'd been into Hinduism, or at least attracted to what her young brain saw as the core of it: the concept of karma and the comfort of stretch pants.

She hardly remembered that girl.

The box made a clinking sound when she turned it over. Her heartbeat picked up. She glanced furtively at the window. The investigators there paid her no heed. Same with the ones behind her in the foyer. She held the box to her ear and shook it. There was definitely something inside.

Squeezing the two long sides, she centered her pointer finger in the middle of the bottom to release the spring. The lid slid open. Inside lay a pair of ancient spectacles, and underneath, a note scratched out in her mother's scrawling handwriting. She tugged both out and read the message.

Bits: bwsmttmzijwcbzmdmvombpmvowpwumn

wttwehpmbziqtbzcabvwwvm

Salem's stomach somersaulted. "Bits" had been Salem's dad's nickname for her growing up. The moniker had cemented itself once she'd discovered her love for computers, though only her mom, Gracie, and Bel had ever called her that. What followed was a secret code.

Her heartbeat thick and loud, she peeked again at the nearest investigators. They were photographing the base of the window, pointing at a spot, talking. Stone and Bel would return from the other room any second. She floated in a bubble of invisibility for the smallest moment.

What do I do with the box?

Salem felt like she was chewing on alum. She glanced a third time toward the window, a greasy sweat trickling down her neck. She clutched the code and spectacles, unsure if they'd been in the balsa wood box for ten hours or ten years, or if they were even meant for her. She didn't want to steal, or pollute a crime scene. Nor did she want to ignore a message from her mother, not under these circumstances. The indecision was agonizing. She was about to close the box and return it to the TV stand when Bel stepped into the living room, Agent Stone on her heel. Salem instinctively shoved the glasses and note into her purse and slid the box closed, her pulse a rocket in her veins.

Stone's intelligent glance flicked at her hands. She held up the now-empty balsa box like a shield, unable to meet the ink of his eyes. "My mom, Vida Wiley, owns this. I made it for her when I was in middle school." Her voice quavered. "She might have been here last night."

Stone stepped toward her and took the balsa box with his gloved hands, examining it from all sides. His voice was a controlled growl. "I told you not to touch anything."

She didn't respond.

He called over the uniformed officer from the window and commanded him to enter the box into evidence without taking his eyes off Salem. "Do you have any reason other than this box to suspect she might have been here last evening?"

Salem shook her head, biting her lower lip to keep it steady. "But she's not answering her phone."

He studied her for a moment longer, an exclamation point of crisp darkness in the dawning light of the apartment, hair shaved close to the scalp, eyes bright and quick, nose strong over sculpted lips. Salem risked a glance, and his gaze laid her bare.

"Are you and your mother close?"

No, Agent Stone, we are not. "I last saw her a few weeks ago." Her cheeks burned so hot that her eyes watered as she stared at her feet. "But she always answers when I call."

He paused a moment before answering. "I'll send officers to her home immediately."

Salem clenched her jaw so no emotions could leak past, only words. "Thank you. Also, I'm not feeling well." She glanced at Bel, passing her a look they hadn't used since high school. "Can you come with me?"

The secret code hummed inside her purse.

It sounded like an urgent, papery whisper of warning.

CHAPTER 4

Linden Hills, Minneapolis

There was a whole lot FBI Assistant Special Agent in Charge Lucan Stone didn't like about this case.

He didn't care for the fact that five victims had been reported in seven days, their throats cut with an identical weapon, their bodies discovered in each corner of the United States from Florida to Arizona to Nebraska—and now Minnesota.

He also didn't like the nagging sense that there were far, far more victims out there than they would ever know.

And as head of a four-man task force, what really pissed him off? He hadn't a single lead.

Not one of the descriptions of the perp had lined up true, but they'd at least had a profile before this Linden Hills discovery.

Their serial killer was certainly male, white, and between the ages of twenty-five and thirty-five. His victims were all women, four Caucasian and one multiracial, two sets of them mothers and their adult daughters and the fifth woman unrelated, none of them sexually violated. According to the FBI profiler assigned to the investigation, the killer had grown up with a domineering mother and an absent father. He also had a job that allowed him to travel without drawing suspicion. He was likely single and heterosexual.

His MO was consistent: locate the victim in her home, slice her throat, vanish. No staging. The only signature was a *lack* of a signature. If not for the peculiar randomness of the victims other than the two mother-daughter connections—a Cuban grandmother in Florida City, a woman who sold sage and crystals in Sedona, a newly married farmer's wife in Nebraska, a Maine attorney, and an elementary school teacher from Southern California—Agent Stone would have marked him for a contract killer.

Then along came this Minneapolis murder of a woman and her dog and the potential kidnapping or murder of Grace Odegaard. This perp's methods were identical—locate the woman in her home, slice her throat, disappear—which is why Stone and his partner had been called in, along with their task force. But this murder had taken place inside a women-only building, and the security tapes, which were as grainy as breakfast cereal and which he'd watched forward and backward twice, showed only women entering and leaving.

He powerfully hoped that it wasn't a serial killer *couple* they were dealing with because the only break they'd had so far was the media not yet connecting the cross-country killings. If it turned out they had a Bonnie and Clyde on their hands, there's no way the press wouldn't catch wind of it. The FBI would lose their meager advantage.

Frankly, it was amazing the connections between the killings hadn't already been leaked. Senator Gina Hayes was likely to thank for that. The woman dominated the media. With the presidential election little more than a week away, she couldn't sneeze without it making headlines.

Stone didn't particularly care for politics. He liked that a Black man was president. He'd like that a woman was president, too, if she did a good job. But he had more immediate issues in his sight line.

"Agent Stone?" The uniformed police officer stood a respectful distance away, shifting his weight from one leg to the other, like a kid who needed to pee.

Stone glanced up from Vida Wiley's FBI file, which he'd pulled the second Isabel Odegaard and Salem Wiley had left for the bathroom. Other than an unusual amount of cross-country and out-of-country flying for a history professor, nothing stood out. The examiners were closing up their murder bags and hoisting Mrs. Gladia into the body sack, which meant the cleaning crew would be arriving soon. He needed to find something, anything, any detail that had been overlooked. "Yes?"

"We've located a human finger." The officer jabbed his thumb over his shoulder, toward the back of the building. "In the dumpster. It's been sliced off like a rat's tail."

Stone was about to reprimand the officer for his cavalier word choice when he noticed his face. It glowed with that waxy sheen that comes right before you vomit. "Belongs to a woman?"

"The techs say they think so." The officer swayed, wiping at moisture collecting above his mustache. "It's a pinkie."

"God*damn*." Stone swallowed past his disgust because he knew what this meant: they might finally have a lead. "Get it to the lab."

"It's already on its way, sir."

He'd have assumed as much. The Minneapolis police techs were the best in the business. He glanced at the uniform's name tag. "Is there anything else, Officer Benokraitis?"

"Not really." The young officer twitched at the loud zip of the body bag closing. "The techs haven't been able to enter the blood samples into the system. Too many cases ahead of you." He nodded agreeably, on more comfortable ground now. "But some patrol cops were in the Powderhorn Park neighborhood and rushed to Vida Wiley's house, like you asked. They radioed that there's no sign of her, or of any trouble."

Stone nodded. That's what he'd figured. He returned to the file, picturing Isabel Odegaard and Salem Wiley blowing in here like a hurricane. Odegaard was all business, scrambling to keep it together and be in charge all at once, an outlook that he understood intimately. Wiley he couldn't read as well. All he knew for sure was that she was so pretty she'd squeezed his heart when he first laid eyes on her.

He didn't like what it meant for either of them that the perp—if it was the same slicer he'd been following—had gone quirky with the finger. A serial killer changing his MO this late in the spree indicated an increasingly unbalanced mind.

The brutality of the crimes was guaranteed to escalate

CHAPTER 5

Linden Hills, Minneapolis

With shaking hands, Salem smoothed the note from her mother on the bathroom counter of the empty third-floor apartment commandeered for police use. Bel stood watch at the door. Since they'd arrived at Grace's, Bel's gaze had grown hollow, her skin ashen, but she still held herself like a rod.

Bel blinked toward the note. "What's it mean?"

Salem shot her a weak smile. "Not anything worth bothering the FBI about. I bet it's a note Mom wrote years ago."

Yet she didn't quite believe that, or they wouldn't be here now.

She reached into her purse and tugged out a pencil and pad of paper before grabbing the ancient spectacles. Their thin, rusting wire was wrapped around misshapen glass lenses. The arms were little more than metal sticks crafted of a copper so old it had turned green. Salem held them toward the light and squinted. The lenses were all scratched up. She set them to the side and pinned her attention on the note.

Bits: bwsmttmzijwcbzmdmvombpmvowpwumn

wttwebpmbziqtbzcabvwwvm

She was most comfortable solving computer problems. All the clean ones and zeros could be perfectly lined up to crack a code as crisply as a key slid into a new lock. Her thesis research had taught her that Charles Babbage's Difference Engine was developed in 1822 and the computer program written for it by Ada Lovelace in 1842, but it was Turing's Enigma cracker, first envisioned in 1936 and built in 1940, that demonstrated the code-breaking power of computing machines.

Alan Turing developed the apparatus for the British government during World War II. Turing's machine built off an earlier model to crack even the most advanced German code, effectively shaving at least two years from WWII and creating the first working model of a general computer. Salem wished for a handheld model now to help her crack the code her mother had left.

"Agent Stone asked me if we knew where Grace or Vida were." Bel's words startled Salem. She glanced up from the note as Bel continued. "When we were both in my mom's bedroom. I told him we didn't know anything. We don't, right?"

"Not yet we don't."

Salem returned her attention to the message, clicking her focus back into processor mode. When she'd initially shown an interest in computers, she'd been excited to discover how many women had been involved in their development. Jean Jennings Bartik was one of six women who created programs for ENIAC, the first electronic general computer, in the 1940s.

A decade later, Grace Hopper led the creation of COBOL, the original wide-use computer programming language. Computer science had been built on the work of women, who in the early years entered through the field of mathematics.

With computers, Salem felt like she was home.

But this code from her mom was old school, which was unsurprising given Vida's general avoidance of computers. With all the *w*'s and *z*'s and the *j*, it was unlikely to be a transposition cipher, where letters were jumbled to create an anagram. It was more probable that her mom had written her a substitution cipher, either a simple Caesar or a Vigenère.

"I don't think the FBI knows anything, either." Bel pressed her ear to the door. "And it looked like the beginnings of a task force out there. Plus, the ME would have come and gone by now if this was a standard homicide. I don't like any of this."

Salem didn't, either. She tapped the pencil eraser on the paper while she pondered. In a Caesar cipher, each letter in the alphabet was replaced by a letter a fixed number of positions down the alphabet. So if the Caesar cipher had a right shift of four, every *a* in the code became a *d*, every *b* an *e*, every *c* an *f*, and so on. It was a fairly easy code to break by using frequency analysis, starting with short words. In English, for example, a single-letter word was only going to be *I* or *a*, and a three-letter word was most likely to be *the* or *and*. Once those letters were established, the cryptanalyst worked out from there, making educated guesses until the puzzle was solved.

Salem began chewing on the end of the pencil. She held up the note so she could examine it from different angles. A Vigenère cipher was a Caesar cipher on steroids. If one didn't know the keyword, the code was uncrackable. At least it had been until Babbage discovered that modular arithmetic and a dash of intuition could break *le chiffre indéchiffrable*.

Salem scribbled Vida's note on her pad, trying the Vigenère cipher first, using *Bits* as the keytext. When that didn't work, she switched to the simple Caesar cipher, testing every possibility in chronological order: right shift of one, right shift of two, right shift of three. It would have been easier if Vida had included spaces between words so Salem could run a frequency analysis, but she worked with what she had. Right shift of four, right shift of five . . .

When Salem arrived at right shift of eight, her heartbeat picked up. She felt the familiar buzz of a puzzle coming together.

Bel shifted at the door. "Any luck?"

Salem nodded. She was close. Letters were turning into words, words into messages.

"Okay." Bel leaned her ear back against the door. "But can you hurry? We've been gone too long."

"Yes." Salem knew that word was the appropriate response, but she hadn't really heard what Bel said. She was almost inside the mystery. She could taste it. She scribbled furiously, decoding the substitution nearly as efficiently as a computer.

"Ah!" The solution flooded through all at once. *Bits* had thrown her off. Vida hadn't meant it as her name. It was part of the code, which a plus-eight Caesar cipher revealed to be:

Talk: to Keller about revenge then go home follow the trail trust no one

The cold tongue of fear licked her spine. This was a fresh note, and her mom had intended for them to find it at Gracie's. That meant that whatever tragedy had befallen Grace had also happened to Vida.

And she had known it was coming.

For the first time, Salem wondered why the FBI had been called in. "Bel," she whispered, "I don't think our moms were randomly kidnapped."

A heavy knock landed on the bathroom door.

Salem, wound tight, squealed. Bel snapped into a fighting stance, her expression steely.

"Ms. Odegaard and Ms. Wiley? Agent Stone would like to meet with the two of you in the lobby, if you don't mind."

CHAPTER 6

Linden Hills, Minneapolis

Salem ran over the words like a mantra as they left the bathroom, kept murmuring them as they entered the elevator, didn't stop when they laid eyes on Agent Lucan Stone in the lobby.

Talk: to Keller about revenge then go home follow the trail trust no one

Stone gestured toward the chocolate velvet couch near the door. "I have some more questions. Do you mind?"

Bel moved toward the sofa. Salem didn't.

Are you and your mother close?

Geographically, less than three miles separated Salem's apartment from her childhood home. Emotionally, she might as well live in China for all the distance between her and her mother. They faked it well—phone calls twice a month and dinner once, erudite conversations on topics that Vida Wiley was passionate about, cards and gifts at all the appropriate holidays.

Someone examining the relationship from the outside would have no idea how high the wall was between Salem and her mother, would compliment the two of them on what good friends they appeared to be. It had happened many times.

You two are almost like sisters.

The chasm between appearance and truth left a vacant spot inside Salem, a tunnel from her heart to her mouth where something solid should be.

"Do we have to answer your questions?" Salem gasped, startled that she'd talked back to Agent Stone—she, who'd spent her adult life avoiding conflict, who struggled to look people in the eye, who valued routine and order. And if she slowed down, she'd have to think about that, and about the repercussions, and about that shiny body bag they'd walked by to take the elevator down. So she floated ten feet above her frame, a gray balloon tied tenuously to the wrist of the shivering woman below.

"Are you asking if I can detain you?" If Salem's question caught Stone off guard, he didn't show it.

"Yes." She watched her own feet. She felt him studying her, the whole energy of him trying to get inside her head.

"I can't keep you here," he finally said, "but the more information I have, the quicker I can locate your mothers."

"Salem?"

Salem glanced at her friend. Bel had splashed water on her face in the bathroom and wore her smooth police officer expression, but worry and exhaustion lurked just below the surface.

Salem felt the same emotions, her brain and body groaning under the weight of Grace and Vida's disappearance. As heavy as that was, though, it was outweighed by the memory of standing onshore as her dad deliberately drowned himself, doing nothing, not even yelling.

Vida's instructions in the balsa wood box had been clear:

Talk: to Keller about revenge then go home follow the trail trust no one

It was the most authentic communication she'd had with her mother in fourteen years. "I want to leave, Bel. Now."

Bel's gaze sharpened. Salem knew she wanted more details on the case, wanted to stay and be the questioner rather than the questioned.

In the end, though, she turned to Stone. "We're going to leave, Agent Stone."

He drew up his shoulders. Salem thought he was going to argue, convince them to stay. He surprised her by instead reaching into his jacket and pulling out a card, which he handed to Salem. She reached for it.

"It's a bad idea that you leave," he said. He didn't release the card, held firm until she finally glanced up. His deep-brown gaze pinned Salem in her spot. She felt it like an electric jolt.

"Vida Wiley is not in her home, and until we hear otherwise, we're assuming she and Grace Odegaard are together and being held involuntarily."

The world tipped for Salem. Still, she gripped the card.

"There is a possibility that the person holding them may target you as well." He finally let go of the card and turned to Bel. "Both of you."

Bel nodded sharply. "Understood."

"Thank you." Salem slurred the words because her mouth was so dry. She tucked the card in her jeans pocket and walked toward the door, Bel following.

"My number is on there," Agent Stone called after them. "Call if you need me."

And you're going *to need me,* Salem thought she heard him say, but by then, they were out the door, crunching over leaves as brittle as bones.

CHAPTER 7

Minneapolis Institute of Art

Salem wasn't well acquainted with Dr. David Keller, assistant curator at the nonprofit Minneapolis Institute of Art. He had been an occasional guest at Vida and Daniel's dinner parties, and then after Daniel's death, Vida would bring Salem by his office when they visited the institute. She remembered him as a stern man who rarely spoke except to critique what someone else was saying.

Talk: to Keller about revenge then go home follow the trail trust no one

They'd been waiting in the car until the institute, recently nick-named "Mia" in a marketing blitz, opened at ten. When the doors were finally unlocked, Salem and Bel breezed past the welcome desk, under the gigantic Chihuly *Sunburst* chandelier, and up the stairs until they reached the Target Galleries. Their impatience condensed around their feet, spurring their movements.

"Excuse me?"

Salem, agitated and out of breath, whipped her head toward the woman behind the special-exhibitions desk. She'd been so intent on their destination that she hadn't noticed her. "Yes?"

The staff member pointed toward the WOMEN IN THE ARTS sign perched on her desk, then toward the doorway of the Target Galleries. "You're going into the special exhibition. It's sixteen dollars for members, twenty for nonmembers. Do you have tickets?"

Salem's brow furrowed. "We're actually looking for Dr. Keller? His office used to be down here."

"Ah." The woman smiled. "All the offices moved a few years ago. Before my time. But I have good news! Dr. Keller curated this exhibit. He's inside right now."

Salem touched her pocketbook without thinking. Teaching at-risk youth how to navigate Excel spreadsheets paid about as well as one would expect. "We have to buy tickets?"

The museum worker put her finger to her coral-colored lips. They matched the beads at her neck. "I won't tell. As long as you're just here to speak with him."

Salem beamed with gratitude and continued through the glass doors. The Target Galleries were quieter than the rest of Mia and crowded for a Monday morning.

"You think he'll help us?" Bel asked, her voice pitched low.

"I think he will if he can."

They hurried across the herringbone parquet floor, their footsteps muffled. Salem scoured the room for Dr. Keller, her attention drawn to the sculptures displayed in the center. A breathtaking Sarah Bernhardt marble sculpture of a grandmother holding the dying body of her grandson dominated the center of the room. Display blocks were arranged around the sculpture to create a movement path. The cubes held ornate silver urns crafted by Hester Bateman and an exquisite silver tea caddy designed by Elizabeth Godfrey in the 1700s, and under glass, an oval tobacco box silversmithed by Elisabeth Haselwood in the 1600s.

Salem was drawn toward the paintings decorating the walls, most especially the Maria Sibylla Merian plates. Her dad was the one who'd introduced her to Merian's botany-based sketches, first created after Merian traveled with her daughter to Suriname in 1699. They were grotesquely, grandly beautiful in their realism. The blending of periods and styles created a gorgeous visual cacophony inside the gallery.

"Salem?" Across the room, a short, trim man in his fifties separated himself from a group of patrons and made his way to Bel and Salem. "How are you?"

"Good, Dr. Keller." The lie was automatic. She held out her hand, and he clasped it briefly. "This is my friend Bel." They also shook hands.

And then Salem was at a loss.

She pushed her hair behind her ears and frowned, grasping for a way to explain what they needed. *My mom and her best friend have disappeared, and Mom left instructions for me to talk with you about revenge, and I have no idea what it means so me and my friend bundled ourselves into a car and drove straight here, and can you tell me who my mother really is because I am beginning to wonder if I knew her at all.* It sounded ridiculous any way she parsed it, even if Dr. Keller didn't intimidate her.

He tossed a sentence into the awkwardness. "You're here to see the exhibit?"

Salem shook her head vigorously. "Um, no. At least I don't think so. I'm wondering if you know anything about this."

She shoved her hand into her coat pocket, yanked out the note, and held it toward Dr. Keller, realizing too late that her scribbles would be indecipherable to him.

"Sorry." She jerked the note back. Was Dr. Keller looking at her strangely? "It's a note from my mom." She held it up. "I'm afraid it's a bit cryptic. I'm wondering if you can help us figure out what it means?"

He barked out a short laugh and glanced incredulously from Salem to Bel. "You want me to translate a note from your mother? Is this a parlor game? Can't you ask her yourself?"

"I'm afraid not, Dr. Keller." Bel used her official-police-interview voice. There was no broaching it. "We really need your help. Now." She shot Salem an encouraging glance, cuing her to share the contents of the note.

Salem nodded, grateful that Bel was taking charge. She'd memorized the translated message, but it was still a challenge to get it past the cotton of her tongue. "The note says 'talk to Keller about revenge.' Any idea what it means?"

All around them, art patrons murmured respectfully, appreciating centuries-old art.

Security guards discreetly patrolled the perimeter.

Dr. Keller didn't immediately answer. Salem couldn't read his expression. He appeared to be annoyed, but maybe he was trying not to laugh? Or, more likely, he was considering the safest route to a phone so he could call the nearest mental institution to haul her and Bel away.

Turns out it was none of these.

Dr. Keller stepped aside so the women had a clear view of the wall immediately behind him. A proud smile bloomed on his face, and he held up his hands, Vanna White–style. "I'd like to introduce you to the greatest representation of revenge ever painted."

CHAPTER 8

Minneapolis Institute of Art

Salem knew from a junior-year art history class that Artemisia
Gentileschi painted in the first half of the 1600s. She was prosperous
during her lifetime, gaining acclaim and making a living in an era when
only a handful of female painters were recognized. She became even
more popular after her death. Modern critics considered the Baroque
painter one of the most gifted artists of the seventeenth century, and she
was known for one depiction above all others: *Judith Slaying Holofernes.*

Salem walked toward the painting as if pulled by a rope. Dr. Keller,
the patrons, the whole museum fell away.

"Breathtaking." She stood inches away from the canvas, Bel nodding in silent agreement at her elbow. The seven-foot-tall, centuries-old
composition was so vibrant that Salem imagined she could smell the
rich oil of the paint, the lead white, the sulfur-scented vermilion, the
chalky clay of red and yellow ochre, the bone black.

The painting featured a powerful Judith poised over General
Holofernes, a glistening blade to his throat, her hands twisted in his
hair as she sawed off his head. Judith's maid was helping to pin him
down. Both women were straining, their muscles and ferocity displayed
as Holofernes's blood spurted into the air and dripped down the white
sheets of the bed. His face was a perfect shock of agony, his hands
futilely pushing the women away as Judith hacked at his neck.

Salem held her own throat, grimacing at the violence.

"It's on loan from the Uffizi in Florence. Stunning, isn't it?"

Salem jumped, Dr. Keller's nearness startling her. He stood less than a yard away, watching them, his expression peculiar.

"We studied this painting in one of my college art electives," Salem said, inhaling deeply to steady her heartbeat. "It always stuck with me."

Bel pointed at Holofernes's agonized face. "Poor guy."

"No," Dr. Keller said, "he's not. The story is from the Old Testament. General Holofernes attacked Israel, raping and killing indiscriminately. He fancied Judith and had her brought to his tent. Judith and her maid waited until he was passed-out drunk and killed him, saving her people."

Bel's facial response suggested that she wouldn't have minded hanging out with Judith and her maid. "Gentileschi was religious?"

Dr. Keller pointed toward the interpretative square. "Not particularly. The portrayal is widely interpreted as Artemisia Gentileschi's painted revenge on her own convicted rapist."

"Huh." Bel looked away from the painting and did a quick and automatic survey of the gallery. "I'm surprised rape was illegal in the 1600s."

Dr. Keller grimaced. "Rape may have been technically illegal, but justice was not swift. Gentileschi had to undergo a gynecological examination and was tortured with thumbscrews during the trial to prove she wasn't lying. Her rapist, her tutor Agostino Tassi, was merely questioned."

"He was found guilty, wasn't he?" Salem asked.

"Yes, in 1612. He didn't serve any time, though. In fact, he wasn't punished at all." Dr. Keller indicated the painting with his chin. "Artemisia Gentileschi completed *Judith Slaying Holofernes* immediately after the trial. We are led to assume that Gentileschi fancied herself Judith and Agostino Tassi became Holofernes."

Revenge.

Talk to Keller about revenge.

"Do you have any idea why my mom may have been interested in it?" Salem asked.

A member of Mia's staff walked toward Dr. Keller, smiled apologetically at the women, and whispered into his ear. He nodded, and then returned his attention to the painting. "I don't. But I can tell you that she requested a private viewing of it."

"She did?" Salem's voice was too loud. She lowered it. "When?"

"She stopped by last Monday, after hours. We've only had the exhibit open for seven days."

"And you showed this painting to her?"

Dr. Keller glanced toward the door, and then at his watch. "Not exactly. She wanted to be alone with it." He raised and dropped a shoulder. "We've been friends for years. It was a small favor."

"Did she say anything afterward?" Bel was scanning the painting with renewed interest.

Dr. Keller shook his head. "I had a dinner meeting and had to leave before she was done. She did email me a thank-you on Tuesday or Wednesday. That was the last time we communicated. Is everything all right?"

"Yes," Salem said, too quickly.

Of course nothing was all right, maybe never had been. Vida Wiley was an enigma to her own daughter.

CHAPTER 9

Seven Years Old

"Time to take the leap, honey."

Salem can tell Vida is losing patience because her mom only refers to her as "honey" when she's trying not to yell. Anyhow, she could call her Wonder Woman and Salem still isn't going into that lake.

"No."

"Please? Mama'll make sure the fish don't bite you. We'll only wade in up to our knees."

It isn't the fish that Salem is worried about, or at least, those are a new addition to her concerns. It's the water itself, the huge, black expanse of it, sun sluicing across the top to reveal a poisonous pool of mercury. Salem knows better than she knows her own name that if she steps into it, into any body of water where she can't see the bottom, no one will ever lay eyes on her again.

She was born knowing that.

It wouldn't be an easy death. There'd be a swirl of silt, and then something horribly cold and muscular would wrap around her ankle and tug her down, down, down into a chill so inescapable it'd freeze her heart. In the final, terrible moment of consciousness, she'd see her mom above the water, just out of reach, the sun haloing her head, safety, love, and home cruelly just beyond Salem's grasp. She would struggle and fight to reach Vida, open her mouth to scream, and the cold water would rush in to fill her lungs, pop out her eyes from the inside, steal her voice and her life.

There is no question in her mind that she can't enter the water. She pushes a tangle of soft curls out of her eyes and repeats herself. "No."

Vida takes an angry drag off her Virginia Slims 120. She cuts quite the figure with her thick black hair tied up in a Pucci scarf, oversize glasses, skin a tawny brown that a Midwesterner couldn't obtain with all the baby oil and summer sun in the world. She still has her accent, too, a faint lilt from spending the first ten years of her life in Iran.

"We didn't drive all this way to sit in the cabin," she says. The "honey" has vanished, both the word and the tenor.

Salem rubs nervously at the webbing between her thumb and pointer finger, trying not to cry. "Daddy wouldn't make me."

"Daddy isn't here, is he?"

CHAPTER 10

Minneapolis Institute of Art

Salem suddenly became aware that Dr. Keller, the Mia staff member, and Bel were all watching her. Dr. Keller's brow furrowed, his body language saying that he didn't want to leave but was forced to.

"If you don't mind?"

"Not at all," Salem said. "Thanks for your help."

He seemed poised to add something but unsure how to word it. Finally, duty winning out, he turned and hurried through the exhibit doorway.

Salem and Bel returned their attention to the painting.

A small group had gathered behind them to admire the Gentileschi, murmuring about the grand drama of it, the beauty, the violence. Bel leaned closer to Salem. "You move to one side, I'll go to the other. Check for notes Vida may have hidden on it as best as you can, okay?"

They both stepped back a few feet, and as surreptitiously as possible, they eyeballed the back rim of the frame in the three inches between the wood and the wall.

Nothing jumped out.

They returned to the front of the painting. Tension made Salem's hands clammy.

"You think there's a secret panel in the frame and that's what Vida sent us to find?" Bel asked.

Salem crossed her arms, analyzing the gilt of the simple beveled mount. Before his death, her father had taught her everything a person could know about concealing drawers and compartments in wood. Looking back, it seemed a weird specialty for a carpenter, but her puzzling mind had loved it. She knew that if a craftsperson had hidden something in the Gentileschi frame, it would be nearly impossible to locate it without physically touching the wood.

"If there is, we're screwed. I imagine they don't look lightly on patrons groping the art."

"So now what?" Bel asked.

"I don't *know*." Salem uncrossed her arms in frustration and felt something odd in her pocket. She reached in, tugged out the ancient spectacles.

Bel spotted what she was doing. Her face reflected an array of emotions, from amusement to desperation. "You're going to put them on?"

"I guess," Salem said, sliding them onto her face. "They were in the box with the note that directed us here. Nothing to lose, right?"

Bel wrinkled her nose. "You look like a superfan in line for the latest Harry Potter movie."

The glasses pinched Salem's nose, and the scratches on the lens were so profound as to render them nearly blinders. Yet her mother had left them in the balsa box for a reason. Salem blinked myopically. "I'm hoping they're like those 3D glasses that came in our Count Chocula. Remember?"

"I remember they were supposed to let us read a secret code on the cereal box." Bel's brow was creased. "Mine never worked."

"Mine either, actually."

With great effort, Salem restrained herself from glancing around to see what stares the glasses were drawing. Instead, she walked forward and peered at the lower edge of the Gentileschi, her nose almost touching it. The painting was darker than it appeared in photographs and flat, the oil paint hardly built up at all. She began systematically scanning every square inch of the canvas from left to right.

Bel stood next to her. "I will kick the ass of anyone who makes fun of you," she whispered.

Salem's lips twitched. She and Bel were still friends, but she worried that that had grown to mean something different, less potent, with Bel in Chicago. For all today's trauma, it was nice to have Bel back as her bodyguard.

After her first complete pass, Salem risked a peek behind her. People *were* staring. She certainly was doing a passable impression of the world's biggest dork, swaying from side to side, nose to canvas, wearing a rusty pair of Coke-bottle, Ben Franklin glasses. It wouldn't be long until someone called the security guards. She returned her focus to the painting and sped up her pace.

Out of the corner of her eye, she saw Bel's clenched hands. Left to right. Right to left. Left to right. Right to left.

It was difficult to make out anything through the scratched lens.

Still, she continued, moving as if mounted on the track of a giant typewriter, methodically scouring the canvas's surface. She reached the first ribbon of Holofernes's blood on the bed, so vivid that it blazed copper even through the brutalized glasses.

She stopped—she'd spotted something. "Bel!"

"What?" Bel swiveled.

Salem peered closer. "Nothing." She released her breath. "I thought I saw some sort of symbol. It was just a paint smudge."

She returned to her rhythmic searching. A loud muttering erupted near the entrance, followed by silence, then more talking. A nearby walkie-talkie squawked. Salem kept surveying the painting, moving even faster, if such a thing were possible.

She was operating so quickly, her heartbeat so loud, that she almost missed it.

She returned to the fringe of the blanket beneath Holofernes's bleeding head, her pulse quickening. Had she imagined something again?

She peered closer, tipping her head. Her breath caught. She hadn't imagined it.

Words.

She yanked the glasses off her face. The words disappeared.

She slid them back on, and the words reappeared. "Oh my god."

Clancy Johnson studied the artwork at the far end of the Target Gallery. According to the placard, he was looking at Hildegard of Bingen's manuscript illustration of the universe, created circa 1140–50. It reminded him of a Persian rug with a fiery vagina drawn on it.

It wasn't really to his taste.

He'd chosen the position because it allowed him to watch the women without appearing to do so. They'd been staring at the gruesome beheading painting as if *it*, rather than the hoo-ha-on-a-rug, held the secrets of creation. Then the dark-haired woman, Salem Wiley, had stuck on those weird little glasses. He didn't know how he was going to explain those.

He wasn't surprised when the security guards showed up. The only question was how long until they kicked the girls out. The two stood out like sore thumbs, their agitation and fear emanating off them like the stink clouds that followed cartoon skunks.

Pepé Le Pew. Now that was some art Clancy could get behind.

He ran his hand over his thinning hair. He couldn't blame the girls for their state, given what they'd been through in the last eight hours. Even their driving from Grace Odegaard's apartment to the art institute had been erratic. He pressed the earbud more firmly into place. It was a small bit of luck that the SIGINT materials he'd packed were identical to the audio guide headphones handed out with the exhibit.

Except *his* magnified sound.

He smiled as he picked up Salem Wiley's voice.

CHAPTER 11

Eight Years Old

"*You know why people hide things, don't you, Salem?*"

Daniel Wiley is hand-sanding a walnut monk's bench. The sun pokes through the shop window's dusty glass, and sawdust the color of heartsblood gambols in the beam. Salem trails her finger through the specks, upsetting their fairy dance. She's on summer break, between second and third grade. The weather's been moody, starting out cooler than usual but winding toward the end of the hottest July on record.

She's helped her dad pick out the wood for this bench. Held tools while he measured, cut, drilled, and Dremeled. Watched in awe as he carved the lion heads that would decorate each end of the two armrests. His woodshop is her favorite place on earth to be, most days.

"*So other people don't find them?*" *she guesses.*

He blows the last of the sawdust off his creation and reaches for the varnish. She wants him to open the can more than anything in the whole, whole world. He's always made her leave at this point in a project. She imagines the varnish must smell like butterscotch.

"*That's right.*" *He is smiling, encouraging. He wears the cut-off jean shorts and faded, paper-thin Led Zeppelin Icarus T-shirt he always wears at this stage in the project, this time of year. "And why don't they want other people to find them?*"

Salem pushes a sticky curl from her face. The Powderhorn Park wading pool closes at five o'clock. It's clear water that stops at her knees. She tells herself it's not scary, it's just a big bathtub, and cooling off an entire third of herself will feel like heaven. Maybe Bellie can ride the bus over and they can skip to the park together, joking about how they're too old for the baby pool but secretly loving it, and then walk home and drink grape Kool-Aid with ice cubes and watch the afternoon showing of Bel's favorite TV show, Days of Our Lives. Bel has promised Salem she'll understand it when she turns the ripe age of nine and that, until then, it's her job to watch and learn. "Because they don't have enough to share?"

He studies her. "You know what, I think you're old enough to stay for the final step."

Her mouth forms a perfect O. "You're going to let me watch the varnish?"

He sets down the can, chuckling. "If you like, but I have something that comes right before the varnish that I think you'll like even better. It's the final test of the furniture."

He reaches into the mouth of a carved lion's head and tugs its wooden tongue. Without releasing the tongue, he turns the head forty five degrees and slides the top of the armrest toward the center. Underneath lies a narrow hidden drawer. He repeats the action with the other lion's head.

Salem is speechless.

"I added the compartments while you were sleeping. I do that with every piece of furniture I make."

He flips the varnish lid and stirs the viscous liquid underneath. She wrinkles her nose against the acrid odor. It doesn't smell like butterscotch at all.

"Remember the question I asked you earlier?" He uses the inside lip of the can to scrape the excess varnish off the stir stick. "There's only one reason a person ever hides something."

She blinks, waiting.

He clicks the lid back into place. It makes a hollow snap, like a metal bone breaking.

"Fear. That's it."

Salem glances at the hidden drawers her father just revealed to her. She is no longer thinking of grape Kool-Aid.

CHAPTER 12

Minneapolis Institute of Art

Fear. If her dad was right, that's what had motivated her mother to hide her instructions in a cipher, which led Salem to this message hidden in *Judith Slaying Holofernes.*

But what level of fear would send her mom to these lengths?

"Amazing!" Bel barked.

Salem snapped her mouth shut, puzzled. Then she caught the shadow of the security guard closing in on them. She yanked off the glasses and stuffed them in her pocket.

"It truly is!" Salem nodded energetically. If they hadn't been drawing attention before, they certainly were now. "A real work of art, this Gentileschi. Ladies are doing it for themselves."

Bel grabbed her arm and steered her toward the door, marching right through the guards. They didn't speak again until they reached the bathroom.

Bel spun her around. "What did you see?" she demanded.

Salem pointed at the glasses in her pocket, her voice disbelieving. "The spectacles must be some kind of moiré device. They showed up a pattern in the blanket's fringe."

"Moray device? Like the eel?" Bel stepped away to peek under the stalls. Finding them all empty, she yanked Salem away from the door.

"Close—moiré. I know it from math, but the principle works on cloth, or canvas, I suppose."

Bel waited, eyes trained over Salem's shoulder, toward the entrance. At 5'11", she was over half a foot taller than Salem and nearly the same weight. She carried hers lightly, on the balls of her feet, ready to pounce on anyone who entered.

Salem massaged her nose where the glasses had left a mark. "It's when you have one lined pattern, and then you slightly rotate a second lined pattern on top of it. If you have something that mimics the initial lined pattern, like etched glass"—she tugged the spectacles out of her pocket and held them up—"it essentially renders the first pattern invisible. Only the lines of the second pattern can be seen. They can be shapes or words."

"And in this case . . ."

"Words!" Salem said triumphantly.

Bel was used to how Salem's brain worked. "And they said . . . ?"

"I could only read a little bit at a time, but I think I got it all before the security guard came over." Salem spoke the words into her phone loud enough for Bel to hear. "We need a translation of '*Il cuore della prima chiesa nel nuovo mondo.*'"

"Is that Italian?" Bel asked. "What's it mean?"

Siri's robotic voice answered: "The heart of the first church in the new world."

CHAPTER 13

Minneapolis Institute of Art

Bel and Salem passed the same clueless expression back and forth in a poor imitation of Laurel and Hardy.

Bel broke the spell. "I don't know what the hell that refers to, but I'm confident you'll figure it out. And the sooner you do, the sooner we rescue our moms." She hauled her own smartphone out of her back pocket. "Tell me what to look up."

Three women entered the bathroom, forcing Salem and Bel to move closer to the sinks. They huddled as far in a corner as they could, Salem talking them both through what they already knew. "The message in Gentileschi said 'first church of the New World.' Mom's note said to go home. So let's google 'first churches in Minnesota.' It's in the New World, technically, and home to both of us, right?"

Bel saluted, and they hunched over their phones, typing furiously.

"There's about a million first churches in Minnesota," Bel groaned. "First Seventh-Day Adventist, First Congregational, First Covenant . . ."

Salem bit her lip. "Let's take out the 'Minnesota' and try it in quotes."

"Try what in quotes?"

"'First Church.' That'll screen out competing names."

Bel updated her search and scrolled through her phone, reading out loud, under her breath. "First Church in Cambridge, First Church in Wethersfield, First Church in Boston, First Church in Texas—wait!" They spotted it at the same time: "First Church in Salem, Unitarian."

Bel's face scrunched up. "'Go *home*.' Have you ever been to Salem, Salem?"

Salem shook her head. "Not unless I was a baby and no one told me." She clicked the link and opened the "About Us" page on the First Church website. "The church was founded in 1629, one of the first in the nation." She pointed toward Bel's phone. "Verify when Gentileschi painted *Judith Slaying Holofernes* while I read the rest of the history."

A woman who had left the closest stall to wash her hands turned off the water and reached for a paper towel. "Historians' best guess is 1614 to 1618. Somewhere in there."

"Excuse me?" Bel asked, hackles raised.

The woman turned from the paper towel dispenser. It was the same coral-lipped staff member who'd let them into the Women in the Arts exhibit. "*Judith Slaying Holofernes*. Artemisia Gentileschi worked on it from 1614 to 1618, give or take."

"Are you an art history student?" Bel asked.

The woman pointed at faint crow's-feet accenting the corners of her eyes. "Ten years ago I was. I'm hoping to be a curator here someday. Or, more likely, at another art institute. They don't like to hire from their own pool in most places. They prefer a 'diversity of ideas.'" She held out her hand. "I'm Sheila. And word is you two almost got yourselves kicked out of the exhibit. If I'd known you were such weirdos, I never would have allowed you in to find Dr. Keller." Her smile belied her words.

Bel shook Sheila's hand. Salem followed. The woman's confident grip, combined with her open expression, made up Salem's mind for her. "Speaking of weird, can I ask you something?"

Sheila glanced at her phone. "Sure. I'm on break for another five minutes."

"Have you ever heard of a secret message, or a code, maybe, hidden in a painting?"

Sheila's soft laughter made Salem think of chimes. "Ah, I didn't peg you two for conspiracists, but it all makes sense now. Were you looking for a message in the Gentileschi?"

"We're just curious," Bel said.

Sheila's eyes narrowed. If she knew Bel was lying, she had the good manners not to call her on it. "I've never heard of anything in a Gentileschi, but there are some famous examples. Da Vinci, of course, painted an *LV* in Mona Lisa's right eye. Domenico Ghirlandaio's *Madonna with Saint Giovannino* depicts a pretty clear UFO flying in the background over Mary's shoulder, and that was painted in the fifteenth century. Michelangelo liked to dig up and dissect corpses, and the ceiling panels on the Sistine Chapel are supposed to be silly with hidden representations of brains and organs, though I don't see them myself."

Her eyes lit up. "My personal favorite Michelangelo is *The Prophet Zechariah*, which, if you look closely, features an angel flipping off Pope Julius II." She lifted her shoulders. "Art nerds love this stuff. It's our social currency. But yeah, I've never heard a peep about anything hidden in a Gentileschi."

Salem was studying a hundred angles a second, trying to line up the painting's dates with the founding of the First Church in Salem. "You said she painted *Judith Slaying Holofernes* from 1614 to 1618. I don't suppose there's any way she could have gone back to the painting to add something new, say a message, around 1629?"

Sheila tapped her upper lip. "Gentileschi didn't die until the 1650s, if memory serves, so timewise, it would certainly have been possible. But she wasn't the only one who could have added something. That painting was incognito for a good chunk of time. People actually mislabeled it a Caravaggio for years, and then it turned up in Boston in the 1840s before finding its way back to the Uffizi."

"So it'd be possible for someone to have painted a secret message into it at any time?"

"Sure," Sheila said, "anytime until it was placed in a museum under lock and key." Either her patience or grace had run their course. She leaned forward, lowering her voice. "Can you tell me what you found in it?"

"Sorry," Salem said. "I wish we could."

Bel nudged Salem, thanking Sheila for the information before leading Salem out and heading toward the main entrance. They wound through crowds to step outside into brisk air that smelled of rotting leaves. A bus full of costumed kids was unloading in the parking loop in front of the institute. They were heavy on the Batman, Disney princess, mermaid, and ninja getups. Normally, the sight would make Salem smile. The day had ground her down, though, her brain a war zone of spinning thoughts and bottomless worries.

"We both know what this means, right?" Bel shoved her hands in her pockets against the cool fall air. They walked briskly toward the parking ramp.

"That we need to . . . ?"

When Salem didn't finish, Bel filled in the words, her voice tender. "That we need to fly to Massachusetts to investigate."

Salem had feared what the Gentileschi message meant as soon as her phone had translated it, but there was something about Bel saying it out loud that drove it home as real as a nail to her forehead. She would need to leave Minneapolis and the routine that had kept her safe all these years. The thought froze Salem's blood, turning it thick and sluggish, choking her veins, tracking toward her heart. She breathed in through her nose, out through her mouth, as her therapist had taught her.

"Hey, it's about time I left the state," she said creakily.

Bel stopped and placed her hands on Salem's shoulders so she couldn't look away. Her voice was firm. "I can go to the First Church alone. You can be my brain on the ground back here, researching for me."

Salem wiped at the corners of her eyes. "It's about time I expand my horizons, right?" She infused her voice with her best imitation of bravado. "If you've got my back, what can't I do?"

Bel's expression was sour with worry, but she matched Salem's tone. "Turn invisible? Make a decent grilled cheese sandwich? Have any semblance of good taste in men?"

Salem punched her arm. "That's enough of that, missy." She didn't know if it was reconnecting with Bel, or the trauma of the morning, but the words spilled past her lips before she could stop them. "Hey, you and your mom are close, right?"

Bel looked taken aback. "Of course. We tell each other everything. Just like you and Vida. Thick as thieves, right?"

Salem bobbed her head, hoping the motion would distract from the flush spreading up from her neck. "Right! So we have a plan. You drive, I'll find us plane tickets. That's what credit cards are for, right?"

Dr. David Keller stood at the glass panels of Mia's second-story walkway, phone to his ear, speaking urgently, his stare glued to Salem and Bel until they disappeared from view. His pupils were dilated despite the daylight, a result of his body's ancient fight-or-flight response designed to provide him with the best possible vision when his life was on the line.

CHAPTER 14

Powderhorn Park, Minneapolis

Clancy Johnson ended the phone call. He stood on Vida Wiley's lawn. The brick agents had left, leaving him and Stone the heavy dry cleaning. They'd discovered nothing—not the woman and no signs of a struggle, just a normal, messy house. They'd been about to leave when he'd gotten the call, one he wasn't willing to answer with Stone in earshot.

He massaged his temples, hoping to delay the approaching migraine.

He didn't like the orders he'd just received.

At the Minneapolis Institute of Art earlier in the morning, both women had struck him as scared. Fear was a hard emotion to fake, and why would you bother if you didn't know you were being followed?

He was positive they hadn't made him. The tall drink of water was a cop, and a good one by her files. But she was young, and only a few hours earlier she'd laid eyes on a pool of blood that might be all they'd ever find of her mother. The poor kid was shell-shocked. He'd seen the same dazed expression and confidence-to-nowhere in his troops in Nam. If she didn't watch herself, she'd convince the both of them to walk off a cliff and believe it was a good idea the whole time.

The other one he hadn't figured out yet. It was funny, because when he'd looked over both their files, Salem Wiley appeared easier to crack than an egg. Born to a professor mom and artist dad, at age twelve, hippie dad swallows a handful of pills and drowns himself right in front of her eyes. Fast-forward a decade plus, and the girl predictably turns to the safety of computers and puzzles and leaves the world behind. Nearly a shut-in, from what he could tell.

But now, she found herself in the same boat as her friend, with her mom a blood puddle and a memory for all she knows. Yet, of the two, it was Wiley who was less twitchy. The girl was either going to crash hard, too hard to recover, or she was going to discover she was a different person than she'd imagined all these years. In his thirty years in the FBI, he'd seen it happen both ways.

And these girls didn't know the half of what they were in for. According to the phone call, Vida Wiley and Grace Odegaard had been leading double lives, both in up to their necks before they'd disappeared. That's what the man on the other end of the line had told him, and he'd yet to be wrong. Clancy never liked it when he took his orders from the H, as he called them, but such was the reality of government work. He'd do what the power asked him to do. He knew where to hide the bodies.

He jogged back toward the Bucar, the nickname all Bureau-assigned cars received, and crawled in. He held up his phone and pointed at it. "Sorry. Urgent business."

His partner, Lucan Stone, glanced at him. At least, he turned his head in Clancy's general direction. It was hard to tell where he was looking with those mirrored frames. "Asshole glasses" was what they'd called them in training. Clancy's reflection bounced off them, a tiny version of himself reflected back to him. He'd been told he resembled the actor Ed Harris enough times that he'd come to believe it.

"Everything okay?" Stone's voice was a deep rumble. The man always sounded like he was about to unleash something.

Clancy nodded. "Just the wife. Wants to know when we're gonna be back in DC."

Stone turned his attention to starting the car. "Don't we all."

Clancy frowned. He didn't know what actor Lucan Stone would be compared to. The movies didn't much interest Clancy Johnson. He was more of a nonfiction guy. Stone did remind him a little of a sculpture he'd passed by when leaving the art institute, though: as black as pitch and carved out of steel.

Stone had exploded through the FBI ranks but didn't have that hotshot air most wunderkinds did, and as a KMA—short for Kiss My Ass, referring to an agent still active but past the age of retirement and so who had nothing to lose—Clancy had worked with more than his share of young guns. Stone was quiet, and he did his job. Clancy Johnson liked him better than fine as a partner, but it was still a mystery whose side he was on.

Given Clancy's latest directive, he suspected he would find out soon.

Definitively.

"I'm flying to Massachusetts." Clancy reached for his Styrofoam coffee cup and took a sip of the bitter, grounds-filled liquid. Like French-kissing a goddamned potted plant. "Salem."

Stone didn't respond, didn't even turn his head. For a crazy second, Clancy Johnson wanted to flick the chisel of the man's cheekbones. He bet it'd make a solid *thunk*. Would hurt his fingers.

"Makes the most sense, given that's where the daughters are flying to, and they're the only assets we've got right now," Clancy continued, as if it were an afterthought. It wasn't unusual for them to work a case from different angles. He'd intentionally been one step behind Stone during this whole one. Allowed him the freedom to complete his real assignment. "What say you get the task force on track here, and we meet up out east?"

Stone seemed to be weighing all the alternatives. Hell, for all Clancy knew, he could be mentally alphabetizing his spice rack.

Stone finally spoke. "I'll meet you in Massachusetts before the end of the week. I have some calls to make."

Who do you answer to? The question nearly leaked out of Clancy before he could stop it, a top-secret burp. He almost couldn't help it. How much easier would this job be if they found out they both had the same goals? But in the end, he dismissed the foolishness. He was too old for that rookie mistake. He didn't know who yanked Stone's strings, but he knew who pulled his.

He shrugged reflexively, massaging the back of his neck.

We all have a boss in this life.

CHAPTER 15

Uptown, Minneapolis

Bel's phone played a snippet of the Beastie Boys' "Brass Monkey" in the lobby of Salem's apartment building. "That's work," she told Salem. She stopped and yanked her phone out of her pocket. "Meet you up there."

Salem nodded and headed up to her apartment. The next seats-available flight to Boston's Logan International left in seven hours, giving them time to shower and tie up loose ends before they hit the skies. She was hoping Skanky Dave was home so she could drop off Beans. Skanky Dave lived across the hall. He'd given himself the nickname, as far as she could tell, and he sold pot, hurt no one, and liked cats. He and Salem had exchanged keys shortly after meeting at the lobby mailboxes. She watered his plants while he traveled, and he promised to sit Beans if she ever needed it.

This would be the first time she'd asked.

When she reached the second floor, she knocked on Skanky Dave's door. No answer. She'd have to text him. She crossed the hall and unlocked her apartment, stepping in. It felt like it had been ten years rather than half a day since she'd been home. "Beans?"

The window to her fire escape was open, and the curtains drifted in on a cold, donut-scented breeze. Dammit. She'd forgotten to close it. The apartment temperature couldn't be above fifty degrees. She needed to shut and lock it quick, before Bel walked in and reamed her out.

"Beans? Are you out with your girlfriend again?"

Salem stopped halfway across the room and cocked her head. Something in her apartment seemed off. It wasn't the open window. She remembered leaving it that way. Everything else was neat and stacked and exactly as she'd left it, including the *Minneapolis Magazine* on her coffee table next to her laptop. All her dishes were put away. No water was running.

Still . . . was it a smell? "Beans!"

No response. But now, the chill grip of terror was massaging her stomach, moving up toward her heart. Something was definitely wrong.

She wanted to call for her cat again, but her mouth was too dry to make a sound.

She yearned to step backward, to turn, to escape out of the apartment, but her feet were frozen to the ground.

She tried to remember basic self-defense moves from the Krav Maga classes Bel had forced her to take, to call on the strength in her thick thighs and the sharp power of her fists, but her feet melted into the ground and her hands hung at her sides. They might as well have been tied to bricks.

Bel! She screamed it, but only in her head. *Help!*

Two cold hands closed around her eyes.

Her bladder released. It was the only movement she could make.

CHAPTER 16

Rosemount, Minnesota
Mosquito Munitions Plant

"Hello?"

Jason relaxed. Carl Barnaby's voice had always been a balm, so blithe and confident. "I located the two managers in Minneapolis."

"Excellent! Did they give you any more referrals?"

Jason's fists clenched, but he smeared butter over his voice. "I'm so sorry. No. Not yet."

"What?" The word was tinged with shock, or anger.

"I had to unexpectedly fire their neighbor. She showed up for a shift earlier than scheduled and brought her dog into work, of all things. I also had to let one of the two managers go." Jason rubbed his thumb over the smooth metal of the locket. "I have the remaining manager with me. She has yet to supply the promised referrals."

There was a pause on the other end. A muffled exchange filtered down the line. Jason imagined he heard the closing of a heavy door, soft footsteps on lush carpeting, the echo of conversation off brocaded walls.

Carl Barnaby returned to the line. "That might be all right. We have word that their daughters are on the way to Massachusetts to retrieve a document from the pulpit of one of the oldest churches in the United States." He took a breath. "We have reason to believe it might be the master referral list."

Jason shook his head, chuckling. Hiding the names in the pulpit of an old church? He'd seen extreme measures in his fifteen years working for the Hermitage, but this came close to taking the cake. You hunt a group of women for a couple hundred years, though, and it made sense they'd find ingenious ways to communicate with one another.

The Hermitage had always taken care of the obvious targets, like Benazir Bhutto, Indira Gandhi, and Anna Mae Aquash, but other than those very public Underground leaders, they'd had to rely on second- or thirdhand information to discover who their enemies were. The five women he'd killed before coming to Minneapolis had *most likely* been high up in the Underground. Same with Grace Odegaard and Vida Wiley, though how high, he couldn't know without the master docket.

But it sounded like he was about to get his hands on the legendary document. Finally, after all these years of searching.

Cut off the head, the snake dies.

Hot goddamn.

"You want me to obtain the referral list, dismiss the daughters, and continue on to the Crucible?"

Jason wouldn't utter her name. His phone was disposable, Carl Barnaby's line secured, but still. A name at that level would be flagged if anyone was listening, and someone was always listening. They were too close to achieving their mission to risk it on a loose tongue.

"Yes, and in that order." Carl Barnaby's voice relaxed into its signature jocularity. "I'll send someone for your current interviewee. We'll keep her in case a position opens up. You stay on task."

Jason nodded, even though Carl Barnaby couldn't see it. He waited as he heard the familiar click of being transferred. When the man's secretary came on, he exchanged directions to the abandoned Mosquito Munitions Plant in Rosemount, thirty miles south of Minneapolis, for the address of the First Church in Salem, Massachusetts. He didn't know if the woman would still be alive when the Hermitage Foundation's cleanup crew arrived.

He glanced at her. She was tied to a chair, hair hanging in her face. Crusted blood had turned her top a muddy brown. Her smell was strong, even from ten feet away, the uniquely sour, musky potpourri of pain, feces, and terror.

It was happy luck he'd discovered both of his Minnesota targets inside Odegaard's apartment. He would have loved to bring them back here for questioning, but because of the neighbor and her dog, he'd only had time to transport the one.

He'd cornered them on the fire escape and grabbed the woman nearest him. Whipping her around to face her friend, he held his fillet knife steady on her throat. Its metal reflected the moon back onto his cheek. The soft, distant purrs of cars driving through the night was the only sound. If either woman had screamed, the police would have arrived in minutes. Most women, he found, did not scream.

"Tell me who the rest of the Underground leaders are, or your friend dies."

The woman in his grasp closed her eyes, silent. The one he faced trembled but did not cry. "I'm the only one left," she whispered.

The soft *ding* of the elevator traveled through the foyer, across Grace Odegaard's apartment, and out onto the fire escape. Jason had locked her apartment door, but that wouldn't buy him much time. He studied the woman across from him, the chilly breeze ruffling her hair. The woman he held was murmuring, probably a prayer.

He opened her throat in one swift and lethal slice.

He stepped aside so the hot blood wouldn't stain his pants.

The woman who faced him, despite her earlier courage, melted as she watched her friend bleed out. She spoke from the cocoon of shock, her knuckles white where she gripped the cool metal railing. "You killed her. I told you what you asked."

He glided forward and held her. His touch was gentle. She recoiled from it. He tightened his grip, slitting her arm with his blade so she'd know not to waste his time. "What else can you tell me?"

When she didn't answer, he punched her once in the base of her neck. She crumpled. He tossed the fresh corpse of her friend over the side. It hit the ground three stories below with a wet *crunch*. He heard a scream on the other side of Grace Odegaard's apartment door, muffled but still clear. They'd found the body of the neighbor and her dog, were surely calling 911 this very moment. He hoisted the unconscious woman over his shoulder and climbed down the metal stairs, loading her into his waiting car.

He grabbed a tarp from the trunk, lifted the corpse onto his shoulder, and tumbled her into the back of his car. Before he could think twice, he sliced off her pinkie, certain that this would be the time he'd have the courage to do it. That impulse lasted until he closed the car door. He tossed the finger into the dumpster, disgusted with his cowardice, and drove away.

Still no sirens. This was good.

He drove straight to the munitions plant, an abandoned, isolated tangle of crumbling monoliths and grasping brown weeds, which he'd selected for exactly this purpose. The woman awoke shortly after they arrived. He'd placed the corpse of her friend next to her as an incentive, and he asked her again, "What else can you tell me?"

He'd asked her this many times over the course of the evening. Despite his persistence, she never spoke another word. He'd started a fire to keep them warm through the night as he sliced and cajoled, cooked his breakfast over it as she bled, and finally, once it was clear he wasn't getting any information from her, he'd wrapped a blanket around her shoulders and called Barnaby.

He admired her for all she'd withstood. If she truly was an Underground leader, she was worthy of the role, as good at her job as he was at his. He massaged the locket in his hand. The silver was warm from gripping it. He never took jewelry from the women he headhunted, had completely ignored the flimsy half-heart charm at her neck, but this trinket felt different. The word *mercy* was etched inside.

He shouldn't keep it.

It was not only against the rules but out of character. He'd already gone too far by cutting off the finger. Yet he couldn't help but drop the locket into his pocket before he stepped outside into the brisk October morning and slid behind the wheel of the rented Chevy Malibu. He updated his face as he drove, the motions automatic, his appearance returning to its normal dimensions. It wasn't magic. It was biology and a trick he'd learned after the first time his mother had broken his nose. He'd been six.

One punch.

The blood had gushed, drowning him in hot liquid. To save his own life, he'd instinctively put his hand to the meat of his nose and pushed.

It'd popped back into place, thinner than before. The bleeding slowed.

Curious, he worked on the cartilage of his nose like a muscle, moving bits, suspending them in place, moving others. It hurt a hundred times worse than any punch, but it was worth it when he discovered that he could change the shape of his nose as readily as other people could crack their jaws or blink.

With repetition and a growing tolerance to pain, he learned to alter the shape of the skin around his eyes and mouth and raise or lower his cheekbones as needed. At the time, he figured it was some rare double-jointedness. When he was old enough, he researched it. As near as he could tell, he had sentient Sharpey's fibers, the microscopic fingers of collagen that connected bone to muscle to skin. If he'd been born a hundred years earlier, he'd have ended up in a traveling freak show, next to the Bigfoot Lady, the Man with Three Eyes, Camel Girl, and two-faced Edward Mordrake.

Fortunately, he lived in modern times.

The ability to modify his appearance at will made him uniquely suited for this job, the one he'd been handpicked for, trained for, practiced two decades for. With wigs, colored contacts, a variety of clothing, and his fingerprints shaved off, he was impossible to trace.

He glanced at his watch, a gift from Carl Barnaby. He estimated it would take him a half an hour to reach the airport. He was Christmas-morning excited to be so close to the Crucible, the ultimate target.

He was the one who would make history, not her.

CHAPTER 17

Chappaqua, New York

Senator Gina Hayes held her first and only grandchild, the plush of the infant's costume soft against her hands. Ten-month-old Tia was dressed as a ladybug and intent on capturing her own antennae, which bobbed just out of reach. One veered close enough to tickle the senator's nose. Hayes sneezed. Her grin was broad and easy. The photographer snapped several photos in a millisecond.

"Don't sell those to the *Enquirer*," Senator Hayes joked. In the next moment, the baby spit up on her suit. Hayes glanced down. "Now *especially* don't sell those."

Her daughter rushed in with a wet wipe. Together, they cleaned up the spot. The baby giggled. Senator Hayes held the infant a minute longer, nuzzling her neck, inhaling her sweet milk-and-honey scent. "Nothing better than the smell of babies."

Her assistant was signaling her from the doorway. Gina Hayes had never had what could be called a normal life, not since her father had been elected fortieth president of the United States thirty-five years earlier, but at least she used to have stretches of hours alone with her family. She missed that since she'd declared her own run for the presidency. She handed her granddaughter back, reluctantly, planting one last kiss on her plump, warm cheek.

"You'll stay for dinner?" the senator asked her daughter. It was a plea more than a question. "Dad is grilling. Probably the last outdoor meal of the year."

"Of course. Baby Tia and I wouldn't miss handing out candy at the old homestead."

Gina was caught off-guard by the wash of relief. She attributed it to the demands of her global schedule. She wasn't seeing her family enough.

Numerous times on the campaign trail, she'd been asked why she was running for president. She delivered the canned answers—she was inspired by her father to a life of public service, it was a calling, she knew she could make a difference—but sometimes, a version of the truth leaked out: she was running for her daughter.

Catherine wasn't beautiful, but she was smart and she was kind, and Gina was proud of her in the deepest marrow of her bones. When Hayes had found herself unmarried and unexpectedly pregnant three decades earlier, however, the future had not looked rosy. She'd thought about and dismissed the idea of an abortion. Instead, she chose single parenthood. Knowing she'd have two mouths to feed, she worked twice as hard to make partner at the law firm, where she put in more hours and acquired and won more cases than any of her colleagues.

Not only *didn't* she make partner, but she also discovered her salary was $20,000 less a year than the man who did. He'd been working there a year less than Hayes. She knew about his salary because he proposed to her after having known her only eight weeks, aware she was pregnant with another man's child.

She said yes, and she and Charles Hayes entered the world of politics together.

Her life wasn't a straight trajectory from there, nothing worked that way, but she always kept close to her heart the fact that being born female was still a handicap in parts of this country.

She would change that for her daughter.

"See you outside?" Catherine pecked her mother's cheek and disappeared through the french doors leading toward the manicured backyard, carrying the baby. The Secret Service detail stepped aside to let her pass. Hayes's lead bodyguard, Theodore, broke from the group of men to stand nearer Gina.

She watched her daughter and granddaughter through the floor-to-ceiling windows. It had been an unusually warm fall. Still, most of the leaves had given up the ghost in a windstorm last week. All that was left were trunks with branches like skeleton hands rising out of the ground. Clouds obscured the afternoon sun and backlit the landscape like a daguerreotype.

Perfect for Halloween, Gina thought, inhaling woodsmoke and the melancholy of fall before stepping into her study. She loved this time of year in upstate New York.

"You look tired." Matthew Clemens had been her assistant since her days as a district court judge. He served as her memory and, some days, as her sanity.

"That's because I am," she responded cheerfully, letting Theodore close the door behind them. The muscled, suited man never let her out of his sight except when she used the restroom, and even then, he waited outside the door. "What's the latest?"

Matthew glanced at his iPad. "You're ahead in the polls. Four points. It doesn't hurt that Americans are growing fond of health care."

Championing universal health care and uniting the Senate vote behind it made the US one of the last, but not *the* last, developed countries to provide health care to all its citizens. It had also painted a bright bull's-eye on Senator Gina Hayes's back for her entire legislative career. Now it seemed the tides were turning. She'd been in the game too long to be surprised.

Matthew continued. "Other than that, Israel peace talks are in the shitter, Afghanistan is a morass, Syria's on fire, and we're running out of oil. Oh, and the media doesn't think the world is ready for a female president of the United States."

Gina stepped to the window, watching her husband and daughter play with Tia. She appreciated Matthew's attempts at humor, even if he usually missed the mark. He reminded her of Stephen Stucker's Johnny in *Airplane!*

Johnny, what can you make out of this?

This? Why, I can make a hat or a brooch or a pterodactyl . . .

"So, nothing new, then?" she asked.

"Just one thing." Matthew's tone was serious enough to make her turn. "The Secret Service wants to up your security detail. With the election eight days away, there is a whole new wash of threats rolling in."

Theodore, who must have had at least one ancestor who was a statue, made no sound.

Hayes nodded.

"That's it?" Matthew asked. "You don't want to know about any of the threats? No specifics on the gun-toting fringers who are scrabbling to make history? Not even a peek at their crayon plans to annihilate the ball-crushing she-bitch with the audacity to run for ruler of the free world?"

Hayes peeked again at her family. Charles was scrubbing the grill's metal grate, and she could almost smell tonight's dill-marinated salmon, which was his specialty. Nearby, Tia was clutching her mom's fingers and trying to stand, her black ladybug antennae bouncing in the breeze. Charles turned to laugh at their antics. He'd raised Gina's daughter as his own.

She turned back to Matthew, smiling softly at his kind, round face. "I can either walk through life looking over my shoulder, or I can do my damn job. It's an easy choice when you look at it that way, don't you think?"

CHAPTER 18

Uptown, Minneapolis

"What the hell, Lemming!" Connor Sawyer jumped away from Salem. "Did you piss yourself?"

Salem stood in the warm puddle of her pants, fear mashing with shame to create a horrible, throat-clogging paste. She turned slowly so she was facing him. Her cheeks were on fire.

Connor laughed, shaking his head in disbelief. He was a beefy man, blond, with the kind of face that would be hard to describe to a police sketch artist without making him sound like a Johnny Bravo cartoon character. When Salem had first spotted him at the law library two years earlier, she'd blushed. He hadn't even glanced her way. A week later, he finally noticed her when he checked out some books. He'd invited himself over that night.

"How'd you get in here?" Her voice was high and squeaky. She wanted to run to the bathroom, strip her clothes off, burn them, never show her face again.

He was still smiling, staring at the drops dangling from the hem of her jeans before joining the pool on the floor. She saw him parsing the words in his head, deciding how he would tell this story to his friends for maximum humor. "The stoner next door let me in. I was heading to a friend's Halloween party up the street. Thought I'd stop by while I was in the neighborhood."

The fear subsided enough for her to notice his costume. He had nickels taped to the back of his T-shirt. He caught her glance. "My favorite band."

In that crystalline moment, she finally saw their relationship for what it was—she was his booty call, plain and simple. He wasn't stopping by to ask her to tonight's party, or to any party. He'd never once appeared in public with her, which was her fault as much as his, but it still hurt. He would never take her to the doctor if she was sick, ask her about her day, or care which of the Jordan neighborhood kids she'd helped or what computer program she'd written.

They didn't have a relationship, never would, no matter what she hoped for or tolerated from him. What was even more painful was the awareness that she still cared what he thought, cared desperately, and here she was standing in front of him drenched in her own urine.

The scraping sound of the hallway fire door made her yelp. Bel was coming! Salem tossed an afghan over the puddle on the floor and leaped toward the bathroom.

"It's normal to lose bladder control when you're scared, right?" Salem asked as they dropped off Bel's duffel at the Delta counter. When Salem had cleaned herself off and worked up the courage to leave the bathroom, she'd discovered Connor and Bel on opposite ends of the couch, paging through magazines, not talking, Beans knitting mittens on Bel's lap. While Connor and Bel had never before met, and in fact Salem had never even mentioned him to Bel, they'd clearly struck up an immediate and lasting dislike for one another.

Connor left shortly after.

Skanky Dave had yet to come home, so Salem was forced to let herself into the apartment to leave a note with the instructions on caring for Beans. She'd also filled several pans with water and several others with cat food, just to be safe.

It had taken her the rest of the evening and the entire drive to the airport to tell Bel that she'd been "seeing" Connor for over a year and that he'd scared the living daylights out of her.

"You need to dump that asshole," Bel stated unequivocally. They'd both packed light, but Bel was checking her bag so she could haul her Glock 19. "Here. You can use my phone."

Salem didn't take it. "Not now. Maybe later."

"How'd he get in?" Bel asked, watching her bag ride the belt out of sight.

"Said Skanky Dave let him in. That's the first time Dave has ever done that."

"You should have kneed Connor," Bel said, accepting her luggage receipt from the attendant. "That's exactly what he deserves for breaking into your apartment and scaring you like that."

She led the way through the crowd, raising her voice to be heard. "Actually, if I read his douche meter accurately, he's earned a good knee-ing simply by being Connor Sawyer. But damn, Salem, a decent guy doesn't jump people. *Ever.* I'm going to bone you up on the Krav Maga."

Salem jogged so she could walk alongside Bel. "You know the weirdest part? When I was walking him out, he offered to watch Beans. He's never offered something like that before."

Bel rolled her eyes. "What a hero."

The security line loomed ahead. As horrible as Connor's surprise had been, it had distracted her from much of the worry about leaving Minnesota. After that wore off, she'd let the Ativan and her rational mind convince her that this wouldn't be so bad, Bel was by her side, the worst had already happened when her dad had died and Grace and Vida had disappeared, and it was time to take action and stop being afraid.

If she passed through security, however, she'd be committing to leaving, to tempting Fate, the Universe, God, whoever, demonstrating to them that she didn't respect their power to rip her world into twitch-ing shreds. That's why she'd never left Minnesota, hadn't left the Twin

Cities since her dad's suicide, had lived her quiet life in its prescribed track.

Chaos lived beyond.

Salem knew she had to walk through security to save her mom and Gracie, but a fear so raw it burned like shame churned the fourteen-year-old memory to the tip-top of her consciousness: Daniel Wiley wading into the cool abyss of Nelson Lake (*Mom, where was Mom*), Salem onshore, twelve years old and wearing her first bikini, so proud of its rainbow colors, of her flat belly, of the way the shadow of her hips curved on the movie screen of the dirty brown beach.

When she looked up, her dad had disappeared, had been underwater far too long, but she was too *scared shocked this can't be real it's happening to someone else* to save him, to even scream for help. A family from Iowa, renting the cabin next door, had found her on the shore, unconscious, bleeding from her left cheek, a cut she sustained when she fainted.

Her dad's body surfaced later that evening.

She had never told anyone, not even Bel, that she hadn't tried to rescue him.

She weighed and measured that reality every day of her life.

"You okay?" Bel asked.

Salem was twirling a chunk of hair with her finger. Twirling, pulling, twisting. Suddenly, the lock was in her hand, loose, something you'd find in the drain. A man wearing a trench coat and pulling a wheelie suitcase pushed against her to get into line. Bel shoved him back. A TSA officer was striding toward them. Salem was breaking into so many tiny pieces that she'd never be whole again.

"Salem."

Bel gripped her hands. Salem saw the gesture but could not feel it. "It's okay to be scared. I'm scared, too."

Salem looked into her eyes, her teeth chattering. She'd stared into those blue pools more than she'd looked at anything except a computer screen.

"You remember the baby ducks?" Bel asked. "You were eight. Nine, maybe. I was sleeping over. You and I snuck to Powderhorn to break into the wading pool, except you heard something." Bel squeezed her hands. "Remember?"

Salem did, distantly, and then with greater focus. There'd been a heavy rain, and it had washed the streets with that bright green smell like the inside of a grass blade. They'd gotten as far as the slide when Salem heard the noise.

"It was a baby duck, trapped in a cistern." Bel put her hands on her hips. "I know you remember. And I wanted to get somebody, but you said we didn't have time. You pulled off your jacket, grabbed one sleeve, and made me hold the other end so you could drop into there."

The pit had been as dark as a grave. They'd only known a duckling was down there from its frantic cheeps. *Maybe it's trying to steer clear of the alligators and clowns that're also down there,* Salem remembered thinking. But she'd gone down, gripping the elastic end of that jacket so tightly that even now, almost two decades later, she could call up that feeling of her hand bones crushing together.

"That's right," Bel said, kissing her forehead. "You've got a super hero in there. And both our moms need her now, so come on."

"Yeah." Salem bit her lip and stepped into line.

"Hey." Bel lightly punched Salem's arm. "How about we make a deal?"

"What?"

Bel's eyes were sad, but there was a twinkle to them. "If we get through this, you and me, next time you see that Connor dude, you flush him like the turd he is." She held out her pointer finger and pinkie for Salem to match in their ritual gesture. "Deal?"

The gesture was automatic. Salem touched her matching fingers to Bel's. "Deal."

But she couldn't meet Bel's smile, as faint as it was, because an icy dread had taken up residence between her heart and stomach. She and Bel wouldn't be coming back to Minnesota, not ever. She was sure of it.

TUESDAY

November 1

CHAPTER 19

Salem, Massachusetts

Jason's layover had been brief. It hadn't gone exactly as he'd wanted, but it was done. Now he was back on track in Massachusetts. The drive straight north from Logan International took more than its estimated half an hour due to thick traffic. The coast was to his right. He couldn't see it, but the kick of salt water washed in through his open windows.

When he pulled into Salem, the traffic worsened as the roads tightened and curved. Cape Cods and bungalows loomed over the four lanes of road, nearly tipping on top of him. The deeper into the center of town he drove, the more regal the architecture became. He motored past Easter egg colored Victorian homes, and Greek Revivals, and Italianates. The streets narrowed even further as he neared the ocean, the roadsides crowded with reclaimed housing for captains and sailors, small, salt air–cured wood-frame homes jammed into one another, seagulls flapping overhead.

The fall had been unusually warm on the East Coast. Late summer bloomed everywhere.

He knew flowers. Loved them. Could recognize most by sight. His mother had taught him all about them. *North American Flowers* was the only book she owned, as a matter of fact, and when she was feeling particularly sad, or lonely, she'd call him over, tug him on her lap, and turn the pages.

"I'll have a garden like this someday."

Not *we'll*. Never *we'll*.

Hydrangeas, dahlias, lavender as tall as a boy, black-eyed Susans. His mom would love it here.

She would never discover that, though, because he wasn't going to let her out.

He patted his blades. He considered himself a sculptor, his knives a chisel revealing the truth under a person's skin. Tonight, after he'd delivered the daughters' heads along with a list of the remaining Underground leaders to the Hermitage Foundation, after he'd basked in the admiration of the greatest men in the world, he would sharpen his knives.

It would be his reward.

His cell phone spoke up, informing him that 316 Essex Street was on his right.

He leaned forward so he could take in the magnificence of the entire building.

If he were a religious man, the Salem First Church would be the type of building he'd feel right at home worshipping in. It was Gothic Revival, constructed of granite so gray and foreboding that it repelled the cool morning sunshine. The building resembled a castle barbican more than anything, with a tall, square, fortifying tower at the center and two shorter walls on each side, their roofs lined with toothlike ramparts capable of hiding medieval archers.

The top center of the tower housed quatrefoil windows on all four sides. Below that but only on the front, enormous intersecting tracery windows were embedded and then echoed in the shorter section of the building on each side below the battlements.

Jason parked across the street and strolled toward the front entrance. Cascading rosebushes along the wrought iron fence softened the appearance somewhat. Red roses had always been his favorite. Their color, their delicate nature, the sweet saltiness of their smell reminded him of the taste of a woman's lips.

He let the magnificence of it all wash over him. He wanted to always remember this moment, the cusp of laying hands on the Underground's leadership docket. Every detail must be stored exactly. Running his hands over the sheath just inside his jacket, he smiled.

"Excuse me, can I help you?"

The smile still lighting his face, Jason turned toward the voice.

It was a man out walking his English bulldog. He visibly relaxed when his eyes connected with Jason's because Jason had donned his everyman face: white, clean, unremarkable, safe. A face you'd want to offer a bank loan to, or apologize to if you accidentally pulled him over for speeding.

"I'm from out of town," Jason said, pivoting from truth to lie with the grace of a dancer. "My parents were married in this church."

The man mirrored Jason's smile, though his bulldog was making a high-pitched growl, its hackles pointing toward the sun. "The building is beautiful, isn't it? One of the oldest congregations in the United States. Are you going inside?"

Jason shrugged. "Maybe. Didn't want to bother anyone." He widened his grin.

The man wanted to help, almost couldn't stop himself. "The office doesn't open until ten, so normally you'd have a half an hour wait, but I saw Samantha go in there just before you pulled up." He pointed toward a walkway leading past the enormous face of the church. "Ignore the big red door. The actual offices are around back."

"Appreciate it." Jason sauntered toward the path.

Though he had reacted well, he didn't like that someone had spoken to him. It made him feel small. Tiny cracks and pops echoed in the courtyard as he lengthened and widened his nose, returning to his natural face with the relief of a man removing his tie at the end of a workday.

He passed a huge old house, likely the reverend's, and walked toward a more modest addition to the church, one with a distinct 1970s feel, twice as long as the original church and laid perpendicular across the back of it. The whole works would resemble a fat-tailed L from the sky. The door of the addition announced the hours. Indeed, the office wasn't scheduled to open for another half an hour, as the dog walker had reported.

Jason tried the door. It was unlocked.

He stepped through it and onto a wheelchair ramp. The interior was underwater quiet in that way that only churches can be. He walked up the ramp, the scent of frankincense surrounding him. He loved the smell, burned it himself all the time. Reminded him how important he was to the Hermitage Foundation.

If he was honest with himself, and he always was, he wasn't ever going to take to religion, not any of the three versions the Hermitage had offered him when they pulled him off the streets of New Orleans. He liked the idea of it, but he knew better. Sleeping in alleys and letting men with beery breath fondle him for money had taught him all he needed to know about whether there was a God.

While he'd never buy into the hopefulness of religion, he respected the orderliness of it, and he particularly appreciated the power enjoyed by the leaders. It was the rabbi, Moshe Haimovich, high up in the Hermitage leadership, who'd ferreted him and the other kids out of the New Orleans building where they'd been squatting. It wasn't a home so much as four walls and a ceiling, empty since the hurricane. And the kids weren't so much friends as wary travelers sharing a shelter.

It had been funny to see a rabbi in the Lower Ninth. Odder still to hear him promise clean clothes and a warm bed. Jason hadn't believed a word he'd said, but he was hungry, and he itched, and he figured he could slice the little rabbi if he asked for anything Jason wasn't interested in giving. Four other kids came with, including Geppetto, the only person Jason had ever been afraid of.

Moshe had been telling the truth. He gathered boys from all over the city, cleaned them up, helped them obtain their GEDs, and then put them through college, and if they showed a special aptitude, he taught them about the Hermitage Foundation. Jason'd been proud that, of the thirty-two boys who'd started the program at the same time as him, only he and Geppetto had been inducted. Rabbi Moshe and Archbishop Christoph del Monte became his personal contacts, and along with Carl Barnaby, they'd guided Jason to his purpose.

The Hermitage Foundation was his life.

And finally, he'd be able to pay them back for all they'd done. He wouldn't let them down. Heart pumping pleasantly, he raised his voice. "Hello?" It echoed back to him. He stroked the knife sheath in his jacket again, for comfort.

A gray-haired woman peeked out of an office up the ramp and to his left. "Welcome!" Her eyes lit brighter when she spotted him. He was accustomed to that. His natural face was handsome, preternaturally so. "What can I do for you?"

She didn't even mention that she wasn't open yet. He appreciated that immediately. Some women liked to shame a man. He could tell this one was different.

"Sorry to bother you. My parents got married here?" He considered smiling and thought better of it. No need to waste a gesture when she was already in hand. "They've both passed. I was hoping for some reflective time in the church. It sounds silly, doesn't it?"

She clutched her hands over her heart. "Of course not. Follow me." She led him through the modern addition, sharing some of the First Church's history on the way. At the end of the hall, past the cabinets featuring teapots and assorted church artifacts, they entered the original foyer. It was huge, groaning with authority.

They stopped in front of an enormous carved wood door.

"The First Church is right through here." She stepped away.

When he didn't say anything, she returned to her office.

He dragged open the door.

CHAPTER 20

Salem, Massachusetts

"Know anything about the town?" Bel asked. "I've only heard of the witch trials."

Salem noticed the cabbie roll his eyes in the rearview mirror, but she didn't care. Something had shifted in her since she'd stepped on the plane. She'd heard it, a small sound like the crack of a robin's egg inside her chest, followed by the tiniest thrumming. She wasn't sure if she'd broken something or started to fix it, but she didn't feel as scared as she'd thought she would leaving Minnesota. In fact, a fire had started burning in her, a desire so powerful that it was imprinted on each of her cells: she wanted to be close with her mom.

She'd never wanted that before, at least not that she'd admit. And not a proximity relationship, but an honest, true one, where they opened to each other, where Salem could be accepted no matter what she did. And she'd do the same for Vida, her mother, the woman she'd placed on a pedestal so high that she forgot how to walk alongside her. Now that her mom had disappeared, Salem wanted nothing more than to hold her close.

Still, she'd started a game with herself on the plane and continued it through to the taxi ride. The rules were simple: on each inhale, she'd count to three, and again on each exhale. If she forgot, she'd have to touch her thumbs to each of her four fingers. Then she could restart the breathing exercise.

If Bel noticed, she didn't comment.

She began the soothing finger routine as she spoke. "They weren't trials so much as mass hysteria at the highest levels." She riffled through her mental notes, finding an island of safety in the sea of facts. "Happened around 1629, 1630. Twenty people were executed, mostly women, based on sketchy evidence and supposed eyewitness testimonial. Five more died in prison."

Pointer to thumb and back again. "Based on what I researched, it was a perfect storm of small-town politics, Puritanism gone berserk, and women who weren't allowed outlets for their creativity or brains. Oh, with a dash of racism. One of the first accused women, Tituba, was a Native American or African or Caribbean slave, depending on what you read."

"And you read *everything*, didn't you?" Bel said. "I was watching you on the plane, you know. You should have slept."

"If you were watching me, that means you didn't sleep, either."

"Yeah." Bel rubbed her face. "Too much on my mind, you know?"

Salem knew.

Bel leaned back in the seat, her eyes closed. "You know what I'm gonna do when we get our moms back?"

The question shot straight to Salem's heart. Since they'd left Minneapolis, they'd avoided talking about their mothers in any specific sense. Salem liked it that way. She thought Bel, who'd acted on her game since the moment the police had called, felt the same. But Salem realized that Bel was used to dealing with *other* people's crises. She didn't have Salem's boots-on-the-ground personal tragedy management experience. She might be crumbling behind the scenes. The thought humbled Salem.

She slid her arm around Bel's shoulders, even though the six inches Bel had on her made it awkward. "Get matching tattoos, all of us, saying 'If lost, return to . . .'?" She'd stopped her finger ritual.

Bel's long lashes stayed on her cheeks, but a smile appeared. "I was going to say that we'd have your mom bake her famous chocolate chip cookies, and my mom would pop her homemade caramel corn, and we'd turn the living room at your house into a pillow fort, just like we did when we were kids. And we'd watch movies. All. Day. Long. Those terrible, smarmy old ones that Mom and Vida always forced us to watch, like *An Officer and a Gentleman* and *Doctor Zhivago*."

Salem sighed deeply. She'd forgotten about those times the four of them would connect, back when both girls were still in high school. "I can see it. Between flicks, your mom would complain about how bad her latest boyfriend was in bed, and my mom would talk about some awful politician she was dealing with, and you and I would roll our eyes and pretend we weren't listening, but really, we'd be soaking it in. We'd inhale the whole first batch of my mom's 'famous chocolate chip cookies,' so she'd have to open another tube, and Gracie would haul out the carton of vanilla ice cream she always brought, and you'd get terrible farts like you always did."

"Exactly," Bel said dreamily. "And you'd burp like a sailor on shore leave, like *you* always did, and we'd hug our moms, and we'd make sure they knew how much we loved them."

Salem's heart twisted. "Yeah. We'd make sure of that."

"But look at you, girl." Bel opened her eyes and leaned forward. "You left Minneapolis and the world didn't end. You're breaking your chains! Going back to how you used to be."

"Yeah," Salem said again. "I suppose." She wasn't sure what Bel meant. Her dad's suicide had shrunk her world, but she'd always been a homebody. It wasn't a time for arguing, though.

The white Metro Cab whizzed by a sign informing them they were entering Salem, Massachusetts, population 44,722.

Salem gazed out the car window, past Bel, at the blaze of fall flowers. Under normal circumstances, she'd find the town lovely, a careening mix of old and new architecture with streets as narrow as thread. She glanced at her phone. "Quarter to ten. That's perfect. We can be at the front door of the First Church the second they open."

She nodded toward a building flitting past their window. "Oh, and Nathaniel Hawthorne is from here. There's the House of the Seven Gables." The lonely widow's walk on the top of the building made her shiver, stark black wood against the sea-colored sky.

The cab driver repeated the First Church's Essex Street address.

Salem nodded. "That's right." Three minutes later, he pulled in front of a wrought iron fence draped with blooming roses, a suitably grand building behind it. Bel handed him her credit card a split second before Salem could. The cabbie ran the Visa, and they grabbed their bags and stepped out into the embrace of a New England fall.

It was love at first smell for Salem: sleepy lavender, car exhaust, the twist of the sea. The ground under her lurched the tiniest bit. She wondered if she'd imagined it. "Do you think this is the door we go in through?" She pointed straight ahead.

The wooden door was old, certainly, but it appeared oddly underused.

"I know how we find out." Bel touched the slight bulge of her holster under her jacket before walking through the wrought iron gate, past the rosebushes, and up the stone steps.

CHAPTER 21

Salem, Massachusetts

They stood outside the raggedy old church. It had looked so abandoned that they'd stopped at the main office to ask the woman working there if they were allowed to enter. She said they definitely were.

Salem thought, for the millionth time, of the two codes that had brought them here.

Talk: to Keller about revenge then go home follow the trail trust no one
The heart of the first church in the new world

"I expected it to be more posh, somehow," Bel said, hands on hips.

Internally, Salem agreed, but this all seemed so bleak and impossible that she had to put a positive spin on it to keep from crying. "We'd be lucky to look this good when we're four hundred years old."

"Truth." Bel held open the door. "After you."

They stepped inside. The cling of mothballs and mustiness scrambled up Salem's nose. She took a quick survey of the small space before pointing toward the ceiling. "This beam is the only part of the original building that remains, according to my research. It was the central support in the meetinghouse that became the First Church."

She indicated the other material inside the building, including ancient-looking pews and warped walls. "A lot of this was added later, when the church was moved."

"So that makes that beam . . ."

"The heart of the first church," Salem said, finishing her sentence. "We need to check it for hidden drawers or messages."

Bel shook her head in disbelief. "What have we gotten into? Mom and Vida disappear and leave some weird code behind, which may or may not have meant to send us to Massachusetts to feel up a four-hundred-year-old chunk of wood. The guys on my beat would love this."

"More feeling up, less talking," Salem said.

"You do the feeling, I'll do the lookout." Bel grabbed a stool and handed it to Salem. "That should get you tall enough. I wouldn't have any idea what to look for. It's your dad who was the mystical carpenter. All my father offered was a onetime sperm donation, remember?"

Bel hadn't meant the words as anything but fact, Salem was sure of it. Still, they stung. "And my dad killed himself, *remember*?"

Bel stared at her cross-eyed. The tension of the last twenty-four hours was finally crackling, pushing them to the edge of one of their rare fights. They'd had three in their lives, by Salem's count. The first happened when Salem was eight and Bel eleven, and Bel was convinced that Salem had purposely wrecked her Furby because she was jealous of Bel's new friendship with a neighborhood girl. Salem had insisted that it was an accident. They didn't speak for a whole month, then one day ran into each other on the playground (Salem suspected their mothers had something to do with that) and picked their friendship up where it had left off.

The second fight occurred seven years later, when Salem told Bel she'd decided not to go to college because she'd found an online coding job she could do from home. Bel had gone ballistic, yelling at her until she wore her down.

The third clash happened more recently, just three weeks ago, when Bel brought Rachel, her new girlfriend, to Minnesota for a visit. Rachel, a petite Korean woman five years younger than Bel, worked the makeup counter at the Macy's in downtown Chicago. She wouldn't leave the house without her hair curled and her eyeliner and lipstick perfect, she texted or checked Facebook the entire visit, and she made velvet jabs at

Bel's low-maintenance look, calling the criticism "professional courtesy" before breaking into an insincere laugh.

When Bel asked Salem what she thought of Rachel, Salem had made the mistake of answering honestly.

Bel had left for Chicago the next day without saying goodbye.

Her middle-of-the-night phone call was the first time they'd spoken since.

This was not the time for a fourth dustup. Salem would absorb whatever was needed to keep the peace. She pushed her curls back from her face and looked Bel in the eye. "Sorry for snapping at you. Will you peek behind the pews while I look up here?" She stared at the beam. "Just in case."

"What am I looking for?" Bel still sounded crabby.

"Anything that seems out of place." Salem bit her tongue. Bel was wired to need the last word, and it wouldn't cost Salem anything to give it to her.

"Like us?" But Bel did as she was told, pacing toward the front of the old church.

Salem rubbed the back of her neck before perching the stool under one of the two ends of the beam. If she stood on the three-legged chair, she was able to feel all sides of the seemingly solid chunk of wood. The truth was, she didn't know exactly what to look for, either. If the beam contained a secret compartment, it would require some sort of trigger, but the thing looked like an unbroken chestnut girder, as dense as rock.

Still, she began to search, inch by square inch.

CHAPTER 22

Nine Years Old

"Can you find the secret compartments, honey?" Daniel indicates the simple desk he's been working on.

"You're silly," she says. There's nothing magical about the plain, boring old desk he's been working on. Besides, she wants to play with the Rubik's Snake her dad bought her from a garage sale up the street. Designed by Ernő Rubik, inventor of the Rubik's Cube, the snake is made up of twenty-four multicolored plastic prisms that rotate four different ways. "Why would I look for anything hidden in there?"

Daniel gently takes the snake from her. He twists the four prisms on one end of the V shape it's currently in, and voilà! It's now a snake with a clubfoot. Salem claps her hands and squeals.

Her dad's face breaks into a grin, a great big crinkly smile that looks like home and hearth and everything right in the world. "You see?" he says. "It feels good to discover hidden things. That's why you should search this desk."

She twists the other leg of the V and creates a club. She is falling into the puzzle, leaving this moment, her focus on the snake. She spots how, thirty-four moves out, she could transform the snake into a uniform ball. Daniel ruffles her hair, pulling her attention back.

"How about you give your old man a moment of your time?"

She doesn't want to. The snake puzzle is calling to her. But he takes his wallet out of his worn jeans pocket, reaches in and tugs out a credit card, and slides it under the rim between the top and back of the unsanded desk.

A secret drawer pops open. It's on the leg of the desk, completely unexpected. Salem drops the snake and peers into the drawer. "A diamond!"

He laughs, a deep, rumbling belly laugh, as she holds the giant Richie Rich gem in the air. "I bought that at the garage sale, too," he says. "You can keep it."

She can't look away from the plastic jewel. "Will you show me where the other secret drawers are?"

"I'll do better than that," he says. "I'll let you discover them yourself, and you can keep whatever you find inside."

She locates two more drawers within ten minutes by knocking along the wood until she detects a hollowness and then sliding her fingernail in nearby cracks to release the spring. The first drawer holds a plastic ruby, the second a Lucite emerald the size of an apricot.

Daniel's pride is written so plainly on his face that Salem blushes. "It wasn't that hard, Dad."

He pulls her into a breath-stealing embrace. She doesn't complain, though, or consider dropping the jewels she clutches in her hands.

"You've got a gift, honey," he murmurs into her hair. "You make me proud."

CHAPTER 23

Salem, Massachusetts

It occurred to Salem, not for the first time, what an odd niche her dad had found with his carpentry. There couldn't have been many crafts-people creating furniture with hidden compartments. She had no idea who his clientele were. They never came into the house.

One day, a white van would pull up—always a white van—and the latest piece of furniture would vanish. That night, like clockwork, Daniel would take her and Vida out for crab legs, and he'd pay cash. Looking back, it had seemed normal because it was all she knew, but she wondered now if she should have paid more attention to who her dad worked for.

She'd been too busy playing, and then learning, at his feet. There'd been so many pieces of furniture that she couldn't pick a favorite. One time, she'd helped Daniel construct a flat-top highboy decorated with cornices. A shallow drawer was hidden behind a broad piece of molding, and it could only be accessed by opening the visible drawer underneath it and sticking her hand inside to release a wooden spring.

Many, many more pieces of furniture followed. The best hiding places were always the simplest, he made a point of telling her, and that's why his secretary with the artless push-drawers hidden in its legs was Daniel Wiley's most popular piece.

She swallowed past the pain that accompanied memories of her father. After all, she should be grateful that he'd taught her what he had. She knocked on the First Church beam, and she stuck her fingernails in crevices, and she pressed. She found a rhythm, and the world fell away. Whatever her mom had sent her here to find, she would discover. Whatever puzzle needed cracking, she would solve it. Whatever information—

"Salem?"

The tenor of Bel's voice carried a warning, but Salem didn't need it. She'd felt it the same time as Bel, a tingle in the back of her neck, a sensation so strong it was almost a smell, almost like . . .

Frankincense.

Bel jogged toward the front of the church, patting the gun at her hip. Salem's eyes shot into every corner of the building. She felt exposed atop the stool. She began to crawl off but was frozen by a voice, deep and angry.

"Stop!"

CHAPTER 24

Salem, Massachusetts

"Stop," Jason commanded the woman. According to the bulldog walker outside the church, her name was Samantha.

She turned, startled. He'd caught her heading toward the bathroom. "Yes?"

"My mother was very specific about the pulpit, which she wanted me to see. It was a shining memory from her wedding. Yet it doesn't look like the original I saw in the pictures. Is it?"

"The original? I'm not sure what you mean."

"Come, I'll show you."

The gray-haired office worker's smile took on a strained appearance. "Of course."

When she walked through the door into the sanctuary, she gasped.

The enormous, gorgeous building had been constructed in 1836, and little had changed in this section of it in the two hundred or so convening years. The ceiling was still covered in quatrefoil molding, replicating the design on the exterior tower. The lancet windows still held the watercolor glory of the stained glass, nearly as old as the stones of the church, depicting biblical scenes. The worn red velvet of the cushions of the box pews that lined the west and east sides of the church was intact. Even the glorious organ in the balcony, which turned the entire upper back of the church into a brass wall, was untouched.

It was the pulpit, the magnificent ten-foot lectern at the head of the church, that Jason had destroyed. Every delicate panel of wood adorning its front and sides had been molested, splintered, ripped open.

The church worker spoke through shaking fingers. "What have you done?"

Jason stared intently at her. The destruction meant nothing to him. He needed the docket. It hadn't been anywhere in the pulpit, and he had to figure out where he'd gone wrong. "Is this the First Church of Salem?"

"Of course it is." She was backing toward the door.

"The only one?"

She began weeping, sniffling, still fumbling backward, her eyes wide with shock. "No. There were four. Didn't you know?"

Jason's mother's face slid over Samantha's. He knew this sniveling woman wasn't Olivette, but still, he heard her speak his mother's words, telling him how stupid he was, not good for anything, a mistake who just made more mistakes.

He should have researched the church more carefully. He'd been too excited, too close to success. He should have known there would be more than one.

You ugly shit. Put a bag over your head when you go out. It's good they come at you from behind so they don't have to look at your face. Don't tell them I'm your mom. And if you get lost, don't bother getting found.

He hit the side of his head to drown out her voice. Olivette couldn't hurt him. Making sure of that had been his first order of business once the Hermitage Foundation had given him the necessary skills and money. He checked on her every week, two at the most, just as he had done on his layover on the way to Massachusetts. It took no more than twenty minutes to change the litter under her chair and pour fresh water in the bottle and tube he'd strung from the ceiling. Only a minute to switch out the IV bag that supplied her nutrients.

She'd given up on begging him to untie her years ago, even before the flesh had grown over the IV needle, consuming it, making it part of her.

Now she didn't even open her eyes when he visited.

He spoke to the gray-haired church lady, his voice terrifyingly calm. "Tell me what you mean when you say there were four."

"Four first churches, three buildings. The original First Church met in 1629." She was talking so fast, snot running from her nose and into her mouth. "About a hundred years ago, that building was moved behind Plummer Hall up a ways on Essex. It's a tourist stop, a tiny old thing, no longer in use."

Her back was flat against the door, but she seemed to have forgotten how to work a doorknob. "Then came the East and North churches, and another First Church. This building was the North Church, built in 1836, but when it reunited with the First Church congregation in 1923, they both moved here because—"

She choked on the slimy yogurt of her own words, the blood draining from her face. It was only when he spotted the whites around her pupils that Jason realized her terror had ramped up a notch.

A second later, he understood why—his bones weren't set. This happened to him in times of great stress, more frequently the older he grew. Only once had he witnessed his face when it was loose, reflecting back at him from a plate glass window.

It was a demon's mask.

He quickly rearranged his bones to support a bland expression, but it was too late. She was melting toward the ground, unable or unwilling to turn her back on him, her mouth opening and closing like a landed carp.

He leaped forward, grabbing her. Her throat was sliced before his feet touched the ground, his hands quicker than gravity. He wished he hadn't made such a mess of the pulpit, but there was no turning back time. He stuffed her in one of the box pews and cleared away the worst of the pulpit's wood splinters. He only needed to buy an hour or two.

Now that he knew his mistake, he could address it. He needed to go to the original First Church, the one that was now behind Plummer Hall, a tiny old thing, no longer in use.

CHAPTER 25

Salem, Massachusetts

"Stop! You're not supposed to be up there." The man's face was flushed with anger. He stood in the doorway of the old one-room church, his hand on the unlatched door. His blazer marked him as a Peabody Essex Museum employee, and his name badge tagged him as "Guy."

Salem hopped off the stool. She gulped three deep breaths to calm herself.

"I'm so sorry!" Bel tossed Salem a glance as she made her way toward the man. *I've got this,* it said. *Get back to work.* "Someone told us Nathaniel Hawthorne had carved his initials into this post, and we wanted a photo."

Guy, who appeared to be in his midtwenties and was built like a linebacker, shoved his hands deep in his pockets. "That'd be pretty cool if it was true, but it isn't. Hawthorne lived here during a totally different time."

Bel tipped her head. "But you do have some Hawthorne artifacts here. Right?"

"Sure, in Plummer Hall," he said, jerking his ear over his shoulder. "You must have walked through it to get back here."

They had. They'd walked through the entire building, out the back door, down the stairs, and up to this itsy-bitsy, single-room church that had, if Salem's research was accurate, been a meetinghouse, and then the First Church of Salem, and then a storage shed before it was found, restored, and relocated behind the Plummer House about a hundred years ago. It was a pointy little red thing, shaped like a Monopoly house, with windows on each side and a blistered old door with a metal loop for a knob.

"Can you point me toward the Hawthorne artifacts?"

Guy appeared doubtful. While Salem thought it would've helped if Bel had been more specific about what sort of Nathaniel Hawthorne "artifacts" she was interested in, she was impressed that her friend had not only recalled Hawthorne's name from their taxi ride but also pulled it out of her ass when they needed it the most.

"That's okay," Bel said, strolling past Guy when he didn't answer. "I'm sure they can help me inside."

Guy either didn't want to let Bel slip through his hands, didn't want to be known as the king of bad customer service, or both, because after a laughable second hooking his glance between Bel and Salem, he decided to follow Bel.

"Go get 'em, tiger," Salem said under her breath, referring to Bel. She loved everything about her best friend, but right now, she particularly loved her quick thinking. She crawled back onto the stool, alone in the whitewashed space.

As she was knocking, exploring, and pressing, she thought, not for the first time, how grateful she was for the internet. No way would she have known there were four First Churches without it. She would have just ended up at 316 Essex Street, where the current First Church stood, and then what?

She liked thinking this. The small victory made standing on a stool, pounding on an old chunk of wood embedded in a ceiling, and injecting her fingers with some of the oldest splinters in America feel less like a snipe hunt. It also made her feel not so exposed this far from Minnesota. That train of thought helped until she reached nearly all the way to the other end of the beam, her knuckles scuffed, her fingernail beds porcupine-pierced with wood. She had less than a foot of the beam left to explore, and she'd discovered nothing, not even an old piece of chewing gum.

Through one of the latticed windows, she spotted Bel emerging from the back of the Plummer House. Guy was with her. Salem's heartbeat picked up. She was almost out of time.

She redoubled her efforts. She refused to let herself think about what it meant if they didn't find anything, if they'd completely misread her mom's message, if the seconds were ticking away on her and Gracie's lives.

Salem had to locate *something*.

Nervously, she glanced out the window, her hands busy. Bel and Guy had stopped. They appeared to be arguing.

They both glanced toward the one-room church.

They resumed walking toward it, Guy in the lead. Bel put her arm out to slow him. He shook it off.

Salem's breathing grew shallow. She had the last four inches of the beam to search. Guy would not be pleased to see her up here. She tapped frantically.

She thought she heard something, finally, a tone different than she'd heard in the hundreds of square inches she'd already tapped. Her breathing was too loud. She tried to compose herself.

She tapped again, on the far side of the beam, the section facing the pulpit.

The results were inconclusive.

She was sure Guy was almost upon her. There wasn't time, but she had to get a better angle. She jumped off her stool and pulled it four inches toward the front of the church. She risked a peek outside.

Guy and Bel were twenty-five feet away and closing in.

She hopped back on the stool. She tapped, locating the hollow spot again immediately. This section looked like it used to be a dovetailed woodworking joint that had been sawed and capped. Pressing her fingers into the sweet spot, she felt the softness of the wood.

Even though every inch of her fought it, yelled at her to run, she closed her eyes so she could better hear.

She tapped, knocking as lightly as a fairy. A drawer released.

She yelped. There it was!

The front door of the church whipped open. Sunlight rained in, outlining Guy's massive shape.

There was no time for delicacy. Salem shoved her hand in the drawer. She felt paper. She tugged it out, as gently as she could, and curled it into her pocket.

She bumped the drawer closed. She hopped off the stool.

It was too late. Guy was furious. "Get. Out."

"Not a problem," she said, grabbing their bags from the floor and slipping past him.

Bel fell in beside her. A quick nod from Salem told Bel all she needed to know. Bel grinned triumphantly and they hurried toward Plummer Hall, ignoring the back door in favor of a side path that would guarantee they wouldn't face any more museum employees. They were giggling as they scurried away from Guy, their heads together.

They were teenagers all over again.

The laughter lasted until they broke out onto Essex Street.

An uncannily beautiful man was exiting a white sedan. His light-brown hair was loose, long, and moved like snakes in the chill fall wind. His build was slight and androgynous, his walk almost feminine as he strode toward Plummer Hall.

He paused, turned, glanced toward both women.

Clouds skidded over the sun, casting Essex Street in abrupt shadows. The atmosphere was lit like a supercharged black-and-white photograph, explosive and static.

Salem's eyes connected with his.

She didn't know him, but he clearly recognized her.

The calculating expression in his eyes, the peculiar, delicate putty of his face, the bulge in his jacket—they all filled her with terror beyond words.

Bel saw the same thing she did.

Both women froze in place, a primal beat pounding their blood. And then they took off running through the pen-and-ink air.

CHAPTER 26

Washington, DC
Russell Senate Office Building

"You're really going through with this?"

Gina rubbed her face. Senate Majority Leader James McCoy had asked her this question a dozen times in the past year. As he sat across from her in her DC office, it was clear that what had started out as a joke between old friends had evolved into something else. He was worried.

The two of them had been born into opposite parties, but James McCoy was an old-school Republican: a fiscal conservative who happened to believe that small government, strong schools, safe streets, and healthy citizens were the best way to govern. He'd always kept his vote out of people's bedrooms, doctors' offices, and church pulpits, and he never played favorites, even after forty-five years in the Senate. He was a dying breed, if there had ever been more than one of him. Hayes had learned more from him about ethics and conduct than from anyone, her father included.

"It'd look a little silly to back out now, wouldn't it, Jim?" She attempted a smile. "You know what the media would say about that."

He held up his hands, spreading them apart to unfurl an invisible banner. *"Gina Hayes Runs Back to the Kitchen, Encourages Other Women to Follow."*

Her smile was genuine this time. "Something like that. You didn't drop by today to talk me out of running, did you?"

"Drop by *today*? I've been trying to track you down for a week. Matthew finally caved and told me you'd be in your office for a few hours. You spend too much time campaigning, Gina, and not enough doing the actual job you were elected to do."

She sat forward in her seat, her smile erased. This was a familiar and favorite debate of theirs. "I agree. If you'd sign off on my bipartisan campaign finance reform bill, politicians would have more time for the real work they were elected for."

He waved her away, not up for the game. "You know that dog has no teeth. Not as long as that scandalous Citizens United stands."

She leaned back, nodding, her eyes sharp. "I could change things. If elected, I would."

Any good cheer dropped off him like a coat. He suddenly looked all his seventy-four years, scalp pink and speckled through his thin hair, hands quavering with the slightest tremble. There'd been talk that he would retire this year. She wondered if it was true.

"Here's why I stopped by, Gina. People are saying that you've met with the Israelis."

She made a mental note to tighten her inner circle. "You know the Israelis have a rule to never meet with candidates, only elected officials."

"Even when those candidates are sitting senators and likely future presidents of the United States of America?" The tremble in his hands increased. How long had he had that?

"I'm worried about you," he continued. "And that's honest to God why I'm here. This isn't going to end well, and your father would say the same thing if he were still alive. No one knows better than this old man how dark politics can get, especially at the top. You have no idea how many forces you're working against."

He coughed, the sound dry and red. "The truth is I want the other guy to win—I'm too old to change parties—but I want it fair and square. At least back off and let the Afghanistan mineral rights bill pass."

Hayes stood. She loved Jim McCoy, but she was too busy to humor his fears. "I appreciate your concern, Jim. You know I do. But it's misplaced. And you know I can't back off of Afghanistan. I'm not willing to risk our troops to line the pockets of a few already-rich."

She helped him to stand. "Now, do you want to go with me to my press conference or not? We'd give the world a treat by appearing together."

In lieu of an answer, he hugged her, grabbed his cane, and limped out through the back door and past her Secret Service detail without another word.

His silence frightened Gina more than anything he could have said.

CHAPTER 27

Salem, Massachusetts

Salem and Bel found themselves on Brown Street, huffing from exertion. There was light pedestrian traffic, not enough to conceal them. Salem glanced over her shoulder. The man was still following them, a hundred or so yards behind, the look on his face beyond intense. It reminded her of the cyborg in *Terminator 2: Judgment Day*. The thought was so ridiculous, every second of the last thirty-six hours so unbelievably ludicrous, that she laughed.

It was a horrible sound.

Bel whipped to look at her. "We have to hide."

Salem hysteria-giggled a little more, then slapped her hand over her mouth. "In there?"

At the end of the block, in a triangle at the intersection of Brown and Washington, a bronze Puritan statue stood on an enormous rock. Behind the rock, a huge Gothic Revival church rose into the sky. It resembled an old castle with battlements, its lanced windows set with red glass. The sign below the central window declared it the Salem Witch Museum.

Underneath the sign, a line of people snaked out the door and around the block, a tour bus behind them. It was the only visible crowd in either direction.

"Yup." Bel grabbed Salem and shoved her toward the crowd. "In there."

Bel pushed through the milling tourists, earning her and Salem a barrage of angry stares. Salem was reminded of the Red Hot Chili Peppers concert Bel had dragged her to during her senior year of high school. Bel was already graduated, living in Chicago. She dressed edgy in ripped jeans and a cropped leather jacket. Salem had felt like a thumb in the mom jeans and T-shirt that had dominated her wardrobe. Somehow, Bel had threaded them from the nosebleed seats almost to the stage. Those fans, while furious at Salem and Bel's passing, had seemed more easygoing than the crowd outside the Salem Witch Museum.

"Hey, line's back there!" It was a dad, three crabby kids under seven in tow. The people around him picked up the grumbling.

"Sorry!" Bel called over her shoulder.

Salem made the mistake of glancing behind her. The man from the white sedan was closing in, just on the other side of the statue. Something odd was happening to his face. Salem shook her head, and the twitch in his cheeks was gone. It must have been a trick of the light.

Bel yanked her inside.

In what must have been the original church's foyer, an older man with a crew cut sold tickets behind a desk on the left. To their right, a tall wooden organizer was stacked with Local Attractions pamphlets. "Hey, get to the back of the line!" This time it was an elderly woman.

"Sorry." It was Salem's turn to apologize.

Bel marched forward, head down, toward the closed doors just ahead. "You can't go in there!" the man behind the counter yelled. "They're about to start the presentation."

Salem wanted to stop so badly, to at least pay to go in, but she'd spotted the top of the head of the man who was following them at the back of the crowd. She had no choice. She let Bel lead her through the pneumatic doors, into the presentation.

The doors swung closed behind them.

They fell into a darkness so complete, Salem couldn't see her own hands.

They were trapped.

CHAPTER 28

Nine Years Old

Enormous, enchanted puffs of snow are falling outside the living room window. The soft crystals dance dreamily toward the ground, a sylphic balance of size and lightness. It's the first snowfall of the year, and Salem and Bel are dying to bundle up, run outside, and build a fort, or a snowman, or play no-touch-me with the falling flakes.

"You're not paying attention," Sensei Pederson says. Vida, Grace, and Daniel have pushed aside the living room furniture so that the sensei can teach them judo in the center of the living room.

"No," Bel says. "I'm not."

Twelve years old and standing up to a stranger. Salem almost yells, she wants to be like Bel so bad. It's not just Bel's courage, or the way she picks up the judo like she was born to it while Salem flails around like a grounded bird. It's not even how TV-show-pretty Bel is.

Well, maybe that is it.

Salem sighs. She'll never be Bel, but at least she gets to be her best friend. She can't wait to giggle with Bel about this later. Who in their right mind brings a private judo instructor to their house on a snowy Saturday night? Vida had said it'd be fun, that she and Grace had thought of it on a whim. They were always thinking of stuff like that—agility courses, first-aid training, dragging Bel and Salem to community ed knot-tying courses or immersion Spanish workshops at the local high school after hours. This is the first time they've brought it into the house, though.

"How's this?" Daniel offers, glancing at Bel, who stands hands-on-hips like an angry soldier. "You two give Sensei Pederson your attention for the next hour—I mean your whole focus—and then I'll take you both sledding."

Salem is sure her dad is the only one of the three adults who remembers what it's like to have fun. She glances at Bel, trying not to smile. Bel has taught her that you never take the first deal presented, but dang, that's a sweet offer on the table.

Bel tosses her golden ponytail over her shoulder. "Ice cream on the way back?"

"Isabel Odegaard!" Grace admonishes.

But Daniel laughs. "You betcha."

Salem grins. She can't believe it. Bel got them ice cream. In the winter! She promises herself that someday, she'll be as bold as Bel.

Someday.

CHAPTER 29

Salem, Massachusetts

The room they'd entered smelled like canned soup. It was an encompassing blackness that crawled over Salem's skin with the weight of dead fingers. To their left, up high, a stage lamp flicked on, bathing a hunched gargoyle in a sick yellow light. The grotesque creature was maybe six feet tall, perched on a second level of the main room. Below it, dead center in the floor of the room, a massive red circle lit up.

SALEM VILLAGE 1692 was written in the middle. Names were scribbled in outgoing concentric circles. Salem recognized Tituba and a few others—people who'd met ghastly fates during the witch trials.

The gargoyle's lamp switched off, and the room was again bathed in darkness as thick as gravedirt. When Salem's eyes had a moment to adjust, she spotted an exit sign at the far end of the room. Seconds later, a stage light to the right fired up. It outlined a peasant man on the gallows, a noose around his neck.

"In 1692, Salem was a peaceful village," began a recorded voice.

Salem blinked. *The presentation.*

The church sanctuary had been gutted to create this gigantic display room. Salem could just make out chairs arranged around the red circle, crammed with tourists. This was what people had been waiting in line for. If she squinted, she could spot the remaining dioramas rimming the upper edges of the hall. They would be lit up one at a time to tell the story of the Salem Witch Trials. It was kitsch at its finest.

Outside the door immediately behind them, they heard a scuffle.

Salem's skin prickled. "It's him," she whispered. She didn't know who *he* was. She knew he was following them, and that there would be nothing worse on this earth than him catching them. The terror of being chased by this predator was so primordial, so unbearably awful, that Salem understood why an animal would leap off a cliff rather than let itself be captured.

Bel pointed across the hall at the dimly lit exit sign. Salem nodded. They wove around the chairs, trying not to draw too much attention.

But they weren't moving fast enough.

The doors behind them opened. Salem stifled a yelp.

The flooding light caused angry whispers to erupt from the viewing crowd.

"Not again!"

"Hey, we paid way too much for this already. Shut off the lights!"

The crew cut worker from the front desk held open the doors. The man who had been pursuing them stood behind, silhouetted. Glancing back at him filled Salem's gut with ice. She pushed Bel forward. "Hurry!"

They stumbled through the exit door. A smaller museum lay on the other side. It featured various depictions of witches behind glass, from the Wicked Witch of the West in all her green glory to a simple midwife surrounded by herbs, and finally, a couple who reminded Salem of Renaissance festival regulars, flowers woven in their hair, holding carved walking sticks.

Salem and Bel ran past all the shtick.

"You know that hotel across the street?" Bel was out of breath. They found themselves inside the gift shop.

"No."

A store employee stepped forward, speaking into her headset, palms facing Salem and Bel.

"The Hawthorne Hotel." Bel glared at the worker. The worker stepped aside, squawking angrily at whoever was on the other end of the headset. "We drove past it to get to the church. We have to slip inside and secure a hiding spot as soon as we can. How much cash do you have?"

CHAPTER 30

Salem, Massachusetts

Jason stood just inside the entryway of The Old Spot, blood pumping pleasantly. He recognized what he hadn't seen in the photos he'd been provided: Isabel Odegaard was beautiful, breathtaking, stunning, even from a distance. She was more athletic than curvy, her strawberry-blonde hair perfect against the cream of her skin.

He felt an electric arousal, one he rarely experienced on the job. He pulled his jacket tighter and glanced at his watch. The women had dashed into the Hawthorne Hotel six minutes earlier. He'd wait ten more minutes for them to check into their room before going to the front desk to retrieve their room number. No desk person would hand it to him, but odds were that they would have the last check-in open on their computer screen. It was industry standard. He'd simply ask the desk person a question that would require them to turn around, and he'd peek over the desk.

He'd done it innumerable times.

He glanced behind him. The pub's overhead TVs were dominated by political ads flashing various unflattering photos of Senator Gina Hayes. "Do you trust her with the troops? She's been lying since her college days—just ask her old roommate. Who will really run the country, her or her father's cronies?"

The propaganda was ugly in a way that sat nicely with Jason, at least until the news showed a day-old clip of Senator Gina Hayes at an Ohio rally. She had an audience of tens of thousands. Their cheers were deafening.

Jason was unaware he was grinding his teeth.

Two men at the table next to him were tossing back draft beer and staring at the TV.

"No *way*," one of them complained.

"I know," his friend agreed. "A woman president? Not on my watch. Uhn-uhn. They're too emotional. I don't need a moody lady with access to the big red button, you know?"

The first speaker had opened his mouth to agree when he spotted Jason watching them. His eyes widened. He held up his hands in apology. "Sorry. We're just talking big, you know? We're both mama's boys."

Jason's chest tightened. Had he given himself away somehow?

Then he realized, gratefully, that on the walk here, he'd let down his hair and, masking it as a sneeze, rearranged his face as a woman's to match the photo on the driver's license he carried. He wore gender-neutral jeans and a plain blue T shirt under his black blazer. The men had mistaken him for a woman, the same disguise he'd used to sneak into Grace Odegaard's building.

He tightened his vocal cords to raise the octave. "Are you kidding me? A female president would be *terrible*. Every woman I know agrees."

The men laughed, relieved.

Jason matched their laughter.

And he went over the Alcatraz plan for the millionth time.

His mission was bloated with urgency. The Crucible was already too powerful. He left the bar and jogged across the street, not willing to wait the ten minutes to dispatch Isabel Odegaard and Salem Wiley.

He wanted to kill them now so he could get out of this ten-cent town.

He had bigger fish to fry.

CHAPTER 31

Salem, Massachusetts

The Hawthorne Hotel was a plush brick cube straight out of the early 1900s. Room 325's wallpaper was beige-on-beige Baroque flocking, buttressed by ornate crown molding along the ceiling and somber carpeting. It was clean and cramped with barely enough room to contain two double beds, a nightstand, a desk, and a TV-concealing armoire. To navigate past one another, either Salem or Bel had to hop on the bed. At least, Salem assumed they would have to. They'd made for the desk as soon as they entered the room.

Salem gently withdrew the paper from her pocket, the single sheet she'd retrieved from the central beam of the original First Church of Salem.

With trembling hands, she flattened it.

The paper was so ancient it felt like calfskin.

She and Bel leaned close to it. It emitted the pleasant mildew scent of old books.

A looping scrawl of crowded, half-cursive words with a sea of white space between them covered the paper. At the top was a title, and below that, a poem.

My Life had stood—a Loaded Gun

Some keep the Sabbath going to church;
I keep it staying at home,
With a bobolink for a chorister,
And an orchard for a dome.

Some keep the Sabbath in surplice;
I just wear my wings,
And instead of tolling the bell for church,
Our little sexton sings.

God preaches, a noted clergyman,
And the sermon is never long;
So instead of getting to heaven at last,
I'm going all along!

—Emily Dickinson

Σ

Bel and Salem stared at it in silence for several seconds. Their entire race from the Witch Museum to the lobby to room 325 had been a child's bed-to-door ghost run, their feet barely touching the ground. And now they were looking at an Emily Dickinson poem scrawled out on an old piece of paper pulled out of an even older chunk of wood, heartbeats thundering to catch up.

"Huh," Bel finally said.

"Yeah," Salem agreed.

"You know," Bel said, cocking her head, "I don't think that title goes with that poem."

Salem reread it. English, particularly poetry, had not been her favorite subject. Too much room for interpretation. She drew out her phone and googled it.

"You're right." She clicked off her phone. "They're two different poems."

Bel smiled. "Who ever thought that English minor would pay off?"

Salem nodded absently. "This doesn't seem like a code at all." She held the paper up to the light. "And I don't see any messages behind it. If it is some sort of cipher, it's an amateur one. Far less complex than the cipher in the Gentileschi, and that was essentially only a hidden message."

Bel walked to the window and pushed aside the heavy tapestry drapes so she could peek out. "We're not facing the Witch Museum, but I don't see any sign of that creep. We paid cash, used false names. I think we're safe. We have time to figure this out."

Salem was studying the paper, face screwed up as tight as a knot.

Bel let the curtain drop. "I see you're in deep-thought mode. I'm going to let you do what you do best and solve that thing so we can locate Vida and my mom. Meanwhile, I'm taking a shower and calling room service. Burgers and fries okay with you?"

Salem nodded, but she wasn't hungry.

Bel called down to the hotel restaurant and placed an order before disappearing into the smallest, whitest bathroom Salem had ever seen. With Bel out of her sight, Salem realized she was coming down from an adrenaline high and, even worse, flirting with a panic attack.

It slithered at the edges, threatening to pounce, to lay its hairy weight over her mouth, nose, and chest, picking out her sanity and flinging bits of it beyond her reach. She scrabbled for the plastic Ativan bottle and popped two of the seven she had left. It was probably conditioning, but she felt better immediately.

Deciding to begin with the basics, she first searched "My Life Had Stood a Loaded Gun." There were no obvious clues in the actual poem. Next, she googled the Sabbath poem.

Same.

Behind the bathroom door, the *whoosh* of the shower came on. "Wow!" Bel squealed. "Cold water."

Their quarters were so tight that Salem heard when Bel squirted out shampoo. She broadened her focus, pulling up Dickinson's Wikipedia page, figuring a wide net would catch more clues. Emily Elizabeth Dickinson lived from 1830 to 1886, was born in Amherst, and thanks to her father, received rigorous schooling, a rare privilege for girls of that time. She was a well-behaved, content girl until Sophia, her second cousin and a close friend, died.

Her parents sent her to Boston in 1844 to recover from her overwhelming melancholy, and when she returned to Amherst, a religious revival was taking place. Dickinson jumped on board for a time, but it didn't stick. More people close to her died, she became reclusive, and she wrote poetry, most of which wasn't published until after her death of heart failure. In fact, during her lifetime, she was known more for her gardening skills, for wearing white, and for being so isolated that she rarely left her house and often talked to guests from the other side of a door.

None of this helped Salem. She pushed her curls out of her face and yanked her focus back to the moment, googling "Emily Dickinson ciphers." She didn't land any logical hits. Same with a variety of synonyms in place of "ciphers."

Still nothing when she searched "Emily Dickinson Artemisia Gentileschi," "Emily Dickinson First Church," and as a last ditch, "Emily Dickinson hides secret in block of wood."

She wanted to scream her frustration. Instead, she opened Google Images and began scrolling through photos of Dickinson. She'd been a striking woman with dark eyes, a full mouth, and fierce hair. She'd also apparently not been big on pictures, because Salem kept seeing the same photograph over and over.

The shower twisted off with a loud protest. Salem heard Bel slide the metal curtain rings down the rod and even heard her toweling off. She shoved the distractions aside.

As she was looking at the pictures of Emily Dickinson artifacts plus the millionth copy of the same Dickinson headshot, she wondered what the woman would have thought of the Hawthorne Hotel. By the sounds of it, the water pressure hadn't improved much since her time. Salem's mind was wandering. She was tired, emotionally and physically. She was scrolling almost too fast to see anything when her finger dropped on the scroll pad.

Her eyes bulged.

She leaned toward her computer screen. She *couldn't* be seeing what she thought she was seeing.

"Bel?"

Bel rushed out, her towel tied around her waist. Salem, long used to how comfortable her friend was naked, didn't even give her a second glance.

"What'd you find?" Bel asked.

Salem swiveled the computer so Bel could see. "Look."

Bel bent forward. The screen reflected like a slumber-party flashlight against her face. "What am I looking at?"

Salem pointed at the image she'd enlarged, wiping drips from Bel's hair off the keyboard. "That letter on the screen. It was handwritten by Dickinson." The note she'd found in the beam lay next to the computer. She held it up. "Check out this note. The handwriting is identical."

Bel squinted, trying to catch up.

Salem explained, her voice belying her incredulity. "Dickinson's name at the end of the note? It's not an attribution. It's her *signature*."

Bel's eyes went wide. "Emily Dickinson wrote the note you found in that old church beam?"

A knock landed on the thick wood of the door. Salem and Bel flinched. Bel shook it off and peered through the spy hole.

"Room service," she told Salem, and through the door: "Give me a minute." She tossed the towel and pulled on her jeans, a bra, and a T-shirt before strapping on her holster, hauling on a jacket, and opening the door.

The guy on the other side was tall and scarecrow-thin, in his late teens or early twenties. He wore a blue uniform constructed of a polyester so cheap that light reflected off. The pants were two inches too short. Probably most pants were for him. He was at least 6'5". He held a toolbox rather than a food service tray.

"Sorry to bother you. Your bathroom has some sort of leak that's affecting the room below. May I come in?"

Bel stepped out of the way. Salem moved her laptop to the bed to clear space on the desk. She set Emily Dickinson's note next to it. Having a false alarm on the room service food made her realize she was starving.

The hotel worker ducked his head and stepped in.

Bel closed the door behind him.

He ate up the three steps it took to cross the room and set down the toolbox on the spot Salem had just cleared. He turned to them both, his expression dark. He crossed his hands in front of him. "You two have to leave. Now."

CHAPTER 32

Salem, Massachusetts

Bel tensed and dropped her body weight to her hips, hand dipping toward the gun inside her jacket. "Excuse me?"

The hotel worker stumbled back toward the wall, his blue eyes wide. "Salem Wiley and Isabel Odegaard, right? Your moms are Vida and Grace?"

Salem's cheeks flushed. She found herself reaching out to him, though her feet didn't move. "You know them?"

He shook his head. "Not really. I met Vida once, never Grace. Heard of both of 'em plenty." After casting a wary glance at Bel, he leaned toward the window, moving a corner of the drapery to peer out. His fingers were so long that they seemed to uncurl.

Salem reevaluated his height. He must be over 6'7". He made the hotel room look like a miniature movie set.

"You guys have got to get out of here."

"Why?" Bel's tone was aggressive, hand still on her gun, but her shoulders had relaxed slightly. "And who are you?"

He turned back to face them. Salem noticed flesh-colored, sparse hair on his face, one shade lighter than the hair on his head. He wasn't old enough to grow a real beard or mustache, but he was trying. "I'm nobody. But you two? You have far more enemies than you realize. And they know you're here."

He spun his finger in a circle, indicating the room. "At the Hawthorne, not just in Massachusetts."

Salem stepped toward him, and then stopped. The Ativan had dulled her brain. "Do you know where our mothers are?"

He dropped his glance, concentrating on a point near her feet. "No." He shot a look in Bel's direction but had no more luck meeting her eyes. He cleared his throat. "One of them is dead, for sure."

Salem's legs turned to pudding beneath her. She dropped cross-legged to the floor as sure as if a giant finger had appeared from the sky and pressed on her head. Bel glided forward and twisted the young man's arm behind his back, driving him to his knees before he had time to react.

"I don't know which one," he whispered. "And the FBI found a finger outside Grace Odegaard's apartment building. It might not belong to either of your mothers, they're not sure." He swallowed hard, his pale skin growing paler.

Bel's voice was fierce. "How do you know any of this?"

"Dr. Keller called me."

Salem's brain was whirling. Dr. Keller had acted strangely at the art museum, but *everything* had seemed so bizarre the last twenty-four hours. "Why?"

His teeth gritted from pain. "He's in the Underground. He said you'd stopped by the institute and would be in Salem soon. I'm the Salem contact. I was watching outside the First Church—we know that's where the trail starts—and followed you here."

He tried to toss his head toward the door, but Bel's grip was too tight. "The tool kit was in my car. I grabbed the jacket from the hotel laundry room on my way up here. I figured you wouldn't let me in otherwise."

Bel's chin was quivering with the effort of holding him. "That explains how you knew where we were, but not *why*."

"The Underground sent me."

Salem and Bel exchanged a glance. Neither had words.

He continued, his breathing shallow. "Your mothers were both part of it. Vida was a leader, I know that, because she came out here once for a history conference and talked to us. Grace Odegaard might have been a top leader, too, I don't know. Nobody knows who's even a member and who isn't. That's to protect us, I guess." He tried shifting. Bel tightened her grip. "Hey, you have to listen to me."

"I'm listening," Bel said. She patted him down with her free hand, searching for weapons. "I can do that just fine in this position. Keep talking."

A bead of sweat rolled from his hairline toward his nose. "The Underground is a network. That's how I know about the . . . situation in Minneapolis."

"Salem," Bel commanded, "call the Minneapolis police right now. Ask them if anything he's said is true."

Salem's upper body reached for the phone. Her lower half was still not responding to commands.

"Don't bother." He sighed. "The police only know about the neighbor and her dog, and maybe the finger. They will never hear of the other body. The cleanup crew has already come and gone. I know because one of them sells information to the Underground. Even if that crew wasn't so good, the bad guys have a plant in the FBI."

He finally looked Salem in the eye. His pupils were a startling blue, like a husky's. "Bits, right?"

A shaking began in Salem's abdomen and traveled to her hands and feet. "What'd you call me?"

"You're Vida's daughter? I recognize your curly hair from her description. She said that if I ever met you without her, it was desperate times. She said to call you 'Bits' so you'd know to trust me. She asked me to tell you about the Underground."

Bel snorted, but she let up slightly on his arm. "Anybody could find out that's her nickname."

Except not really, Salem thought, *because the only people alive who know about that are you, my mom, and Grace.* "What else did she tell you?"

The drop of sweat rolling down his face was joined by others. His already-pale complexion was shading green.

"Bel, I think you should let him go." Salem didn't know where that had come from. Her legs still weren't working, for Christ's sake. She was literally in *no position* to defend against him. But up close, he looked exactly like a scared kid, more boy than man for all his height, wearing his too-short pants and blinking his too-serious eyes.

Bel glared at Salem, but she released her grip and stepped back, returning her hand to her gun while she watched him warily. He moved his arm slowly back into position, grimacing. He cradled it while he sat on his heels.

"What's your name?" Salem asked.

"Ernest Mayfair." His eyes flicked to Bel.

She leaned against the wall, her posture still rigid, right hand near her gun. "All right, Ernest Mayfair. Let's start at the beginning. How do you know we're in danger?"

He nodded as if his teacher had just asked him to give a speech he'd stayed up all night rehearsing. "Both your moms were in the Underground, and Vida was one of the leaders," he repeated, "and every so often, the Hermitage Foundation does a 'harvesting' of Underground leaders, who're mostly women, to try and wipe out the organization."

"*The* Hermitage Foundation?" Salem asked. "That lobbying group that's always in the news for its donations?"

Ernest twisted his mouth. "That's their public face. The truth is much darker." He rose to his feet, offering his good hand to Salem. She stood with his help, her legs still creaky. "The Hermitage Foundation is an old, old organization that was dying out until Andrew Jackson revived it in the 1800s. He gave it new life and a new mission: run the world. They renamed themselves after his plantation."

Bel rolled her eyes. Ernest caught her expression and blushed, but continued despite her disapproval. "The Underground was resurrected at about the same time as the Hermitage, early 1800s or so. The Underground's mission was basically to protect women, because the

Hermitage viewed them as a threat to their power. At least that's what everyone says." He tipped his head at both of them. "Your mothers might have known something more specific. Most of us members are only contacted when we're needed for something."

He tried to draw himself up to his full height, but the 1920s room had not been designed for 6'7" people, and so he bumped the hanging light. "Like today." He rubbed his head. "I was called on to pass a message to you two. To let you know that you're not safe here. The Hermitage Foundation came for Vida and Grace, and now it's coming for you."

"But why us?"

He shrugged. "Vida said it'd be guilt by association. Usually, female leaders pass on the Underground membership to their daughters. I guess they wanted to protect you two from that, if this is the first you've heard of any of it."

"So the Hermitage Foundation regularly kills off women, and no one even notices?"

Ernest answered her question with a look.

Bel blew air through her nose like a bull. "Okay, let's say everything you've said is true. The Hermitage Foundation is a front for some shadowy cabal that secretly runs the world. Their main opposition is an organization of women who call themselves the Underground. Our moms were leaders, and because of it, one of them might be dead, and the other is, what? Kidnapped?"

Ernest nodded. Bel paled, but she continued. "So what scavenger hunt are we on now? What are we after with all these clues?"

Ernest shook his head sadly. "I don't know. I just know that it's the only way to stop the Hermitage Foundation and protect yourselves, maybe keep your, um, one of your mothers alive."

Salem was ticking through all the information he'd offered. "What can we do to stop them?"

Bel threw her hands in the air. "You're not really falling for this, are you?"

Salem looked from Ernest to Bel. "It makes as much sense as anything this last crazy day, doesn't it? Maybe more. It fits right in with a hidden message in a Gentileschi painting and another in a wooden beam just as old." She sat on the edge of the bed, her legs still trembly.

For the first time, Ernest smiled. "You found the note at the First Church?"

When neither woman responded, he continued. "We all knew, or thought we knew, anyhow, that's where the trail began. The First Church. But no one except maybe Salem's mom knows what's at the end." His eyes lit up. "We just know that it will somehow destroy the Hermitage Foundation."

Bel rubbed her face. "This is such a bullshit story. If finding whatever's at the end of this trail would destroy the bad guys, why didn't my mother, or Vida, or the Underground, or whoever, just do that a long time ago?"

Ernest thrust out his hands, palms forward. *Surrender.* "They've tried. Every leader of the Underground since it was revived has. Whatever is at the end of that trail was originally hidden two hundred years ago, and hidden well so that the Hermitage couldn't discover it. Whoever knew what and where is long dead."

He dropped his hands and exhaled slowly. "When Vida was here, she said she was training a code breaker to finally track down the document."

He directed his glance toward Salem. "She said it was you, Bits. She's been training you your whole life. You're the one who can save the Underground."

CHAPTER 33

Washington, DC
Russell Senate Office Building

Senator Gina Hayes's aide, Matthew Clemens, showed the two representatives from Women Rise into her office. Gina was familiar with the organization and their chief mission to eliminate acid attacks on Southeast Asian women. She had seen photos of what an acid attack could do, melting through flesh and bone, liquefying noses and eyes and mouths, dissolving, fusing, hardening skin and muscle into unbending leather, destroying lives.

She knew that the two representatives who were ushered into her office had been attacked, the first doused with sulfuric acid by a husband who thought her beauty drew unwanted attention, and the second whose boyfriend, whom she'd met on Facebook, melted her face with nitric acid when she ended their relationship.

But none of this could have prepared her to sit across from the women as they unwound their scarves.

Despite possessing a poker face honed across decades of public service, Gina found herself shaking with anger.

"Thank you for seeing us."

"Of course," Gina said. She did a mental body scan, calming herself. These women didn't need her fury or her pity. They needed her influence. She looked them in the eye and gave them the only things she could: respect and attention.

They continued their introductions, and then Anchali, whose mouth was so destroyed that she had to hold a handkerchief to it to catch moisture as she spoke, dived in. "It's not just the acid attacks we would like to speak with you about. They are the most obvious markers of a culture that does not protect its women, or allow girls access to a living wage or advanced education. I was one of the lucky ones."

Her voice was lilting and lovely, crisp on the consonants and rolling through the vowels. She had been enrolled in medical school at the time her husband melted her flesh, she explained. She'd had to take a reprieve from her education, suffering twenty-seven surgeries since the attack.

Khean, the other representative, pulled out facts and reports and photographs that made Gina want to call her daughter that moment and tell her how much she loved her. Gina listened, taking notes, waiting to speak until they paused.

"Your bravery is humbling." She spoke to both women. "Tell me more, and tell me what I can do."

Their meeting lasted a half an hour. Gina wished she had more time, but her schedule was full. It always was.

"Ready for your next one?" Matthew said after leading out the Cambodian women. He set a steaming cup of chamomile tea with a squeeze of lemon in front of her.

Gina was still scribbling notes to herself. She didn't look up. "What sort of world do we live in where a man would drive a seventeen-year-old girl twenty miles from the nearest hospital, pour battery acid on her, and drive away, Matthew?"

He sighed. "One that needs a change of guard, Gina. And that's why you and I are here on the first day of November, fighting through paperwork and malarkey so deep, a shovel couldn't touch it. And while we're on the topic, your next appointment is with the Speaker of the House. Should I toss a sheet over the furniture before I let him in?"

That drew the tiniest of smiles from Gina. "Not necessary. But let's have him wait an extra five minutes, shall we? I don't recall him ever making one of our meetings on time before I earned the nomination."

"That's the spirit," Matthew said, glancing at his iPad. "As long as you keep it under twenty minutes, you'll be on schedule."

He tapped his screen. "Capitol meetings all day, and then tonight, you're getting together with representatives from Veterans for Peace. Tomorrow, we return to Iowa for a rally. Actually, you're out of town every day until the election. Sure you don't want me to squeeze a second in there for you to sleep, or wipe your nose?" He glanced at her, his eyes lasers. "I wouldn't mind canceling the Alcatraz stop on Monday, for example. You already have California in your pocket. Getting to and from that island is going to be nothing but a hassle."

"I'm not changing my schedule. A promise is a promise." She blew on her tea. "I'm ready for the Speaker."

CHAPTER 34

Ten Years Old

Salem skips up the sidewalk of the blue-and-white bungalow. The air smells like the inside of a freezer. The corpses of flowers and weeds alike, brown and jaggy from an early frost, hang over the sidewalk. A year ago, Vida gave her lawn over to what she calls "an English garden."

Salem lost a friendship bracelet in there that she has yet to find.

She walks up the three stone steps, one of them bearing her left handprint. She disliked the cold, messy feel of the cement when her dad pressed her kindergarten fingers into it five years ago.

At the top of the stairs, she curls her grip around the familiar C-shaped handle, depressing the tongue with her thumb. The door is unlocked. She steps inside.

She shouldn't be home. It's the middle of the school day. But it's picture day, a day she dreads because she looks like a frog with her poofy hair, green eyes, and big lips, and she doesn't want that in the yearbook. Again. So she told the nurse she was sick and that she was going home. The nurse, one year from retirement, either hadn't heard or didn't care.

One bus ride later, and she's standing inside her home. Her mom prefers a "tousled" household, so all cleaning is done by Salem and her dad. Vida's disorganization is a side effect of her peculiar genius, Salem's dad tells her. He should be in his shop, working, and Vida should be teaching at Hill College. Salem is going to sneak an Orange Crush out of the refrigerator and bring it to her room before she goes to his shop so she has something to drink up there, because her dad is for sure sending her straight to bed when he sees her home this early.

She is almost around the hallway corner and in the kitchen when she hears them arguing. Her mom and dad. Home in the middle of the day. Her throat tightens. She wishes she really were sick.

"She's too young," Daniel is saying. "Let her be a child yet."

Her mom answers. "She's perfect, Danny, and you know it. The girl's a genius."

"Yes, but she's our *girl."*

Is Daniel crying? Salem has never seen either of her parents cry. The thought terrifies her. She peeks around the corner.

"She sets us free," Vida says, "and we're free forever. All of us. You, me, Gracie, Isabel. So many more. It's not just about one person, you taught me that."

Vida's hair is in a bun. She's wearing hoop earrings. Daniel has on a faded T-shirt. They stand in front of the refrigerator, the grocery list secured with a Salem-crafted button magnet visible between them. Vida reaches for Daniel, who is indeed crying, his lashes dripping with tears. Salem gasps. They both swivel, spotting her.

What happens next is vague, a ghost memory of letting her watch movies and eat popcorn even though both her parents, normally strict about school, know she is playing hooky.

Yet they spoil her that day.

CHAPTER 35

Salem, Massachusetts

Ernest Mayfair's words echoed.

When Vida was here, she said she was training a code breaker to finally track down the document. She said it was you, Bits.

His announcement hung in a silence so intense that it became a living thing.

Bel slayed it. "That is absolutely, 100 percent *enough* horseshit for one day. I am full up." She reached for her duffel and began packing up her toiletries.

Salem felt hollow. Hollow and lonelier than she'd ever been in her life. She believed her mom would use her—in a heartbeat, in fact—but her dad?

"Sorry." She shot Ernest a miserable smile. Bel was being harsh with him, even though he clearly believed every word he'd said. "This is a lot to digest. We're both pretty freaked out that our mothers are missing."

Ernest's shoulders slumped. "How else can you explain their disappearance, and whatever you found at the First Church? You both know this is big. I can see it in your eyes."

Salem was struck by his bearing, an unlikely mix of innocence and defiance. If she believed what he'd said about the Hermitage Foundation and her parents training her to solve this code, that meant she'd have to believe that either Vida or Grace was dead. Gripping that thought was like squeezing a live coal.

"The only thing I know for sure," Bel said, "is that if *you* know we're here, that means someone else could, too. We have to get the hell out of Dodge."

Ernest nodded eagerly, as if they were finally all three on the same page. "I'll come with you."

Bel snorted. "No way."

Amazingly, Salem trusted Ernest, but she trusted Bel more. She powered down her laptop and slid it into its case. Next, she grabbed the Dickinson note and refolded it gently into its original shape before sliding it in her jacket pocket. She moved past Ernest to reach the door.

"Sorry," she told him.

He didn't seem to hear her. "The man who chased you into the Witch Museum is waiting outside. He's at the restaurant across the street or maybe in the lobby. I can show you a back way out." His voice was little more than a whisper.

"We'll pass on that generous offer." Bel's voice was sleek with sarcasm. She opened the door and held it ajar for Salem. "Walking down dark halls with strangers is one of the first no-nos they teach you at the police academy. We'll go straight from the lobby into a cab, so it doesn't matter where that creep is. He won't grab us in public, and he won't know where we're going, just like you won't."

Ernest nodded in resignation. Salem had never seen anyone look so sad. She opened her mouth but realized she had no way to make him feel better. She stepped outside room 325, and the door closed behind her. Bel was already halfway down the hall.

Salem hurried to catch up. "You didn't have to be so mean to him."

Bel sighed and waited for her. "It's not mean to stand up for yourself. We didn't know that guy from Adam."

"But he knew *us*."

"Nothing an internet search and a solid dose of evil couldn't get him."

"Why would he bother?"

Bel stabbed the elevator button. "I don't know. Where are we headed?"

Salem glanced over her shoulder. The hallway was empty. She lowered her voice anyhow. "Amherst, Massachusetts. It's where Emily Dickinson grew up."

"You think there's another message there somewhere?"

"I don't know, but we have to get out of this town, and that'll buy me more time. Amherst is a couple hours west, I think. If we rent a car, I can research while you drive."

They rode the elevator in silence, the air between them charged. When they hit the main floor, Bel held up a hand and peered around the spacious lobby. Three women reclined on the ornate couches in the middle of the atrium, paging through wedding planners. A gray-haired guy sat across the couch from them, back to the elevator, reading a magazine. The same efficient man who had checked them in was working the front desk, helping a woman in a black blazer. A group of people were talking loudly around the corner from the elevator, out of Salem's and Bel's sight line.

"Do you see him?"

Bel shook her head. "All clear. Stick close."

They stepped into the lobby. Salem's pulse thumped in her temples. She felt conspicuous, and like she wanted to look into all the corners at once. "I'll ask about a rental at the desk."

"I'll watch for him out front. There's too many damn entrances to this lobby." Bel turned toward the foyer.

Salem walked to the counter and stood in line behind the woman with the black jacket. The woman glanced toward Salem, then back to the hotel employee. Her shoulders drew up, and she abruptly ended her conversation and turned back toward Salem as if to leave.

Her face was bland, unremarkable.

Salem would have let her walk right past, but they locked eyes. The same eyes she'd seen in the man outside Plummer Hall.

The same eyes that had followed them into the Witch Museum.

Evil eyes.

The woman stepped toward Salem, a smile licking her mouth. Salem tried to yell for Bel. A low moan escaped instead. The woman reached into her interior jacket pocket.

Salem smelled metal. Fear grabbed her, touched her where she didn't want to be touched.

She learned what it was like to be hypnotized by a snake's eyes, to watch, frozen, while a deadly creature slithered toward you, unable to so much as breathe. Her feet sank through the carpet, into the floor below, holding her so she could be harvested.

If she hadn't been bumped from behind, violently, she was sure the woman in the black blazer would have swallowed her whole. She fell forward.

"Excuse me." Agent Lucan Stone grasped her arm, scowling at the woman before turning his full attention to Salem. "Are you okay?"

Salem threw her hand onto a nearby pole to steady herself. Her heartbeat, which had been suspended, returned with a pounding force. "What are you doing here?"

"Coincidence." His smile was brilliant.

Salem felt an electric surge. They stared at each other for a moment too long. When Salem glanced around the lobby, the evil-eyed woman had disappeared.

"Not likely," Bel said, appearing at Salem's side. "You must have news for us."

Agent Stone's grin disappeared. "I'm afraid not. I do have questions, however."

"Sorry," Bel said, grabbing Salem's hand and leading her toward the door.

They stepped into the chilly November afternoon, the tangerine and gold of the setting sun at odds with all the darkness in their lives.

CHAPTER 36

Salem, Massachusetts

Clancy was the first person Agent Stone had spotted when he'd entered the Hawthorne Hotel lobby from the rear moments earlier. His partner had been sitting on a couch in the center of the spacious room, pretending to read a magazine.

The second person Stone saw was Salem Wiley, frozen in terror as the eerie woman in a black blazer turned from the front desk and walked toward her, *predator* written on every inch of the woman's creepy skin. Stone had seen death row gangbangers with less hate in them.

Clancy had witnessed the same thing Stone had, but he didn't appear alarmed. Rather, he looked like a man who'd ordered the steak and been brought chicken instead but was willing to make the best of it. Stone wasn't surprised Clancy had been expecting it to go down like this. He'd discovered early in their pairing that Clancy was clandestine, his backstop deeper than Stone could dig, which was why Stone didn't always share ops with him. He assumed Clancy returned the favor.

It was unusual for Clancy to sit by on something so aggressively public, however. Clancy had been letting the woman in the black blazer advance on Wiley, and she would have gotten her if not for Stone's intervention. The woman had since disappeared like a ghoul.

As Stone watched Wiley and Odegaard scurry out of the hotel, he wondered if Clancy had gone hard. Stone let Clancy grab him.

"What in the hell are you doing here?" Clancy's face was red. He clutched Stone's lapel, twisting it, his free hand fisted at his side as if itching to throw a punch.

Stone's brows drew in and his jaw tightened. It's not what he'd driven here expecting, but maybe it was time to work this shit *out*. Rather than remove his partner's hand, he gave Clancy thirty seconds to consider how badly he didn't want to throw down with younger, taller Stone.

It took twenty.

Clancy unclenched Stone's lapel and swore, stalking toward the parking lot entrance. "You should have notified me of your location," he muttered over his shoulder.

Stone followed, pissed by Clancy's rage. "We agreed to meet here, remember?"

Clancy grunted and walked away, straight toward an illegally parked sedan.

Stone walked to the driver's side door, blocking Clancy. "Keys?" It was a low blow, but Clancy should be grateful Stone was working his anger out with words. That's not how he'd learned to play growing up in Detroit.

"How'd you get to the hotel?" Clancy snarled.

"Cab."

Clancy slapped the roof of his rental and tossed Stone the keys before sliding into the passenger seat, avoiding eye contact. "We're tailing the girls, right?"

"Best plan." Stone slid in and started the car. He didn't know how all the murder victims were connected, or how that extended to Wiley and Odegaard, but he intended to save their lives. That's why he'd slipped the tracker in Wiley's pocket back in the lobby.

He could still smell Salem from where their clothes had touched—something spicy and clean like cinnamon, and under that, a raw animal fear. For a moment, he wondered how long Clancy had been hiding in the lobby. He ultimately dismissed the thought. Worrying about another man's motives was a sure way to drive yourself crazy in this business.

All you could complete was your own mission.

CHAPTER 37

Salem, Massachusetts

"It was the same guy from the art institute in Minneapolis." Bel was chewing on the inside of her cheek. "I don't know what he was doing at the institute or in the freaking Hawthorne lobby in *Salem, Massachusetts*, but it was him both times, I promise. Chubby Ed Harris–looking guy."

"Forget Ed Harris," Salem said. "Who was the snake-eyed woman?"

The cab was ferrying them to the Enterprise Rent-A-Car on Canal Street. The cabbie had assured them she was driving as fast as she could. It didn't stop Salem from wanting to strap jet packs to the roof and rocket them across town.

"I wish I knew. Maybe we're being followed by a brother and sister? That would explain why they have the same eyes." Bel touched the outline of her handgun. She'd assured Salem that she could carry the piece across state lines as long as she kept proof of her law enforcement status handy. Salem didn't like guns, but she was happy to make an exception in Bel's case. Their situation had gone from upside down to deadly.

Salem started her finger-touching routine. "Maybe we're just being paranoid? I've read about heightened stress causing delusions."

"Paranoia might be all that keeps us alive here."

Salem flinched. "If what Ernest said was true, it didn't work for our moms. At least for one of them."

"I won't believe that without proof."

But they both settled into the heavy blackness of the possibility. It had the ring of truth, as did every word Ernest Mayfair had uttered. It was simply too large to process all at once, though Salem had tried to fit those words into the slots that would elicit the correct emotions. *Conspiracy. Hermitage. Underground. Death.*

She cleared her throat. "I think it was a mistake not to talk to Agent Stone back in Minneapolis. Or here. My mom said not to trust anyone, but we have to trust *someone*."

Bel shrugged. "No looking back, only forward. Besides, I don't like that Stone showed up in Salem, and that he was in the lobby the same time as the snake-eyed woman and Ed Harris. There's no good reason for the FBI to be following us."

"Are you thinking about what Ernest said about the Hermitage having a plant in the FBI?"

Bel ran her hand over her face. "I'm thinking about your mom's warning. I intend to beware. We both should."

Salem hugged herself and glanced out the window at the bayside city sliding past. *One two three breathe.* They would look forward, not back. They would talk about things as if both their moms were alive, because the alternative would hurt too much. *One two three breathe.*

Wherever the messages took them, they would follow, because her mother had set them on this trail.

One two three breathe.

"He looked pissed," Bel mused.

"Who?"

"The Ed Harris guy. But not at us. At Agent Stone."

"Think they know each other?"

"Stone for sure has a partner. Could be him. But right before the Ed Harris guy looked angry to see Stone, he looked *surprised* to see him. Just for a split second."

Salem rubbed her eyes. Blinked. Her vision was blurry. When was the last time she'd slept? Two days ago? Three? She took a whiff of her armpit. Definitely past due for a shower. She envied Bel's rapidly drying silken hair.

The cab stopped abruptly in front of a strip mall, the force of the sudden halt banging Salem into the seat back.

The driver clicked a button on her meter. "Here you are."

Salem handed her a ten, told her to keep the change, and squeaked out with her and Bel's duffels in hand, rubbing her shoulder where it had hit the seat. She slammed the door and glanced around. Bel did the same. They stood in front of a Jackson Hewitt Tax Service. A Family Dollar was around the north corner, occupying most of the strip mall. On the south side, a white garage with shredded paint leaned against a graffiti-stained warehouse.

The setting sun turned the sky a dull red.

Besides one car parked in the strip mall lot, the neighborhood was deserted. Salem knocked on the cab door. "Hey, I don't see—"

But the cab sped off. Salem had to hop to keep from having her toes run over. "Dang it!"

"Over here," Bel said, jogging north. "The Enterprise is right around the corner, tucked behind the—"

Her words cut off as a shadow separated itself from the bushes and stalked toward her.

CHAPTER 38

Salem, Massachusetts

Bel leaped forward, grabbed the assailant's wrist, and twisted it as she ducked under in a move that reminded Salem of square dancing. They'd learned the basics in a middle school gym class, except in Bel's current version, she kept moving underneath and behind, twisting the man's arm to the point where Salem could hear the sinew protesting, at which point Bel shoved the sharp side of her foot into the back of his knee, pushed in and down, and used her weight to pin him long enough to yank her Glock out of its holster and press it deep into his temple.

"Don't!" A girl no more than seven, all jutting bones and greasy hair, jumped from the shadows and shoved Bel, oblivious to the gun and the danger. "Don't be mean to my brother!" She beat Bel with her tiny fists.

"Ernest?" Salem asked, recognizing the lanky man in Bel's grip. "Bel, let him go."

"Not until he tells us what he's doing here. And get the kid offa me." A car motored by slowly, the driver certainly wondering at the tableau of Bel overpowering 6'7" Ernest while being pummeled by a little girl.

Salem reached toward the child, but the girl moved to Bel's other side, just out of Salem's reach.

"Don't hurt her!" Ernest's voice was tight with panic, his flesh white from the pain of Bel's hold. He jerked his head toward the girl, whose face was streaked with tears and dirt. "I think they're after her." She was still pounding Bel but hadn't the strength to do damage. "Mercy, stop it."

The girl paused, stepping around front so she was face-to-face with Bel. Her eyes were wide, scared, their lashes impossibly long. "Will you let him go?"

Bel didn't answer.

Ernest tried again. "I need to get out of town to protect Mercy. You two need to get out of town to save your *own* lives. The Hermitage Foundation sicced one of their best assassins on you, and the FBI is in Salem, too. No telling whose side they're on today. I figure you have sixty seconds before one or both locates you here."

Bel ground her knee into his back. He grunted.

"Bel!" Salem said.

"Fifty seconds." His jaw was clenched. "No way can you get a car rented in that time. Even if you did, it'd be traceable. We can take mine."

"That's as traceable as a rental," Bel barked.

"But it's not tied to you two." He glanced away from Mercy, who was twisting a soft-looking blanket in her hands. "And anyhow, it's not mine."

"Stolen?"

"Yes," he said. "Forty seconds."

Bel glanced at Salem.

"Please," the little girl begged, turning to Salem. With her huge eyes and wringing hands, she reminded Salem of a Keane painting.

"You don't have to trust me," Ernest said. "You don't even have to like me. Just get in my car, let's drive somewhere safe, and I can explain the rest. You know you can overpower me if you need to. You've done it twice."

Still, Bel paused.

"Thirty seconds," he pleaded. His upper body was trembling from the pain of Bel's hold. "That old brown sedan over there is mine. We can still get out of this."

"Go. Now!" Bel holstered her gun, released him, and all four of them raced to the car.

CHAPTER 39

Massachusetts

The phone buzzed like a rattlesnake nest inside Jason's jacket pocket. It was almost certainly Carl Barnaby calling him for an update, but if Jason didn't check, he wasn't technically avoiding talking with him. And there was no need to speak with Barnaby until he had something to report.

He signaled left to stick close to the brown sedan the women and the tall man and the child had tucked themselves inside of, jabbing the window button to allow the brisk breeze to wash through the car, cleansing him of Salem Wiley's scent. The woman had been a frightened rabbit, eyes wide, shivering. If not for the FBI agent's interference, he would have slid the knife into her gut and his hand into her pocket to retrieve the document, then stepped to the rack of brochures while Isabel (she was so beautiful up close that he called her Isabel now) rushed to Salem's side, thinking her friend had fainted.

He would have knelt to help Isabel, puncturing her kidney so cleanly she'd feel only a strange punch before bleeding out. And then he'd stand with a different face, making room for the bystanders rushing to assist the two women, and stroll out the front door, into his car, and fly to San Francisco to celebrate and wait.

Sixty seconds, start to finish.

He opened the cracked windows to their full extent, fresh air collapsing itself around the cinnamon particles still clinging to him and sweeping them out to sea. The gray trees and brown grass matched his mood, the garish shops designed to cash in on the witch trials annoying him. It didn't even make him happy to see that there were no police cars in front of the First Church, either of them.

The sedan turned left on Washington. He did the same. The women had made contact with the man and girl just ahead of his arrival at the strip mall and were fleeing to the airport or the train station. It didn't matter to him which.

He punched the radio. Whoever had rented the car before him had tuned it to NPR.

"Her husband, Charles Hayes, nearly negotiated an Israeli-Palestinian peace deal during his tenure as secretary of state. With local DC news station WLJA posting grainy photos that appear to be Israeli Ambassador to the United States David Meridor and PLO Ambassador to the United States Yousef Ziad ar-Reefy leaving a Washington, DC, office building separately and minutes ahead of Democratic presidential candidate Gina Hayes, pundits are speculating that she intends to finish the job her husband started if elected. This means . . ."

He slammed his fist into the console, cracking the plastic. The radio squawked country music before he punched the off button. Concentrating on his pulse, he reminded himself how close he was to his goal. Ahead of him, Salem Wiley was driving, with the strange man in the passenger seat and Isabel Odegaard next to the girl in the back. Wiley surely had the master list stuffed in her front left coat pocket, the one she'd kept patting in the hotel lobby.

The Crucible would be on Alcatraz Island on Monday, November 7, the day before the presidential election. That gave him six days to catch the women, nab the list, and kill them.

He wouldn't need six days.

Once their car stopped, he wouldn't need six minutes.

CHAPTER 40

Ten Years Old

Daniel has joked that Bel has two switches: on or off. She never does any-thing halfway, which is why Salem isn't surprised when Bel signs up for law enforcement camp the summer after she graduates from eighth grade. She's given up looking for her dad; at least, she doesn't talk about it anymore. Now it's all about arresting the bad guys.

The week without Bel is excruciating. Salem tries helping her dad, or going to the park, or reading, but it's not the same knowing she can't call Bel when she wants to. When Gracie asks Salem if she wants to go with to pick up Bel at the end of the week, it's all Salem can do not to yell her yes.

Bel seems different on the drive back. Distant, maybe, or like she's guarding something. When the two of them are alone in Bel's bedroom, she spills it.

"I kissed a girl."

An unpleasant heat burns in Salem's chest. She's seen people kiss, of course—her parents, people in movies—but she thought it wouldn't be something she'd have to worry about until high school at least. "What was it like?"

Bel gets a faraway smile. "Warm. Wet. I liked it."

Salem feels the chasm growing between them. She's a girl, ten. She still wears a helmet when she bikes. She owns a training bra, but she doesn't need it because she hasn't even got what the boys call "mosquito bites." Bel is growing up without her. The heat moves to her eyes, and she thinks she might cry. She adjusts her shirt, its front emblazoned with a dorky Saved by the Bell *iron-on. She feels fat and stupid and out of place.*

"But not as much as I liked the rope wall. Salem! I can't wait to be a real police officer! I have to show you what I learned about climbing. Come on."

Bel takes her hand and tugs her outside. They take their secret path to the limestone caves by the river, and Bel teaches her all her tricks. They giggle and finish each other's sentences and Bel flashes her gorgeous smile, and everything is right again.

CHAPTER 41

Massachusetts

Salem tried to cover herself with the warm recollection of that smile as she drove the brown Buick Century, wrapping the memory around herself like a sweater.

Or a bulletproof vest.

Ernest sat next to her, massaging his arm. Mercy rested in the seat directly behind him, looking even younger curled around her blanket, and Bel rode next to the girl, her back against the door, eyes and maybe gun trained on Ernest. Salem couldn't tell from the driver's seat. All she knew was that Bel had patted down Ernest before she let him in the car and she'd ordered everyone where to sit, all in the span of one of the tensest twenty seconds of Salem's life.

Salem blinked against the setting sun. Her eyes felt gritty enough to make pearls if she could only close them for more than a second.

She needed to talk to stay awake. "How did you find us?"

Ernest shrugged, then winced. "Lucky guess. Figured you'd take a cab to the nearest car rental."

Bel cursed from the back seat.

Salem asked another question. "Back at the hotel, you said the Hermitage Foundation came after our moms, and now they're after . . . your sister?"

She glanced in the rearview mirror. The girl appeared asleep. She imagined Bel was glaring at the back of Ernest's skull, her eyes shooting bullets into him. Salem had seen her friend agitated before, but never to this level. They both needed sleep, food, and to get their heads on straight.

"That's right." Ernest fidgeted. Salem first thought his height made it difficult to get comfortable, but then she realized he was trying to check on his sister in the mirror.

Salem craned her neck so she could glance deeper into the back seat. "I think she's sleeping."

"Yeah," Bel said from the rear. "I can hear her breathing. You should tell us anything you left out back at the Hawthorne, and quickly. We have somewhere we have to be."

Salem knew better than to say *where* they needed to be—Bel would be furious if she spilled their destination to Ernest. That was unfortunate, because all Salem had was a vague idea that Amherst lay about two hours away on the western side of the state, combined with an awareness that the sun set in the west. She had no idea which roads to take and was following the fading light.

"Can I cover her with my jacket first?" Ernest looked pained.

"Of course," Bel replied. "You're not hostages."

He was too tall to remove his parka without bumping Salem two separate times. Other than the chicken-soup smell announcing he was past due for a shower, she didn't mind. He unbuckled, leaned over the back seat, and tucked his jacket around Mercy. She didn't stir. He returned to his spot and rebuckled.

"You're not going to like this," he began, "but I don't know much more than I told you at the hotel. The Hermitage Foundation was formed by Andrew Jackson back in the early 1800s. He invested his fortune into it. I think he envisioned a secret group of men who would get rich and stay rich, sort of orchestrating the world behind the scenes. Part of their mission entailed keeping women in their place."

"Why?" Salem asked.

Bel echoed her. "Yeah, weren't religions and governments doing just fine at that?"

"That's just it." Ernest swiveled to face her. His voice was sincere, begging Bel not to make fun of him. "The original founders were the heads of *everything* at the time, including churches, businesses, and the government. They wanted to keep it that way. They've done a pretty good job, too."

"I thought I heard something in the news sometime about the Barnaby brothers being active in the Hermitage." In response to Bel's questioning stare in the mirror, Salem explained, "Those two rich guys taking down unions all over the country."

Ernest nodded. "One of them, Carl Barnaby, is the Hermitage's CEO. His brother, Cassius, is on the board. They oversee the American arm of the Hermitage. Their mission is to help the rich get richer, starting with themselves. It's the original good old boys club."

Bel glanced out the window, taking her eyes off Ernest for the first time. "Let me guess: women's inequality is a conspiracy, created and funded by the Hermitage Foundation."

He misread her sarcasm as buy-in. "Exactly! Women are the majority. If they unite, they can take their power back. The Hermitage knows that. Sanctioned wartime rape, acid attacks, how impossible it is in some places to get an education—or even birth control—if you're female, unfair pay, erasing women from the history books . . . they're all movements funded by the Hermitage Foundation. They're so good at it that they have people thinking all of that is their own idea. They even have *women* speaking out against their own interests. And your mothers"—he turned his attention to Salem—"were instrumental in keeping the Hermitage in check, even though it's always been an uphill battle."

He coughed. "You're going to want to get on Highway 2."

Bel spun her eyes back into the car. "What?"

The shadow of a smile appeared on Ernest's lips. "I peeked at the note back at the hotel, when you had me in that lock hold? I saw Emily Dickinson's signature. I figure you're going to Amherst, right?"

Salem sneaked a peek at Ernest. He was so tall he had to bend his shaggy head forward to fit in the car. He otherwise sat as straight as he could, long fingers spread out on his knees, face too young to grow a proper beard but a couple weeks past a shave nonetheless. He'd proven himself to be resourceful and smart, and he clearly loved his little sister. He was growing on Salem. "I think we should trust him, Bel."

A flash of light appeared in the back seat as Bel fired up her phone. "The directions he gave look good."

Ernest nodded happily. Traffic was heavy enough to keep the sedan at forty miles per hour, gray cars full of gray people on gray roads streaming past like groupers against a current. The only color in the severe fall landscape was the sun, which had nearly dipped below the horizon, a vivid corona of blood orange marking its passage.

Bel's voice cut into the silence. She was still researching on her phone. "The only Minneapolis homicide stories mention Mrs. Gladia." She aimed her words at Ernest. "No mention of her dog, no mention of our mothers disappearing, both facts that you knew."

"Not to mention my nickname," Salem said.

Bel dropped her phone and rubbed her face with both hands. "Okay. The kidnapping of two women, one of them a local celebrity, should be headline news. Goddammit."

Salem's eyes grew hot. If she started crying, she wasn't ever going to stop, so she swallowed the cresting wave of loss. No one was looking for Grace and her mom, no one but them.

"Your mom was right, Salem," Bel said softly. "We have to beware. We're on the run, officially, until we figure this out." She put her hands on the front seat and pulled herself forward. "Ernest, I *don't* trust you, but it's not personal. It's common sense."

He bobbed his head. "Understood." His voice dropped. "Your moms knew the Hermitage was coming for them. They set something in motion before they were . . . taken care of. Emily Dickinson's note must tell us what it is."

Salem's hand flew to the cloth of her jacket. She pushed lightly and heard a crinkle.

Dickinson's poem. Safe and sound.

Relieved, she let out her breath. "Where are you from, Ernest?"

His shoulders slumped. "Everywhere. Me and Mercy have camped in Massachusetts for the last few months."

"How'd you get caught up in all this?" Bel asked from the back seat.

Ernest glanced at the shadows racing outside his window. "We were living in Georgia. My mom died giving birth to Mercy. The Underground found us soon after. They give us places to bunk up and down the coast, help me with Mercy when I run errands for them. We can't ever stay in one place too long. I don't want them to find her."

The jacket in the back seat moved. "I'm hungry," Mercy said.

Salem covered her mouth with her hand. *How much had the girl heard?*

"You know what, honey?" Salem said. "I'm hungry, too. I'll take the next exit and—"

A deer leaped out of the ditch, scaring the words from her mouth, hurtling toward the hood of their car.

CHAPTER 42

Massachusetts

Salem shrieked and jerked the steering wheel to the right. She narrowly avoided colliding with the animal but had overcompensated, careening toward the ditch. A bevy of horns blared and lights flew at her from every direction as the sedan's tire caught loose gravel and the car spun. Salem slammed her foot on the brake and held it rigid. The brake's screams matched her own as the smell of burning rubber filled the air.

Finally, the car slid to a halt, one back tire in the ditch, the two front tires creating a perpendicular line with the passing traffic. The deer, a twelve-point buck at least, continued to wreak havoc on the traffic going the other direction before bounding safely into the far woods.

"Everyone okay?" Bel asked.

"Mercy?" Ernest nearly jumped over the seat to reach his sister.

Her voice was tiny. "I'm okay."

Salem released the steering wheel, realizing too late that it was all that was anchoring her hands, which took to the air like palsied birds. "I'm all right," she croaked.

"Then let's get out of here before the police arrive." Bel unbuckled herself and stepped out of the car. She tapped on Salem's window, helped her out, and hugged her quickly before sliding into the driver's seat. Salem hobbled into the back seat, adrenaline rattling her bones, the brisk air a small help in clearing her head.

"I'm still hungry," Mercy said, so quiet that Salem was sure she was the only one who heard it.

"Bel," Salem said, "we need to rest. You and I haven't slept in over two days. It's dangerous. And I need to research what Ernest told us plus figure out exactly where in Amherst we're going. A shower wouldn't kill me, either."

"I'd feel better if we kept moving." Bel timed her reentry into the traffic. "Can you do the research on your phone?"

Salem glanced over at Mercy. Ernest's jacket had slipped off in the near accident, revealing the girl's painfully thin arms. *When was the last time you ate, baby girl?*

"I need to use my laptop," Salem said firmly.

"And lemme guess, you were too cheap to pay for a hot spot on your phone?" But Bel's tone was acquiescent. Salem knew it would be a relief for all of them to stop.

"Look." Salem shoved her hand between Bel and Ernest to point ahead. "Right up here—a motel and a pizza restaurant, all advertised on the same billboard. It's a sign from the universe. This exit, please."

Bel did as requested, pulling into the parking lot of the Holiday Motel just off the ramp. Its vintage neon sign was at odds with the crumbling strip of rooms to each side of the office. A gas station that looked like it'd last pumped fuel during the Reagan era was the only other building on the scabby patch of road, which led south to Littleton and north to the highway they'd just exited, the latter so close Salem could read the license plates of the cars zooming past if she squinted. She marched into the Holiday Motel office and exited four minutes later with the key to room 11, two double beds, no smoking.

The room was at the far north end of the motel, so Bel moved the car, and the four of them trudged into the room, quiet as a prayer.

When the door closed behind them, Bel slid the chain lock into place and secured a chair under the knob as an extra precaution.

Outside, a gray sedan pulled into the abandoned gas station parking lot and killed its lights.

No one got out.

CHAPTER 43

Massachusetts

"Does the pizza place deliver?" Bel asked, stepping out of the bathroom.

The room was worn but serviceable, containing two beds as promised and not much else. Ernest stood at the window, peering out past the industrial curtains. Mercy sat cross-legged in front of the TV, watching a staticky *Seinfeld* rerun. The jokes would go over her head, but the light and laughter had a soothing effect, entrancing her. Salem pushed aside the Bible to get at the stack of take-out and delivery menus in the nightstand.

"Yup," she said. She shook her head to clear the cobwebs. "What's everyone want?"

She scribbled down the requests—extra cheese for Mercy, *all meat any meat please* for Ernest, Bel wanted her usual cream cheese, pineapple, and Canadian bacon, and for Salem, jalapeños and mushrooms. She added a garden salad to the order. The way Mercy's shoulder blades poked out of her camisole indicated it'd been too long since the child had eaten fresh vegetables. Salem wondered how Ernest supported the two of them, if it was stealing like he'd done with the car, or if Underground members paid him for running errands. Probably both.

As if reading her mind, he reached into his jacket. "I can help pay."

He brought out his wallet, but something was caught in it. Salem reached for it, the chain uncoiling in her hand as softly as water.

It was half of a pink quartz heart, the word *love* etched in it. Her guts twisted, forcing an *oof* out of her mouth.

Bel looked over from the window, where she'd taken up Ernest's watch. "What is it?"

Ernest tried to snatch the necklace out of Salem's hand, but it was too late. Bel had walked over and spotted it herself.

She and Salem had discovered the matching necklaces ten years earlier when shopping for Mother's Day gifts. They'd seemed perfect, pull-apart rose quartz, each half identical to the other, symbolic of the love the four of them shared.

A month later, Salem and Bel decided the necklaces were corny and stopped wearing their halves.

As far as they knew, their mothers had never taken theirs off, even to sleep.

"Where'd you get this?" Bel's voice was rust and bile.

Ernest's face shaded a waxy red. "Dr. Keller overnighted it to me. It was found on the body of one of your moms. He said if the 'Bits' didn't convince you, then the necklace would."

Mercy looked away from the television, attracted by the thick tension.

"Why didn't you show us earlier?" Bel demanded.

Ernest groaned. "I couldn't. It was hard enough to tell you that one of them was dead."

Bel had grown so pale that Salem could see an aqua-colored vein running from her forehead to her ear, pulsing. Salem wanted to touch it, but she was floating, no longer body and bone but pure white fear.

Bel was monotone. "How did Dr. Keller acquire it?"

Ernest's eyes swam with tears. He couldn't look at either of them. "Two Hermitage employees in Minneapolis were called in to dispose of the body. One of them also works for the Underground. He went straight to Dr. Keller afterward with the necklace."

"Our mothers were together. What happened to the other one?"

"The assassin took her to some plant outside of Minneapolis. She was still alive."

The words dropped out of Bel's mouth like bombs. "Which one of our mothers did this necklace come from?"

His shoulders crawled toward his ears and stayed there. "I don't know. The Hermitage employee who disposed of the body didn't offer a description when he gave Dr. Keller the necklace."

Bel reached over to Salem and clung to her, grounding her despite the trembling that passed between them. They'd been forced into this conspiracy, trained for it apparently, and it was a world where people were *murdered*. The cold shock was too thick to pierce, but Salem felt something toxic and hot squirming just outside it.

Betrayal.

Their mothers hadn't warned them about any of this.

They hadn't asked if Salem and Bel wanted to be a part of it.

Their mothers had led a double life, and it had gotten one of them killed. Salem had been dreaming of a loving relationship with her mom, and Vida had been training her for war.

"I'm hungry."

Salem glanced over at Mercy and then exchanged a look with Bel. *There is nowhere to go but forward,* it said.

Bel slipped the necklace into her jeans pocket and returned to her post at the window. "Order the pizzas," she muttered over her shoulder.

Salem patted Ernest—he looked miserable—and tried to smile at Mercy, testing her speech. "I'll get us food."

She called in the order and then tugged the Holiday Motel Wi-Fi password out of her jeans. She walked to the bathroom to grab a towel, placing it over the bedspread, and set up a small workstation. She retrieved the Dickinson poem from her jacket pocket and placed it next to her on the towel. With her back against the headboard, she left the pain and fear of the hotel room and fell into the rabbit hole of research.

Salem had studied the note so many times that she knew it by heart:

My Life had stood—a Loaded Gun

Some keep the Sabbath going to church;
I keep it staying at home,
With a bobolink for a chorister,
And an orchard for a dome.

Some keep the Sabbath in surplice;
I just wear my wings,
And instead of tolling the bell for church,
Our little sexton sings.

God preaches, a noted clergyman,
And the sermon is never long;
So instead of getting to heaven at last,
I'm going all along!

—Emily Dickinson
Σ

She recognized the symbol below Dickinson's signature. The original Greek letter sigma, used frequently in modern mathematics, was usually referred to as *lunate sigma*, or the female sigma, because of its crescent shape. Salem had already decided it was either a shorthand symbol for the Underground or, given its *E*-like shape, an affectation of Emily Dickinson's.

Yet she must have overlooked something. She retraced her earlier research, locating the actual "Loaded Gun" poem, finding the title for the Sabbath poem, investigating Dickinson, her family, her education, any link to the Underground or other famous women of her time who might have connected her to the Underground. Other than the brief period in 1844 when Dickinson's parents sent her to Boston and she met Lucretia Mott, there were no other historically remarkable women Dickinson may have encountered.

Salem tied up her hair with a band that she wore at her wrist and scratched her chin, selecting the Emily Dickinson Museum from the list of Google offerings. The museum was closed for the day and wouldn't reopen until eleven tomorrow. It consisted of two buildings: the Homestead, where Dickinson was born and spent much of her life, and the Evergreens, home of Dickinson's brother, wife, and children. If Salem didn't discover anything on her computer, the museum was the likely place for them to travel to tomorrow.

But how could there be nothing in Dickinson's note? No substitution cipher, no transposition cipher, just a poem with the wrong title, the whole works written by one of the most famous poets in history. Salem exhaled the frustration through her nose. Maybe it was a code, with each word representing something else, the key forever lost to the ages.

"What are those for?"

Salem jumped, her tunnel vision expanding to include the towel, and the bedspread, and finally, little Mercy Mayfair, who stood right next to her, peering at the note with her liquid brown eyes.

"The words?" Salem asked, steadying her heartbeat. "It's a poem by Emily Dickinson. Have you heard of her?"

"Not the words," Mercy said. "I can read those. What are the dots under them?"

Salem's heart thudded against her rib cage. She held the note up to the light. The paper was faded and yellow, but still, how could she have missed it? Dickinson's note hadn't contained a code or cipher. It was steganography, the act of concealing a message in plain sight—Morse code knit into a scarf, an itty-bitty message hidden under a stamp, invisible ink, a still frame planted within a video.

Dots under letters revealing a secret message.

Salem squealed and pulled Mercy into a hug. The girl neither struggled nor returned the embrace.

Bel ran to Salem's bedside, Ernest at her heels. "What is it?"

"Mercy solved the code in the Dickinson poem! It's a pinprick encryption. See these dots under certain letters? They spell out a message. Victorian lovers used it to send secret meeting times to one another in seemingly innocuous notes. Check this out." She pointed under the word *Gun* in the title. "There's a tiny dot under the *G*. That's the first letter in the code." She jabbed her finger at the notepad and pen on the side table. "Write these down!"

Bel did as commanded, scribbling each letter as Salem spelled them out: *G-u-n-s-a-m-u-e-l-l-u-c-r-e-t-i-a.*

"Gun Samuel Lucretia!" Bel hooted. "Who are they?"

Salem shook her head in amazement. "Samuel and Lucretia Dickinson were Emily's grandparents." She glanced down at her computer. "Let's hope the Emily Dickinson Museum still has their gun collection, and doesn't mind us poking through it."

Knock knock.

All of them except Bel jerked. She slid her hand into her holster and unsnapped her gun, finger over her mouth. Striding quietly toward the door, she peered through the peephole.

"Pizza." She reholstered her weapon and opened the door.

She stepped outside while Salem paid for the pies. If the long-haired, high school–age delivery driver thought it odd that two women in their late twenties, a giant about the delivery kid's own age, and a little girl were spending the night in the Littleton, Massachusetts, Holiday Motel, he kept it to himself.

He didn't even remove his earbuds, though Salem was gratified that he turned down his music when he took her money. He'd been playing 2Pac and Dr. Dre's "California Love" if she wasn't mistaken, and it reminded her of her Jordan neighborhood kids. The connection gave her a sharp pain. She'd be helping them after school right now if she weren't here, teaching them how to cut and paste and save and upload and, if they showed the aptitude and interest, program a computer.

"Wow, thanks!" the kid said in response to the five-dollar tip. He was grinning as he walked past Bel.

Bel shut and locked the door behind him, not bothering with the brass-plated chain. "I think we need to keep moving."

"Wha—" Ernest had a slice of steaming pizza halfway to his mouth. Mercy had carried hers to the floor in front of the TV, completely disregarding the salad.

"The pickup that was parked next to the office when we pulled in is still there, but there's a sedan next to it now, and another in the gas station parking lot. I don't like it."

"It's a motel, Bellie." Salem wanted to be strong, but Bel's paranoia was creeping up her neck like fingers. "We have to sleep somewhere."

"I agree." Bel pushed Mercy's pizza box closed. "It's a two-hour drive to Amherst, and we have three drivers. We sleep in shifts."

Ernest and Mercy didn't argue, likely a side effect from years of constant movement. They both appeared long-faced, though. Maybe it was simply hunger. Salem was stacking the pizzas when her phone buzzed. She set the greasy cardboard boxes on the bed and reached in her pocket.

She flipped over the phone and saw that she had gotten a text. From her mom.

CHAPTER 44

Massachusetts

The interior of the sedan was redolent with the fried sugar-salt smell of McDonald's mingling with Clancy's Old Spice. If it were up to Stone, there'd be no fast food stops, no cologne you could buy from a drugstore shelf, no gum chewing allowed in the car. But Clancy was still pissed at him for the double op in the Hawthorne Hotel lobby and Stone didn't want to waste any more energy on him.

He kept his thoughts to himself.

The lurid neon of the Holiday Motel sign didn't quite reach their car parked tight to the abandoned gas station. Still, Stone kept his iPad on no-see mode, covered with an FBI-issue filter that gobbled up the light using reverse night vision technology. This allowed him to read in the dark with no telltale glow. He was in the passenger seat. Clancy was behind the wheel, eyes on the door to room 11. They'd swapped when they'd filled up on gas.

"The girls just got a pizza delivered," Clancy said. "Four pies, it looks like. Any luck finding out who their two ragtags are?"

"Have you *heard* my phone ring?" It was out of character for Stone to snap at his partner. He kept emotions out of the business. It'd been a long two days, though, and Clancy knew better than him that the lab would call if they got anything on the photos they'd been sent.

Clancy grunted.

Stone never glanced up from his search, which, despite the high-end tech allowing him to use the device unseen in the dark, was research anybody with access to a free desktop at the library could do. He was looking for national, or at least Minnesota-local, news on the suspected kidnapping of Grace Odegaard and Vida Wiley.

Back in Minneapolis, he'd been relieved that the media hadn't stumbled on the serial killer cases he and his team had been following, but since the Hawthorne Hotel lobby, he'd decided to get suspicious. His luck had never been that good. In fact, in his experience, if it looked like luck, you were missing something. So he'd started sniffing around the news sites. He'd located information on the five murders leading up to the Minneapolis case, but it was buried and it was brief, which was not how the media normally handled the murders of four white women.

Then he'd decided to see what a regular citizen could find out about the kidnapping of a successful Realtor and a high-profile history professor in Minneapolis.

Turned out, nothing.

Not one peep on all of the internet, though Mrs. Gladia's murder had been reported.

Goddamn.

This went up high, up to someone powerful enough to muzzle the media and buy Stone's partner. In this age of the internet, where everyone with a phone had a camera and could find an online audience, that took bank and connections of a staggering scope. Stone pulled his eyes from the device and refocused them onto a spot about four feet in front of the hood of the car.

God*damn*.

Since the lobby, Stone had upgraded Clancy from neutral to enemy, which added another level of hassle to a situation that was already so far out of control as to be a joke if there weren't lives at stake. But what Stone knew that Clancy didn't was that he'd finally received a break, the tiniest thread of hope that might lead out of this pit. It had come moments earlier in the form of an email from a forensic scientist in the New Mexico Regional Computer Forensics Lab, the closest RCFL to the first murder and the location to which Stone had sent the hard drives and phones of all five murder victims.

She'd found something. A connection.

Three of the victims—the New Age woman from Sedona, the Maine attorney, and the Nebraska homemaker—had all attended the same conference a month earlier, an all-female retreat in San Diego. He googled the conference, called Women in Numbers.

The site was simple, consisting of a single page, soft blues and browns behind black lettering. The conference had been held October 1 and 2 in the Los Milagros Resort and promised two days of panels and breakout sessions designed to explore the role of women in history as well as their current role in politics, education, and the sciences.

The keynote speaker? Dr. Vida Wiley.

A hot rush of triumph had pumped through Stone. Finally. He finally had a lead. The bottom of the page included an email address and a phone number, plus a tagline: **Let's Not Do Our Work Underground Anymore.**

Bookmarking the page, Stone let his eyes drift back outside, into the space of night. He thought his mother would have liked that, a group of women standing up and claiming what was theirs. She'd look up from the hamburger and noodles and canned peas she was pulling together for her two sons after a ten-hour shift cleaning houses, right before going to whatever floating part-time job she juggled to keep food in their bellies and a roof over her head, and she'd say, "Goodness, Luc, doing our work underground? We've been doing that shit right in front of your eyes for years. Just open 'em up." Then she'd laugh that sweet, deep laugh that pushed aside every dark thought a person had ever entertained.

He'd give up his career, the one he'd scratched and fought and sacrificed for, just to hear that laugh one more time.

"They're coming out," Clancy said, starting the car. "Looks like they're on the move."

CHAPTER 45

Eleven Years Old

"You know how magicians make their magic, don't you?"

It's the winter Salem decides to try bangs. Rather than looking like Uma Thurman in Pulp Fiction, *which was her goal, she resembles a poodle at Westminster. Bel tells her she looks fine—fluffy—and subsequently talks Salem out of dropping out of sixth grade.*

Salem's dad's shop is insulated, and he's working on a simple TV stand. She doesn't understand why he's wasting his time on something so basic—a cube of wood with two drawers in the front, big enough to support a twenty-three-inch before the US got rid of the fat-backed cathode-ray TVs. You could pick up something just like it at Sears.

"I suppose," Salem says, though she's never really given it thought before, "that they get you to look one way and do their trick another."

Daniel slaps his knee. "Exactly!"

Salem feels the warm drops of his pride speckle her skin, just like she always feels when she works with her dad. She points at the ugly lump he's working on. "Is that what you're doing here? Is there a prettier piece of furniture inside?"

Daniel laughs. He's never been mad at Salem, not that she can remember. "If there's ever been a smarter child, I don't want to meet her. No, this plain piece of furniture is all there is to it. Unless," he says, holding up a finger, his eyes twinkling, "you try to open the drawers."

Intrigued, Salem reaches for the round knob holding the top drawer. It doesn't budge. She tries the bottom drawer.

Same.

Vida dances out to the workshop to inform them dinner is ready, bringing in the solid cold of winter. Her cheeks are flushed. Vida's happy because her parents are visiting, and she's made all their favorite foods—a chicken, walnut, and pomegranate stew aromatic with saffron and cinnamon, rice and fava beans flecked with fresh dill, lamb kebabs flavored with lemon and salt. Their house has smelled succulent all day. Vida kisses Daniel on the cheek, and he slips his hand around her waist and dips her for a full kiss. Salem looks away. She's embarrassed and proud that her parents love each other so much.

Vida giggles and pushes away from Daniel.

"Mom," Salem says, "Dad made a TV stand with drawers that don't work."

Her parents exchange a glance. Daniel speaks. "Think of the magicians, Salem. Move your focus away from what you see."

Salem works at it for ten minutes, but the drawers are solid, no trip switches on any of them. Vida murmurs something to him. Daniel's smile drops. He leans forward, grips the top edges of the stand, and turns the whole rectangle forty-five degrees counterclockwise. Underneath lies an unfinished piece of wood.

Next, Daniel pulls out both drawer knobs exactly as if they are the handles on cigarette vending machines. Finally, he places a hand flat on each side of the stand and presses gently. The front of the unit pops open, not two drawers as the design suggests but one.

"But it's just a drawer, exactly as it appears!" Salem exclaims. "Why would you make it so difficult to open?"

Daniel's smile has returned. "The best place to hide something is always in plain sight."

This is one of Salem's earliest exposures to the furniture equivalent of steganography. In a year, she will use the same principle to craft a balsa box etched with an Om *for her mother.*

CHAPTER 46

Massachusetts

Salem's hands were shaking.

Bel and Ernest watched her from the doorway. Mercy was dragging her feet, trying to soak up one last second of television. Time had become a great syrupy broth.

The text from Vida Wiley was twenty-one words long:

Follow the trail to the end, no matter what. Stick close to Bel. Trust no one else. I love you, always.

"Salem? Who texted?"

Was Bel watching her oddly? Well, of course she was. Salem was not answering a direct question, shivering, holding her phone like it was both a scorpion and a life raft. An idea was birthing itself, ripping through Salem's stomach, shredding her throat, too big to push past her mouth, tearing through sinew and skin in its effort to escape: if her mom was texting her right now, that meant Gracie was dead.

Beautiful, sassy Gracie, who lit up any room she walked into and treated everyone like she was their best friend.

Gracie, whom Salem had always secretly wished was her own mother. No way could Salem tell Bel that Gracie was gone. She couldn't destroy her best friend's life the way her own had been razed by her dad's suicide.

She *couldn't.*

She closed her eyes, her brain pounding against the prison of her skull.

Because maybe the text didn't mean Grace was dead. Maybe *both* their mothers were still alive, and Ernest had lied or gotten bad information or found out what sort of necklace Grace and Vida wore and located a replica. Or maybe Salem's own mother was dead, and somebody was using her phone to get to Salem and Bel.

Somebody who wanted to lull her into believing them, trusting them, revealing information she shouldn't.

Or her mom was alive and Grace was dead.

Salem couldn't control the racing thoughts, couldn't look Bel in the eye. She dropped her phone into her pocket and hugged her elbows. "It's Connor. He wants to know when I'll be back in the Cities so he can come over for a booty call."

Bel snorted. "A gentleman to the very end." She stepped aside so Ernest could pass her. "Come on, Salem. I want to get going."

Salem drew in a shaky breath. "I have to pee. I'll meet you in the car, 'kay?"

Bel began to walk toward her. "Are you feeling all right?"

Salem backed into the bathroom, her hands up. "Fine. Just a quick pee. Promise." She closed and locked the door behind her and dropped onto the closed toilet. Her bones were vibrating. She pulled out the phone and reread the message.

With thumbs as cold as the lie she'd just told, she typed a reply: Mom? She breathed in through her nose, out through her mouth, ten times. She counted backward from twenty. No response. She slipped her phone into her pocket, flushed the toilet and washed her hands in case Bel was listening, and shoved down the lava flow of guilt that was searing her insides. She would tell Bel, she would figure out how, but not just yet.

She stepped out of the bathroom.

The hotel room was empty. Salem did a visual sweep to make sure they hadn't left anything. Finding it all clear, she dropped the key on the nightstand and made her way outside. The air was bracing, the moon a waxing crescent, a judging wink staring straight into her yellow heart. She yanked open the Buick's door and slid into the back seat next to Mercy.

Ernest adjusted the rearview mirror. "You sure you're okay? You look pale."

"Just hungry," Salem mumbled.

"Here you go." Bel passed back one of the pizza boxes. Mercy was already tearing into hers. The oily smell made Salem's stomach clutch. "Thanks." She took the box, knowing she couldn't eat, certain the pizza would taste like cardboard and shame.

"That sedan's gone," Bel remarked as they pulled out. "The one that was in the gas station lot. I never got a look at who was driving it."

Salem watched the glow of the hotel's neon sign from the back seat and nodded, the only response she could muster.

She was falling through smoke.

As the dark Massachusetts highway rolled away beyond the Buick's window, her brain drifted from the lie she'd told to a burning question: Had her parents and Gracie pushed her and Bel into their future careers of cryptanalyst and police officer, not by force but by planned, manipulative gestures? Things like a new codebook brought home from the library for Salem, or math camp sold to Salem and law enforcement camp to Bel every summer, like it was the lottery they'd won?

The thought that her dreams and passions had never been her own sent her into an emotional free fall. She didn't want to believe it, that her parents' support and encouragement of her had been so calculated.

Salem didn't even know she'd fallen asleep until Bel's scream woke her.

CHAPTER 47

"Thank you for meeting with us, ma'am."

"My pleasure." Gina took the seat across from the two veterans and indicated they should also sit. Her Secret Service shadow and her ever-present aide took the table behind them. She wondered what Theodore and Matthew talked about.

Probably not the price of tea.

"We see your campaign is going well." Staff Sergeant Samuel Wringson smiled. He was a veteran of the current war in Afghanistan, where he had lost both legs below the knees and his right arm to a roadside IED. His companion, Lieutenant Louis Palakiko, had been stationed in Iraq during the most recent US invasion and was a well-known national speaker on PTSD. They were both active in Veterans for Peace and had managed to land on Senator Hayes's schedule in this campaign crunch time.

The press took the remaining tables in the Red Hen, whose rustic main room had been reserved for this brief meeting.

"I think it is." Gina thanked the waiter for her water. She took a sip, sighing inwardly as the press corps snapped photos. She seldom ate or drank in public since Matthew had shown her the photo of her taken a month ago from outside a restaurant, a magnified shot of her gaping mouth as she forked fish into it. The caption underneath read, Senator Hayes Hunts for Krill.

"Screw them," Matthew had said. "That line isn't even funny. They should have used, *We're Gonna Need a Bigger Fork.*"

She didn't think either of them was funny, but she'd gotten used to attacks on her weight—she was a size twelve, unforgivable for a woman in the public eye—and didn't want to fuel the fire. So she ate behind closed doors. Her company didn't need to, however.

"Are either of you hungry?"

"No, ma'am," Wringson said. "We know you're busy. We wanted to speak with you about the Afghanistan mineral rights bill up for vote in the Senate. We were hoping we could persuade you to vote against it."

The same bill Senator McCoy had mentioned yesterday. She had no intention of voting for it whether or not she'd met with these men. The bill was a pet project of Barnaby Industries, a multibillion-dollar, multinational corporation based in Kansas City, Missouri, and owned by the Barnaby brothers, who also sat on the board of the Hermitage Foundation. Barnaby Industries had many offshoots; one of its most profitable was mining. They were the only producers of the type of equipment needed to access Afghanistan's nearly $1 trillion mineral trove, which included copper, iron, and carbonatite deposits. Barnaby Industries was also the lead contractor providing security to private enterprises in Afghanistan.

A Missouri senator was conveniently the one who had proposed the bill, with the blessing of Afghanistan, as a way to pay off their mounting war debt. Barnaby Industries stood to make billions if it passed.

"You must know I've publicly spoken out against the bill," Gina said.

Lieutenant Palakiko leaned forward. He had the skin tone of a Native Hawaiian and eyes that twinkled. "We do. We also know lobbying groups can be very persuasive. We can't match them in money or numbers, but thanks to this meeting, we can match them in access."

He provided data on the proposed mineral rights bill, all of which she'd seen before—collateral and financial costs, timelines, alternatives.

"Thank you." She took the file he offered her. She'd have Matthew add it to the ones she'd already acquired. "Is there anything else?"

The veterans exchanged glances. Senator Hayes estimated they were about the same age as her daughter, Catherine. She wondered if they had partners and children of their own.

"We want you to know that you're the first viable presidential candidate who's been willing to meet with us, ma'am," Lieutenant Palakiko said. "We won't forget that."

Gina smiled warmly.

One of the press caught the expression perfectly.

The caption under it in tomorrow's *Times* would read, A Leader for the People.

CHAPTER 48

Twenty Years Old

"Who's familiar with Marie-Sophie Germain?"

It's October of Salem's first semester at the University of Minnesota. It's taken her two years after high school to work up the courage to attend college. The campus is picturesque, the mall full of street preachers and gyro vendors hoping to catch students between classes. Different languages mingle with the Minnesota accents, the fluid threading the nasal, and students argue Karl Marx and Britney Spears with equal fervor beneath century-old oaks that drop their leaves like blessings. The air smells of woodsmoke and possibility, and despite her agoraphobia, Salem feels a tremor of excitement when she's on campus.

She also harbors a deep crush on Dr. Ventura, her only unmarried male professor. Yet it's not because of her embarrassing attraction to Dr. Ventura that she doesn't answer his question.

Rather, she has no idea who Marie-Sophie Germain is.

She isn't alone. Dr. Ventura scans his CS236 cryptography class, one of the most popular on campus. There are over a hundred students registered and almost all attend regularly. Not one has raised their hand.

Dr. Ventura nods as if he expected this. "Sophie Germain was one of the greatest mathematicians who has ever lived." As his students whisper their surprise, he advances the PowerPoint slide, introducing a sketched profile of a strong-nosed woman in her forties, hair tied in braided buns Princess

Leia–style. Her name is written underneath the profile, and below that, the years 1776–1831.

"She was born in France at a time when women were not taught math unless they were aristocrats, and then only enough to make polite conversation. The single textbook these women were allowed to read on the subject was Francesco Algarotti's Sir Isaac Newton's Philosophy Explain'd for the Use of the Ladies. *Because Algarotti believed women could only understand math and science if it was put in romantic terms, he presented Newton's theories as if they were a discussion between a man and the young woman he was courting."*

A student behind Salem snickers.

"So you'll be unsurprised to learn that in this climate and time, women were not allowed entrance to the institutes of math, which is why Germain had to impersonate a man to attend the École Polytechnique in Paris." Dr. Ventura unconsciously runs his hands through his thick, graying hair in a move that he'd likely be embarrassed to find out was called "the Fabio" by giggling sorority pledges. "Despite this, Germain reached out to and was mentored by the leading mathematician of her time, Carl Friedrich Gauss. She also built the foundational insight upon which Fermat's Enigma was eventually solved and wrote a paper on the elasticity of metal that was so revolutionary that her findings are still being used today, over two hundred years later."

He pauses.

If their silence is a marker, the class is suitably impressed. Salem is busy scribbling down notes. She'll email him for the PowerPoint after class to make sure she hasn't missed anything.

"Do you know why I'm telling you this?" He moves toward the front row to stand directly in front of Salem. Is he looking at her?

"Because it's important?" a student yells from the back. Salem turns to look, flustered by Dr. Ventura's nearness. She recognizes the student who hollered from the football team.

"No," he says, smiling, "but thank you for giving me hope for today's youth. I'm telling you this because in Sophie Germain's story is everything

you need to know about cryptography." He smacks his hands together, but he doesn't need to. He commands the attention of every mind in the room.

"When you are breaking a code, whether a cipher or the most intricate computer encryption, countless apparently insurmountable barriers will be thrown your way. The solution will seem impossible. You'll reach a point where you think it's more likely you could grow wings and fly than crack it. But if you persevere—and you must persevere—you will solve your puzzle."

This time he definitely makes eye contact with Salem.

CHAPTER 49

Massachusetts

Bel's yell from the front passenger seat was so loud, so startling, that Ernest swerved, pushing Mercy into Salem. The girl was sleeping deeply enough that the sudden shifting didn't wake her. Salem lifted her gently and laid her against the door again, tucking Ernest's jacket under her for a pillow.

"What is it, Bel?"

Bel turned, tears coursing down her face. She held her phone toward Salem. "It's a text." Her voice was hoarse. "From Mom."

Fear slammed into Salem's throat as strong as a fist. She blinked the sandy sleep out of her eyes, focusing on the phone. The message was short.

If you found it in Salem, keep going, no matter what.

Salem's heart plummeted. Someone was toying with them in the most horrible way. She couldn't share her fears with Bel, not now that she'd hidden the text she'd gotten from her own mom.

If her mom had even sent it.

"Oh, honey, I'm so sorry," Bel said, misreading Salem's expression. She unbuckled and crawled over the back seat to hold Salem.

Salem couldn't speak. Bel thought the text meant Vida was dead. And she very well could be. The only thing Salem knew for sure was that she had lied to her best friend, the one person who'd always been straight with her, always stood by her side, and that she'd let the lie grow too old to tell Bel the truth now. She felt the cold, private fingers of a panic attack curling around her neck, preparing to pull her under.

Ernest was watching them in the mirror. "You both need to toss your phones." The reflection of his eyes, which was all that Salem could see, was dead serious.

"What?" Bel asked.

"Think about it." His tone was apologetic but firm. "You're a woman who's been kidnapped, and you get your hands on a phone. What's the first thing you do?"

"Call the police," Bel said. A whole scene played out over her face, realization followed by a surge of denial. "But then you text your daughter," she said defensively, "who you know is worried about you."

Nobody spoke. They didn't need to because Bel worked it through. "And you tell her where you are, what happened to you, who did it, and why because you know she's a police officer and will need these details." Her words were cold and empty.

"You have to get rid of your phones," Ernest repeated. "Both of you. They can be traced. I shouldn't have let you keep them this long. Same with any credit cards. They have to go, as soon as you draw as much cash as you can off them." His eyes flashed to his left mirror, and then back up again. "I should get us a new car, too. If we're going to survive, we have to go totally off the grid."

Bel's face was cloudy, but she didn't argue. Neither did Salem.

They had an hour and a half of road left between them and Amherst.

The driver of the car that had been following them since the motel kept a healthy cushion between his vehicle and their Buick.

CHAPTER 50

Massachusetts

Jason didn't normally listen to classical music, but the thunder and roar of Stravinsky's *Rite of Spring* captured his mood when he was scanning through stations. The Hermitage Foundation had Clancy Johnson in their pocket, so Jason wasn't worried about the FBI following the women. The man with Isabel and Salem Wiley was huge, but too young to wield his body, and so he represented an annoyance rather than a barrier. Jason only needed them to stop in a relatively nonpublic place long enough for him to pounce.

With six days until the Crucible's assassination, he should be worried, but rather, he found himself growing excited at the thought of watching her die at his feet.

In fact, he was feeling powerful.

He wondered what his mother would think of him if she could see him now. Olivette had sold whatever she could to get by, including her son's body. Maybe that's how she'd been raised, but it didn't matter. Jason had never known a moment of safety in his life. The beatings, the starving, the rapes all congealed into a writhing snake ball of memories, one horror barely discernible from another.

Only one recollection claimed its own stage, and he'd never understood why.

He'd been maybe ten years old but half the size he should have been. He was malnourished, under the radar of the New Orleans school system, living the life of a dog on the edge of the Upper Ninth. His mom had sent him out to make money for food. He scored twenty bucks much sooner than usual and returned home. He'd found his mother with her boyfriend, a man from the Garden District who drove a Camaro and had hairy knuckles. The man owned a famous restaurant, renowned for being at the front of trendy food fads.

Jason knew because the man had bragged to him before taking Olivette into the bedroom.

This day, when Jason returned early, his mother and the man had been eating sushi.

Jason didn't have a name for it then, but he smelled it and his eyes feasted on it, the perfect circles of fish, slivers of fresh vegetables tucked next to them, sticky rice, all laid out like a quilt, like jewels, like the most beautiful thing he'd ever seen. His mouth had filled with saliva.

His mother slapped his hand and laughed when he reached for it. "You're not man enough to eat something raw."

She'd exchanged a raunchy laugh with the hairy-fingered restaurant owner. Jason's cheeks had burned. Underneath her derision, Jason recognized his mother's glazed expression. She didn't enjoy fish, never had ("swamp food," she called it), but she would swallow the sushi, pretend like it was the most amazing delicacy she'd ever eaten, because she wanted to pass for cultured. She got the same look when her boyfriends brought her thick liqueurs and gooey candies from other countries.

After the men left, she'd always say the same thing. "Those fancy fuckers think they know best. Give me a cold Abita and a bag of cracklin any day."

Jason understood that his mom was as attractive to other men as she was stupid.

He hadn't gotten to taste the sushi, not that day.

You're not man enough to eat something raw.

Jason smiled at the woman squeezed in the passenger-side footwell, the same easy grin he'd used to lure her into the car. Duct tape covered her mouth, bound her ankles and wrists, and crisscrossed her waist like a silver spider's web to keep her in her place.

He'd procured her at the truck stop where Isabel and her friends had stopped to use the facilities a half an hour back. He'd have harvested them there, but there were too many people around. The captive taped inside his car was a holdover or a warm-up, depending on how you looked at it.

His eyelid twitched. Taking the finger outside Grace Odegaard's apartment had been brazen, reckless. That's why he hadn't gone through with it. This woman, however, wouldn't be missed. She was a lot lizard, someone who rode from one stop to another to make her money from the long-haul truckers.

"How are you, baby?" she'd asked, bored or tired by the sound of it. She smelled like cigarettes and cheap floral perfume. Once she slid into his car, though, she pushed her shoulders together, smiled suggestively, putting a little back into it. Jason thought that was nice, considering he was a sure dollar and she could have just gotten it done and over with.

One of her canines was twisted. Beyond that flaw, her teeth were shockingly white, straight. He'd slapped duct tape over her mouth before she could change expression. Her hands reflexively flew to cover her genitals, likely a leftover habit from her childhood.

It was a reflex he understood, but she needn't have bothered.

That wasn't the part he was interested in. At least, not like she thought.

This time, he was going to go through with it. He was going to eat something raw.

He smiled and cranked *Rite of Spring* as loud as it would go.

WEDNESDAY

November 2

CHAPTER 51

Amherst, Massachusetts

Salem's eyes were dust-storm dry. It had been forty-eight-plus since she'd had a full night's sleep, longer since she'd showered. Sleep deprivation at this level felt like walking next to her body, floating over it, making a sandwich out of her brain and then eating it. Her muscles were tight and sore, aching from long rides in a cramped car.

They didn't have the energy needed for small talk. The adrenaline marking the last two and a half days had drained out, leaving an after taste of ozone and lye. When Ernest parked the car three blocks from the Emily Dickinson Museum, the sun was four hours from rising and the air felt heavy, like it'd be night forever. The somber cloak seemed like a natural fit for Amherst, a town straight out of the Colonial period, for all its paved roads and electric lights.

Ernest yanked a baseball cap and dark sunglasses out of his backpack, the only piece of luggage he carried. "I'm going to get two burner phones and another car. I'll be back at sunrise."

"Is that a disguise?" Bel asked listlessly, pointing at the cap. She didn't ask where he'd acquire the car or phones. Her body language suggested she'd reached a grudging acceptance of him.

Ernest shrugged. "As much of a disguise as I can pull off. It's hard to blend in when you're this tall. You two toss your phones"—he pointed at the nearby Dunkin' dumpster—"and you should try sleeping. You look . . . crusty."

He tucked his jacket tighter around Mercy, even though he'd be freezing without it, and stepped out of the car, unwinding himself from the confined interior like a jack-in-the-box finally freed. He jogged down the street, not glancing back.

"I'll take care of the phones." Salem laid her hand across the front seat. Bel placed her cell in it without a word. Salem stepped out of the car, inhaling air as crisp and juicy as a fresh-sliced apple. The ground was spongy with a pre-frost. Despite being in an urban area, a wall of scrub and trees lined the road across from the donut shop. Salem considered running rather than walking to the dumpster, but by the time she made up her mind to do so, she was already there, inhaling the grease and sugar and sour of the alley.

She glanced back at the Buick. Bel and Mercy were inside, their scalps pressed against the passenger windows, probably asleep. Bel's phone was warm in her hand. She yanked out the battery and SIM card and tossed the rest.

As a safety precaution, she charged another block up and flung Bel's battery and SIM into the receptacle outside Kelly's Restaurant, a mom-and-pop joint at the end of a strip mall. Her breath came out in white plumes.

Next up, her phone.

She tugged it out of her pocket, holding it for a moment. A sleek black rectangle, it was both phone and computer, and now, possibly a lifeline to her mother. She fired it up and checked for new messages. There were none. But there *could* be. A message *could* arrive that would save Grace or Vida. Something that would make it okay that she'd lied to Bel about the original text.

She had to keep her phone.

Salem powered it down and inserted it into the inside pocket of her parka, the one where she kept spare tampons and a black-and-white tube of Chapstick.

She glanced around. No one was up yet. The city-country of Amherst didn't even have cars moving at predawn. She felt silly with exhaustion, wired and loopy, like she could have run all the way back to the car and kept on running until she hit Mexico, and then leaned over to touch the border just like in the relays they used to complete in phys ed, and then charged back up to Amherst before Bel and Mercy woke up. That sounded like a plan, but when she returned to the side of the Buick, she realized she couldn't move another step if her soul depended on it.

She fell into the car and a bottomless sleep.

She realized something just before she plummeted. She and Bel would not talk about the fact that one of their mothers was dead. They would just keep moving forward, racing toward the end, pretending it wasn't true.

CHAPTER 52

Amherst, Massachusetts

"Rise and shine." Ernest peered inside the driver's door. He held three coffees and a hot chocolate in a carrier. Salem had never smelled anything so good. "Our new ride is behind the museum, about a ten-minute walk from here. We can ditch this car. Make sure you grab everything you own out of it."

Mercy sat up like a little soldier, handed Ernest his jacket, grabbed her Dora the Explorer knapsack and the hot chocolate, and stood next to the car, her eyes sleepy, blonde hair soft-looking and messy. She must have done this early-morning-car-switch maneuver a lot.

Bel was slower to rise.

"There's an ATM on the way," Ernest said once they were all outside the car. "You can withdraw cash on your credit cards, and then don't touch them again. You got rid of your phones?"

Salem sipped the coffee. It burned her lip. She nodded, wiping at the pain. It amazed her how easy it was to lie, to not feel anything, not even guilt. The day had warmed considerably since her predawn jog. The fuzzy peach glow had made good on its promise, delivering a golden globe hanging above the horizon. The sun had burned off all the fog and taken with it their visible breath.

They set off toward the museum. Salem wondered what time it was, reached automatically for her phone, and then stopped, her pulse lurching. "You got us phones?"

"Yeah," Ernest said, his face lighting up. He pulled two black flip phones out of his pocket and handed one to Salem and one to Bel. "They're precharged and aren't traceable, unless you start making regular calls to someone you know, and someone the FBI knows you know. They can watch the accounts on that end."

Bel handed her coffee to Salem so she could power up the phone she'd just been given. "You've been on the run awhile?"

"My whole life, seems like." He was matter of fact. "Hey, Mercy, I want you to stay in the park outside when we go into the museum. You can hide in the bushes."

Salem's head jerked toward Ernest. "What?"

Ernest scratched his hair just above the ear. "I don't want her recorded on any cameras or near any danger."

"No way," Bel said. "We're not leaving a child alone in a strange town in November."

"It's okay," Mercy took a long draw off her hot chocolate. "That's how we do it."

"Not anymore." They reached the bank, and its outdoor ATM. Bel slapped her hand over the camera, withdrew the maximum from her credit card account, and kept the camera covered while Salem did the same. They tossed their empty coffee cups and credit cards in the nearest trash bin.

A woman inside the lobby of the Emily Dickinson Museum was unlocking the front door just as they walked up.

Salem rubbed the back of her neck, beginning her counting exercises to soothe her unease.

If the museum didn't house Samuel and Lucretia Dickinson's gun, they'd reached a dead end.

Whichever of their moms was alive, she wouldn't be for much longer.

CHAPTER 53

Amherst, Massachusetts

Agent Stone didn't approve of Clancy's diet, that much was clear to him. Stone also managed to look completely put together despite spending the same twenty-four hours as Clancy had in this tin-can car.

Clancy pegged Stone for a food stamp kid, the way he kept himself so tidy, his suits impeccable. Poor kids grew up, but they never grew past the need to show the world that they weren't dirty. He also figured his maneuver in the Hawthorne Hotel lobby had put to rest any chance of them becoming friends.

Still, Clancy held the open box of donuts out to Stone. "You want any?"

Stone didn't acknowledge him. Somewhere between the Hawthorne and here, Stone had gone from reserved to monolithic. It was either the ream-out Clancy had given him for showing up at the hotel without checking with him first or Stone had figured out who was pulling Clancy's strings, though Clancy had racked his brain every way but Wednesday and couldn't figure out how that would be. He'd been neat.

All his covert ops, like texting the daughter from her mom's phone, Clancy did in the bathroom, door locked. The phone had come to him via the Minneapolis cleanup crew with instructions to use it to make sure the daughters were on the right track. Seemed they'd gotten further in cracking the hidden codes than tens of agents before them, stretched out over two hundred years. The Hermitage saw it as good business to have them continue.

The Hermitage's assassin hadn't gotten the message, though, and that's surely who'd almost taken out Salem Wiley in the Hawthorne Hotel lobby. Or maybe the communication had broken down on Clancy's end. He was following the last instructions he'd been given. That's all he could do.

"They've got someone following them," Clancy said.

Stone, his eyes trained on the group of four walking toward the Emily Dickinson Museum, put down his granola bar. If Clancy had to bet, he'd lay money it tasted like sweet-n-salty dog shit.

"You see him now?"

"Naw." Clancy dropped his glance, biting into a powdered circle of flour and sugar. He was rewarded with a bright squirt of lemon curd. "Saw the same car downtown as I did back at the truck stop, but I don't see anyone here now. Just a feeling in my gut."

Clancy was pleased that Stone refrained from glancing at his stomach. "You watch too many movies," Stone said.

But Stone sat rigid, as he had since the moment the daughters came into view. He might have a different mission than Clancy, but he had the same instinct warning him that something big and hairy was about to go down.

CHAPTER 54

Twenty-One Years Old

"It's okay, Salem. I understand."

Salem feels terrible. Isabel is graduating from Loyola with her BS in criminal justice. She wants Salem to attend the ceremony. The thought of leaving the state makes Salem's heart buck. "I'm sorry, Bellie. I wish I were—"

Bel interrupts her. "I love you just the way you are. I'll have Mom videotape it, and we'll have a private viewing at your place, okay? You can meet my new girlfriend, too! She said she wants to come to Minneapolis and check out my friends."

Salem smiles into the phone, but she feels the crack in their friendship like it's a tear in her own physical body. She knew things would change when Bel left for college, but they had Skype, and the phone, and Bel came home for every holiday and the summers.

Not this year, though.

She'd just been accepted into summer skills training, the next step to being hired by the Chicago Police Department. Working for Chicago PD was her dream job, the one she'd been training for her entire life.

"That sounds good, Bel. I can't wait to meet her." But Salem feels it in her gut.

The two of them are growing apart, their friendship crumbling under the impossible weight of adulthood.

CHAPTER 55

Amherst, Massachusetts

A crazy thought entered Salem's brain: maybe this whole scavenger-hunt adventure she and Bel were on was one of her mom and Gracie's elaborate schemes to teach them something, or to reunite them.

A moment of elation was followed by a mental picture of the thick blood pooling in Gracie's hallway. Salem shuddered.

She, Bel, Ernest, and Mercy stood outside Emily Dickinson's earliest home. It was a Federal-style mansion. They marched up the museum's cement steps, past the white columns, and through the green door. Salem knew from her research that Emily Dickinson had been born in this house, the Homestead, in 1830. She and her family left for a number of years and returned in 1855. Dickinson lived here until her death in 1886. Amherst College bought the house in 1965, and in 2003, the museum opened its doors.

According to the museum's online furnishing plan, the Homestead and its sister building, the Evergreens, contained a wealth of historically accurate items, many of them owned by the Dickinson family, from Emily's childhood piano to a ruby decanter and matching glasses. Salem had found no mention of pistols or rifles in the collection, but they had agreed beforehand that it was better to search the rooms themselves than be marked as the nervous, sleep-ragged foursome who asked to see Samuel Dickinson's guns.

"Four tickets, please," Bel said. "Three adults, one child."

"Excellent!" The woman was dressed in period gear, a bishop-sleeved, blue-and-white checked day dress that reached the floor. She paused to smile at two new people entering immediately behind Salem. "We'll have enough folks for a tour in no time."

"We don't need a tour, thanks." Bel flashed her brightest smile. "We have to get back on the road. We want to show ourselves around, if you don't mind."

"Of course. I'm afraid I still have to charge you the forty-two dollars, though."

"No problem." Bel pulled out three twenties. She grabbed the tickets and her change, and they walked up the purple, twisting stairs, Bel whispering instructions. "Two of us to a room. Me and Ernest are a team. Salem, you take Mercy. You find any guns, you locate the other team and we look them over together."

Salem nodded. Bel and Ernest stepped into the room at the top of the stairs. Salem and Mercy continued to the end of the hall and opened the door, stepping inside.

"I think this was her bedroom." Salem took in the tiny writing table perched in front of the window, the sleigh bed surrounded by a matching washbasin cupboard and dresser. She thought of Dickinson's passion for knowledge, and her reclusiveness. It was rumored that at her sickest, Dickinson wouldn't let her doctor take her pulse, would merely walk past an open doorway and require him to diagnose her from afar.

She and Dickinson would have gotten along just fine.

"I like it here," Mercy said. "I want to live here."

Salem pushed a lock of the girl's hair from her eyes and smiled. "It's nice, isn't it? Clean. No surprises. And," she said, visually sweeping the room, "no old-fashioned rifles."

Such was the case in every room they were allowed to enter in the Homestead as well as the Evergreens next door. As a last-ditch effort, they scanned the brochures near the front counter, scouring for any mention of a gun belonging to Dickinson's grandparents.

"We have to ask someone," Bel said. "It's the only way."

By now, there was a line at the desk. When it was their turn, Bel slapped her smile back on. "Excuse me. Can I ask you a strange question?"

The woman nodded. "Believe me, I've heard them all."

"Are there any guns on the property? Antique ones that belonged to the Dickinson family, specifically Samuel and Lucretia, Emily's grandparents?"

"Hmm," the woman said. "That's a new one. I don't remember seeing any, but let me pull up our records." She slid her glasses from the top of her head to her nose and turned her attention to her computer. She stroked the keys and studied the screen intently.

Salem found herself standing on the balls of her feet, leaning forward, as if she could step inside the computer and pull out the information they needed. *Follow the trail*, the text from her mom's phone had read, but what if the trail died here? Salem felt like someone was sitting on her chest.

"I'm sorry," the woman finally said, perching her glasses back on the top of her head. "No guns. A lot of the original Dickinson possessions were sold over the years, before the museum was formed, I'm afraid."

"Any idea how we could track down where it all went?" Bel asked.

The woman made a *tsking* sound. "I wish. But if you want to leave your name and number, I could talk to our curator. She's on vacation now but will be back next week."

Bel nodded. To an outsider, it would look like she was considering her options. To Salem, it was clear she was trying to keep from punching a hole in the wall.

Salem flipped open her phone and stepped to Bel's side. "Here's our number," she said, reading it from the inside of the phone. "Please do call if you hear anything."

She and Bel walked outside, Ernest and Mercy trailing behind them. The sun hit their face with a cruel brightness.

"We don't have a week," Bel said. She seemed to have shrunk. "Whichever of our mothers is alive doesn't have a week."

"I know." Salem's chin trembled. She could hear her mom's life ticking away, or Gracie's. "The note led us nowhere."

Mercy was glancing across the lawn in front of the Homestead. "It had more dots."

"What, sweetie?" Salem asked.

"The note had more dots." She said this with the absolute certainty only a child can pull off. "You got excited, but there were more after that."

Salem, Bel, and Ernest stared at each other. Salem reached into her pocket, and with wobbly hands, she yanked out the note and smoothed it on the column in front of her. She spotted what Mercy was referring to in the poem's last stanza:

My Life had stood—a Loaded Gun

Some keep the Sabbath going to church;
I keep it staying at home,
With a bobolink for a chorister,
And an orchard for a dome.

Some keep the Sabbath in surplice;
I just wear my wings,
And instead of tolling the bell for church,
Our little sexton sings.

God preaches, a noted clergyman,
And the sermon is never long;
So instead of getting to heaven at last,
I'm going all along!

—Emily Dickinson
Σ

G-r-a-v-e.

"Grave." Salem's voice shook with excitement. "We have to go to Samuel and Lucretia's grave!"

She charged back into the Homestead and barged ahead of the others in line. "I'm so sorry, but we just have one more question. Can you tell me where Samuel and Lucretia Dickinson's graves are?"

The woman wore a puzzled smile. "Why, Samuel Fowler and Lucretia Gunn Dickinson are buried here in town, in a single grave. They were reinterred in the family plot in the Amherst West Cemetery over a century ago." She pointed northwest. "It's a ten-minute walk, as the crow flies."

Salem had almost stopped listening after the woman said Lucretia's full name. Lucretia *Gunn.*

Gun Samuel Lucretia grave.

The "gun" in the code hadn't been referring to a weapon! There must be something hidden behind the first three letters of Lucretia's maiden name on her gravestone.

Salem squealed. "Thank you!"

She ran outside, Ernest's, Mercy's, and Bel's faces staring desperately at her like baby flowers to the sun. "The cemetery is walkable from here. Let's go!"

CHAPTER 56

3 East 70th Street, New York

Carl Barnaby held one end of the oversize check. Three wiggling kids held the other end, giggling and shuffling to get in the shot. The check was for $1 million, made out to the Inner City Education Fund. The money would be used to provide a laptop for every inner-city elementary school student in New York City who kept their GPA above 3.0 for an entire year.

It would change lives.

The nun who had founded the ICEF fifty years earlier, Sister Simone, was still alive. She hobbled into the photo. "Thank you again, Mr. Barnaby. You're investing in children, our most valuable resource."

The photographer captured all five of them grinning at each other. "It's my pleasure," Carl said, handing her the check. "You'll get the real one in the mail within a week. It'll be easier to cash."

The three kids laughed. She passed the mock check to one of the children's parents. After more pleasantries, they all filed out. When the last child waved goodbye, Barnaby stepped to the window, staring across Fifth Avenue, toward the low stone wall that hedged all of Central Park, into the dusty brown that marked fall in Manhattan. His hands were clasped behind his back. His steel-blue, $25,000 Zegna bespoke suit had been tailored to remind people, subtly, of a uniform.

The protesters gathered on the street below him. Their signs were not particularly clever: ARREST ONE OF US, TWO MORE APPEAR. ROBIN HOOD WAS RIGHT. NO BLOOD FOR OIL. GET YOUR RELIGION OUT OF MY DEMOCRACY.

While he was angry the good people who'd just left his office would have to walk through the picket line, the last sign amused Barnaby. He was an atheist, but religion had made the Hermitage's work easier from the beginning. Maybe even made it possible.

The Hermitage, an organization that advertised itself as "Founded on the Values Made Great by Andrew Jackson," had always been cloaked in shadows, an eventual target for every conspiracy theory that floated.

Killing of the Romanovs? Check. Roswell UFO landing? Yes. Kennedy assassination? Obviously.

Then came the internet, and the theories gained traction. The Hermitage found itself connected to a bloody coup in Nicaragua, a successful assassination in Latvia, an election in Florida. The attention made their work more difficult. Carl Barnaby, as current CEO of the nonprofit Hermitage, cared. Then the Hermitage's address was publicized—3 East 70th Street, on Central Park in New York—and rumor chasers began to gather on the sidewalk, bothering guests and members equally.

That's when Carl convinced the board to bring in a new PR team. Historically, the Hermitage's public face, when they were forced to reveal one, was as a modest organization working toward global religious and political cooperation. The one group with any power who believed otherwise, the Underground, was being systematically downsized, had been since Andrew Jackson's time. If Jason secured the master list of leaders, the Underground would finally be put out of business, and the Hermitage Foundation would be free and clear.

But they'd still have the annoyance of the internet.

A motley group of bloggers—hackers, socialists, feminists, and the like—was painting them as a cabal of rich white men and religious leaders pulling the world's puppet strings. The Hermitage had initially met this challenge by ignoring it, allowing the natural weight of conspiracy to fall back in on itself and crush the truth in plain sight. With the protesters outside, however, legitimate news outlets were picking up the story.

The new PR company proposed that the Hermitage host a conference in Florida, invite the public, and swing wide the doors to the media. Give them something sweeter to chew on besides the meaty conspiracy theories, the firm argued. They manufactured a suitably meaningless name—the First Universal Conference on Religious and Social Synergy—and lined up politicians, CEOs, rabbis, archbishops, imams, and even a handful of NGOs to speak, 99 percent of them unaware of what the Hermitage actually was.

Carl hadn't made an appearance. He had real work to attend to. But he'd heard it had been going well, with wonderful initiatives being discussed and photo opportunities captured, when a married Texas senator attending the conference was caught with three prostitutes in his room. Damn Texas politicians, every last one of them too dumb or too liberal, never both at once. Fortunately, the Hermitage's PR team had quickly distanced the senator from the organization and the conference by uncovering and then distributing records showing his improper use of campaign funds. The senator quietly stepped down from his position, the crisis was averted, and the Hermitage's public relations men were back at work.

But the protests continued outside.

Carl sighed. "Don't they have anything better to do on a workday?"

Geppetto didn't answer. Carl had expected as much. The assassin was taciturn and, frankly, terrifying, sitting quietly in the corner for the entire photo op. Where Jason reminded Carl of a Machiavellian prince, handsome and flirtatious, Geppetto was taciturn, more tool than man. He looked nothing like his namesake. His age and ethnicity were unclear, his appearance unremarkable, with one exception: his fingers were as strong as steel.

Carl had studied them once, during Geppetto's induction into the Hermitage. Most of the recruits were nervous in the fancy offices of the

Hermitage—most, but not two. Jason melted into his surroundings like he'd been born there. Geppetto was expressionless. He sat, hands resting on his thighs. Carl had heard about what Geppetto could accomplish with those weapons, and when they'd first met, he'd expected to see fists like boulders, fingers like sausages.

He hadn't been disappointed.

Still, at that first meeting, Carl was considering whether Geppetto was a good fit for the organization. That's when Geppetto turned to him as if reading his mind, his gaze as flat and black as a shark's. Without breaking the stare, Geppetto lifted his hand and set it on the shoulder of the man next to him. It might have appeared to be an encouraging gesture, but not to the man under Geppetto's grip. He'd trained with Geppetto. He knew what Geppetto was capable of.

He moaned.

And with the effort Barnaby would use to squeeze a lemon into his ice water, Geppetto pinched the front and back of the man's shoulder, pressing until only the densest inch of bone separated Geppetto's pointer finger from his thumb.

The sick *crack* of the bone, the *pop-squish* of muscle turning to soup, would forever stick with Carl. He hadn't doubted Geppetto since.

"I need you to go to Alcatraz." Carl finally turned, facing his office and the Ziegler Mahal Persian rugs, the Florentine ebony chests, the tables inlaid with garnet, lapis, and malachite. The walls were draped with lush tapestries sewed in Jesus's time and oils painted by Van Gogh, Rembrandt, and Monet. Baccarat chandeliers dripped prisms of light from the ceilings. It had all been here before Barnaby's time, collected by Andrew Jackson and the men who came after him.

Geppetto sat on the other side of Barnaby's desk, hands clasped in his lap, black eyes eating the light in the room. Barnaby had been told that Geppetto did hand and finger exercises constantly when he wasn't working. He believed it.

"Jason was in charge of that." Geppetto's voice had the flatness of one who was deaf. His hearing was fine.

"He still is." Barnaby rested his hand on his kangaroo-leather chair. A surge of annoyance flashed through him. Gina Hayes was scheduled to deliver a prison reform speech on Alcatraz the day before the election. The plan to dismiss her had been put in place a year ago, a desperate measure that they should never have had to use. The regular arsenal should have been sufficient to remove her from the political field: swift-boating with directed media attacks on her family, her appearance, her Senate votes, bribes to her closest staff members, goddamn it *her gender*, should have been enough.

But the woman was like a Bobo doll.

Every punch she took, she bounced back up, a smile on her face, her hair perfect. The final insult? Her Republican opponent was a cartoon of a human being. All the woman needed to do to stroll into the presidency was survive this next week.

It was Carl's mission to make sure she didn't.

"You'll be there to help, if needed." He didn't share with Geppetto that he had a third line of defense in place in case both Geppetto *and* Jason failed.

It wasn't just that Hayes's election to president would cut into the Hermitage's cash flow, with her promise to remove troops from the Middle East, reduce US dependence on oil, and put an end to no-bid government contracts. It wasn't Senator Hayes's impending Mideast peace deal, which threatened to shift power on a global scale. It wasn't even her opposition to the Afghanistan mineral rights bill currently up for vote in the Senate. If she made it to the Oval Office, that bill was dead in the water, guaranteed, and Carl and his brother didn't have the money to cover the promises they'd made. That was bad, but it wasn't the ultimate reason Hayes needed to be stopped.

She had to be stopped because she was a woman.

A female figurehead on that level would undermine centuries of work.

There were *no lengths* to which Carl would not go to keep the second-class status of women, and by extension his and his colleagues' fortunes, intact. It was a full-time job, but the men of the Hermitage had the time, the money, and the incentive.

"The Underground leader Jason captured in Minneapolis has arrived?" Carl asked.

Geppetto blinked, which passed for a nod.

"Bring her up. I have questions."

Geppetto stayed motionless just long enough to show that he acted of his own volition. The man never looked like he was taking orders. It made Carl uneasy. He'd like to fire him, except he was scared to be on opposite sides of the playing field.

Finally Geppetto stood and walked toward the door. He paused when Carl issued a second instruction. "I'll want you to stay here during the questioning. We need her to be completely forthcoming. And I'll want you to find everything you can about her daughter. About both their daughters."

Carl didn't want to admit to himself that he might have to call Jason off the daughters and the Underground leader docket they were after to concentrate on the main prize—Hayes. He wanted it all. "I need to know where the girls work, how much money they have in their accounts, who their boyfriends are, their favorite foods, *everything*."

Geppetto continued without responding. Carl returned to the window overlooking Central Park, confident his instructions would be followed, even if Geppetto ended up delegating them. In the moldering coolness of fall, beyond the protesters, his eyes followed a mother pushing twin boys dressed in green in a stroller. Carl thought of his own grandson, three years old, blond hair, blue eyes, and the most beautiful thing Carl had ever seen.

The power cannot shift.

A sudden thought eased the weight on his chest. He didn't want to be the dog that dropped his bone in the river to bark at its reflection, but maybe he *could* have it all. He would just have to place the two daughters and their list in storage until Gina Hayes was killed.

Barnaby reached into his jacket and yanked out his cell phone.

CHAPTER 57

Amherst, Massachusetts

Two days past Halloween and the decorations still reigned in the shops and houses surrounding Amherst West Cemetery: wiggly white skeletons, cotton cobwebs, black plastic spiders, gigantic blow-up lawn ornaments in the shapes of ghosts and witches. Clancy Johnson was raised in the wide, flat bowl of Wyoming. He'd already grown tired of Massachusetts without the added ornamentation.

It almost felt like claustrophobia, what he was experiencing. The buildings were too close to each other, the trees crowding for attention like five-year-olds at show-and-tell. It didn't help that he had a twitchy feeling he was out of the loop on this one. One of his three phones buzzed. It wasn't the one his wife and kids called him on, which he kept in his breast pocket. The vibration also wasn't coming from the Android taken from the woman killed in Minneapolis, sent to Clancy via the Hermitage. It was coming from his work phone, which he kept looped on his belt. He tugged it out of his pocket.

"Clancy Johnson."

The instructions were clear, terse, and set Clancy back on his ass as hot as a punch. "Tell me again," he said. It was a reflex, a way to buy time while he figured this out. The instructions were even more succinct the second time.

He hung up without a goodbye and whistled, low and surprised. "You still got eyes on Odegaard and Wiley?"

Stone had the binoculars firm to his eyes. "Yup."

"Good. Cuz I just received a phone call from the SAC saying we have to take them in. They're wanted for conspiring to assassinate Senator Gina Hayes."

CHAPTER 58

Amherst, Massachusetts

The late-morning sky over the West Amherst Cemetery was aggressively slate in color. There must be a poultry farm nearby because the smell of fowl was blowing in, coating the headstones, rolling like fog over the low spots, carrying with it a primal scent of butchery.

"We're looking for Lot 53, Grave D." Bel held the cemetery map and led the way, the graves laid out in a roughly triangular pattern.

Salem was jittery, a leaf before a storm. *One two three breathe.*

"1737," Ernest said, pointing at the tipping white tongue of a gravestone, its inscription so worn by rain and sun that it had nearly disappeared. "Mercy, you see this? Think of it. The person buried here was alive three hundred years ago."

The girl stayed close at his heels, not saying a word. Salem thought that if they made it out of this alive, the first thing she'd do was buy Mercy a doll. No little kid should be without one.

Bel stopped so suddenly that all three of them almost bumped into her. She glanced down at her map and up again. "There." She pointed ahead at a wrought iron fence surrounding four headstones, three of them tall, thin marble tablets and the fourth a squat marble monument. A bronze plaque mounted in the fence read IN MEMORIAM, EMILY DICKINSON, POETESS.

The first thin tablet inside the wrought iron marked Emily's sister Lavinia's grave, the second Emily Dickinson's, decorated with flowers, coins, and trinkets, and the third belonged to Edward, Emily's father. The fourth was inscribed for Dickinson's grandparents:

SAMUEL FOWLER DICKINSON

DIED APRIL 22, 1838 AGED 62 YEARS

———

LUCRETIA GUNN

HIS WIFE

DIED MAY 11, 1840 AGED 64 YEARS

"Why's that grave different?" Mercy asked, pointing through the fence.

"Emily Dickinson's grandparents weren't originally buried in this cemetery," Salem answered. "They were dug up and brought back here, to their hometown. Maybe that's why?"

Mercy's eyes grew wide.

Salem knelt in front of the gravestone, the wrought iron separating them. Mercy stood at her shoulder.

"Keep watch," Bel ordered Ernest, kneeling next to Salem.

Salem stuck her hand through the four-inch-wide opening in the iron and felt the cool stone of Samuel and Lucretia's grave marker, running her fingers over the grooves spelling "Gunn." The name was an inch high, four inches long. The stone around it felt solid. In fact, other than the line separating the information on Samuel from Lucretia's, the whole inset name panel appeared to be one unbroken chunk of rock. The gray of the sky pressed on Salem's shoulders.

"Do you see anything?" Bel asked.

Salem shook her head. "I've never worked with stone." She didn't want to alarm Bel by telling her that she didn't even know what to look for. If this were a dresser, or an armoire, or even a wooden beam, she'd at least know where to start.

Mercy threaded her hand through the fence and knocked on the face of the gravestone. She had to grip Salem's shoulder for balance. Her hand felt warm and tiny. Salem found herself protectively covering it with her own hand.

With her palm over Mercy's, she felt something unexpected.

"Do that again." Salem listened carefully, still covering Mercy's hand with hers.

Mercy knocked the inscription panel again.

"Now knock on the stone outside the panel." Salem's heartbeat danced.

Mercy did as directed.

"Do you hear that?" Salem asked. Bel shook her head.

"Here." Salem transferred Mercy's hand to Bel's shoulder. "Mercy's body is serving as a sound transmitter. You have to feel it rather than hear it."

Bel closed her eyes and listened as Mercy repeated the knocking. Her eyes shot open. "It sounds different. The panel. Hollow, maybe?"

Salem nodded, a smile playing across her lips. "I think so. It's still thick, though, even if there's a compartment underneath." She stuffed both hands through the fence and began feeling the edges of the panel. "If we can find a trip switch, we won't have to bust it open."

"Hey," Ernest said, softly. If they hadn't been standing so close together, they wouldn't have heard him.

"What?" Bel asked crossly.

"Suits," Ernest said. "Two of them."

Salem glanced over her shoulder. Agent Lucan Stone and another man—a guy who looked like Ed Harris—were charging up the hill toward them.

Her throat hitched. "They're FBI."

Ernest grabbed Mercy and threw her over his shoulder. "Run!" he yelled.

CHAPTER 59

Amherst, Massachusetts

Jason's jaw was hanging. He stood at the window of the Speed Wash Laundromat on Pray Street, across from the Amherst West Cemetery, watching the fiasco play out. Agent Clancy Johnson and his partner were cuffing Salem Wiley and Isabel.

Those women were *his*. Clancy Johnson had been directed to keep his distance.

Jason had never missed a target in his life. He was both pleased and amazed to see his hand steady as he withdrew his phone.

Carl Barnaby picked up on the second ring and spoke without preamble. "They've been arrested?"

Jason felt the fall-stop of deep unease. Wiley and Isabel's arrest hadn't been a mistake. Barnaby had ordered this. "My instructions were to harvest the women and get the list. I can't do that if they're in FBI custody."

Barnaby chuckled, but his conviviality lacked its usual soothing effect. "Consider it a favor. The women are on hold, perfectly preserved until you are done with the real job: the Crucible."

It was as if someone had set fire to Jason's stomach. "I had planned to take care of *all* of it. There's time. We have five days until I need to be in San Francisco."

"True," Barnaby said. "But there's too much at stake. The Crucible is more important than any other woman in the world right now. If she wins, she'll be untouchable. I want you in California early to make sure everything is in place. But listen to this."

Jason was trying to heed, but he was so angry that the world was going white. He could have done it all. He'd had the situation under control. All his power was being snatched from him, leaving him a small, trembling boy, skinned by the world, nowhere to hide.

You're not man enough to eat something raw.

"The FBI is arresting the women for a planned dismissal of the Crucible." Barnaby's laughter deepened. "Isn't that rich? Her maintenance team will need to divert resources from actually protecting her to investigate the girls. Meanwhile, if the two of them already possess the list, our contact will retrieve it when he drops them off at the local police station. If they don't yet have it, I've been assured that they'll be held for at least a week, until long after your work with the Crucible is done. By the time they're released, we'll have a new corporate structure. You can follow them to the list, dismiss them once they have it in hand, and use the names on the list to shut down the Underground once and for all."

The white was fading, leaving pulsing red dots. "I could have taken care of them here, and still gotten to the Crucible."

"Jason!" Barnaby's tone was acid. "Are you arguing with me?"

Jason exhaled through his nose, moderating his breath so it didn't make noise. "I'm sorry. This job is so important."

Barnaby continued, mollified. "Of course it is. I appreciate that you value that. Remember, you'll still get the glory. You just have to wait a bit."

"Yes, sir. I can do that."

"I thought so." Barnaby lowered his voice. "There's one more thing. I'm sending a colleague to support you. He'll meet you in Boston, and you'll fly to San Francisco together, first thing tomorrow morning. Both your flights are booked."

"A colleague? Who?"

But Jason knew. The black pit that his stomach had become was certain that it was his nemesis. They'd all been troublemakers in the Lower Ninth, every last one of them, but they'd also been victims. The unspoken rule among them was that they never hurt one another, and they all followed this imperative—all but one, the one who spent every spare moment exercising his fingers, performing endless rounds of fingertip push-ups, punching rocks with them, using them to lift impossible weights.

That one hadn't earned his name because he was kindly, crafty, or Italian.

He'd gotten it because he would stick his fingers inside you and make you do things you desperately didn't want to but would forever if only he'd remove them.

"Geppetto," Barnaby said unnecessarily. "You'll remember him. We harvested you both from New Orleans, didn't we? You worked together in Minnesota, what, ten, twelve years ago? Looks like you'll finally get a chance to finish that business together."

Jason robotically hung up the phone and walked outside to his car parked at the far end of the lot. It had actually been fourteen years ago they'd worked together, fourteen years since Jason had last seen Geppetto. Jason had wept on that assignment. He'd been an adult but still sobbed like an infant, the pain had been that bad. His face grew hot with the memory.

He sat inside his car, sipping air. He needed music to mask the noise he was about to make, so he turned on the radio. He recognized the song that came on: "99 Problems." It wasn't Jay-Z's version, but something thumping, sexier, devil blues, commiserating with him about girl problems.

He ghost-smiled, the expression a raw gash of red against white flesh. The universe had a sense of humor.

Some days, that was the most you could ask for.

He pulled out of the Laundromat lot and drove to the outskirts of town, steering into the driveway of an abandoned farmhouse. The song was winding down. He wished it wouldn't. He'd like to hear it again. He glanced over at the woman in the passenger-side footwell.

He hadn't been able to do it, to eat her flesh. His mom had been right about him. He wasn't a proper man. The woman was alive and physically unharmed. Crusted tracks on her cheeks and neck marked the path of her tears. She wouldn't look at Jason.

He parked the car behind the tilting barn. He unbuckled.

He reached inside his jacket with one hand, turning up the last morsel of the song with the other.

His smile was gone as he leaned toward the woman.

The first spurt splashed the interior light with a haunted-house red. When he was finished, blood would paint the doors and ceiling. In the distant part of his mind that was freed to think, Jason decided that once he was done here, he'd clean up and go back to the Amherst police station, find out where Salem Wiley and Isabel were being held. His flight out of Boston didn't leave until tomorrow. He had time to prove to Barnaby that Geppetto wasn't needed after all.

The realization was so relieving that he laughed out loud as he sliced.

CHAPTER 60

The Amherst Police Department was new construction, designed with a redbrick turret to make it blend in with the church next door. Despite its exterior warmness, its holding rooms were the same sterile white cubes as any police department Lucan Stone had ever been in, the coffee the same bitter pitch.

He and Clancy sat across the table from Salem Wiley and Isabel Odegaard.

If there'd been a shred of oxygen to the bullshit assassination charges, the women would have been questioned separately. As it was, both men were going through the motions until their SAC told them differently.

"Tell me what you know about Senator Gina Hayes," Clancy asked, taking the lead.

Bel knew the routine. "She's running for president. She's a Democrat. I intend to vote for her. I have no intention of assassinating her."

Salem stared at her hands, massaging the webbing between her thumb and forefinger. Her hair was glossy from three days on the road, her natural body oils morphing her fuzzy curls into smooth ringlets. Both women smelled ripe, musky.

"Salem?" Stone asked softly.

She glanced up. Every inch of her was fierce-scared. She reminded Stone of the kitten he'd discovered walking home from school when he was fifteen. The Detroit neighborhood he'd grown up in was broken glass and rusting steel. You'd be more likely to find a used syringe than a four-leaf clover in the playground grass, at least until they tore up the playground to build a parking lot. So when Stone happened across that little spitting ball of fur in the crook of the only tree on the block, he'd known it was something special. He'd coaxed the kitten down, let it scratch and bite him, tucked it in his coat, and ran all the way home. His mother had made him take it to the animal shelter. He understood why. He'd still named it on the way.

"I know what Bel knows." Salem returned her attention to her hands.

Stone wished he could hold those hands until she felt safe enough to look at him. Something about her eyes—he wanted her to *see* him. He managed to keep his voice neutral, barely. "What are you two doing in Massachusetts?"

Isabel Odegaard certainly knew she could request a lawyer. Probably she also knew what a waste of time it would be.

"Touring. It's a beautiful state this time of year. Look," she said, slapping her palms on the table and leaning forward, "what's the score here? Do you need us to tell you something about our mothers, and you'll let us go? Because we don't know anything."

"Like we said at the cemetery," Clancy said mildly, "you two are under arrest for a conspiracy to assassinate Senator Gina Hayes. We've found evidence on her"—he made a gun out of his finger and fired it at Salem—"home computer that implicates both of you. Hayes's schedule, her security detail, information on her upcoming Alcatraz speech that *no one* without clearance should have."

Salem's eyes shot up, her mouth a shocked O. "Someone hacked into my computer?"

Stone thought she sounded surprised rather than scared. Made sense. With her computer science and cryptography degrees, she was sure to have secure firewalls. The woman was something of a legend, from what Stone had gathered from his friends in computer forensics. The FBI had had a file on her before any of this happened. Same with the NSA. They all wanted Salem Wiley to come work for them.

He just wanted her to survive the week.

"You can hold us, what, forty-eight hours without pressing charges?" Bel asked.

Clancy rubbed his nose. "Massachusetts says seventy-two."

"Then get on it." Bel sat back, her cheeks flushed. She crossed her arms. "Because we don't have anything else to say."

Stone understood their frustration. Based on their behavior and demeanor, the two women believed that one or both of their mothers was still alive, and they were on some sort of mission to save them. He almost wished he could let them go, but the orders to hold them had come from the top. Either someone had called in a favor or the SAC had been presented with evidence he could not disregard.

Clancy's phone buzzed on his belt. Did he go pale for a moment? He reached into his jacket and pulled it out, glanced at it, turned the phone's face to Stone. Stone saw it was the senior agent in charge phoning. Clancy stood and walked outside to take the call.

"I think we're done here." Stone pushed his chair back. "Someone will be in shortly to show you to your cell."

He waited a moment in the hopes that Wiley would finally look at him. She didn't. Odegaard, however, used her eyes like swords to slice him from tip to toe. He almost couldn't tamp the smile down in time. In his five years in the FBI, he'd never run across a pair like this: tough, terrified, and as smart as a slap.

He locked the door on the way out and gave instructions to the officer waiting outside to ready a cell. Clancy was hanging up the phone.

"SAC wants us in Iowa. Senator Hayes's next public stop." Clancy jabbed his thumb at the holding room. "He's worried about these two, has a tip that the slicer is connected to plans to kill what's gonna be the first female president, and that it's gonna be on his hands because we didn't catch the guy in time."

They walked toward the exit. Stone examined angles. "What do we do in Iowa?"

Clancy grabbed a toothpick from his shirt pocket and stuffed it in his mouth. "I dunno. Tell Hayes to watch out for bad guys? Juggle our nuts?" He switched the toothpick to the other side and stopped abruptly. "Hey, Stone."

His tone of voice made Stone pause. They'd been partners for two years. They'd slept in the same hotel room, eaten more meals together than apart, and seen things that would give a combat vet nightmares. In those two years, until the Hawthorne Hotel lobby, Stone hadn't developed strong feelings either way for the man. But now, something in Clancy's eyes made Stone wonder if they could have been friends had they met outside this business.

"How high does this stink to you?" Clancy asked.

"To the moon," Stone agreed.

"You saw what was taken off of 'em, right? Two burner phones, Wiley's iPhone, Odegaard's licensed piece, pocket junk, a bottle of prescription pills, that tracker dot that I assume you planted back at the Hawthorne, and a goddamned handwritten Emily Dickinson poem. What are we supposed to do with that?"

Stone had seen all those things. He'd also witnessed Clancy's reaction to the poem. The man had seemed puzzled, and then annoyed, and then tossed it back into the holdings pile like dirty toilet paper. Stone wondered what he'd been expecting to find. "We leave it. Whoever the uppers call in to finish this trumped-up case can sort it out."

"Yeah," Clancy said, his voice quiet. They resumed their walk to the front door, the hive buzz of the police station swarming around them. "So why do I think those two won't make it to the end of the week, even if neither of them does a damn thing wrong?"

Stone held the door for Clancy. Neither man attempted to meet the other's eyes. There was no need. They were both thinking the same thing.

And the only reason Stone could walk out these doors was because jail at least what passed for jail in this town—was currently the safest place for Salem Wiley and Isabel Odegaard.

CHAPTER 61

Twenty-Six Years Old

"Salem, this is Rachel. Rachel, Salem."

The woman holds out her petite hand. Everything about her makes Salem feel like a huge, torpid moose.

"I've heard so much about you!" Rachel says.

Salem shakes her hand. She realizes it's the first time she's been in the same room as Bel in a year. "You too." It's not true, but it's the polite thing to say. Salem and Bel circle each other like strangers, relatives who only connect on holidays.

"How's work? You still at the community ed center?" Bel asks, before turning to Rachel. "She teaches computer to kids who otherwise wouldn't have access. A computer genius with a huge heart."

Salem smiles. Or at least she thinks she does. She's not sure if it reaches her face. "Yep. And I got offered a research assistant job at the college."

"Think you'll take it?" Bel asks.

"I think so." The stilted small talk squeezes Salem tighter and tighter until she's trapped in an airless box. When Daniel died, Bel had moved into Salem's house and slept in her bed until she relearned to fall asleep on her own. When Salem's mom forgot to shop for groceries or make meals, Bel made sure to tell Gracie so that there was always food in Salem's house. When Michael Dingboom asked Salem to senior prom "as a friend," Bel

had driven back all the way from Chicago to help her get ready and give her kissing pointers, just in case.

That same Bel stands across from her now, a million miles away, twitchy, her and Rachel acting like they'd rather be anywhere else in the world.

Bel makes alone time for Salem only once during that visit. It is to take Salem aside and ask her what she thinks of Rachel.

Salem makes the mistake of telling her the truth.

They won't speak again until Halloween morning.

CHAPTER 62

Amherst, Massachusetts

Bel had spotted Salem's phone when the Amherst police took it off her.

She knew Salem had lied to her. She had not spoken to her since. It was even worse than being locked up, this burning shame at lying to her best friend.

"Bel."

"We have to get out of here." Bel strode to the holding room door and checked it. Locked. The admitting officer had come in to inform them that he was prepping their cell and it would be thirty minutes, and did they need to use the restroom? When they both declined, he'd left. "That officer was nice, but I wish he'd left this open."

Salem kept her seat, watching her friend's frantic movements. "Bel."

Bel returned to her chair and knelt next to it. "Did they take all your money?"

Salem leaned back to dig in both her front jeans pockets. She pulled out a copper coin, her expression empty. "They left me a penny."

"Perfect." Bel snatched it from Salem's hand and went to work on one of the chair legs, using the coin like a screwdriver to loosen a thin cross bracket. "Put your ear to the door. Let me know if anyone's coming."

Salem stayed seated. Regret and resignation churned in the cement mixer of her stomach. She'd felt naked and alone since Bel had seen her phone taken from her, the phone she was supposed to have dumped back at the Dunkin'. "Bel."

"Got one!" Bel let the first screw drop and went to work on the second. "I learned this trick from one of my arrests. Never thought I'd have to use it."

"Bel."

Salem's steady insistence finally earned Bel's attention. She glanced at Salem, her eyes wild. She didn't stop rotating the penny. "What?"

"I know we've grown apart the last few years."

Bel's brow furrowed.

"And as horrible as all of this has been, I'm grateful that it's brought us back together. That's why it hurts so much to tell you this." Salem's head drooped. "Back at the first hotel room? The one where we got the pizza delivered and left before we ate it?"

The words hurt like razor blades, but she finished. "I received a text from my mom's phone there."

Bel dropped the penny. Her breathing grew shallow.

"I didn't tell you because I couldn't do that to you. I couldn't be the one to say that Grace was dead. I was going to eventually, I swear."

Bel rose to her feet, slowly, the color draining from her face. Salem wished she could halt the hot rush of words scalding her lips, but she'd opened the gate. "And then you got that text from Grace's phone, and that made it worse."

"Stand up." Bel's voice sounded as if it were coming from far away, maybe underwater, maybe the other side of the world.

Salem left her chair, her blood growing thick, but still the words gushed. "I didn't throw my phone away. I didn't! I lied. I said I would, and then I just tossed yours. Now the police have my phone, the one my mom texted me on, and I know you saw them take it when they made us empty our pockets. I'm glad because I never should have kept it. I never should have lied to you. A real friend wouldn't have done that." A fiery, painful gasp pushed past her lips.

"Come here."

Salem's feet propelled her forward, ready for the punishment she'd earned. Her father was dead, probably her mother as well, and she'd betrayed the last person who loved her. She hoped Bel would punch her so hard that she'd pass out, with such force that she'd never wake up again. Nothing would knock this burning guilt out of her, but if Bel hit her with enough force, at least unconsciousness would bring temporary relief.

The only thing Salem couldn't stand, what she wouldn't be able to survive, was Bel telling her what she already knew: *You're worthless, you mess everything up, even your own father didn't think you were worth living for.*

Salem stood in front of Bel, as vulnerable as she'd ever been. She waited for the blow, either fists or words.

"I was fired."

The *click-clack-click* of the round wall clock, its black skeleton fingers snapping a beat to mark the seconds, was the only noise in the room.

"What?" It felt like a joke, what Bel had said. Salem didn't get it.

"Not exactly fired, at least not until the results come back." Bel cleared her throat, but the sound escaped as a sob before she pulled it back. "I'll be out of a job for sure after that."

"What?" Salem repeated. Bel had only one goal her entire life: to be a police officer. She'd gone through all the right training, taken all the right classes, was the best at *everything*. Salem would have been less surprised if Bel had told her she'd grown a tail.

"Yeah. Turns out they frown on you doing drugs on the job."

Salem shook her head. "But you don't do drugs."

Bel continued as if she hadn't heard her. "Rachel turned me on to it. Said it would keep me on my game, alert." She grimaced apologetically. "You know me, I always need to jump twice as high, run twice as fast. But in the Chicago PD, I was nameless, just one of hundreds trying for the same promotion. I swear I only did it occasionally, only when I had to pull a double shift. Turns out one of those shifts included a random drug test."

Salem had thought the worst thing that could happen was hearing Bel say she hated Salem for lying to her about the phone. She'd been wrong. Seeing Bel's shame—proud, perfect, strong Bel—was a million times worse. "Oh, Bellie."

Bel dropped her eyes. "I got the call about the scene at Mom's apartment a few hours after I took the drug test. I figured the timing was perfect. Cosmic punishment."

Bel's glance rose. A pained grin creaked across her face as she wiped at Salem's face. "Don't cry! I was trying to make you feel better. Let you know you're not the only bad guy in the room."

Salem wrapped Bel in her arms, pulling her so close that their heartbeats matched. At first Bel tried to pull back, but then she squeezed the breath out of Salem and kept hugging her past that point. She didn't let go until both their tears stopped, and still Salem held on. When she finally released her, Bel used the cuff of her sleeve to wipe Salem's eyes.

"You're on your own with those boogers," she said, pointing at Salem's nose.

Salem laugh-hiccuped. "I'm so sorry."

Bel sighed. It sounded like a rusty bucket being pulled up a dry well. "We're a fine pair, aren't we? A liar and a druggie."

"I won't ever lie to you again."

Bel's smile was still sad, but it grew. "I know. Because I *will* kick your ass next time. And as terrible as the last few days have been, it got me away from Rachel. There's hope for both of us."

Salem tried to draw a deep breath, but her chest hurt too much from the crying. "Do you think there's hope for our moms?"

Bel put a hand on each of Salem's cheeks, her expression fierce. "You and I are in this together, until the end, until we figure out what happened to them, so no more secrets. Understood?"

Salem nodded, using her own sleeve to swipe at her nose.

Bel studied her for a second, planted a kiss on her forehead, and returned to her work on the chair. "We've got to forgive ourselves one of these days, Salem. It's not my fault my dad didn't stick around, or your fault Daniel killed himself."

Salem didn't respond. She was floating in the limbo between lightness and emptiness, that unmoored clarity that comes with absolution.

Bel glanced up from her work, an eyebrow raised. "I didn't mean we needed to do all the forgiveness shit right now. First things first, we have to get out of this holding room. Can you stick your ear up to the door and tell me what you hear?"

Salem blinked two or three times before walking to the door and pressing her head to it. "I hear a bunch of people talking, but I can't make out what they're saying."

Suddenly, a thunder of footsteps raced past outside the room. Bel shot forward and pressed her ear to the one-inch crack between the door and the carpeting. She listened intently for two or three minutes. When the din passed, she stood, the chair bracket in hand. Sliding the thin metal between the strike plate and the door latch, she began to wiggle it. "They've found a body," she said as she worked. "Outside of town, sliced up pretty bad, missing her fingers, eyes, and other stuff I couldn't catch."

Salem felt this information with the force of hands on her neck. Sliced up. Missing fingers. *The killer had followed them to Amherst.* If he could trail them here, he could find them anywhere.

"I know what you're thinking," Bel said, "and you're right. That's why we have to get out of here. Now." The door clicked open as she finished her sentence. She stood back, blinking in surprise. "I didn't think it'd work. They really should make these holding room locks more impressive."

She peeked into the hall, waited a few seconds, and then yanked Salem out with her. "Walk alongside me," she said. "Don't look scared. Don't look anything, in fact. Tell me a story."

"About what?"

"It doesn't matter!" They reached the end of the hallway, opened the door, and stepped into the police station's main room. It housed twenty desks. They'd all been full when Stone and Clancy had brought them in. Now, there were only a handful of officers around. Bel chuckled softly.

Salem stared at her, alarmed, before she realized Bel was holding up her end of the fake conversation. Salem matched her smile, and spoke, her light expression out of sync with her words. "Any chance we can get our stuff before we leave?"

"None!" Bel said, as if providing the punch line for a joke. Salem grinned appropriately.

"And the best part," Bel said, leaning in to share a secret, "is that we need to walk past the front desk like nothing has happened. The remaining staff has no idea who we are or what we're being held for. All right?"

Salem did her best imitation of a thoughtful expression. "Of course. And then what?"

Bel laughed again, an artificial tinkling sound. Her eyes darted into every corner of the room. A middle-aged officer on a computer shot them a glance, then returned to his work. No one else paid them any attention.

"Then we hope Stone and Clancy aren't outside, and we run like motherfuckers."

CHAPTER 63

Amherst, Massachusetts

"They had a tracker on you."

Bel and Salem were speedwalking the three blocks from the Amherst Police Department to West Cemetery, both grateful that the graveyard was near since they no longer had even the penny between them. The night was full-on dark, though the Bank of America sign they passed informed them it was only 7:23 p.m.

It hadn't been even seventy-two hours since Bel had received the call about the blood at Grace's apartment. Not three full days, and their lives had been ripped out from under them, hurtling them all the way to the East Coast.

"Who?" Salem's hands were shoved in her jean pockets to keep her warmth close to her body. Amherst's downtown was speckled with light pedestrian traffic, people leaving restaurants or walking to a movie, their fall parkas pulled tight around them against the forty-degree air. The Colonial and Gothic buildings of Amherst lent it a similarly witchy feel as Salem.

"Agents Stone or Johnson, is my best guess. It was that round white thing they pulled out of your pocket same time they took your phones. Johnson was the Ed Harris look-alike that I spotted watching us in the Mia and again in the Hawthorne lobby, by the way."

"That's probably when one of them slipped it into my pocket." Salem glanced over her shoulder. "If we find whatever is in the gravestone and save Grace or my mom, does it matter?"

"As long as the killer isn't using a similar means to trail us," She swore. "I should have patted us both down already. Hold still."

Salem complied. Bel checked her top to bottom, then did the same to herself.

"All clear, unless they have some newfangled technology I can't find." Bel grew quiet. The low stone wall of the cemetery appeared a block ahead. "You think you can get inside the gravestone?"

Salem was chewing the ragged edge of a fingernail. "I'm going to try my best." She made an empty laughing sound. "It'd be easier if I had a crowbar."

Bel tipped her head to the left, toward a CVS Pharmacy. "What about a penknife?"

Salem raised an eyebrow. "That'd be nice, but we don't have any money."

Bel winked. "One of the best parts of being a cop is that you learn how to impersonate a criminal." She jogged across the street and was gone from sight for four minutes before reappearing outside the CVS with the fingers of her left hand flashing a V for victory at her waist.

She was out of breath when she returned to Salem's side. "Got it!"

Salem frowned.

Bel patted her cheek. "I'm not going to turn into a regular crook, if that's what you're worried about. I learned my lesson back in Chicago. What I'm doing here is about survival." She held out the knife. "You don't mind an Emily Dickinson memorial penknife?"

Salem couldn't bury the smile. "I wouldn't have it any other way. We'll send the CVS a check when all this is said and done?"

Bel flashed a brilliant grin. It lit up the dusk. "You are perfectly perfect, Salem Wiley. When we are at the end of this, I promise you I'll pay the CVS back for the stuff I took, and I'll raise you one better. I'll come clean with the Chicago PD and voluntarily check myself into rehab."

Salem squeezed her arm. "Will it be enough to keep your job?"

Bel shrugged and started toward the cemetery. "I don't know, but it'll be the right thing to do."

Salem slipped her hand into Bel's, holding Bel's smile close to her as they walked, letting it fill her with its healing warmth. The two of them were right again, and if they were together, they could survive anything.

The metal gates to the cemetery were closed, so they rested their bottoms on the waist-high stone wall and slid their legs over the top. They jogged straight to the wrought iron–enclosed Dickinson plot on the far side of the graveyard. A healthy crescent of cheddar moon dangled in the sky, but the clouds scudding over it fractured the light. The wind was chill and moody, bullying the brittle fall leaves one second and cowering the next.

"I don't suppose you stole a flashlight?" Salem asked.

She was answered by a *click*, followed by a tight circle of yellow light the size of a fifty-cent piece.

Salem chuckled. "Bel Odegaard, master criminal. Hold that beam on the face of the stone, okay?"

She played her fingers over Lucretia Gunn's name for the second time that day, tracing the letters' curves and depth, pressing gently, pulling back to test for trip switches, searching for any construction anomaly that would indicate a secret drawer. Finding none, she expanded her exploration to the rest of the words on the inscription, and then even wider, to the lips and edges of the name panel.

Still nothing.

She knocked on the face, other hand over her heart, and felt the same hollowness that she had earlier with Mercy's help. She was certain there was something back there, but she didn't care to destroy the stone to get to it, even if she'd had the tools to do so. Flicking open the blade of the knife, she explored the same crevices and loops. She was rewarded with marble dust.

She sat back on her heels, blowing a curl out of her face. It had been almost three days since her last shower, and for the first time, she became aware of the smell of her own body, the sourness of sweat, her natural musk. She studied the rock.

It waited patiently, gripping whatever secret it had housed for over 150 years.

"Bel, where did your parents meet?" Salem was tracing the knife over an irregularity she'd just discovered leading from the ornamental line separating Samuel's information from Lucretia's. "High school, right?"

"That's the story." Bel held the flashlight steady, checking over her shoulder periodically. The only noise in the graveyard was the dry whisper of leaves tumbling one over another, scrambling to spy on the two trespassers. The distant hum of passing cars barely penetrated the trees guarding the cemetery. "He was on the competing football team, homecoming of her senior year. They hooked up at some party in a field later that night. She never saw him again."

"Ah, young love." Salem frowned and pressed the tip of the blade deeper into the stone. "And my parents met in college. Imagine how our lives could have been different. Let's say your dad didn't go to that party, or my mom didn't register for that same art class my dad took."

"No they didn't."

"What?" Salem asked, absentmindedly. There was definitely a crack running from the ornamental line to the *G* in *Gunn*. It was invisible to the eye, but the point of her knife was picking it up.

"Your parents didn't meet in college. They met in high school, just like mine."

Salem stood, hands on hips, so she could study the gravestone from a different angle. "Huh?"

Bel moved the flashlight beam to her face. "When I helped Grace move to Linden Hills, we found a box of old photos. There's one of Grace, Vida, and Daniel, and it was taken at my grandparents' house in Iowa. That house was sold the year I was born, and a chunk of the money put into an eighteen-year CD for me. I cashed it in to go to college."

Salem's brow wrinkled. The wrought iron fence she'd threaded her arms through was providing too much interference. She'd need to sneak inside the fence. "I'm positive my mom said they met in a drawing class in college."

Bel returned the beam to the face of the gravestone. "It doesn't matter, does it?"

Salem didn't know. There was a lot she didn't know anymore. "Help me over."

Bel held the flashlight with her teeth and created a hoist with her hands. Salem placed her foot into it and hopped the fence. Bel crawled over without help.

"Give me the light, okay?" Salem asked. "I want you to try and twist the top of this while I watch the face."

Bel raised her eyebrows but didn't object. She pushed on one end of the gravestone's top. Nothing moved. She tried the other end. Still nothing. Finally, she leaned over and put her shoulder into it. "Hulk mad!"

The marble top made a shrieking, scraping noise before moving an inch.

Bel's face appeared behind the gravestone, eyes wide. "I didn't think that would work."

"Keep pushing!" Salem knelt in front of the inscription. The crack from the line to the *G* had grown deeper. She jacked the tip of her knife into it. Bel earned another screaming inch from the marble. The crack widened.

"Do you smell roses?" Bel asked, panting.

"Push harder." The crack was now three inches long and wide enough for Salem to stuff her finger in. She did so, with a murmured apology to the Dickinson family. She felt the trigger at the bottom of the crack, a cool shelf of metal the size of a fingerprint.

She pushed.

A perfect rectangle of panel shot out, the *Gun* of Lucretia's name centered on its front.

Behind the panel was a drawer.

Inside the drawer was a metal container the size and shape of a pencil box. Resting on the container was a dried red rose so fragile that it crumbled when Salem's finger brushed it.

Her blood stampeded through her veins. She set what remained of the flower gently to the side and reached for the metal box, sliding her fingers around it. "Bel, do you really think my parents trained us for this?" She pulled out the box. It was as light as a bird.

Bel stared at it, her voice husky with amazement. "If so, they did a kick-ass job."

Salem was just starting to lift the lid when two hands reached across the fence, grabbed her by the shoulders, and hauled her off her knees.

CHAPTER 64

Amherst, Massachusetts

"Ernest!" Bel leaped over the wrought iron fence of the Dickinson family plot, but he'd already released Salem. He appeared abashed more than anything, maybe for taking advantage of their concentration to sneak up on them.

Mercy stood next to her brother, her face red and swollen from crying. "He ran away," she said.

"What?" Salem was trying to get her bearings. She brushed the grass and leaves off her knees, careful to hold the metal box steady.

Mercy pointed at her brother. "He shouldn't have let those men take you."

Bel scanned Salem to make sure she was all right. The juicy crescent moon broke free of its cloud cover and lit them from above, four lost souls in a Massachusetts graveyard. "It was a good idea to leave us," Bel said, her focus still on Salem. "In fact, it was the best thing you two could have done. There was no point in all of us being arrested."

"We have to go," Ernest said. He hadn't stopped surveying the dark corners of the cemetery. "This is the first place they'll look for you."

"He didn't just want to leave you *here*." Mercy glared at him despite the trembling in her thin shoulders. "He wanted to leave you forever. But I wouldn't let him. I knew you'd come back."

Ernest ducked his head, pulling his sister closer. "I'm sorry, but I gotta look out for Mercy. She's my number-one priority, you know? But I'm here now, and it's time to split." He glanced uneasily toward the road. "There's a sedan been driving by."

"We have to replace the gravestone," Salem said. "Put it back together as much as we can."

Ernest made a frustrated noise. "There isn't time!"

"It's someone's grave," Salem insisted.

Bel hopped over the fence. "The sooner we do it, the sooner we can go. Trust me, you can't change her mind when it's made up."

Salem flashed Bel a grateful smile, her grin widening as Ernest stepped over the fence to help Bel straighten the headstone's cap. Salem threaded her hand through the fence and pushed the drawer back in. The *Gun* no longer blended in with the rest of the face, and the crack she'd widened with her penknife was obvious.

Bel glanced at it, hands on hips. "That's the best we can do," she said firmly, directing her words at Salem. "We have to go. Ernest, we'll follow you."

The two of them climbed back over the fence, and then all four jogged toward the northeast end of the cemetery, Ernest talking as they traveled. "I need to get rid of this car before we travel any farther. If the FBI knew enough to find you at this cemetery, they know what we're driving."

"But you just got it!" Salem objected.

"No choice."

Salem cradled the box, breathless from running, but her words were clear. "Okay, but I need light, a computer, and Wi-Fi. Now. We need to see what I pulled out of the gravestone."

CHAPTER 65

Iowa City, Iowa

"You look beautiful."

"Charles, it's the new millennium. Don't you mean I look power-ful? Smart? Capable?" But Senator Gina Hayes's broad smile showed she was teasing. Her husband always said exactly the right thing. It was one of his gifts.

"I mean it." He pulled her into an embrace rare enough that Matthew Clemens stopped juggling seven different appointments, hundreds of texts and emails, and a phone conversation with CNN to stare, agape.

The three of them were backstage at Kinnick Stadium on the University of Iowa campus. Outside, an unusually plump crescent moon was crawling up the night sky, and the winter-washed air carried ice currents that nipped at noses and fingers. That didn't keep the record crowd of thirty-five thousand supporters from bundling in parkas, hats, and scarves to hear a historic speech by who looked to be the first female president of the United States of America.

The election was in six days. News stations were predicting the highest voter turnout in history. Technicians, news crews, and security personnel bustled backstage. Since no moment of Senator Hayes's life was private, at least two different cable stations were showing a live feed of her husband's embrace. She knew this, or at least guessed.

She didn't care.

She was going to steal these five seconds in her husband's arms, safe, grounded, a blink of selfishness before she stepped in front of thousands—millions with television and the internet—and gave them everything she had. She'd been raised in the ideal of public service, taught by her father that your life only had meaning if it helped others. She'd seen the sacrifices he'd made right up until his death of a heart attack two years earlier. She knew how proud he'd be of her, and that was one of the sparks that kept her fire burning.

Gina pulled out of her husband's arms, letting her hand linger on his cheek for a moment. "Do I still look okay?"

He flashed the charming smile that had disarmed men and women—too many women—his entire political career. "You've never looked more powerful, smart, or capable."

He leaned close to her ear and whispered, "And I've never seen you look more beautiful. If you need help getting out of that suit later, you know where to find me." With a wink, he stepped back and let her hair and makeup crew complete their final touches. Gina threw him one last glance before returning to work, wondering how he could still surprise her, still make her feel so attractive, even after all these years.

She called over her shoulder, "Matthew, has someone tested the teleprompters?"

"Yes, but you won't need them." Matthew didn't pause his typing to answer but did stop to issue a threat to the cable news anchor creeping closer to Hayes despite multiple warnings against direct questions until after the speech. With a single gesture, he also managed to have her pre-speech chamomile tea brought to her.

Gina smiled as she sipped. American voters were worried they'd be electing her and her husband to run the country when, in fact, they should be worried about the package deal of her and her assistant. Matthew had chosen her outfit (a slimming pantsuit in deep "power" red), her hair ("less of the Matronly Martha, more Assertive Annie with a dash of Sexy Susie"), and her makeup ("*Chop-chop!* I need her to look like she's actually slept since last May"). Gina had chosen the content of her speech, however, and written most of it through the night, working with her team of speechwriters.

The address hit the three points she'd based her campaign on: economic power, global stability, and environmental protection. This one also contained an Easter egg, something her speechwriters had begged her not to include: a nod to the so-called kitchen-table issues that had been important to her as a law student and continued to define her. She would address women's reproductive freedom, gay rights, income inequality, the pay gap, the minimum wage, immigration reform, and veterans' rights.

She would represent the people.

"Are you ready?" Matthew held his iPad in one hand and her mobile mic in the other.

Gina nodded briskly and handed him the empty teacup. "Always."

Matthew appeared wistful for a moment.

"What is it?" Gina asked.

"I hate to say it, but Charming Charlie was right. You look beautiful."

Gina actually laughed, a ruby-colored chuckle seldom heard in public. "You're not getting a raise, Matthew."

He winked and stepped away, the melancholy smile still on his face. Gina was escorted into the wide-open arena, the applause deafening. Tens of thousands of people jumped to their feet, screaming, waving signs, some of them crying. Gina walked to the center of the stage and held her hands in the air. The teleprompters to her left and right were suspended like thin prisms. The space heaters on the stage created a visible barrier against the frigid November air, a wavy storm front that Gina had to stare through like a mirage to see her audience.

But it didn't matter. This was where she was supposed to be. These were the people she was fighting for. She let the cheers wash over her.

"Thank you for inviting me to your lovely stadium, Hawkeyes!" Impossibly, the volume of the cheers rose.

Gina's smile widened.

She had her mouth open to begin her speech when the first shot rang out, popping like a car backfire, the bullet piercing the mirage of the stage.

Two Secret Service agents were on top of Gina's body before the second shot was fired.

CHAPTER 66

Northampton, Massachusetts

"What's in it?" Mercy asked. She was perched on the cheap motel bed-spread, leaning against Salem.

Ernest had driven them west to the Road King Motel, a roadside two-beds-and-a-bathroom that wouldn't require them to walk through the lobby to reach their room. Salem and Isabel were wanted women. Ernest had requested the farthest room from the office, paid cash, and settled Bel, Salem, and Mercy before leaving to trade cars, obtain two more phones, procure a handgun if he was able, and refresh their cash supply.

Bel and Salem hadn't asked any questions.

"We don't know what's inside, hon," Salem answered.

Bel was working at the metal box with the penknife. Salem couldn't tear her eyes away from the container. It was rust-free, constructed of tin or some other flimsy metal, with a simple goat's eye. Bel had inserted the tip of the knife into the clinch and was jiggling it.

Their room was nonsmoking, which apparently only meant no ash-trays. Black lips had seared themselves into the edges of the Formica-topped nightstand from cigarettes laying themselves to rest. The air was stained with the dark undersmell of mold. The motel was right off the highway, and cars zoomed past outside.

Salem put her arm around Mercy. "We hope it's something that will help us find out what happened to our moms."

The words were like magic, and the top of the box popped loose with a sigh. Bel set the container on the bed and silently pushed it toward Salem, across the stained flower bedspread.

Heart fluttery, Salem lifted the lid all the way. The hinges shrieked, the noise hurting her fillings. In that second, she realized that her Ativan was back at the police station, but that she hadn't missed it.

Inside the box lay a roll of yellowed papers tied with a bit of ribbon and lace.

Salem slid her fingers around the bundle. It was old enough to feel feathery.

She unwound the ribbon and laid it on the bed, gasping as she recognized it. "It's the collar Emily Dickinson wears in the daguerreotype—that famous photo of her that everyone's seen."

"Oh my god." Bel reached to touch the lace and then yanked her fingers back. "Unroll the paper."

Salem laid the scroll on the bed next to the collar. She held one side and smoothed out the other. Inside were three handwritten sheets of paper penned with the same looping script as the note they'd found in the First Church's beam. Salem began reading out loud:

> *To the Journeywoman—*
> *If you are reading this—please! You are an Explorer of the highest Order. If your Heart matches your Intellect, then we possess Spring's Hope.*
> *Hear my Story.*
> *It Begins with the estimable Lucretia Mott, Elected leader of the Underground in 1817.*
> *(O—for you to be True, and protect this Secret World!)*
> *What is now the Hermitage was sleeping, an old Dragon that had lost its way. But the Underground kept*

watch on the Cave, wary, and their Fear was Rewarded when General Andrew Jackson sought to Revive the organization.

The Underground was all that stood in his Way.

General Jackson killed hundreds—Women!—Negroes!—Indians!—to get at the Underground. Mrs. Lucretia Mott was forced to hide the names of the leaders, the treasure of the people, and this: the Truth of the waltz the Dragon and the Underground had been dancing for 2,000 years.

"What's that mean?" Mercy interrupted. "There's a dragon?"

"I think she's saying that the Hermitage, the organization that came after our moms, is a lot older than we thought," Salem said. She set aside the first sheet of paper, which snapped back to its scroll shape with a *swish*, and began reading the second.

Mrs. Lucretia Mott employed the noted Thomas J. Beale—an Explorer, like you!—to Buoy the cause. Mr. Beale coded the Truth in an unbreakable Cipher and hid it, with the Treasure and the Membership Docket, in Virginia. He entrusted Mrs. Mott—no one else!—with the Key that would open the cipher.

Salem's breath shot out of her as surely as if she'd been squeezed. "Holy crap," she whispered. "The Beale Cipher."

"You've heard of it?" Bel jockeyed impatiently for a better view of the scroll.

Salem tilted her head, examining the scroll with reverence. "It's one of the most famous unbroken codes in history. It's actually a set of three ciphertexts. The first is rumored to contain the location of a massive treasure, the second an accounting of the treasure, and the third, supposedly, a list of names of the people the treasure belongs to. Only the second cipher has been broken, using the Declaration of Independence as the keytext. The Declaration didn't work to decode the first and third."

"Where'd the treasure come from?"

"According to legend, Beale and his gang of adventurers discovered it near Santa Fe. Beale returned to Virginia, befriended an innkeeper, and gave him a cryptic story about buried treasure and someone trying to kill him. Beale also gave the innkeeper a metal box and ordered him to open it only if he—Beale—disappeared."

Salem pushed her hair back from her face. "If you guessed Beale was never heard from again, you'd be right. When the innkeeper opened the box, maybe around 1840, he discovered the three ciphertexts but couldn't crack them. Someone eventually published the codes in a pamphlet in the 1880s with an offer to share any treasure they yielded."

"How much treasure?" Mercy asked, her eyes bright.

"Tens of millions of dollars, according to the second ciphertext, the only one that's ever been broken." Salem's legs were falling asleep, so she shifted on the bed, scaring up the sharp odor of industrial detergent. "Some people think the story was a hoax used to sell the pamphlet itself."

She tapped the Dickinson scroll. "No one knows, though, because the first and third ciphertexts the ones that supposedly contain the location of the treasure and the list of names—have never been broken in all this time, even with all the technology we have."

"Well, keep reading," Bel said. "It sounds like they're not going to remain unbroken for much longer."

Salem inhaled deeply.

Alas, Mr. Beale could not pause for rest—or (Faith, this is Important) to explain the application of the Key to Mrs. Mott—because General Jackson became President Jackson, and he conducted the slaughter of innocents on a National scale, with the Flag behind him.

Mr. Beale and his men rode out, taking it upon themselves with Sweat, Blood, and the Love of God, to risk their lives yet again to obtain the Lightning Bolt that would strike down President Jackson and destroy the Hermitage in its present incarnation.

With Grace and Fortune, Mr. Beale succeeded. Mrs. Mott received word that he'd secured the Lightning Bolt and placed it in the same hidey-hole in the hills of Virginia as the Treasure and the Docket, and that he would return anon to explain the Key's application and impart the exact location of All.

Mrs. Mott wasn't worried—don't you see? She knew the Docket by her Heart, had counted the Treasure, had nurtured the Truth, and Mr. Beale was on his way to share the Downfall of Jackson.

All Mrs. Mott was lacking was the exact coordinates of the hidey-hole wherein Mr. Beale had stored it All, and she held the Key that could whisper that to Educated Ears.

But the Future did not unfold as planned.

My Tears testify that Mr. Beale was never heard from again.

I was called into this story 18 years later, in Boston, as so many of us were in those years after Mr. Beale disappeared. We were to put our Honeybee Minds to the task of employing Mr. Beale's Key to solve his Three-fold Cipher, but we failed. The Wall was too High.

Like Children who Scheme to hide their Sweets from their Brother, we'd actually hid the Secret from ourselves. We could only wait, patiently, for You—finally, the wisdom to break the code and Set Free the souls of the Gentlest Women in History.

Salem and Bel exchanged a look charged with amazement and something deeper, almost sacred. Salem wiped her sweating palms on her pants, set the second scroll to the side, heard it *whisk* back into its 150-year-old shape, and began reading the third and final page of Emily Dickinson's letter:

> As my Winter rose, I was assigned the task of hiding the Key three levels deep.
>
> You are now intimate with my work—a message hidden in a brilliant Gentileschi currently on loan in the home of a Boston Brahmin—leading you to a secret drawer in a Church that afforded me solace—directing you to the headstone of my beloved grandparents.
>
> Craftspeople of the highest order have assured the subterfuge of the Clues, but I will have to trust the Whispers of the Women to carry through the ages the beginning point and the spectacles that reveal the secret in the painting. (That my Investment was Sound and that you are Reading this gives me Pleasure that echoes through Time to reach my Hand as I Write!)
>
> When you Apply the Key correctly, Beale's Cipher will crack as an Egg, revealing the location of the Lightning Bolt that will destroy the Hermitage, the treasure of the Underground, and the Master Docket of Underground leaders. Protect this final Knowledge above all else. It's a timeless, Fragile Butterfly the Hermitage would seek to Crush under its Boot.
>
> We are at this Moment.
>
> Mr. Beale's Key is thus: SF Dolores Bell
>
> I Trust, Dear Explorer, that you will take this Beacon and Set Us Free.
>
> —Emily
>
> Σ

The silence in room 23 pulsed. Encountering such far-reaching knowledge in the tight, dirty grip of the motel was disorienting. Salem was working through solutions, synapses firing, lighting up passages, gray matter straining, but it all led her to the same alarming conclusion. "*SF Dolores Bell* isn't the keytext to the Beale Cipher."

Bel jumped off the bed. "How could it not be?" She pointed at the scrolls. "There's no way anyone went to all that trouble—that *we've* gone to all this trouble—for nothing."

Salem shook her head sadly. "It's too short."

"Can't it be one of those ciphers you talked about in your thesis? I remember you wrote that the key could be a short word, even four letters long."

Mercy was burrowing into Salem, eyeing Bel, whose voice was raising.

"I wrote about Vigenère ciphers, which are polyalphabetic." Salem tried to keep her tone level, but she was feeling the same panic. They couldn't dead-end here. "The Beale Cipher is numeric. It needs a full keytext to decrypt it, a work long enough to include all the letters of the alphabet at least once. That's why the Declaration of Independence worked to decipher the second of Beale's texts."

"Okay, that's okay," Bel said, pacing. "Then *SF Dolores Bell* is something else, something that will lead us to the actual keytext. It's not supposed to be easy, right? How about this?" She reached toward her hip for a gun that wasn't there, a soothing, habitual gesture. "How about *SF* stands for Samuel Fowler. Right? That makes sense. And maybe Dolores Bell is a relative of his? Or a friend of Emily Dickinson's?"

Bel's enthusiasm was edged with hysteria, and it was contagious. "It could be that there is no Dolores Bell, and we're just meant to use those initials," Salem offered, her heartbeat picking up.

Bel clapped her hands, making Mercy jump. "There you go! *SF* DB. Samuel Fowler Dickinson . . . Boston?"

"Why don't you google it?" Mercy asked. She'd shrunk into herself. Noticing how scared the girl looked calmed Salem down a notch.

"We don't have a computer, honey, or that would be a great idea."

Mercy reached into her pocket and yanked out an Android phone tucked inside a Dora the Explorer case.

Salem pulled her into a hug. "You're the best, sweetheart!" Her thumbs flew as she pulled up the browser and typed in *SF Dolores Bell.* Bel crowded her shoulder. Mercy tried to peek at the screen, too.

The connection was slow, and the screen went blank for several seconds.

Finally, the hits appeared.

The first was the Wikipedia entry for Dolores Park in San Francisco, California, home of a replica church bell erected to honor the memory of Manuel Hidalgo, father of Mexican independence.

Bel exhaled. "It looks like we're going to San Francisco."

Salem nodded numbly, scribbling down notes. "To look inside a bell for a key that will crack the world's most famously unbreakable cipher, leading us to treasure, a master docket of Underground leaders, and some sort of lightning bolt that will bring down the Hermitage." She needed a shower, and dinner, and sleep. The weight of her mom's life, or Grace's, weighed on her shoulders like stones.

"You stopped reading too soon *again*," Mercy said condescendingly, pointing at the scroll that lay next to Salem and pulling her out of her exhausted spiral. "What's at the bottom?"

Salem tossed her head as if pulled from a dream. She picked up the third sheet of the scroll, glancing to the foot, to the section she'd skipped over after reading the key Dickinson provided. "It's a postscript," she said. "It looks like a poem."

> *P.S. Indulge me as I gift this Blessing on your Journey—*
> *"I know where the pink flower grows*
> *But,—I ne'er pick it*
> *Let it follow its highest path*
> *Female freedom, think it!"*

"That's pretty," Mercy said. "I like pink flowers."

Jason hadn't had time to dispose of the rental car and obtain a new one. In fact, he'd barely had time to deposit the body inside the tilting barn when a group of joyriding teens screamed into the rutted driveway. Cursing his bad luck, he'd waved at them and hopped in his car, using the lot lizard's shirt to clean the blood off the windows, and driven straight to the police station in time to witness Salem Wiley and Isabel walk out of the Amherst Police Department like they owned the world.

He didn't mind the meaty, slaughterhouse smell of the car's interior. The outside air was cool enough to keep the biomatter from rotting, at least for as long as he'd need the vehicle.

Besides, the scent kept him company while he waited in the parking lot across from the Road King Motel, killing time until the light in room 23 winked out.

CHAPTER 67

Iowa City, Iowa

Senator Gina Hayes's eyes were open to the night sky.

That crescent moon, curved and plump, almost orange, was a Cheshire cat smiling down as the world collapsed.

Two Secret Service men covered her body with theirs. Three more flew off the stage like night creatures taking flight. A second bullet flew. Police swarmed toward the source of both shots. They reached the shooter in five seconds, a full second after the Secret Service, but they could have taken a minute, or ten, or an entire day, because the shooter would not get off another round. Two civilians in black-and-gold Hawkeye jerseys held him face down, three fingers on his left hand broken in the effort it took to wrest his gun from him, his left arm hanging peculiarly from where they'd chicken-winged him.

All this took place in a vacuum, suspended in time and space. The world, watching via live video stream, held its breath.

And then the sound came rushing back.

"Get her offstage!"

"Has she been shot?"

"Move the camera closer!"

Gina was carried off by the Secret Service agent who'd initially pushed her down, Theodore, her first line of protection since she'd declared her candidacy.

"Theodore," she said, surprised at how calm she sounded, "I can walk. You don't need to hold me like an infant."

"Sorry, ma'am." He didn't put her down.

A phalanx of men in suits appeared alongside him, shielding her as much as possible. Through their shoulders, she spotted Charles, his face raw with worry. She heard Matthew issuing commands, ordering back the media, her soldier to the end. Theodore didn't slow until he reached her car, which he tucked her into before sliding next to her. He gently pushed her head down, below window level. The passenger door opened and another Secret Service agent slid in on her other side, and two more in the front. They sped away.

"I haven't been shot."

"I know, ma'am. The bullet passed three inches above your right shoulder, through the recording wall behind you, and lodged itself in the stadium wall." He kept his hand on her back so she wouldn't sit up. Both he and his partner in the back seat were scanning the world sliding past, their muscles thrumming with adrenaline. The driver was doing the same. The agent next to him was on the phone, talking in a low voice.

Gina smoothed her pant legs as much as possible from this bent position. How were her hands not shaking? "I need to let my husband know I'm all right."

"Protocol, ma'am. We have to remove you from the scene and transport you to a safe location."

She felt the back of her head. She'd have a nice goose egg where Theodore had thrown her down. Her right shoulder was tender, as well. She was damn lucky. "Thank you for saving my life."

"My job, ma'am."

They drove in silence for another minute. "Theodore, we've been together for what, almost a year?"

"Eleven months and fourteen days, ma'am."

"So you can guess what I'm going to say next, can't you?"

He reached into his jacket pocket, pulled out his phone, and handed it to her without taking his eyes off the passing crowds. The faintest of smiles tipped his mouth. "Call a press conference and then get back to work?"

She took his phone and punched in Matthew's number. "Damn straight."

CHAPTER 68

3 East 70th Street, New York

Carl Barnaby wished he'd given the woman an opportunity to bathe before he'd requested her company. She had washed her hands and face on the private flight here from Minneapolis, but her clothes were crusted with blood and worse. She smelled like a farm animal.

"You know who I am?" he asked. She was staring at him in an unpleasantly direct way.

"Carl Barnaby, one of two Barnaby brothers and current CEO of the Hermitage Foundation." Her voice was scratchy from disuse.

He studied her. Her glance was bold, but she was a small thing, so slight up close. Supposedly, she was one of the Underground leaders, but what were they? A group of scattered women and a few neutered men. The Hermitage had them outfinanced and outgunned, had since the beginning of time. He was past due to swat this annoying fly once and for all.

His tone was measured. "Your daughter is still alive, as is her friend." She flinched. Good.

"Where are they?" Her expression was no longer defiant.

He steepled his fingers and leaned back in his chair. He'd received word that Isabel Odegaard and Salem Wiley had escaped from jail. Jason wasn't answering his phone. If the girls eluded Jason's grasp and located the list, he might never get his hands on it. He would make sure the media covered their jailbreak to help locate them, but that might not be enough. He needed the woman sitting across from him to tell him where the leadership docket was. "Massachusetts. They're getting close."

He paused, but she didn't say anything. He continued. "If you tell me where the list is, we don't have to kill them."

She opened her mouth to laugh, but she was too damaged. Jason had taken bits and slices out of her, twisted her fingers, done what he needed to extract information. Only a low moan escaped. "If you have the list, you'll kill them and more," she said.

"Not true." He dropped his hands and leaned forward in his chair, his expression grandfatherly. "We only need the one."

"Gina Hayes."

He shrugged. *You've got to crack a few eggs.* "She's risen too high. Once she's eliminated, we could live in peace, the Underground and the Hermitage."

Her eyes were burning again, pinning him in his seat, accusing him. "This war is older than you and me, older even than Andrew Jackson." Her voice was rising, shaking, white with fury. "I'm fighting for my life, and the life of my daughter, and our right to live in this world without fear, with opportunity, with control over our own bodies and destinies. Do you even *know* what you're fighting for?"

Carl stood, abruptly, and turned toward the window. "A man tried to assassinate Senator Hayes in Iowa just an hour ago." Out of the corner of his eye, he saw her pale. "A rural man, from what I understand. Uneducated and angry. He didn't want to answer to a woman, didn't want the shame of living in a country run by a female."

Carl walked around to the front of his desk and sat on the edge. "He didn't succeed."

He pulled a burgundy handkerchief from his pocket, shook it out, and held it over his nose to mask the stink of her. His words fell like sleet, their syllables sharp and cold. "His methods were rudimentary, but his mission was not. You can't possibly understand the terror of losing your power after growing so accustomed to it."

He pulled the handkerchief away. He was no longer able to maintain his cool exterior. "Imagine if you woke up one morning and discovered that someone was going to slice off your hands, or amputate your legs, and use them for their own." Spittle flew from his mouth. "Would you fight? Would you *kill* to keep what you knew was yours?"

She rose to her feet in a single swift move that must have cost her immensely. He drew back, his free hand flying up instinctively to shield himself. But she wasn't going to attack him. She turned toward the door she'd been brought in, shambling away.

"Monday," he called after her. "Alcatraz. We kill Hayes, obtain the list, harvest Isabel Odegaard and Salem Wiley, and wipe the Underground off history's ass. I might let you live to see the end. You'd be the last. A dodo bird."

Carl realized he was shouting. He nodded to Geppetto to escort her back to her cell. The woman shuffled out the door without another word, not so much as a glance over her shoulder.

Geppetto paused at the lip of insubordination before following her.

Back in her belowground cell, she waited until the door closed and locked to slide her hand under the mattress. She'd been brought to this building, ironically, through the underground entrance, and she didn't know where she was, even what city, though it had looked like Central Park outside Carl Barnaby's office.

Her cage was windowless, an eight-by-eight-foot cement box containing a sink, a toilet, and a bed. She had requested antiseptic and bandages to dress her wounds, which were starting to fester, the infection burning and setting into her bones, the smell thick and rotten.

Her request had been ignored.

But there was a singular brightness. They hadn't searched her. She was just a woman, small and beaten, so why would they?

Only 3 percent of her battery remained. She must choose her words wisely.

CHAPTER 69

Northampton, Massachusetts

The light in room 23 of the Road King Motel had been extinguished thirty-two minutes earlier. Jason wasn't in a hurry. Salem Wiley and Isabel were not professionals. They'd been on the run for three days.

They were falling into the heavy sleep of the shattered, a tiredness so complete that it weighted your bones with opium and called you down like a lover. If he gave them time to process the last dregs of adrenaline, he'd be able to dismiss them without waking them.

Yet the moon agitated him.

It was too bright for such a thin crescent. Pure orange, not a hint of red or yellow. And Barnaby had been calling nonstop, certainly to shout at Jason and order him back to Boston. Jason would talk to him after both women and the mewling child were dead. He could bring the list of Underground leaders they'd surely retrieved from the gravestone to Barnaby in New York.

Then Geppetto wouldn't be needed.

Jason's eyes flew open. It was time.

The Hermitage training he'd received had been exhaustive: a business degree with a psychology minor, hand-to-hand combat, weapons training, DNA cleanup, surveillance technology, breaking and entering.

Room 23's lock was so easy to pick as to be an insult.

He glided into the room like smoke, closing the door behind him before the moon's bossy orange light had a chance to follow.

He took stock.

The room smelled like it had been water damaged at some point. Mold and old cigarettes. Heavy shades were pulled over the single window. When his eyes adjusted, he made out two beds, one with a single figure—tall, Isabel—and the second with Salem Wiley, the child curled against her. Holding his breath, he measured theirs. Isabel was snoring lightly. Wiley and the child breathed in sync.

All three were sleeping.

His eyes adjusted further. A white scroll of paper lay on the table between the two beds.

The list.

Jason scanned the floor. It was clear of noisemakers. He stepped, reaching for the scroll.

Isabel stirred.

His hand shot to the smooth bone handle of his knife, holding it like a promise.

Isabel's snoring resumed.

Jason released the knife and picked up the scroll. He floated across the carpet to the bathroom. He closed the door gently and paused. Patient, never rushing, even though his blood was a red rocket shooting through his heart and exploding in a bright fireworks display.

He needed to make sure he had what he'd come for before he killed the sleeping females in the other room.

The list.

Two hundred years, and the Hermitage had never gotten this close. When no sound came from the other side of the bathroom door, he unrolled the scroll and scanned the three pages, plus a fourth page of scribbled notes that made clear the women were headed to San Francisco. And then he scanned all four pages again, processing them in the dim orange moonlight.

A third time.

He'd heard of the Beale Cipher. He knew it was unbreakable and led to hidden treasure in Virginia. That Beale's hiding place contained the Underground master docket and the secret to bringing down the Hermitage?

New information.

His mind reeled with the possibilities. If he held all the cards, he could trade them for Geppetto's life. His shoulders relaxed for the first time since learning Barnaby had assigned him Geppetto.

Using a bar of soap and a washcloth to pin each end of the papers, Jason snapped photos of all four pages.

He needed to let the women live for a while longer.

Until Salem Wiley solved the final code.

He could be a good loser, if it was temporary. San Francisco, eh? He was going there anyhow.

He thought of his mother. *If things are working out, you know you're doing something wrong.* She'd loved that saying. Maybe she still did. He'd have to ask her next time he changed out her IV. Or maybe he could wheel her to a window to see the outside. It'd been years. That was more than she'd ever done for him, but he was feeling generous. He slid his phone back into his pocket, replaced the soap and washcloth, and let the scroll snap back to its natural shape, the sheet of notes tucked inside. Holding his ear to the door, he checked for sounds in the other room. There were none. He stepped out, replacing the scroll.

Isabel's snoring had stopped, her mouth open slightly, a gentle susurration of air passing in and out. He thought of placing his mouth on hers, thrusting his tongue inside, tasting the sweet warmth of her. The embrace of darkness softened her already-impressive beauty, caressing her glorious hair, riding the curve of her cheeks, blessing her lips. He could smell her. Cheap hotel shampoo honeyed by her natural scent, water to wine.

The child whimpered in her bed. He tensed and held his breath, turned only his head. The girl snuggled deeper into Salem Wiley's arms but did not wake.

Jason glanced back toward Isabel.

Being this close and not touching her? Impossible.

He returned the scroll to the table. Then his hand slithered inside his jacket, coming out with his favorite knife. Strawberries and cream, that skin and that hair.

He reached for it, held a soft lock between two fingers. Isabel closed her mouth, made a *hm* noise, and returned to her soft snoring.

Slice.

Jason slid the lock of hair into his pocket and the knife into his sheath, leaving as silently as he'd arrived.

He'd read Barnaby's text when he'd taken out his phone to photograph the scroll.

> Back to the original plan. Follow them until they acquire the list, then fire them.

How nice that Barnaby had given him permission to finish what he'd started.

SATURDAY

November 5

CHAPTER 70

Twelve Years Old
Daniel's Last Month

It's May of Salem's twelfth summer. The sun is a giant lemon floating in the plum pudding of the sky. Lilacs bloom and drowsy dandelion fluff drifts in the air. Her world is bracketed by overalls and fanny packs, double pony-tails, and pastel-colored shirts.

Daniel and Vida have planned a surprise birthday party for their only child. It is to be just the three of them, though the Odegaards and all Salem's neighborhood friends are invited over for cake afterward. Her dad covers her eyes. Her mom takes her hand. They have a surprise for her. They lead her from the bungalow's living room to the backyard.

She hopes it's a puppy.

When her dad pulls away his hands, she realizes it's even better: a refurbished Macintosh PowerBook. She squeals, twirls, flips cartwheels. Her dad stands behind her mom, tall, his arms wrapped around her, both of them smiling. Salem knows that Daniel has made this happen. He's the one who notices when Salem's thrift store jeans, too old to be fashionable and too new to be retro, reveal most of her ankles. Despite being as terrible a housekeeper as Vida, it's he who has always made sure Salem showers every night before school and has her wild curls professionally cut twice a year.

Salem's kind, foggy-headed dad is her rock, always stable even though he is perpetually dreaming, creating new and more intricate cupboards and furniture and introducing his daughter to each piece of work as if it were a friend.

And three weeks after she receives the PowerBook, he kills himself.

CHAPTER 71

Sacramento, California

The car changed speeds, waking Salem. She jerked into an upright position, nerves jittering like they always did when memories of her dad's last days sneaked past her barricades. Her mother had started her with a therapist after Daniel's suicide. The woman was kind. She told Salem it wasn't her fault. She also told her that the full memory of that day at the lake would come back to her someday.

Salem hoped not.

She stretched the sleep out of her joints and glanced around. The back seat of the Honda reflected the forty-six hours they'd been on the road—bags of sunflower kernels, empty water bottles, maps. The car's interior smelled swampy.

Ernest hadn't returned to the Road King Motel until the next dawn, but he'd acquired a Honda Civic, two iPhones—one a 4 and the other a 5S—car chargers for each, over $2,000 in small bills, and a .380 Colt Automatic that delighted Bel. Ernest's face had hung as he displayed his loot. It hurt Salem to see him ashamed of his work, to know that he had to steal for them.

They'd left immediately, following the sun that first day.

Salem and Bel had filled him in on the Dickinson letter immediately.

"If we can get our hands on that treasure," he'd mused when they finished, "we could use it to buy off the Hermitage, maybe save your . . . mom." He didn't direct the word at either Salem or Bel.

"It would definitely be more useful than the leadership docket." Bel used the meat of her hand to wipe condensation off her window. "That's got to be nearly two hundred years old. All those people will be long dead."

Ernest ran his hand over his face, the other on the wheel. Salem wondered when he'd last slept. "I wish it worked that way," he said. "Underground leadership is usually passed down through the family. If your mom was a leader, you would be, too. When the Hermitage finds out about a connection, or thinks they've discovered one, they destroy all the women in the family."

Whenever Salem thought of the ridiculous scope of this—she and Bel on the run from the FBI and a serial killer, hidden messages from Emily Dickinson, shadowy organizations wiping out women, an impending assassination—she thought back to Grace's apartment, and the blood, which had been as real as her legs.

Salem felt, surprisingly, a fire begin to burn in her belly. Fear alchemizing to anger. "I've been thinking about the lightning bolt Emily refers to, the thing that can take down the Hermitage. It must be some sort of paperwork, something that would expose their origins, or the murders committed in its name back in Jackson's time. It would be too ancient now to destroy them, probably, but it could slow them down."

"That sounds like a plan," Ernest said.

"Hey, can I ask you something?" An unclosed loop had been niggling at Salem since she'd met Ernest.

"Yup."

"How'd you know what room we'd be in at the Hawthorne?"

He kept his eyes on the road. "Like I said, I followed you. Man, you two looked scared."

Bel shot him the stink eye, and he held up a hand. "I don't blame you. That guy following you for sure works for the Hermitage. You were so busy watching for him that you didn't see me. I was right behind you when the Hawthorne front desk guy told you your room number. All that was left was figuring out a way to get you to let me in."

Salem stuck the end of a curl in her mouth and chewed. "And Dr. Keller is in the Underground?"

Ernest adjusted his sunglasses. "Yep. I never know who's who until they call me. They phone when they need someone in Massachusetts, like when your mom came, and they give me a code word before they fill me in."

She rubbed her neck. Her body hadn't grown accustomed to sleeping in a car so much as resigned itself to the tweaking coil of mobile slumber. They continued to drive directly west, cutting a shaky diagonal across the country, following 1-90 until it became I-80 in northern Ohio. East Coast fall morphed to Midwest winter turned to Southwest canyons. They stopped only for food, gas, and the bathroom, alternating drivers between the three adults. They held to the speed limit, as Ernest was the only one in possession of his driver's license. At least, Salem hoped he had one.

The four of them fell into a quiet camaraderie. Salem used some of their cash to buy Mercy a coloring book and sharp, perfect crayons—no doll yet, but she'd get the child one soon, as soon as they stopped somewhere other than a gas station—and a bag of M&M'S. When they were in the back seat together, Salem taught her math and gave her a smooth, bright candy for each question she answered correctly.

Bel had bought an "I heart Iowa" T-shirt on the way through the state and had worn it since, her hair in a twist on top of her head, her face makeup-free. Ernest mostly kept to himself, making sure everyone selected their gas station foods before paying for everything, including his beloved ranch sunflower seeds with a side of Dr Pepper. Bel was progressively thawing toward him, Salem could see it. Bel was taking Ernest under her wing, punching his arm playfully, even opening up a little bit about her job as a police officer.

That made Salem happy.

The last time Salem had been awake, before the catnap featuring her dad, the Honda had been crossing from Nevada into the forests of eastern California. Now, she didn't know. Mercy was buckled next to her, staring out the window. Salem tucked a loose chunk of the girl's hair behind her ear and leaned toward the front. "Where are we?"

Bel glanced at her in the rearview mirror. "Sacramento, sleepyhead. An hour and a half east of San Francisco. We need gas, and I've had to pee for two hours."

The gas station they were pulling into was an ugly plug of cement off the highway next to an industrial park. They'd stuck to no-name stops the entire trip, not really agreeing to it beforehand, just all three of them independently deciding to keep as low a profile as possible. Bel pulled up to the nearest pump.

The sun was just rising. Salem stepped outside into air that was California-cool, an earthier chill than they'd felt on the East Coast. She waited until Mercy came around the side of the car, grabbed her hand, and walked toward the gray building. Ernest began to wash the windshield. Bel sped past to reach the bathroom first. They had a routine.

Mercy ran to the carrel of magazines just inside the gas station door. She turned it. It made a creaking sound. Salem peeked through the glass partition dividing the cash register from the rest of the dusty store. She smiled at the man behind the counter. He was watching TV and didn't acknowledge her.

Salem let Mercy pick out a word find book, cheese crackers, and an orange juice.

"Hey, Mercy, do you think we can get through today eating only orange food?"

Mercy screwed up her face, so Salem tickled her to elicit a giggle. She grabbed a cheese stick and some cashews for herself. They walked to the front counter and set their bounty on it. Still, the man ignored them. Salem raised her hand to knock on the glass when she spotted her own face on his television set.

It was her senior photo.

Her hair was bigger, and she wore cat's-eye makeup, but it was unmistakably her.

"... *for the planned assassination of Senator Gina Hayes. Both women are believed armed and dangerous and on the run. You are asked to call the authorities if you have any information on them. Do not attempt to* ..."

Salem was backing away from the partition, her hand still in the air, the knock unfinished.

"Salem?" Mercy asked. "You didn't pay. I want my word book."

The man finally turned. His eyes were tired and rheumy behind the glass. He didn't recognize her immediately, but then Bel appeared at Salem's side, smiling.

"Not the worst bathroom I've ever seen," she said brightly.

The man's glance flicked from his TV, which now displayed Salem's senior and Isabel's police academy photos side by side, and back to the women.

"Salem?" Bel asked. "You okay?"

Salem shook her head, but no words came out. Quicksand was welling up from the floor, sucking her down. She grabbed Bel with one hand and Mercy with the other and backed toward the door.

"Salem!" Mercy pouted. "I want my book!"

The man reached for the phone.

"Go!" Salem yelled.

CHAPTER 72

San Francisco

Switching out the Civic for a Toyota RAV4 cost them an hour, but they had no choice. A quick search with their phones showed their cross-country run was one of the top trending stories, right next to a rap star getting married, Senator Hayes's next speaking appearance, and the recovering economy. As they pulled into San Francisco, every glance from a passing driver felt like it lingered too long. It made Salem itchy. She wanted to locate Beale's keytext and get the hell out of this city.

She'd never traveled to San Francisco before, of course. Even in her stressed state, she had to admire how pretty it was as they descended 1-80. They drove up almost-vertical hills, the clanging of streetcar bells filtering in their open car windows, followed by the *clack clack clack* of the trolleys and the sounds of gears grinding.

Ernest followed the GPS instructions up Nineteenth Street toward Mission Dolores Park.

Scrubby acacia and palm trees skirted the perimeter of the park, and beyond those, white and gray buildings ringed the field of green like castle battlements. Dolores Park was an oasis in San Francisco's center, the bay a straight shot behind it.

"You two stay inside the car," Bel commanded Mercy and Ernest. "Be ready to drive away if we come running."

"There it is!" Mercy pointed through the two front seats. "I see a bell!"

Salem spotted it, too, a pewter-colored ornament at the entrance to the park, a rolling expanse of grass falling away behind and to each side of it. The bell was suspended in a white cement U, the whole structure no more than ten feet high top to bottom. They'd be able to peer inside the bell without stepping on their tiptoes.

Salem's itching morphed into a humming. "It can't really be that easy, can it?"

"It's about time something is." Bel glided out of the car as soon as it stopped. Salem followed her, the warm sunshine working its way through her greasy curls to massage her scalp. The ocean smelled different here than in Massachusetts, more lake than sea, at least from where Salem was standing. The park was already filling up. It was a sunny Saturday morning with a predicted high of sixty-six degrees. Frisbee, soccer, dog walking.

Salem had learned her lesson back at the Amherst Police Department: walk like you know what you're doing.

"Take my picture!" She tossed a smile in her voice and stepped onto the white stand of the U. She peeked inside the bell. Smooth metal. She ran her hand around the interior, just to be sure, but it was solid. She gonged it with her hand. The low *ting* garnered a stare from a couple walking by. Salem pulled her hair over her face and pretended to pose for Isabel and waited for them to pass.

When the couple was no longer looking their way, Salem ran her hand over the cool exterior of the metal bell, feeling for any abnormality. Was that guy with the Frisbee staring at them funny? She kept working, sweat sliding down her spine. The bell seemed solid. She turned her attention to the wood that held it, which was slatted and old-looking. Potentially, it could be disguising any number of secret messages.

Was the Frisbee man taking out his cell phone while ogling her and Bel?

Salem ignored the fear-thump of her heartbeat and stepped off the stand so she could get a better look at the whole unit.

The man with the Frisbee and the phone was most definitely staring at them. He called over a friend and pointed at her and Bel. Salem's heartbeat moved to her throat.

She turned to Bel.

"I see it," Bel said. "Hurry."

Salem nodded and faced the bell again, the commemorative plaque at her feet. She scanned it and choked when she got to the last line: PLAZA AND MONUMENT PRESENTED TO THE CITY OF SAN FRANCISCO BY LIC. GUSTAVO DIAZ ORDAZ, PRESIDENT OF THE UNITED MEXICAN STATES, SEPTEMBER 16TH, 1966.

"No." The word came out low and long, air leaving a tire.

Bel stepped to her side, her voice worried. "What is it?"

"This bell." Salem pointed her chin toward it. Her dad had taught her better than this, and yet she'd fallen for the oldest trick in the book: seeing what she wanted to see rather than what was really there. She should have researched more, but it had all fallen into place so neatly that she hadn't questioned this location for the SF Dolores Bell.

"This is a replica crafted in the 1960s. No way could Thomas J. Beale have hidden anything here."

Salem's blood had been replaced with powder.

The man who'd been watching them had dropped his Frisbee and finished his phone call, and was walking toward them with his friend, his expression grim.

Salem and Bel speed-walked back to the car, heads down, and told Ernest to hustle off and not look back.

CHAPTER 73

Chinatown, San Francisco

San Francisco's Chinatown was the first in North America. When the twenty-four-square-block enclave was established in 1848, it was the only place the Guangdong immigrants were allowed to live.

Founded on the fruit of laborers, spiced with world-famous madams and disciplined, bloodthirsty tongs, the stew remained to this day an exotic microcosm of tea shops, pagoda roofs, temples, stores selling cheap jade and fans, butchers who threw nothing away, and a vibe almost like sorcery.

Salem felt more at home here than she ever had anywhere.

It was disorienting. It was also exhilarating, with so much going on that it became its own soothing white noise. Salem marveled at how far she'd come, not only geographically but in terms of being comfortable in her own skin. She was no longer afraid of crowds. She'd discovered there were much scarier monsters out there.

Ernest had ditched the car on Bush Street, near the famous Dragon Gate marking Chinatown's northern entrance. An autumn art fair in progress had closed off the neighborhood roads to cars.

"There *is* a dragon," Mercy said triumphantly, clambering onto one of the fierce statues guarding the green-roofed gate.

Ernest yanked her off. "That's a lion, not a dragon. It keeps the evil spirits away."

Good. We could use a lot more of that.

They passed under the gate and dived into the current of Chinatown. Salem found herself glad just to be here. She felt like she was both anonymous and a part of something, the busy crowd moving past her and with her, salmon swimming upstream together. Every one of her senses was being stroked. Clean laundry fluttered overhead, swaying and slapping in the breeze. She smelled five-spice powder, sesame oil, caught a whiff of fried fish and fragrant fruits and veggies. She heard the murmur of different dialects. When she stepped aside to let a group of kids in school uniforms pass, she almost tripped over an ancient Chinese man with a face like a riverbed. He was sitting on an upside-down milk crate playing a one-stringed instrument.

She wanted to twirl, to cover herself in Chinatown's essence.

Ernest had sworn he had a connection here, someone who could help them figure out why the trail had dead-ended. He promised his connection would also provide a place to lie low. Vida's original message and the text from her phone both had said to trust no one, but they had no choice. Ernest had been true. Hopefully, his friend would be, too.

Her stomach growled loud enough to garner a glance from Bel.

"Sounds like you have a bear in there." Mercy giggled. "Bear cave belly."

Salem shot her a wan smile. None of them had eaten since last night, and it was lunchtime. She'd never seen so much amazing food all at once, but she wasn't going to be the one to slow down the group.

Mercy didn't have that compunction. "I'm hungry," she declared.

Ernest nodded absentmindedly and hung a sharp left into a yellow-fronted shop, its windows covered with spidery red lettering. Salem would not have guessed it for a restaurant, but once inside, she spotted the naked chicken carcasses hanging from the ceiling like a 1950s comedian's set piece. The place was dingy, small, with room enough for two card tables, four chairs each, and a front counter. The smell was heaven, though—roasting garlic, smoked meat, fresh and dried herbs that spoke to her tongue and stomach directly.

Ernest placed their order without asking them. All four sat at the table nearest the door. Shortly, the same man who'd taken Ernest's order and then disappeared into the kitchen returned with four steaming plates and four sweating cans of some beverage Salem had never seen before.

Ernest pointed. "Tamarind soda." Then he dug into his food. Mercy did the same. Bel and Salem exchanged a glance and followed suit.

It was the best thing Salem had ever tasted.

Slivers of delicate chicken, crunchy-soft steamed broccoli, sautéed onions and garlic, and a squash-like vegetable Salem wasn't familiar with were all blended together in an aromatic brown sauce that tasted like home and love. A crispy pork skin crumbled over the top provided a counterbalancing texture. The rice that accompanied the meal was sticky enough to ball up and dip in the sauce, which was exactly what Salem did, following Ernest's example. She almost moaned as she swallowed it.

The tamarind drink took some getting used to, sweet like a raisin rather than treacly American soda, but it was ice cold and the carbonation balanced the thickness of the brown sauce perfectly.

The food was gone in under five minutes. Salem wondered if she'd even bothered to chew, and whether it'd be rude to lick the plate. Ernest cleared the table, sparing her that embarrassment. He slipped something to the man behind the counter, and they dived back into the river of Grant Avenue.

Ernest kept to the road, where the foot traffic was lighter but the noise of throngs still constant. He weaved around white tents featuring local artisans—painters, potters, candlemakers. He led them past a market featuring enormous glossy fish, their silver heads still intact. In a cardboard box below, tiny crabs crawled over one another to escape, the whole pile tipping backward short of the brim. Another store, narrow as a hallway, was lined with hundreds of tiny drawers, floor to ceiling. The single counter inside held large glass lab bottles stuffed with powders and leaves.

Just past the Ocean Pearl Restaurant ("Best Snails in San Francisco"), Ernest hoisted Mercy on his back so they could travel more quickly. Salem and Bel hung close. Abruptly, he dipped into an alley. A wall of reflective sunglasses had caught Salem's eye and she would have missed his turn if Bel hadn't tugged her by the shirt.

"What's down here?" Bel asked.

She was answered by a smell—the delicious perfume of cookies fresh out of the oven. Ernest pointed overhead and ducked under a tiny green awning, GOLDEN LUCKY FORTUNE COOKIE COMPANY printed on it in one-inch letters. The factory would be nearly impossible to locate if a person weren't looking for it.

The vanilla and sugar aroma was even stronger inside the wee front room. An Asian woman, her hair more gray than black, walked under the cloth separating the foyer from the back at the tinkling sound of the front door.

She stopped and stared at all four of them.

Her brow furrowed and her lips tightened. Salem glanced from the woman to Ernest. He still held Mercy piggyback. His eyes were pleading.

Her accent was thick but her English unmistakable. "You bring president killers into my business?"

Lu informed them that the broccoli chicken they'd eaten at Ping's earlier was trash, sautéed shit and vegetables that Ernest never should have fed them. That's how she talked.

"I will make you real food." She'd hugged them a lot since they'd arrived, treating Bel and Salem like long-lost daughters. "I met both your mothers. Yes. Great women." She winked at Salem. "And your father."

They were in her kitchen—not the factory kitchen she used to bake the fortune cookies, but the smaller one in her upstairs apartment.

Mercy was napping on an overstuffed couch upholstered with windmills and tulips, Ernest snoring next to her. The entire second floor was a cacophony of cultures and colors, kitsch and castoffs.

Lu hadn't stopped talking since they'd arrived three hours earlier. She wasn't mad that they had come here. It was the opposite. She was angry that Ernest hadn't brought them to her immediately. She wasn't the head of the Underground, but Salem got the impression that she was close to it. She seemed to know everything about everyone.

"You knew my dad? Daniel Wiley?"

"Yes. A good man. He recruited both your mothers for the Underground when they were only in high school." Lu stopped stirring the luscious-smelling pot of broth, lemongrass, and shrimp. "He made furniture for the Hermitage."

Salem and Bel swapped the same dumbfounded glance. "He worked for the Hermitage?"

Lu clucked her tongue. "He worked for *us*. He told those men where to hide their secrets. He told us, too." She cackled. "We went in and got what we needed when we could. And bugs! We put plenty of bugs in the furniture." Salem cast a doubting look around the kitchen. The most high-tech item was an electric can opener. Lu grabbed a clean spoon from the counter without breaking her stir and swatted Salem with it. "You don't think this is fancy. It's not. It's my kitchen. The technology is in back."

"Computers?" Salem asked hopefully.

"And other things." Lu's gaze grew secretive.

"Can I look at them?"

"Later!" Lu said, too loud for the small room. "Now, you eat."

She carried the steaming pot from the stove and poured savory broth and plump shrimp into each of their bowls. Gliding to the fridge, she yanked out a tray of tiny blue quail eggs and cracked two in each of their soups. The hot broth poached the whites immediately, turning them milky. Finally, she drizzled lime juice over the top and stood back.

Salem wasn't sure whether to dig in. She didn't want to get swatted again. Bel seemed unsure as well.

"Eat!" Lu yelled. She settled into a chair across from them, smiling like a proud mother as the two women slurped the soup. Her short hair was permed, her eyebrows shaved and penciled in, her lipstick a fire-engine red. She wore a *Twilight* T-shirt and yoga pants. "Good, eh?"

It was better than good. It was heaven. The broth flowed into Salem's depths, filling her with warmth, the citrus-scented chicken broth as sweet and glowing as the sun. When Salem bit into one of the quail eggs, the rich, creamy yolk added an impossibly lush layer to the already complex flavors. She could tell the way that Bel was chewing, her eyes closed in ecstasy, that she had just tried one of the eggs in her own soup.

"You like it!" Lu sat back, satisfied. Then, like a rerouted train, her mood switched. She scrunched her face and pointed at Salem and then Bel. "So, why did the two of you never join the Underground? Did you think you were too good?"

"No!" Bel set her spoon down. "We'd never heard of it. Our moms didn't tell us that it existed."

Lu nodded and stroked her chin. "That's what I thought. They protected you. Or they *thought* they did." She tapped her head. "No one is safe if one woman is unsafe. No one. You young kids. You think you don't have to fight for anything. You think it's always been this way. But we fight, us old ladies."

"It's not like that," Salem objected, but Bel talked over her.

"We're fighting now." Her voice was deadly serious. "We've been on the run since Monday. We don't know if our mothers are even alive."

Lu stood. Salem thought she might yell again, but instead, the smile returned to her face, as if they'd just passed a test. "Yes. You're fighting now. But first you eat, little birds. Then you shower. You two smell like unhoused people and crotch. Then I'll show you the computers and we'll make you look different so you don't get arrested, and then you'll go to the *correct* SF Dolores Bell."

"There's two?" Salem asked, barely able to refrain from sniffing at her armpits.

"Of course," she said, as if Salem had just asked if the sky was high. "You went to Mission Park and looked at their silly bell. You should go to *Dolores Mission*, three blocks from where you were. That Dolores has been there for hundreds of years. Before the Chinese, even."

"Does it have bells?"

"Three. Outside, on the second level, for all the world to see."

Lu's tiny bathroom was decorated with a Nemo shower curtain, an orange bathroom mat, and bleach-stained towels in jewel tones. The inset medicine cabinet had a mirror front. As Salem peeled off her reeking clothes, she thought back to her last shower. Five days ago? The cargo pants and T-shirt she'd been wearing the entire cross-country drive had taken the shape and smell of her body. She dropped them onto Lu's bathroom floor and stepped into the most delicious shower of her life.

When water met body, the steam and heat melted her, washing the crust from her eyes, massaging the tight knots in her shoulders, creating hot rivulets that followed the curves of her belly, running between her thighs, washing gently down to her feet. She ran her hand over her stomach, marveling at its flatness. She'd been developing a computer programmer's pooch, but a near week of adrenaline and sporadic access to food had erased it.

She lathered her hair first. After they'd finished the soup, Bel had trimmed Salem's curls into a short bob. Salem was amazed at how little time it took to suds up her shorter hair. Lu's shampoo was cheap, but the ginger grapefruit seemed like the sweetest nectar Salem had ever smelled. She tipped some into a washcloth and used it to scour away road dirt, dark odors, and accumulated fear. The water washing into the drain went from a dirty brown to clear, and still she scrubbed until her flesh felt raw and new. Then she shaved her legs. Bel had warned her she might need a machete, but her stubble had grown in soft and came off cleanly.

She'd been in the shower so long that it was almost out of hot water when Bel, who'd already showered, entered the bathroom. "Better than an orgasm, right?"

Salem sighed by way of response, reluctantly shutting off the water and reaching around the Nemo curtain for a towel. She dried her bob, thinking she could get used to the ease of the short hair. She wrapped the towel tightly around her upper chest and slid the curtain open with a sharp *whisk*.

Bel stood in front of the mirror, wiping off the condensation. "Rachel would have loved this." The foggy swirls of the mirror were reflecting a short-haired brunette Bel. Before her shower, Salem had dyed her friend's hair light brown with a box kit Ernest had brought them and then hacked most of it off, leaving one inch. It stuck up in the back around the queen of all cowlicks.

"Would have?"

Bel nodded. "I think that relationship might have run its course."

Salem smiled happily and stepped out of the shower to stand behind Bel. "I didn't like her."

"Really?" Bel made a mock *no way* face. "I couldn't tell. Except wait, didn't you come right out and *tell* me so the only time you met her?"

"You asked me!" Salem's indignation would normally have caused her curls to fly into her eyes, but not any longer. They were too short, drying in an alarming fright wig pattern, a few canary-in-the-coal-mine curls beginning to break free of the weight of water and test the air atop her head.

They locked eyes in the mirror. Bel opened her mouth to argue. A laugh escaped instead. "You look like Buckwheat."

Salem was going to protest but caught her own reflection. She chuckled. The mirth was contagious, inciting more giggles from Bel, the first in days, and they grew to a full-on belly laugh. Soon, Salem and Bel were doubled over, sweet tears leaking out their eyes, howling so hard they could hardly speak.

"Or maybe you look more like Screech," Bel finally managed.

Salem nodded in complete agreement as she pictured the lead from their favorite high school TV show, a cramp forming in her stomach from the laughter. Still, the giggles rolled on. "You did such a terrible job cutting my hair!" she managed to choke out.

"I really did!" Bel squealed. "But at least you look old enough to drive a car."

That set off a new wave of howls. They'd have laughed all night if Lu hadn't knocked on the door.

"You girls are too loud! This is not a party!"

"Sorry," Salem said, trying to hold her breath to halt the laughter. She snorted instead. They had the funeral giggles, which had to run their messy, healing, hilarious course. "It's getting a little hairy in here."

Bel punched her arm, wiping laugh tears from her eyes. "That's dumb."

Salem giggled in agreement.

"You know," Bel began.

"Yes?" Salem said, falling onto the closed toilet seat to ease her side.

"I love you."

"Olive juice too!" Salem said, harking back to a joke they'd passed around in junior high. If you mouthed "olive juice," it looked just like you were confessing your love. They'd do it to the boys, and laugh and prance away. Salem waited for Bel to return it, or begin laughing again, but she didn't. "Bel?"

"I'm serious." And she was. The happy tears were still on her face, but the laughter was erased. She faced Salem, placing her hands on her bare shoulders, and looked her straight on, the short, dark hair making her appear waifish. "I would do anything for you, Salem. I *will*. I don't know which of our mothers—"

"Stop." Salem's mirth disappeared.

"No, I have to say this." She swallowed. "I don't know which of our mothers is still alive, but my heart tells me it's yours."

Salem's hand flew to her mouth.

"And I will survive that, because you will be by my side."

Salem tossed her head side to side. "Grace is fine."

"I don't think she is, Salem. You've heard everyone talk, Ernest, Lu. Vida's the leader of the Underground. It makes sense to keep her alive. She'd be more of a bargaining chip."

Salem wanted to argue but couldn't find the words.

"You and me forever, right?" Bel held out her index and pinkie finger in the blood sister's salute they'd invented about the same time as "olive juice."

Salem touched her identical fingers to Bel's and sighed. "They should have told us, you know?"

Bel's sweet blue eyes deepened. Salem thought the lines around her mouth were new. She looked older than her twenty-nine years. "Our parents?" she asked.

"Yes." A hot pool of emotion was swirling inside Salem. "Our entire childhood was a lie, you know? They knew about this world, and they hid it from us, left us to discover it on our own."

"You heard Lu. They were trying to protect us."

"That made sense when we were little girls, Bel. Not now that we're grown women. They manipulated us. They chose what was easier for them, not what was best for us." Her voice was spiraling upward. "They didn't have to stay in the Underground. They didn't have to risk our lives. One of our moms didn't have to die."

"Stop." Bel's eyes were blazing, her voice sharp. "They did the best they could. What's done is done. There is no advantage in looking backward."

For the first time in her life, Salem felt like she understood people better than Bel. Or maybe she was behaving like a child. She was too exhausted, too disoriented to know the difference. "All right."

"It *is* all right," Bel said. "Or at least it will be. Let's get to work and save Vida."

Salem watched Bel exit the bathroom. She stayed behind to clean up. She needed to collect herself. She tossed her road clothes into the trash, tugging on the clean underwear, sports bra, khakis, and surprisingly low-key peasant blouse that Lu had provided. They actually fit reasonably well, the pants loose around her slimmed-down waist. She ran through the plan as she dressed. Now that she and Bel had disguised themselves, Ernest would drive them to Dolores Mission, where an evening wedding guaranteed a large crowd and relative anonymity.

Mercy would stay behind.

Once they'd recovered Beale's keytext from the bell, they would return to Lu's, where she promised them she would show them the "best computer bank in the world." Salem would use it, hopefully, to crack Beale's Cipher, and she, Ernest, and Bel would fly to Virginia, where the treasure was rumored to be. They would use the cracked cipher to pinpoint the treasure's location, retrieve it, and bring it back to Chinatown. Lu would know what to do with it, how to use it to save whichever of their mothers was alive. Mercy would continue to stay behind for her own safety. The girl deserved at least one day without running.

Salem thought for a moment about stealing a look inside the medicine cabinet. What could a woman as resourceful and unique as Lu stock inside?

What the hell. Small satisfactions, you know?

Salem opened it and peeked inside. Noxzema, a toothbrush, whitening toothpaste, and a tube of rash cream.

Huh.

She was closing it quietly when the door was yanked open and Bel stuck her head in, eyes wide.

"You have to come see this. Now."

CHAPTER 74

Chinatown, San Francisco

Agent Lucan Stone stood just inside the Powell Street grocery store on the northwest end of Chinatown. When he'd spotted a short-haired, brunette Isabel Odegaard through the second-story window, there was only one reasonable reaction.

"Well, I'll be damned."

Clancy Johnson was in downtown San Francisco with Senator Hayes's people, going over the plans for the Alcatraz speech in two days. No one liked it. The optics would be brilliant—talking about prison reform on one of the starkest piles of rock in the country—but dropping Hayes on an island was a logistical nightmare. Stone didn't envy the Secret Service in charge of that security detail. Realistically, there was nothing Clancy or Stone could do to help, but the government liked to stack everything one (or a hundred) too high.

Stone knew his speedy rise through the FBI ranks had pissed off a lot of agents he'd stepped over. He'd made peace with that. He wasn't in the field to placate colleagues.

He was here to make his mother proud.

She'd died before he graduated Quantico, even before he'd gone to college, the victim of a heart attack.

"Life gives you defeats," she'd say, "but don't ever let yourself be defeated."

That had gotten him through the first year after her death. Her second favorite saying, "Life doesn't work unless you do," earned him a full ride to college, and his 4.0 GPA opened the door to Quantico. Turned out growing up in the streets of Detroit had prepared him well for FBI training. After that, there was no secret to his success. He worked hard, he listened to his gut like his mother had taught him, he always made good on his word, and when possible, he kept his mouth shut and eyes and ears open. That's how he'd acquired the tip that had sent him here, across the street from the Golden Lucky Fortune Cookie Company.

According to Stone's contact in the NSA, a female agent he traded intel with (and sometimes more), the NSA had been collecting SIGINT from the Golden Lucky ever since a protocol search had intercepted unusual emails being sent from their server, messages containing words guaranteed to draw the government's attention: *state of emergency, executions, terrorism, Iraq, North Korea, fundamentalism.* The communications, once decoded, were vague enough that the NSA assumed they were still a code within a code, things like *the fundamentalists are funding North Korea, the executions have begun.*

The messages were not yet grounds for a search warrant, but they were suspicious, coming from a fortune cookie factory.

But then came words that spoke directly to Stone's current mission—*Gina Hayes assassination, Vida Wiley, Isabel Odegaard,* and one that threw him for a loop even though he'd read the decoded message four different times: *the Hermitage.* The NSA cross-referenced their files, found Stone and Clancy assigned to the Wiley and Odegaard case, and Stone's contact passed on the intel. Stone had skipped out on Clancy's San Francisco snipe work with Hayes to follow up on the lead, and here he was, discovering a whole lot more at the Golden Lucky than he'd bargained for.

"How about that."

Salem Wiley had just passed in front of the same second-story window as Isabel Odegaard, her hair short enough to send her corkscrew curls into a straight-up halo, but it was her, nonetheless. Stone's heart thudded. He hadn't thought he'd ever see her again, not since he received word that she and Odegaard had escaped from the Amherst holding cell. He'd almost laughed when he'd heard about their prison break. Those two were either the worst double agents or the best women on the run he'd ever encountered.

Wiley and Odegaard squatting inside Golden Lucky spun the NSA's findings in a new direction. It also made Stone dislike even more the fat-fingered suit across the street.

The man'd been leaning against the melon stand adjacent to the Golden Lucky for far too long. Stone didn't care for the lethal, compact shape of the man, or the girth of his fingers, each like a muscled sausage. Stone guessed from the way he squeezed an exerciser in each that his digits were as strong as they appeared.

The sun was beginning its downward trajectory. Stone estimated he had half an hour of natural light left. The creeping twilight brought out the natural witchiness that he'd always felt in San Francisco's Chinatown. He possessed a healthy respect for the culture of the place, and there was a lot of it—people taking care of each other, family secrets passed down through the women, medicine that treated your spirit as much as your body. It reminded him of his MawMaw, his mother's mother, who cooked her own salve out of almond oil, beeswax, and boiled herbs. He could recall the acrid, green scent at will, and craved it even to this day when he was cut or burned.

An exultant yell caught his attention, yanking him out of his MawMaw memories. He glanced out the window to the north, up Powell. A parade was starting, probably forming to celebrate the art festival. Like most in displaced, close-knit communities, the people of Chinatown would find any reason to celebrate, and they'd do so often. Children in red silk robes led the parade. Behind them, four women in heavy white face paint and ornate headdresses followed, and to the rear of that, one of Chinatown's famous parade dragons rippled and swelled, spitting sparklers running the length of it, tossing hot bits of light into the street.

He needed to figure out what he was going to do about Wiley and Odegaard and soon. They were known fugitives, and with the parade, this street was going to be chaos in a matter of minutes.

"Can I help you?"

Stone glanced at the shopkeeper. He'd been standing in this exact spot for twenty minutes, taking up valuable space.

"Sorry," Stone said. "Can I buy some mango juice?"

"In back." The man pointed toward a cooler humming against a far wall and returned to his till.

Stone nodded. His phone buzzed, and he yanked it out of his pocket as he turned back to the window. The fat-fingered man was also pulling his phone out and gluing it to his ear. A chill passed through Stone. Why did he feel like they were both about to talk to the same person? But of course that was impossible. Caller ID told Stone that his SAC was on the other end of his line.

"Hello."

"Stone, where are you?"

Stone didn't answer immediately. He couldn't. Across the street, a dozen men in full SWAT gear were swarming upstream from the parade and toward the Golden Lucky Fortune Cookie Company factory, silent as mice, lethal as deathstalker scorpions.

CHAPTER 75

Chinatown, San Francisco

Salem hurried out of the bathroom after Bel. "What is it?"

"I can't even describe it to you. You won't believe it."

Salem followed her across the apartment, weaving around the old couch, to the north end of the building. She noticed, for the first time, that Lu had pasted a strip of wallpaper imprinted with a photo of molding just below the ceiling in every room. They reached a door, its paint chipping, a red scroll emblazoned with gold lettering covering the worst of it. Bel tossed Salem a loaded glance, grasped the rusted doorknob, and turned.

Salem felt the heat of the computers before the door was fully open. Inside the room, the familiar smell of charged ions and stationary people greeted her. A tower of green lights to her left told her that Lu had her own server, which made sense given the ten computers inside, each one with its own person typing furiously.

The space was dark except for the glow of ambient lights, quiet but for the sound of fingers clacking on keyboards and the hum of a heavy-duty air conditioner near the server. The windows must be painted on the inside to keep any natural light—or prying eyes—from leaking in. Salem thought she heard music outside the building, but there was no way to know.

"If this doesn't teach me once and for all not to judge someone by how well they speak English, then nothing will," Bel whispered into

Salem's ear. "See the ID maker over there, by the camera? This is a full-service lab."

"Out of my way!" Lu pushed past Salem to stand over the shoulder of a portly Asian man wearing round glasses. She commanded in Chinese that he do something. At least that's what it sounded like.

Salem coughed to get Lu's attention. "I thought you weren't going to show us the computers until we returned from the Mission."

"We got new information," Lu said without looking away from the man's computer screen. "Made it extra urgent that you get the code before Gina Hayes comes to Alcatraz. The Hermitage plans to kill her there. I'm eccentric, not stupid. I need to know if these computers work to break Beale's code so we don't waste time."

"You have to tell the police," Bel said.

Lu rolled her eyes. "No idea whose side they are on. I told Hayes, and she did not even care. She said they are trying to kill her all the time, so what makes Alcatraz special?"

Salem cocked her head. "You know Gina Hayes?"

"Duh. Now you tell me—are these computers good for you?"

Salem walked over. The man was working on an HP Spectre laptop. It appeared to be the old model but running quickly. Next to him, a woman with her hair tied up in a pink bandanna typed on a Mac. "I can't be sure until I see the keytext, but if it has access to the internet and is fast, I'm sure it'll work fine."

If the cipher is even crackable. People have been trying for 150 years.

But she didn't see a reason to express her doubts. Instead, she tried to peek at what the man was typing, but he had a privacy screen that made it impossible to read his screen unless she looked at it dead on. "Is everyone here working for the Underground?"

Lu's eyes were sharp and black. "Yes."

Bel stepped next to Salem. "What are they doing?"

Lu sighed. She was wearing a 49ers T-shirt, sweatpants, and men's slide sandals in a camouflage pattern over Christmas socks. "Depends. Sometime, we intercept messages. Other days, we move groups of women and children to hiding, lobby for women's causes, deliver crisis supplies where needed. Mostly cleanup. We'd like to be in front of the horse rather than behind one of these days." She smiled. It creased the corners of her eyes.

Salem indicated the computers. "Who pays for all of this?"

"Bad guys are not the only ones with money." Lu full-on cackled this time. Then her switch flipped, exactly like it'd done earlier in the kitchen. "You know someone tried to kill Hayes in Iowa?"

Salem nodded. "We heard it on the radio driving here. Was that the Hermitage?"

"We don't think so. When it is the Hermitage, they don't fail. We think they are going to try something else. We got a text."

What was it that Salem saw behind Lu's eyes? "Who was the text from?"

Lu glanced away. "No matter. You have your plan. If the computers look okay, you should go to Dolores Mission. Now."

"All right," Salem said. "Should we—"

The commotion outside the painted-over windows became louder. At first, Salem thought it was more music, but then she realized it was coming from inside the fortune cookie factory.

"SFPD! Come out with your hands up!"

CHAPTER 76

Chinatown, San Francisco

Every one of Lu's computer workers responded to the takedown like they'd rehearsed for it. Two women and two men ran outside the room. A fifth followed to the doorway, locking the door behind them, sliding a second door made of soldered iron bars over that, and then locking it as well.

"The people who ran out? They are stalling for you." Lu patted Salem's bottom and pointed toward the opposite wall. "You go out the window."

"What?"

Lu nodded, smiling. "Don't worry. There is a fire escape out there. SFPD come up through the living room. Maybe they are also on the roof, so be small. Blend in."

"Why is SFPD here?" Bel was following Lu to the window.

Lu shrugged. "Slow day. Sometimes, they just want to come check on us." She pointed at the five people still on their computers, each of them leaning to work two machines simultaneously. "We only need seven minutes to hide everything. They will find nothing but a digital mah-jongg club, no gambling, when they get here!"

Her laugh was punctuated by the screech of Bel forcing open the window.

A flood of cool air and the refreshed smell of baking cookies flowed in. The discordant Chinese music below was almost too loud to be heard over. "A parade! You so lucky," Lu said, exaggerating her accent. "Like the fortune cookie. Now go."

She stepped aside and shoved Bel out onto the fire escape. Bel scanned the perimeter, assessing the situation, before offering her hands to Salem.

"My damn gun is back in the room," Bel muttered. "I almost don't deserve one."

Salem stepped onto the fire escape, too scared to respond to that. "Is this a good idea?"

They were perched a story above the sidewalk, floating over a group of boys who waved red ribbons and wore red and gold silk robes. Salem's eyes followed the long, looping dragon behind the boys, four men wide and at least fifty feet long. Sparklers glittered and popped inside its nostrils, and ornately dressed soldiers flanking the dragon set off small fireworks that erupted green and blue in the sky. These were met with cheers from the throngs on the crowded sidewalks. The setting sun added to the visual noise, raspberry dusk blending with caramel celebration.

"I don't even know what a good idea looks like anymore," Bel said, shoving on the fire escape's rusty metal ladder to release it to street level. It wouldn't give. She kicked at it. It yelled back at her and moved an inch. "Help me!"

Salem began kicking the ladder along with Bel. A few of the parade children glanced up as heavy rust flakes rained down on them.

From inside the apartment, violent knocking sounded on the other side of the caged door. The noise was muffled by the volume of the parade, but Salem still heard it.

"SFPD, we know you're in there! Open the door or we'll break it down."

"Hurry," Salem begged.

Bel knelt so she could put her shoulder to the ladder. Salem did the same. They pushed until sweat broke out on their foreheads, but it wasn't budging. The dead drop was at least twenty feet.

"Get help!" Bel said.

Salem stood and turned back to the window. Lu was now seated at a computer station, all the workers typing so fast that their fingers nearly disappeared.

Suddenly, the wood of the door splintered, revealing the head of an axe.

"They're breaking down the door!"

Bel stood and peered over the side of the fire escape. "God help us, I hope we don't weigh too much."

"What?" Salem was frantic.

Bel pointed below. The parade dragon was just weaving its way under the fire escape. Salem could make out the forms of people below the rich, brocaded material of the beast. They seemed to be holding the dragon's body over their head like a blanket.

"We can't jump on them!"

The axe swung against the door again, this time sending a foot-long splinter of wood halfway across the room.

"It'll be like the parachute game in school," Bel said, leading Salem to the edge of the fire escape. "Remember? We'd all hold the edge of a parachute, and someone would roll into the middle, and we'd toss them in the air like popcorn. Their weight would be spread out. Easy peasy."

"But we didn't jump on each other's heads!"

The axe slammed through the door a third time, ripping the knob free. The wooden door opened. A masked man in all black knelt to begin work immediately on the iron bars, the only barrier between him and the computer room.

It was either stay, get arrested, and lose any chance at saving Grace or Vida; jump twenty feet to a sidewalk and crack their anklebones like toothpicks; or aim for a soft spot on the back of a parade dragon.

Salem didn't give herself time to think. She let Bel grab her hand, they both hoisted their legs over the iron side of the fire escape, and they tipped forward. They fell through music, firecracker smoke, the strident song of the parade actors, and their own yelling.

Thump. Thump.

Salem landed first, her stomach still back on the fire escape. Bel followed immediately. If they'd thought it over, they'd have spread out their weight more, but the people underneath held them as firmly as a palanquin.

"Are you okay?"

Salem nodded. The dragon's back was a thick felt. It smelled like mothballs. Underneath her, hands adjusted, and what sounded like swearing in another language assaulted her ears. She didn't blame them one bit. The dragon carried them down the parade route, jostling them above the crowd. The noise was even louder at street level, people yelling and pointing at them, music pounding, colors swirling, the sizzle of sparklers threatening them from every angle.

Bel glanced up toward the fire escape they'd just flown from, raising her voice to be heard. "The SWAT hasn't made it outside yet. I hope Lu had time to hide what she needed to hide."

But Salem didn't hear her.

Her eyes were drawn somewhere else—across the street, beneath the blue awning of Powell Grocery, and into the bemused stare of Agent Lucan Stone.

CHAPTER 77

Mission District, San Francisco

The Misión San Francisco de Asís, nicknamed Dolores Mission, Spanish for "Mission of Sorrows," was founded in 1776, making it one of the original missions in the United States and the oldest San Francisco building still standing. At the time of its construction, missions were not merely religious centers. They were settlements that housed people, contained animals, raised crops, manufactured goods, educated, and healed. At one time, the mission encompassed 125 square miles.

Bel and Salem were interested in a single building, the only remaining original construction: the adobe mission chapel, dedicated in 1791, along with its three bells: San Martín, San Francisco, and San José.

Lu had conjectured that the priests of the mission, themselves friends to the poor and dispossessed and particularly the Native population, may have been Underground members, or at least sympathetic to the cause. It made perfect sense to her that Beale would have hidden his keytext there, inside bells that would stand the test of time.

Salem and Bel stood side by side on the Dolores Street median directly facing the whitewashed adobe mission. The mission was a story and a half high. The upper level was surrounded by a copper-colored metal railing. The three bells and a short door were inset into the wall behind the balustrade.

A wedding was taking place next door, in the basilica erected over a century after the adobe chapel. People were filing into the basilica. The hosts must have been offering some sort of hors d'oeuvres to hold guests over, because white-coated caterers were unloading a van and heading toward the breezeway between the chapel and the basilica.

"Maybe we should steal one of those hats and jackets," Salem joked. "You can sneak in anywhere in a caterer's outfit."

A limo pulled up on Dolores Street, unloading six women dressed bright as peacocks along with one resplendent bride. Her strapless gown cascaded over her body, her streaming veil dusting her shoulders. The seven women were talking animatedly and laughing. Their entrance elicited applause and hollers from those assembled on the sidewalk.

"Now's a good time." Bel pushed Salem off the median. "All eyes will be on the bride. Let's sneak into the chapel."

They crossed the street. Salem had felt super-visible the whole run to the Metro station, riding the M, and walking here, as if her haircut looked as amateur as it felt. But the self-consciousness was even more acute here, surrounded by wedding guests wearing their finest and catering staff in immaculate white. Salem's frumpy hair and informal clothes felt like a beacon.

"We'll do fine," Bel said, reading her mind.

"How do you know?"

"Because we don't have a choice." Bel used her weight to yank open the mission's heavy wooden doors.

A wave of incense washed over them. The interior was glorious Spanish Baroque, with a multicolored chevron-design ceiling that reminded Salem of a pair of corduroy pants her mom used to wear. Behind the altar, a wall of bronze stations of the cross dominated the area, floor to ceiling. The church was empty except for a handful of women sitting in the front pews, their heads bent, and a single elderly woman lighting a candle. The space had an aura of song.

A spiral staircase immediately inside the door and to their right led to the second-story bells. The steps were so narrow that Bel and Salem had to climb single file. Salem was too scared to glance behind and see if any of the supplicants were watching. What would she do if they were? At the top, they crawled out a door so small they barely fit and emerged into the jasmine-scented night air.

Salem risked a glance down. They were as high as they'd been on Lu's fire escape, give or take, with no dragon below to land on. The wedding must be starting—the crowds outside the basilica were thin, and the catering van had pulled around to the side. No one seemed to be glancing their way. The only sounds were the occasional car passing or the chatter of a distant conversation. Salem studied the three bells anchored in the mission's alcove.

"Which do you think it is?" Bel remained in a crouch.

Salem pointed at the middle bell. "The San Francisco. Lu said it's the only one mounted in its original rawhide and wood bind."

Bel turned to watch the sparse crowd below. "Then get to it. You know the drill."

"Yeah," Salem muttered. "Find centuries-old messages in wood, copper, and bronze. Easy peasy." Except Beale's note couldn't possibly be inside the bell because that would affect the sound. It *had* to be concealed in the wood. Right? "Can you kneel here?" Salem asked. "I need to stand on your back."

Bel quirked an eyebrow but obliged, dropping to all fours so Salem could reach San Francisco's ancient harness. She climbed on Isabel's back and managed to shove her knee into one side of the bell's alcove, using her hand to hoist herself onto the rim of the cavity.

"Hey!" A man pushing a stroller stopped near the church door and hollered up at them. "You're not supposed to be doing that!"

"It's okay," Bel called down. She stuck her hand through the balcony and waggled it at him. "This is part of an all-city scavenger hunt. We'll be careful."

He wasn't buying it. He yanked his phone from the top of the stroller, next to the sippy cup, and started punching in numbers, pausing every second or so to glare up at them. His toddler protested the stop.

"Hurry," Bel commanded.

Salem struggled to focus. She reached for her phone and turned on the flashlight function so she could light up the area, but her hands were slippery with sweat, and she dropped the cell in the recess. She had to dig through bug carcasses and pigeon poop until she located it. She tried again, this time succeeding.

She ran the light over the bell.

San Martín and San José were big bells, colored a silver-green with age, nearly three feet long from crown to clapper, but San Francisco was half the size, more harness than bell. Her light didn't reveal anything she couldn't spot from the ground, so she shoved her cell back into her pocket and began exploring with her hands. The bell's metal was cool. She touched it gently to hoist herself higher, toward the ancient wood, smooth and grooved from decades in the elements.

"The police are on the way," the man with the now-screaming toddler informed them matter-of-factly, raising his voice to be heard over the wails.

"Thank you, sir!" Bel called down. "I'm sure the people being burglarized and assaulted will understand the reallocation of resources to two women in a harmless scavenger hunt."

"Bah." The man waved his hand and walked away.

Salem heard sirens. "That could be for anything, right?"

"Could be," Bel muttered, "if you don't consider our luck."

Salem examined the face of the wood, holding her body at an impossible angle. There were no visible hiding spots, but of course then they wouldn't be hiding spots. She strained to touch the back of the harness, grunting at the effort. She started at the bottom and ran one hand up, swallowing her pain as she embedded a splinter deep into her middle finger. She switched hands so the wounded one could anchor her, and ran her other hand up the back.

The sirens were drawing closer. "Anything?" Bel's voice was tight.

"Not yet," Salem answered. "Can you be any taller?"

"Not on all fours."

Salem tried to grow. She needed to reach the rawhide at the top of the mount, but it was an inch beyond her grasp. She stretched, adjusting her knee to buy length. She was almost there, the rawhide kissing her fingertips.

Then she slipped

Her hands wheeled in the air, scrabbling for any purchase. It was happening too quickly to scream.

Her phone fell out of her pocket in the panic, crashing below.

She grabbed the lip of the bell, catching herself at the last possible second. It *donged* solemnly. Her sweaty fingers dug into the alcove, gaining purchase, and she hugged the wall as her pulse pounded in her ears.

She paused, eyes closed, nauseated from terror.

"Salem. We don't have to do this." Bel's voice was urgent, worried.

The police sirens were almost on them.

Salem steadied her breath. She rearranged herself so she was back on her knee. She balanced so she could use both hands to feel the wood. She retraced her pattern on the face of it. This time, she felt the smallest cross-grain bump on the upper left corner, just below the leather harness. Her bleeding finger was the closest, so she pushed with it, biting back the pain.

A drawer popped open.

Salem grabbed the cool metal cylinder inside, the size and shape of a Magic Marker, didn't pause to close the drawer, and slid off Bel's back.

"I have it."

The police cars turned on the end of Dolores Street, screaming directly toward the mission.

Bel crawled toward the tiny door leading them back into the chapel, pushed it open, scuttled through, and reached back to help Salem. Everyone inside was most definitely staring at them now. Salem and Bel stood to their full height once inside, Bel's back and Salem's knees creaking, hurried down the spiral stairs, and hopped onto the main floor.

A priest was whispering to a woman at the head of the sanctuary. She pointed at Salem and Bel. The police sirens were just outside. A panic attack bubbled in Salem's belly, battery acid eroding her safety and balance. She needed to run, or yell, or simply collapse.

Bel grabbed her, her eyes darting to the front door and the back, calculating the best escape route.

The police sirens passed.

Salem and Bel exchanged a look of surprise.

The priest was walking toward them, his face an uncomfortable mixture of displeasure and kindness.

"Front door," Bel said, tugging Salem after her.

"Sorry!" Salem called over her shoulder. "We didn't hurt anything!" Outside, people were moving normally. No one was staring. There were no police. Salem grabbed the pieces of her phone from the ground and glanced up at the bell. She wished she'd closed the tiny drawer. You couldn't spot it from the street unless you were looking for it, but still. She patted the cylinder inside her jacket pocket.

"Excuse me!" Bel said to a man who bumped into her.

Salem's attention was drawn back to the moment. She glanced at the man who'd pushed Bel.

Her heart stopped. She recognized him.

CHAPTER 78

Twelve Years Old
Daniel's Last Week

"Who's buying that dresser?"

Pickup day is the first Wednesday of every other month. On that day, a white van drives down the alley to Daniel's shop, furniture is loaded out of sight, the van motors away, and Daniel's space is cleared to make new furniture. During the school year, Salem never sees the pickup happen. In the summer, Daniel makes sure she's absent on those Wednesdays, but on this one, she's sick.

A fever, nausea.

The stomach flu.

She stays home. She promises her father she won't come outside.

But her stomachache turns for the worse, and she's scared to throw up without her dad nearby. So she tiptoes to his shop.

She lets herself in. A fat-fingered man carries one end of a dresser, Daniel the other. Salem stands in the doorway, guilty, curious, sick.

"Who's buying that dresser?" she repeats.

Daniel drops his end of the furniture. The fat-fingered man doesn't change expression, but his eyes walk over Salem's twelve-year-old body like flies. Salem's face grows hot, and she glances down to make sure she's still wearing clothes.

"Salem!"

She looks back up. Daniel is scared. The fat-fingered man looks satisfied. That makes no sense. Salem runs back into the house, and she throws up.

Her dad finds her over the toilet. He wants to tell her something, she's sure of it, but instead he holds her hair away from her face and rubs her back until the spasms stop.

In the end, all he says is, "I'm sorry."

They never talk about it, and Salem never sees the fat-fingered man again. At least, not that she'll let herself remember.

CHAPTER 79

Mission District, San Francisco

The fat-fingered man stood in front of Mission Dolores, solid, wearing that same satisfied pickup-day expression that stripped Salem fourteen years earlier. His fingers were grotesque, rippled and scarred, as large as bratwurst but evilly muscled, disappearing into Bel's flesh deeper than they could possibly go without snapping bone. Bel cried out and grabbed at his wrist, trying the same move that had brought Ernest to his knees in Amherst, but the powerful man didn't flinch.

Salem pushed him. It was like shoving a concrete wall.

Another man appeared from the shadows and walked toward them. He had the same eyes—those snake eyes—as the man and the woman from Amherst but completely different features. His face was gorgeous, stunning, the immaculate image of a Renaissance angel, too perfect to look at except in short bursts. He smiled and its prettiness hurt. Salem was suffocating in his sugar.

She moaned. She couldn't force the fat-fingered man to release Bel, and she knew he intended to kill her. Salem would rather die a thousand times herself than watch it, but she felt utterly helpless. All she could do was scream from the bottom of her lungs.

A voice called out from across the street. "Salem! Isabel!"

CHAPTER 80

Upper East Side, New York

The Audubon Society was a pet project of tonight's host. He was charging $75,000 a plate for guests to mingle, dine with Senator and presidential candidate Gina Hayes, and learn about the blue-throated macaw. He'd first learned of the bird on a hunting trip to Bolivia when one of the gorgeous creatures followed his party, flying particularly close to him. When he learned the birds were endangered because their ecosystem was being destroyed by cattle ranchers, he'd asked his billionaire father to buy him a nature park in the country. He'd also taken his passion—and several birds—home with him.

On the drive to the fundraiser, Matthew Clemens labeled their host a silver-spoon hippie. "Imagine if he used all that money to save *people* rather than *birds*."

Gina watched the city stream by outside. "He's using it to help *us*."

Matthew would not be mollified. "I bet he serves chicken for dinner. Idiot."

Matthew was entitled to his opinion, but Gina didn't share it. Tonight's host wasn't spending his money on cars, or planes, or *things*. It was being spent on the environment, and she could use all the help she could get on that front. Besides, she was tired. No, she was past tired, through exhausted, and taking up residence in walking dead. She didn't have the luxury of rest, however, not this close to the election, so she strapped on her game face and stepped out of the car immediately behind her security detail.

Photos were snapped, quietly. She walked the blue carpet leading to the apartment, thinking it was a bit much. On the way, she shook hands and smiled. Inside the door, she let a woman in a black and white french maid uniform take her coat.

"Thank you."

She was led into the main room. Over one hundred people were drinking cocktails, many of the women wearing hats. *Fascinators encouraged*, the invitation had read. Hayes knew Matthew would be itching to speculate where all the feathers in the hats had been procured. He was too professional to say anything in public, of course. He was already lining up the meet-and-greet list. Gina would not stay for the dinner. She would spend an hour inside this Upper East Side mansion, speaking with the prescribed people, and then she would leave for her next event.

She would raise $1 million in that hour.

"Senator Hayes." Matthew appeared at her elbow, his voice level. "I don't believe you've had the pleasure of meeting Carl Barnaby."

Gina turned.

That Carl Barnaby was first on her meet-and-greet list meant that he had paid an extra $100,000. Gina owed him three minutes in return. She'd seen photos of Barnaby—a grandfatherly man, hair white and slicked back in that way men of the previous generation favored, shoulders still strong, clothes immaculate—but she'd never met him in person. She was surprised he'd arrange their first meeting in so public a place. She'd imagined she'd be afraid if they were ever in the same room together.

She discovered, instead, that she was curious.

"Mr. Barnaby." Gina had learned about the Hermitage at her father's knee. They'd tried to buy his ear. She didn't think they had, but with politics, even with your own father, you couldn't be sure. She'd never doubted the conspiracy theories that surrounded the organization, had in fact witnessed firsthand proof of their power and reach.

The Hermitage was the very skeleton of the political system in some countries and certainly at least a kidney in the United States government, with loyal members in the FBI, CIA, and NSA. She suspected the Hermitage was behind the Iowa assassination attempt. She knew they'd historically executed leaders of the Underground, an organization that she'd been born into and that she, along with Vida Wiley, Lu Zhang, and Grace Odegaard, currently ran.

He took her hand and shook it. "It's a pleasure, Senator. Thank you for your time."

Her eyes sparked as she realized that not only was she not afraid, she was exhilarated. *Oh yes*, she was up for this challenge. "Do you prefer small talk, the truth, or political bloviating, Mr. Barnaby?"

His gaze narrowed. "I was hoping we could chat about the Afghanistan mineral rights bill you plan to vote down. That would be a mistake."

"Really, Mr. Barnaby. Please tell me more." She examined him as he spoke, taking his measure. If she lived to reach the Oval Office, it would be because the Hermitage, an organization Carl Barnaby headed, had failed in its attempts to kill her.

She would give him the three minutes he had paid for, nothing more.

CHAPTER 81

San Francisco

Someone in the wedding party stepped out of the basilica to see what the commotion was about. The priest also walked out of the adobe mission. The street was suddenly very crowded.

The fat-fingered man gave Bel one last squeeze, then jogged to a car parked at the curb. The beautiful man followed him, rage contorting his features. They were pulling away when Agent Stone reached Salem's side.

Stone's hand was inside his coat, eyes on the departing car. "We have to go somewhere."

Salem didn't spare him a glance. "Bel?"

Bel was ashen, gripping her own arm. It hung loosely in the socket. Her voice was hoarse. "He dislocated it. He only used his thumb, and he pushed it out."

Stone stepped between Salem and Bel. "Hold her," he ordered Salem.

She grabbed Bel around the waist.

Stone held up both hands, palms out. "I'm going to touch you. This will hurt."

Bel nodded.

He placed his right hand on her good shoulder. With his left, he jerked and pushed her loose arm in one swift movement.

Bel's knees buckled, but Salem kept her upright.

Stone pushed back the cloth of Bel's jacket, revealing her shoulder. Her skin was contused, a deep purple circle over the joint. Four matching circles ridged Bel's shoulder blade.

"There's a coffee shop up the street. She needs to sit down, and we need to talk."

"Tell me what's going on."

Salem held a steaming mug of tea. Bel drank black coffee. Some of her color had returned, but she was still nursing her shoulder. Neither of them responded to Stone.

"All right, I'll start." He loosened his tie and scanned the room. "Your mothers were leaders in an organization called the Underground. Their job was to take down the Hermitage. Same with the other five women who were murdered. The Hermitage got sick of their interference and started taking them out."

He studied both women. "Ah, I was right. I wasn't sure about that last part."

Salem was too exhausted to be either excited or scared by his presence. "Are you going to arrest us?"

His eyes landed on her. "You're up against the Hermitage? You probably *want* me to arrest you. While following you here, I called in some favors to find out what the organization has been up to. Safest place for you is in jail."

"Why did the SFPD raid Lu's?" Bel's voice was sullen.

"NSA sent them, near as I can tell. They've been watching Golden Lucky for quite a while. With Senator Hayes coming to San Francisco in two days and a lot of suspicious comms leaving the factory, they had to follow through. No choice."

Bel nodded.

"Has either of you heard from your mothers?"

"We've each received a text from one of their phones," Salem said.

"But at least one of them was a lie because one of our mothers is dead," Bel muttered.

"Bel!"

Stone rested his palms on the table. "How do you know?"

Bel tried to shrug and paled with the effort. "The Underground told us. They've been right about everything else."

"Dammit." Stone sat back and rubbed the tops of his thighs, clearly weighing something.

Salem found herself able to study him dispassionately. He was handsome, his features strong, his skin smooth and dark. Normally, she'd be terrified to sit this close to him, to talk to him.

She'd been through too much to care anymore. "Help us," she demanded. "Or let us go."

He stared at her, his eyes lingering on her face. "Your cat is fine."

She laughed. She didn't know where the sound came from. "What?"

"I asked the Minneapolis field office to check on him when they searched your apartment. Your neighbor across the hall has him, and he's fine. Your cat sitter might want to be more subtle, however. He offered to sell a bag to my agent."

Salem nodded. Skanky Dave and Beans seemed like characters from a dream.

Bel came to a decision. "Salem's right. We need you to help us, or to at least let us go. You know we haven't done anything wrong or you would've already arrested us. Let us finish what we're doing. Give us until Monday."

Stone shook his head. Salem thought he was coughing but realized it was soft laughter.

"You two are going to rescue whichever of your mothers is alive and dismantle the Hermitage, one of the best-funded and most well-connected organizations in the history of the world?"

"In that order," Bel said fiercely, leaning forward.

Stone's expression grew serious. "You know what? I believe you can. Because you two are some combination of lucky, strong, and smart that I've never seen before. But I can't just let you go. It's a million to one that you've even survived this long. Plus, Senator Hayes is coming to town. No way can you roam San Francisco. Your faces are too hot, even with those disguises."

Salem's brain raced, the metal cylinder burning a hole in her back pocket. If she held Beale's keytext, they could travel to Virginia, retrieve the lightning bolt—whatever it was—and hand it over within a day. She didn't tell him about the potential assassination. Salem figured there was no point. If they took down the Hermitage before Alcatraz, Hayes would be okay. If they didn't, there was no protecting her.

"Thirty-six hours," she said to Stone.

"What?"

"Give our luck thirty-six hours. And then we'll bring you what you need to solve the murders of those five women, plus Mrs. Gladia, and take down the Hermitage."

His forehead rutted. "Will you tell me what it is that you're after?"

"We can't," Salem said, "because we don't know. Thirty-six hours."

Still, he hesitated.

"If you want to get to the roots of why those women were killed, you can't do it without us." Bel pointed to Salem. "You can't do it without *her*. In five days, she's blown through codes that have been hidden for over a century."

Stone stared at Salem. The fear of being seen and coming up short raged inside her, burning muscle off bone, but for the first time in her life, she didn't stare at her feet, didn't hide from the attention.

She held his gaze.

It was Stone who finally looked away after something passed between them.

She didn't know what, but it felt *good*.

He rubbed his chin and laughed again, this time more of a growl of amazement. "I can't believe I'm saying this, but you've got it. Thirty-six hours."

CHAPTER 82

San Francisco

"Lightning never strikes the same place twice."

Ernest was attempting to reassure Salem and Bel that the SFPD was gone as he followed them into the rear of the Golden Lucky Fortune Cookie Company.

"That's not true," Salem said quietly. "Lightning can strike any location twice."

"Did the ninjas get anything?" Bel asked, referring to the SWAT team's uniforms.

"Nope." Ernest raced ahead so he could hold the door to the second-floor apartment open for them. "Lu hid it all before they broke through. She's gonna need a new door for the lab, though. They shredded the wood one and then the metal one."

"Anyone arrested?"

"No."

"Good."

Stone had assured them that he'd do his best to keep the local police and FBI off their backs for the next day, and Salem needed computer power. Returning to Lu's made the most sense, as long as the police were gone and the computers were intact.

They met Lu in the kitchen. Her arms were crossed but her eyes were dancing. "Dragon riders come home!" She squeezed Salem's arm as she walked past. "You found a clue at the Mission, too. I can see it in your eyes."

Salem held up the cylinder and asked for dish towels. When Lu handed them to her, she made a sling for Bel and let Lu remove the splinter from her finger and bind it before marching to the computer lab.

The shards of the wooden door had been swept up and removed, and the iron prison gate was leaning against the wall, off its hinges. All ten techs had returned to their computers as if no interruption had occurred, a symphony behind the scenes, trying to stay one step ahead of the Hermitage. The window Bel and Salem had slipped out of was closed and locked.

Mercy ran across the lab and hugged Salem around the waist. "I knew you'd come back! You always do."

Salem smiled, surprised at the wave of emotion the hug elicited. She kissed the top of Mercy's head. "I missed you. What've you been up to?"

Mercy smiled at Lu. Salem realized for the first time that the girl had dimples, sweet valleys on each side of her pink rosebud mouth.

"Lu taught me how to make fortune cookies!"

"She's shit at it," Lu said, winking at Mercy. "She eats them all up before they cool. Now, enough chatter. Time to get to work."

Salem gave Mercy a squeeze before breaking free and walking to a table covered in computer parts. She stacked them to the side to clear a spot. Bel and Ernest stood at her elbow. Lu commanded someone to prepare a computer for Salem. Two techs hurried to comply.

Salem felt oddly embarrassed by all the attention.

"Can I get a lamp?" While Ernest went to grab one, Salem screwed off the cylinder's metal cap and tipped the case upside down.

Nothing fell out.

For a heart-stopping second, she wondered if someone had already retrieved the clue, but when she peeked inside, she spotted a yellowed curl of paper. Using a pen, she teased out the scroll.

Ernest plugged in and flicked on the lamp, illuminating a looping scrawl of black ink on ancient paper.

The Declaration of Independence. Second first alone.

Last first third, first and third make one. Miss Gram guards the truth.

Salem's stomach thudded into her spine. *Hell on wheels, it's another code.*

Bel's brow furrowed. "Didn't you say the Declaration of Independence had already been used to crack the second cipher? Wouldn't someone have already figured out if it was the keytext for all three?"

Exactly. And how many decades dead was this Miss Gram?

Salem pushed aside the worry that was beginning to fog the edges of her vision and stumbled to the computer that had been opened for her. A flurry of keystrokes, and she pulled up a copy of the three Beale Ciphers. She pointed at them.

"See how they're constructed? Each of Beale's three ciphertexts is a string of numbers separated by commas. In the second one, the one that's already been decoded, each number represents a word in the Declaration of Independence, and the first letter of that word is what Beale used to write his message."

She enlarged the image of the second cipher. "Check it out. The first number Beale used in the second cipher was 115. *Instituted* is the 115th word in the Declaration of Independence, so we know that the first word of the second Beale Cipher is *I*."

"What does the second cipher say?" Lu asked.

Salem cleared her throat. "It gives an accounting of all the treasure in Beale's vault—gold, jewels, and silver, worth over $60 million in today's money."

Lu whistled.

"The treasure is supposedly stored in a stone-lined vault, in massive pots, six feet underground somewhere near Montvale, Virginia, but no one has ever located it because they haven't cracked the first cipher, which is supposed to contain the exact coordinates."

"But when you had that first cipher up, it looked long," Ernest said. "Nearly as long as the second. How can it just be coordinates?"

"A lot of people have wondered the same thing." Salem sighed. "And the third cipher doesn't seem long enough to be a list of all the heirs, like the Underground legend says."

"How does the story change if you know about the Underground, and Lucretia Mott, and their hiding of the contents of Beale's vault until someone friendlier to their cause was running the country?" Bel interjected.

Salem spread out her hands. "I don't know. No one does, not without the keytext."

Lu pointed at the scroll. "It is the Declaration of Independence for all three! Dummy."

"The man who solved the second cipher tried that. So did a lot of people." Salem returned to her computer screen. "The Declaration of Independence, *Pride and Prejudice*, *Little Women*, the Bible, the Articles of Confederation, the Louisiana Purchase. Every single major document from that era, and a lot of minor ones, was tested. None of them worked. The first and third cipher remain encrypted. The innkeeper Beale entrusted with the box eventually handed all three codes over to James B. Ward in 1885. Ward published a pamphlet asking for help in solving them, and that's how everyone came to hear of the Beale Ciphers."

Lu jabbed her finger at the scroll Salem had retrieved from Mission Dolores. "Now you have the key. You figure it out."

"It's not that easy," Bel said defensively, moving closer to Salem. "This has been unbroken for a hundred and fifty years! She's not a wizard."

Lu directed a dismissive sound in Salem's direction, something like a raspberry. "I know her type. She looks fragile, but when a wave hits, she goes deep. Women have been doing it forever, the strong ones. She can sit at the computer and figure this out. It's not so hard."

Lu patted Salem's head before shuffling toward the door. "Go deep. I will make more food. You solve this." She held out her hand to Mercy. The girl ran up to her and they disappeared out the door.

That left ten strangers staring at Salem, plus Ernest and Bel. Salem drew in the deepest breath of her life. "Okay. Who has programming experience?" Four hands shot up.

She let out the breath, slow and sweet. "Wonderful. I want you guys over here helping me modify an online decrypter I created in grad school. Maybe we can program in what the scroll says and pick up a pattern I'm just not seeing. The rest of you, start googling solutions to the Beale Cipher."

A woman in a striped shirt laughed.

"I'm serious," Salem said. "Sometimes the truth hides in plain sight."

CHAPTER 83

3 East 70th Street, New York

Carl Barnaby loosened the bow tie of his tuxedo as he rode the elevator to the second basement level of the Hermitage headquarters. His computer forensics department had hauled him out of the Audubon Society dinner with a single-word text: pink. The code word indicated they had found information on the Underground, and that it was urgent. Carl hoped it was the positive kind of urgent.

Gina Hayes's condescending "audience" with him, where he had to plead his case like a supplicant, had left a bad taste in his mouth. He was of a generation that didn't call women names, but he believed his son would refer to Gina Hayes as a Class-A Bitch. Carl wouldn't miss her when she was gone.

The elevator stopped at -2. The door slid open, revealing a billiards room. Carl inserted a plastic card into a slot, and the elevator's back panel slid open directly onto the forensics lab. Abhay, head of computer forensics, rushed toward the elevator.

Carl couldn't tell if the sheen on Abhay's face was triumph or worry. "Sir!"

Carl's mind was still rolling over the Audubon event. Hayes hadn't seemed intimidated. In fact, she'd acted *confident*. "What did you find?"

"Over here."

Abhay led him to the north side of the lab, where a white LCD screen was set up. "Blake, pull it up."

Carl didn't recognize Blake. He must be a new hire. Whatever he had on his screen was coming into focus.

"What am I looking at?"

Abhay cleared his throat. "We believe you are looking at the same computer screen Salem Wiley is currently looking at."

Carl stood straighter.

"We've been monitoring all of her online activity. She logged into her University of Minnesota Dropbox account approximately twenty-four minutes ago."

"She's back in Minnesota?"

"No. San Francisco." Abhay paused for Carl to get his bearings.

"Chinatown?"

Abhay smiled. The Hermitage's computer forensics staff had been lurking on the Golden Lucky Fortune Cookie Company server since one of their best men had discovered it at the beginning of the year. They assumed the server belonged to the Underground, maybe was their technological hub, but it had so far served them better to monitor it than shut it down.

"Yes, sir."

"What's she doing?"

"We believe she's modifying a decryption software that she developed a few years ago. It's quite good, actually. NSA is using a version of it on most of their computers. It works by—sir, are you all right?"

Carl had gone the color of tapioca pudding. "The Beale Cipher."

Abhay glanced at the screen. "Yes, sir. She appears to be trying to crack it. We don't know why—maybe to access the rumored treasure to fund the Underground? But there's no way . . ."

Carl was no longer listening.

His body was ice-bath cold.

It wasn't the docket these women were after. It was the destruction of the Hermitage.

His voice sounded froggy. "We need it all."

"Sir?"

"Every word she types." He gained volume. "Save it, store it. I want the directions to Beale's vault the very minute that Salem Wiley discovers them. Understand?"

"Sir, there's no way she can, that anyone can, solve—" Abhay saw Carl's expression and gulped. "Yes, sir."

Carl turned toward the elevator. His legs carried a slight tremor. Jabbing the elevator button, he pulled out his cell phone and was unsettled to see an incoming call from his counterpart in Europe. The man would not be pleased with how the US branch of the organization was faring.

He ignored the call and punched in the number to the guard station one level below him. "I want the woman from Minneapolis taken out of her cell, bathed, fed, and sent to Jason. The two of them are going to Virginia."

So much was at stake.

He needed all boots on the ground, every chip on the table.

CHAPTER 84

Chinatown, San Francisco

There came a time in a person's life when they were shoved into the quick, that moment of truth when they found out if they were made to fly or were merely a four-legged creature putting on airs.

For Salem, that moment was now.

Hollering suggestions to the other programmers, manufacturing lines of code, her fingers flying like Mozart's over piano keys, she conducted the most important symphony of her life. Binary digits floated past her eyes. She grabbed them from the air, stuffed them in their place, stacked them like the sticks and stones they were to design the Trojan horse that would sneak through Beale's Cipher, crack it open, and deliver the glory inside.

Previously, computer life had been solitary for Salem. She'd spent thousands of hours hunched over a board marked with letters, celebrating private victories, discovering thrilling knowledge and having no one to share it with. Working in a room of people all bent toward the same goal was exhilarating. Running ahead of them and yelling back instructions, and then having someone do the same for her, energized her like never before, leapfrogged her past any level that she could have obtained on her own.

That's why when the woman in the striped shirt, Margaret, jumped out of her chair and yelled, "I got it," Salem wasn't jealous. In fact,

Salem shot out of her own chair and hooted. She was happier than she'd been in days. They all rushed over to Margaret's computer, staring over her shoulder to see what she'd discovered.

"So, I started with Beale's clue that you found in the bell." Margaret pointed at her screen. "*The Declaration of Independence. Second first alone. Last first third, first and third make one. Miss Gram guards the truth.*"

She smiled shyly. "I've been focusing on one part: *Second first alone.* I think *second* refers to the second cipher, *first* refers to the fact that the numbers of that cipher correspond to the first letter of their assigned word in the Declaration, and *alone* means that the second cipher is a stand-alone."

"That makes sense." Salem tried not to sound disappointed. The second cipher had already been decoded over a century ago.

Margaret continued. "With that in mind, I moved to the next line of Beale's clue: *last first third, first and third make one.* So, based on what I just told you, I posited that maybe the two unsolved ciphers, the first and the third, are actually one cipher spread across two separated codes."

Salem's pulse picked up. That had never occurred to her. Everyone was staring at her, but she was studying the whiteboard inside her head. Numbers were landing, words were moving, ideas were lining up.

That's where she saw it, finally, with Margaret's help: the solution to the Beale Cipher laid out as clearly as the future of quantum computing had been when the clear blue line had shone across Babbage's Vigenère cipher solution to his Differential Engine research.

She rushed back to her computer to input one more level of code to her program.

Her fingers were a blur.

"Salem?" Bel asked. She sounded anxious. "Do you have it?"

"I . . . think . . . so." She didn't slow her typing. "I'm inputting *last*, *first*, and *third*, running all those possible combinations against the

Declaration of Independence to see if the computer can find anything that looks like a—wait!"

Her exclamation brought the other programmers over.

"It's the median letter!" she yelled. "The first and third cipher are clues to alternating letters of one complete document, like Margaret said, but rather than using the first letter of a word in the Declaration like the second cipher, they use the median letter!"

"What if there's an even number of letters in the word?" Ernest sounded doubtful.

"Then it uses the letter gotten by adding the alphabetic positions of the two middle letters and dividing by two, rounding up if it's a half number, just like in math," Margaret said triumphantly, reading over Salem's shoulder. "Your program is genius, Salem!"

Except that her computer was spitting out jumbled letters that looked almost but not quite like words. Salem's balloon began to deflate. It didn't make sense. She returned to her mental whiteboard.

Miss Gram guards the truth.

She mentally studied the sentence. All the letters fell away except for four: *gram.*

She inhaled. Everyone in the lab did the same.

Just as Salem's father had taught her, the best place to hide something was always in plain sight.

Miss Gram is Ana Gram. The code is an anagram.

Salem made a final tweak to the program, adding an automatic unscrambler that would input every possible combination of a letter string to provide the most likely and recognizable English equivalent.

After completing the tweak, she only had to wait three seconds. Latitude and longitude coordinates began unspooling on her screen. She yelled with joy.

Everyone who wasn't already crowded around her rushed over.

Bel used her good hand to copy down the information.

Suddenly, Salem's computer froze.

She tried to unlock it, pushing several keys. It was still frozen.

A tiny cowboy appeared on her screen. "You're being rode, missy," he hollered, before yelling "Yeehaw!" and pixelating as he galloped off her screen.

"What happened?" Bel asked, her voice frantic.

"We were piggybacked." It felt like someone was grinding her guts. "If it was the Hermitage, they saw the same stuff we just saw. Coordinates and everything."

"Maybe not," Margaret said, racing back to her computer. "We have a thirty-second lag programmed in. Get your machine offline!"

Salem followed her instructions without question. Killing the Wi-Fi unfroze her screen, revealing that her program had decoded the entire cipher while the cowboy rode off into the horizon:

Latitude three seven point three eight four six zero four Longitude negative seven nine point seven three zero nine four five, in Bedford County, Virginia.

Here you will find the Treasure, and the Lightning Bolt, courtesy of intelligence obtained in the southern territories, notes which will take everything from Jackson and his descendants and return it to its rightful owners.

A list of names immediately followed.

The Underground leadership docket.

Salem felt her world shrinking to a pinhole as she recognized many of them: Sanger, Nightingale, Ross, Curie, Hayes.

Bel pointed at the screen. "Look."

Wiley was on the list. So was Mayfair, Ernest and Mercy's last name. Odegaard was not present, but neither was Vida's maiden name. The list was over a hundred names long.

Ernest left and brought back Lu. She read Salem's screen. The lab was as quiet as a church.

Lu spoke into the momentous, charged air. "That settles it. Looks like you two are going to Virginia. I will keep Mercy safe here. You take Ernest. We'll get you IDs. You don't have much time. Only thirty-six hours until Hayes comes to Alcatraz."

CHAPTER 85

Twelve Years Old
Daniel's Last Day

Three days ago, the fat-fingered man stole something from her with his grabby eyes, sticky like fly feet over her body, as if he could see the breast buds under her training bra, the soft triangle of hair between her legs. Salem hadn't mentioned anything to her mom. Somehow, she knew she shouldn't. But she wants her body back, and she thinks she knows how to do it.

"A bikini?" Vida asks. They're at JCPenney. It's June, and Salem has grown two inches up and one inch out since last summer. They're going to the lake today—Daniel, Vida, and her—and she needs a new swimsuit. "Persian girls don't wear bikinis."

"I'm not Persian. I'm Minnesotan."

"What about this?" Vida holds up a black one-piece with a skirt, the brown molding of the cup liners off-center and peeking out. "The fabric is lovely."

Salem hasn't asked for a lot from her parents. Even at twelve, she's aware of this. "Please, Mom. I'm growing up. I'm becoming a woman."

She rehearsed that line on the drive to the mall. In her head, it didn't sound so corny.

Vida's eyes fill with tears like someone left the hose on behind them. Salem reviews her words, panicking. Her mom never cries, never. Except that one time she fell while biking and had to get stitches, but that doesn't count. That was pain.

"*Mom?*"

Vida tips her head as if gravity can send the tears back where they belong. Salem thinks her mom is going to pretend like the crying isn't happening— hopes she'll pretend that—but Vida comes to a decision. She untips her head and the tears run down her cheeks. She looks straight at Salem. The message is clear: I'm crying. It's okay to cry.

It's kinda late for that bit of info, *Salem thinks. She's learned a lot from her mom—how to articulate arguments, how to cook Persian food, how to be a good friend. She's seen Vida Wiley stand in front of a crowd of thousands and deliver a speech on women's rights that has people standing on their chairs, yelling their support, as if her words are keys unlocking something precious inside them.*

She has not *learned emotion from her mom.*

That has come from her dad. Daniel was the one who held her and stroked her hair when she cried about Peter Miller calling her Salami Willy in third grade. Daniel's was the face she could count on in the audience of her band concerts and at her science fairs. She even went to her dad rather than her mom when she got her period last winter. It wasn't comfortable, make no mistake, but it made more sense than confiding in Vida.

Salem doesn't know what to do with a weeping Vida in the swimsuit section of the Minneapolis JCPenney, so she hands over the most important thing to her in this moment, a sacrifice that hurts but it's all she can think of. "I don't need the bikini, Mom."

Vida wipes her face. She sniffles. She reaches for one of Salem's unruly curls, holding it, running her fingers down it. "You make me proud every day, baby. Do you know that?"

Salem's stomach drops. She'd hoped her mom wouldn't take her up on her offer, but she knows that once you make a deal, you stick with it, no matter what. She musters a wan smile.

Vida pulls her into an embrace. "But of course you need a bikini, because you are *becoming a woman. A strong, proud woman."*

Salem is confused. What did Vida mean about being proud of her if it wasn't that she'd conceded the swimsuit battle?

But she doesn't worry too long. She's getting a bikini.

When they arrive home, Salem runs immediately to Daniel to show him the new swimsuit. He says it's pretty, and that he's happy she got what she wanted. Daniel and Vida kiss.

Salem is so used to seeing their affection, the way they share secret looks, how she can hear them some nights laughing and talking well past the time they should be asleep. She knows that deep friendship is what it means to be married.

Daniel has packed for their day at the lake. He takes the cooler, Vida the beach bag with their books, sunglasses, and sun cream, and Salem lugs the beach towels. They are almost out the door when the phone rings.

"I'll get it," Vida sings, setting the bag on the floor. She's happy, Salem can see that. They always have fun at the lake.

The conversation doesn't go well, though. When Vida hangs up, her expression is heavy. She tells them that Beth, her colleague, has gone into labor early. Someone needs to cover her classes. She has a guest speaker booked, a famous lecturer, and the college has paid too much for him to cancel.

"You can take Salem alone, honey." Vida plants a kiss on Daniel's nose. "Remember that one time I took her when you had to work late? This will make us even."

Salem feels sad, but then a thought buoys her: she'll get to wear her bikini without her mom staring at her sideways all day.

It will be the first day Salem and her dad go to the lake without her mom.

It will also be the last.

CHAPTER 86

In Flight

The Virginia-bound plane pitched and dropped, yanking Salem out of her light sleep.

For as long as she could remember, Salem had thought her mother had grown cruelly selfish after Daniel died. Vida always put her work before her daughter. But a simpler, equally painful realization was twisting its way free. Adult Salem realized her mother had likely struggled with depression after Daniel's suicide.

To twelve-year-old Salem, it had felt like someone had iced the sun.

Their house became gray. Frozen dinners replaced home-cooked meals. Vida worked or slept, never smiled unless Gracie was around. Vida treated Salem like an inconvenience. When Salem won the eighth grade science fair blue ribbon for a tornado-predicting computer program she'd back-rigged to break into any word processing program and warn the user of approaching dangerous weather, Vida had not been there. Same with band concerts, parent-teacher conferences. Her mom was competent, distant, and after Daniel's death, Salem grew up without her.

But what had Vida given up when she'd lost Daniel? The plane dipped again. Salem glanced over at Bel.

Her friend had claimed the window seat. Her head leaned against the cold oval of the closed screen, her eyes closed, undisturbed by the brief turbulence. Salem had the middle seat, and Ernest the outer. One of his knees was halfway up the seat in front of him, and the other looked like he'd unrolled it into the aisle. Salem thought of waking Bel to talk about Daniel with her. She hadn't, not really, since his funeral. She'd shut Bel down when she asked questions—what was there to say?

But suddenly, for the first time since her father had killed himself, a new thought was tossed to Salem like a rope: Where had Daniel gotten the sleeping pills the day he'd drowned?

She sat up straighter. She had carried the beach bag after Vida left, shoving the towels into it. There had been no pills in there. They weren't in the cooler, either. Daniel could have stolen the sleeping pills from out of the lake cabin's medicine cabinet, but Salem knew there hadn't been any there, either, because she'd peeked inside when she'd used the bathroom (toothpaste, Visine, mint floss, a generic bottle of ibuprofen, two toothbrushes). She supposed they could have been in the pocket of his swim trunks.

"I have to use the bathroom."

Ernest got up to let her pass, leaning over. He was too tall to fully stand in the plane. The red-eye flight Lu had booked for them was surprisingly full. The bathroom line was three deep. Salem was okay with that. It gave her time to uncramp her legs. She thought about all they had to do—land, rent a car, buy gear, follow the coordinates, crack Beale's vault, fly back to San Francisco to hand over to Agent Stone what they'd found—and how little time they had to accomplish everything.

The man in front of Salem turned, smiled. He wore sunglasses. She didn't smile back. Something about him made her uncomfortable. Was it his smell? But if he had an odor, it was too mild to pick out on the plane. His face appeared pleasant enough around the metal rims of the sunglasses. She didn't recognize him. She looked away, but he didn't.

"Been to Virginia before?" His voice rumbled just above a whisper. A couple sleeping in the seats next to him shifted, the woman pulling the thin airplane blanket closer to her.

Is he really picking me up on an airplane? Salem shook her head and looked away. She hoped he'd get the hint. Did it bother her that he was wearing sunglasses at night, in the air?

He nodded and turned back toward the bathroom door accordioning open. A woman squeezed out and another sardined in. The line was now down to two, plus Salem. The man in sunglasses returned his attention to her.

"Where in Richmond are you going?"

Salem felt trapped. She wanted to be polite, but his attention was making her uncomfortable. Her body language should have made that clear, but she gave it one more shot, shrugging by way of an answer.

That must have registered loud and clear, finally, because he turned away from her. Thirty seconds later, though, he turned back, his lower lip trembling. "I'm just trying to make conversation, you know? I don't know if you think you're too good to talk to me, or what, but I think I deserve some decent human interaction here."

Every one of Salem's fears came crowding back in. She felt terrible for making him feel bad. She opened her mouth to speak, but found Ernest at her side, crouching.

"She doesn't owe you anything, man."

"It's okay, Ernest."

"No, it's not." Ernest didn't look mad, just that mix of resigned sadness he got when he was stressed. "You get to stand in line any way you want to."

"Really, it's fine." She appreciated Ernest's brotherly reaction, but she didn't want a scene. She certainly didn't want to make this man mad. They were going to be stuck on this plane together. "You can sit down. I'm okay. This gentleman is going to leave me alone, and everything will be all right."

Ernest glanced at her, hesitated, then nodded and shuffled back to his seat.

Salem stopped herself short of apologizing to the man in sunglasses—barely—and shoved her hands in her pockets. She wished she had a phone to look at.

The bathroom door opened again and places were traded. The man in sunglasses was next in line. Salem was glad she wouldn't have to stand next to him much longer.

"You never said where in Richmond you were going," he said, without turning to face her.

Her breath caught. *Really?* She opened her mouth to say something to him directly, then snapped it shut. The plane ride was almost over. She could keep her peace until they landed. Besides, the man wasn't even looking at her.

Then he did. He turned. She saw her own face reflected in his lenses, upside down and tiny. "Northern Richmond is pretty this time of year. Are you visiting friends?"

She didn't know what exactly it was that dug up, dusted off, and pushed her *screw it all* button after all these years, and especially after the last five days. Maybe it was his simpering aggressiveness, his shaming of her for not doing his bidding, the way he'd ignored all her nonverbals. Maybe it was that she realized she'd gone without Ativan for four days, and that she was surviving. *Better than surviving.* Probably accumulated stress had something to do with it, too, but suddenly, she found herself caring much more about her own comfort than his.

"You're being a dick."

He jerked as if she'd hit him. "What?"

"I clearly don't want to talk to you, and you won't let it go, so screw you. Screw you for thinking I have to speak with you because we're both standing in line and screw you for your creepy sunglasses on a plane. I will stand in this line until it's my turn, I will not talk to you, and you *will* respect that."

"Hell yeah," the woman under the blue airplane blanket muttered sleepily.

Salem realized her chest was moving up and down rapidly, her heart racing. She waited for the man to react. He opened and closed his mouth. Time unspooled at a snail's pace. He finally responded, sort of. He pushed past her and returned to his seat four rows ahead of hers. She waited until the bathroom door opened, went in, and slid the lock closed.

She leaned against the bathroom door, laughing quietly. There may have been tears mixed in.

SUNDAY

November 6

CHAPTER 87

Montvale, Virginia

The woman was slumped in the back seat of Jason's car when he deplaned from one of the Hermitage's private jets onto the Richmond International Airport tarmac. She was bound, blindfolded, unresponsive. The agent who handed him the keys also handed him a Christmas tree–shaped air freshener.

When he slid into the car, he understood why.

The Underground leader's flesh was a swampland of infected wounds, her body running a fever so high that Jason could feel the heat of her from the front seat.

It enraged him.

Surely her wounds were the cuts he'd inflicted back in Minneapolis, but that was in the line of duty. If the Hermitage chose to keep her, they needed to tend to her. Jason would be lucky if she stayed alive for the four-hour drive to Montvale, and what good would she be to him dead?

He slammed his hand into the steering wheel.

When Barnaby had called, his command had been clear: "Take her with."

"She'll slow me down. Why do I need her?"

"Geppetto tells me you failed outside the Dolores Mission."

Jason's cheek twitched, took a new shape, popped back. When he'd met Geppetto outside Mission Dolores, Geppetto had placed his hand on Jason's shoulder.

He'd squeezed.

Just a bit.

Enough to steal Jason's breath.

To remind him of those nights in the Lower Ninth, when it was his turn with Geppetto.

To make sure he remembered that single job in Minnesota fourteen years earlier.

To let Jason know that his crack could come again, at any time.

Jason despised Geppetto for that, but he hated himself worse for not reaching for a knife and skewering that meat hook of a hand like a kebab, for not even pulling away. That was Geppetto's power, to teach you that attempting escape hurt worse than letting him have his way, to brand that message deep into your soul.

Adding insult to the promise of injury, the women had escaped their grasp outside the mission. Jason had watched across the street as Wiley fumbled with the middle bell, nearly falling before popping a drawer hidden in the bell's harness and removing something. He saw them exit the front door, and he'd issued a terse command to Geppetto: *Hold Isabel, don't hurt her.*

Even with her hair chopped, she took his breath away.

But then the FBI agent arrived, followed two hours later by this phone call from Barnaby.

"Yes, *we* failed. The daughters weren't able to stay for the interview as we'd hoped." Jason didn't like that his voice sounds whiny, or that Barnaby's good cheer had disappeared days ago and had not returned.

"It's not just the docket anymore," Barnaby says. "They have the location to Beale's vault. This is a Code Blue. I need you."

That announcement knocked the whine directly out of Jason. He felt himself grow.

Barnaby continued, "I need stealth. If I send in the entire work-force, Wiley and Odegaard might run before they open the vault, and we'll have nothing. That girl is the only one who can get inside, so make sure she does. A plane is waiting for you at SFO. We'll have the Underground leader in a car for you when you land."

Jason didn't want to ask again. "Why do I need her?"

A pause announced Barnaby's displeasure. "You may not, but if it comes to it, what would you do if someone was about to dismiss your mother in front of you?"

"Anything."

Jason meant it. Killing his mother was *his* job.

Barnaby's genteel voice broke into Jason's mental stroll. "Wait until they enter the vault to be sure it's possible. Then downsize them all. We won't need their work any longer. We won't need any outside employ-ees." His tone became reverential. "Once we have what's inside the vault, the Hermitage will be untouchable."

"What do I do after they've been dismissed?"

"We'll have a human resources crew on hand, just out of sight, poised for cleanup. You'll tell them when to arrive. I don't want them there until everyone is terminated. Understand?"

"Yes, sir. Thank you."

Barnaby cleared his throat, his tone chiding. "They're your backup, too, if you aren't able to decruit everyone on your own. You'll inform HR when you go in. You'll have ten minutes from that point to finish the job. If they don't hear from you within that time, they swarm. But that won't happen, will it, Jason?"

The words stung. "No, sir."

"Good man."

Barnaby had better believe it.

Everyone would be dead when Jason was done.

CHAPTER 88

Montvale, Virginia

The three of them picked up a rental car at the airport, purchased shovels, pickaxes, and a high-powered GPS at a Home Depot just outside Richmond, and inputted Beale's coordinates.

The GPS led them to Montvale, Virginia, then south to Porters Mountain Road. A sugar maple and pine forest hugged the sides of the winding highway. Mountains—or at least they looked like mountains to Midwest-raised Salem—circled the robin's-egg blue of the sky. Although they had yet to pass a farm, the air had the earthy smell of manure and spicy plants, like tomatoes or dandelions.

They'd been cruising Porters Mountain Road for three miles when the phone commanded them to drive straight into the center of the woods. Bel parked the car on the shoulder, and they packed up their equipment and started hiking into the forest's heart, Bel carrying her share of the load even though her shoulder was clearly still bothering her.

The trees stayed dense, but the ground transformed from spongy to stone. In the distance, Salem heard water crackling along a rocky creek. It reminded her of the sound of bacon frying. Birds screeched overhead. Sweat began to inch between her shoulder blades despite the maple-syrup-thick shade of the trees. When they reached a rocky outcropping shaped like three triangles, the GPS informed them that they'd arrived. They went to work on the middle stone, trying to pry and budge it.

They were taken completely off guard by the man.

"Hands up. All three of you."

Bel, Salem, and Ernest dropped their tools and turned slowly.

"Tell me what you're doing." The elderly man's singsong accent was at odds with the shotgun he had trained on them and his gnarled face. He wore a flannel shirt and faded jeans tucked into work boots. A noon sun shone overhead, speckling the forest.

They didn't have a weapon of their own. Bel couldn't risk an unregistered gun in her bag, even if they'd had time to check it.

"Sir, put the gun down." Bel's voice was steady. "You can see we're unarmed."

"Please," Salem begged, her hands in the air. To have come this far, to be so close to saving their mothers, only to be gunned down by this stranger was inconceivable.

"I can see you're trespassers, and I'm within my legal rights to shoot you." He tossed his chin at the pickaxes they'd dropped at their feet. "Treasure hunters?"

"Yes, sir," Ernest said.

"Bah." The man spit to his left, but he didn't lower the gun.

"Is this your land?" Salem asked.

He nodded. "And my father's, and his dad before that. And I'll be g'all damned if you get to come and go as you please on what is rightly mine. If I chase off one treasure hunter a week, I chase off ten."

Salem licked her lips. "Has Beale's vault been discovered?"

"Hell if I know. I'll ask you kindly to pick up your equipment, walk back the way you came, and never return."

Salem's stomach dropped, but she followed his instructions, as did Ernest and Bel. They grabbed their tools, including the GPS, and started walking away.

"Sir," Ernest said, stopping.

The man's gun was still trained on them.

"Do you have a mother?"

"A'course," he said. "And two legs and a dog. What's that to do with anything?"

"We're trying to save one of these women's mothers."

The man made a sound like air leaving a tire and cocked an eyebrow at Salem and Bel. "Which one?"

"Please." Salem stepped forward. He'd let the tip of his gun fall, but he raised it back. "We don't know. We just know that somebody kidnapped our mothers, but one of them may still be alive. If we can get to the vault, they might return her."

He laughed, then paused. "You serious?"

"Yes."

"That's a new one." He dropped his gun again, scratching his chin. "I'm quite sure I don't believe you, but a good story deserves a reward. I tell you what, though, I've been hunting these woods since I was knee high to a grasshopper. If there were a treasure in these rocks, I'd have found it."

"Sir?" A hunch burned Salem's throat.

"Yup."

Miss Gram guards the truth. What if it was more than a clue to the anagram contained in the ciphers? What if it marked the actual vault? "Have you noticed any symbols around here, ever? You know, when you were hunting?"

"Like pentagrams or something?"

"Probably not," Salem said. "Something smaller."

"Nope," he said, yanking a handkerchief out of his back pocket. He blew loudly and returned the cloth. "Just the electric company's stamp over the yonder hill."

Salem forgot to breathe. *Miss Gram*, rearranged, made *Ma Rigs Ms*, *Mags Rims*, and *Mass Grim*.

It also made *Mrs. Sigma*.

The original Greek letter sigma, used frequently in modern mathematics, was usually referred to as lunate sigma, or the female sigma, because of its crescent shape.

Mrs. Sigma guards the truth.

Emily Dickinson had included the symbol below her name in both messages she'd written. Writers were taught to represent sigma with more of a buckle in the middle, comparable to an English capital *E*, like the first letter in *electric*.

Exactly what you'd expect to see for an electric company's stamp.

"Never would have found the stamp," the man said, pointing at it. Once he'd made up his mind about the three of them, he'd been a genial host, introducing himself as Ronald. "Except a burrow of groundhogs set up here. I don't mind 'em, but the wife didn't like what they did to her garden. I tracked them back to their home and made to set up traps.

"You have to secure the trap to the ground or the animal runs away with it," he explained to Ernest, as if the 6'7" city boy were the only one who could truly understand. "I stuck one in right here and it wouldn't go. Not surprising, since much of this is rock. I moved the grass aside to be sure, and there was the electric company stamp. Funny, because there's no electricity over here."

He kept talking to Ernest while Salem and Bel dropped to their knees, ripping out grass and pushing aside dirt. Their work revealed the metal disk—bronze, the size of a dinner plate, a large Σ stamped in its center.

They both sat back on their heels. Salem's skin tingled.

Ronald stepped over to them. "That's it. There you go! Good work, girls."

"You found it, Salem," Bel said. "I can't believe it. You found Beale's vault."

"We all found it," Salem insisted. Was it possible to have an excitement-induced heart attack?

"Maybe," Bel replied. "But you're going to be the one to open it."

Ronald leaned his gun against a nearby tree. "How's that? Open the electric company marker?"

"We think this is the marker for the Beale vault, sir." Bel stood awkwardly and brushed off her knees with her good hand. "If you're familiar, the second cipher says the treasure is six feet under."

Ronald took Bel's place next to Salem, his gun forgotten. "Well, I'll be. You know people been looking for this for lifetimes, right?"

Salem felt all the grooves on the stamp. In mathematics, sigma usually represented the sum of a series. She suspected Thomas J. Beale used it to represent the lunar, or feminine. Neither piece of information helped her. "Hand me the pickax."

"You're not going to destroy it, are you?" Bel asked.

"I want to dig around it." Salem took the tool Ernest handed to her, using the blunt edge like a spade to clear the area immediately surrounding the bronze stamp. A wider metal circle emerged under that. "Help me!"

All four of them went at it, digging until their shoulders ached and sweat stung their eyes. They widened the circle, and then another circle around that. After an hour, they had discovered the top of the vault. The stamp was welded to a circle the size and shape of a manhole cover, which sealed what appeared to be a room-size, rusted metal container buried in the ground, sloping out and down from the manhole. Salem guessed it would be shaped like a giant whiskey jug if she could see it from the side.

"Now what?" Bel asked. They'd stopped, panting, the circle of earth they'd cleared forming a natural ledge they could all sit on to study the manhole cover. "A blowtorch?"

"Let's get these pickaxes between the lid and the base and see if we can pry it open," Ronald offered. He tried first, but there was no crack to stick it in. Even after a few directed swings with the pickax, there was no purchase.

Bel scratched her head. "I think it needs your sweet touch, Salem."

"I don't know what to do," she wailed. "I've felt every square inch of that cover, pressed and pulled on every bit of it."

"What about pushing together?" Ronald asked. "You pushed down, but how about toward? Like squeezing?"

"What would you squeeze?"

"The edges of this *E*." Ronald pointed toward the tips of the sigma symbol. "It's itching to meet up with itself." He leaned forward and demonstrated, his long fingers touching the points and pinching.

The vault underneath them shifted. "Do it some more!"

He squeezed again. The earth rumbled some more, and the manhole cover popped up an inch with a pneumatic hiss. The air it released was bitter with age.

"Help me push this lid open," he said. They all came around to his side and put their shoulders into it. The manhole cover slid to the side, still attached but no longer atop the opening. An absorbent darkness stared back at them.

Ronald whistled low. "I hope one of you brought a flashlight."

CHAPTER 89

Beale Vault

They'd brought two.

Bel shined hers into the vault. It was no more than ten feet deep with waist-high terra-cotta pots lining the floor and shortening the distance between outside and in. The hole was only wide enough for one person at a time to stick in their head. Bel volunteered, tipping her upper body over the edge while Salem held her feet.

"More clay pots," she said, her voice echoing. She yanked herself back out and pulled off her sling. "I'm going first."

"I'm going to tie your rope around that tree while you go in," Ronald said, pointing at a pine. "Only a fool and a groundhog go into the ground without a way out."

Ernest went second. He was tall enough to stand on one of the clay pots and pull himself out, if need be, so Salem lowered herself down last with his help, the second flashlight tucked into the waistband of her khaki pants.

She eased her feet between a cluster of pots and flashed her light into the farthest reaches. The vault was indeed shaped like a jug, the floor a circle with a twelve-foot diameter, clay pots lined three high on the perimeter. There were at least a hundred of them.

Salem slid the lid off the waist-high pot nearest her. It made a scraping sound. It was packed to the brim with circles of gold. She grabbed a fistful, the sun shining through the opening of the vault and glinting off the treasure.

A shadow dimmed the sun overhead.

Salem glanced up, throat tight. One of them should have stayed on the surface. They were at the mercy of Ronald, a stranger.

His face peered down, followed by a rope. "That what I think it is?" he asked.

She held up her hand to him. Five feet separated them, but he still reached for the gold.

He smiled. "I'll be hot-damned. I'll stay up here. One of us should."

Trust no one.

Salem shined her light toward Bel, whose back was to her. "Find anything?"

"Every urn I've opened contains gold, or jewels, or silver."

"Same here," Ernest said.

"Keep looking. We need to find whatever it is that's going to ruin the Hermitage."

The scraping of terra-cotta pots being opened filled the space, echoing off the walls, interrupted by the occasional gasp as Bel uncovered a container of rubies, or Ernest found a small cask filled with loose pearls, like a vase of creamy marbles. It was amazing, glorious, beyond belief. Without a car and GPS, it would have taken months to locate this spot, if it would have even been possible. Thomas J. Beale couldn't have conceived the world his treasure would be born into.

"Wait!" Salem said. Her light shined off a pot different than the rest. It had a lightning bolt cast into its side.

Here you will find the treasure, and the Lightning Bolt . . .

She waded through the maze of pots until she stood in front of it. The lightning bolt pot was stacked on top of another and stood at chest height. She slid off the cover and tipped the pot to peer inside. It contained rolls of paper. She pulled them out.

"Come here and hold my flashlight!"

Ernest reached her side first, Bel seconds after. With shaking hands, she unrolled the paper on a nearby ledge. The first one was a letter signed by Thomas J. Beale and dated 10 August 1814:

> *Major General Andrew Jackson altered the Treaty of Fort Jackson, falsely, after the Chiefs entered their signatures. My men have intercepted the one true original, which rests herein. If the accurate Convention is brought before the Nation's eye, Jackson cannot rewrite history. The whole of Alabama and the valuable parts of Coosa and Kahawha containing in all approximately twenty-three millions of acres are NOT articles of the Creek's cession. Major General Jackson has created copies that cast out this fact, but they are unconsummated by the signatures of the Chiefs of the Creek Nation and contain only the letter X where a name should be. With the Truth herein, and the strength of the Creek Treasure encased in this vault, the Indians keep Alabama and Georgia and Jackson's fortune and reputation are struck a fatal blow.*
> *—Thomas J. Beale*

"Holy cow," Salem said. "Alabama and Georgia legally belong to the Creek Nation?"

"Let's see the treaty," Bel insisted.

Salem set Beale's note aside. The three pages underneath were a thicker parchment. The top started out with this:

> *Articles of agreement and capitulation, made and concluded this ninth day of August, one thousand eight hundred and fourteen, between major general Andrew Jackson, on behalf of the President of the United States of America, and the chiefs, deputies, and warriors of the Creek Nation.*

Salem skimmed the section blaming the Creeks for starting a war against the US until she got to the First Article.

> *The United States demand an equivalent for all expenses incurred in prosecuting the war to its termination, by a cession of all the territory belonging to the Creek Nation within the territories of the United States, except that lying west, south, and south-eastwardly, of a line to be run and described by persons duly authorized and appointed by the President of the United States.*

The treaty then went on to describe in great detail the land the Creek were to keep, with Article 2 underscoring the Creek's claim to most of Alabama and southern Georgia:

> *2nd—The United States will guarantee to the Creek Nation, the integrity of all their Territory within said line to be run and described as mentioned in the first article.*

The rest of the treaty was devoted to the language of peace, including the Creek agreeing to no longer collude with the British, to remain in their designated lands in Alabama and Georgia, and to never again engage in conflict with the United States. The entire third page was signatures, the spiderwebs of ink impossible to read in some places, though Salem clearly made out Andrew Jackson's name along with some others—Faue Emautla, of Cussetau; William McIntosh, for Hopoiee Haujo, of Ooseoochee; Eneah Thlucco, of Immookfau.

"Are these official?" Bel asked.

"They sure look like it," Salem said. "You know what this means?"

"Andrew Jackson not only stole Indian land. He broke established law to do it," Ernest said.

"I don't know." Bel rubbed her cheek. "Weren't treaties broken all the time?"

"Yeah, but that was then. This is now." Salem swiveled to count all the pots of gold and gems the vault contained. "With this treasure on their side, the surviving Creek Nation could muck up the courts for years while this gets figured out. Jackson built his fortune on a falsehood, which means the Hermitage Foundation did, too. They might survive this going public, but they might not."

Bel whooped.

Ernest leaned over and scooped them both into his arms. "I can't believe you two did it. You're going to put a vault-size dent in the Hermitage!"

"Not if we don't get out of this hole," Bel said. "Salem, you first. Tuck those papers into your pants and let's go."

"Wait, what's this?" A slip of paper freed itself from the roll. It was half the size of the land deeds but tucked between them. She picked it up and shined the flashlight on it. "It looks like some sort of code."

"Gawd, no," Bel groaned.

"I'm taking a picture." Salem lined up her phone. "We can deal with it later."

The code consisted of columns of seemingly random letters as opposed to the numbers Beale had used in his famous ciphers. She snapped a couple shots, rolled the papers back up, and tucked the works into the back of her pants.

They'd parked their car on the side of the road over five hours ago.

They'd changed history in that time.

Salem held her arms toward the fading sunshine, her shoulders stiff with fatigue. "Ronald, I'm coming up!"

Ernest climbed on top of the clay pot immediately under the hole and made a bridge with his fingers. Salem stepped into it and used his leverage and the rope to wrench herself up and out. The warmth of the dappled fall sunshine was a relief after the close air of the vault. She hoisted one knee over the edge, and then the other, turning to look for Ronald.

She found him lying on the ground, blood pulsing from a gash in his throat.

A man stood behind Ronald's corpse, holding a knife to the throat of a woman.

Her face was swollen and battered, but she was recognizable. The killer looked tired, his clothes rumpled, but he was still breathtaking.

His snake eyes studied her.

He held his finger to his gorgeous mouth, his meaning unmistakable.

Make no noise or sudden movement. I want your friends here for this.

CHAPTER 90

Montvale, Virginia

Salem ignored his silent threat and lunged for her mother.

She wrapped her arms around Vida, who fell against her. Her skin felt hot and loose. "Mom?"

Vida was too heavy to hold, but it was a sick weight, the heaviness of infection and swelling and pus. Salem slid her to the ground as gently as she could.

Vida's eyes fluttered open.

"Mom? It's Salem. Mom!" A sob escaped Salem's lips. She felt hands at the back of her pants, sliding out the papers. She didn't care. Her mother was burning, her skin a purple-green all over. Her clothes were matted to her, bloody, melding and scabbing into her flesh.

"Salem!" Bel was climbing out of the hole.

Salem felt the sudden pressure of a blade against her neck as a response. The killer turned her around, never easing up on the pressure at her throat. He was deceptively strong. She knew in that moment that Grace Odegaard was indeed dead.

Bel seemed to realize the same thing, her whole body melting to the ground as her eyes traveled from the man to Salem to Vida and back to Salem.

"Noooo," she breathed.

Ernest climbed out next. He glanced over at Ronald and paled. He stood to his full height, pulling Bel to her feet, careful of her shoulder.

"Wonderful," the man with the blade said. He was the same person who'd tried to take them outside the Dolores Mission, the friend of the fat-fingered man. His voice was velvet. Salem thought she detected a slight Southern accent underneath.

He kept his knife pressed to her throat as he shook out one of the pieces of paper he'd pulled from her pants. "The land deeds exist. Not for long, eh?" He laughed, the good-natured sound you make when a friend forgets something that you could have easily forgotten yourself.

Ernest stepped forward. The blade pressed deeper into Salem's throat, opening an edge of flesh with a tiny pop. Warm blood trickled down her neck.

"If you want to live two more minutes, I invite you to tell me exactly what else is in that vault," the man said. "I'll find out in any case after I kill you."

"Gold." Bel's voice was scoured steel. "Jewels. Pearls."

"The master list of Underground members?"

"That too," Bel said.

Salem's eyes shot to Bel. The list was on the computer back at Lu's. Why would Bel lie about that? They were going to be dead in two minutes, all of them, and the killer would find out the truth. So why lie?

Salem read the answer in Bel's face loud and clear: *Because fuck him.*

There was one basic rule underlying all of Krav Maga: use your opponent's strength and weight against them. With a knife at your throat, that meant your enemy was pushing into you. He expected you to hold still as a rabbit. It was instinct. It would never occur to him that you might push back.

Giving you a second's lick before he regained his balance.

Salem didn't think. She leaned forward and then rolled backward, away from her mom, away from the knife and into her captor, knocking him off balance hard enough that he released her, stumbling back a step.

He readjusted quickly and turned toward her, murder in his eyes, the knife thrusting toward her in a blow meant to kill, not capture.

Ernest launched himself with an incoherent yell. The killer turned his blade to the more immediate threat, slashing the knife in a vertical arc that sliced through Ernest's throat with buttery ease. Ernest's eyes widened in shock as a glut of red spurted out from the gash below his chin. He slumped to the forest floor, solid and motionless, as the killer swiveled on Salem, who had not moved.

Bel had hurled herself into motion the same time as Ernest, but swifter and sleeker. She flew underneath, grabbing a rock the size of her fist, and slammed it into the killer's brain stem before his blade could claim Salem.

The killer fell toward Salem. She pushed him away, screaming. He landed on his back next to her. Bel hurried to check his pulse, rock still in her hand. She was panting, her eyes wild.

"He's dead. Look at his face."

It was a horrifying patchwork puddle of melting flesh.

Salem was panicked, confused. "Did you smash the rock into his face?"

Bel shook her head, her pupils huge and black. She couldn't drag her eyes off the man's pooling face as she went through his pockets. She discovered no ID, only a set of knives in an intricate sheath, a silver locket, a hank of strawberry-blonde hair, and the papers he'd snatched off Salem. She took all but the hair.

Salem crawled over to Ernest. "Help me turn him over!"

The earth was sucking greedily at the blood pumping out of Ernest's throat, absorbing the pool before it could form. Salem pressed her hands over the wound, the heat of his life pulsing against her, growing softer.

"Mercy." The word cost him. Blood sprayed from his mouth. "Protect Mercy."

"Bel! Go get help."

Ernest wheezed, and his breathing stopped.

Bel clasped Salem around the waist, straining to pull her away.

"What are you doing? He's still alive. He's still got a heartbeat." Salem looked away from Ernest to search Bel's face. It was a tapestry of sadness.

"We have to get Vida to a hospital, honey. We can send an ambulance for Ernest, okay?"

Salem glanced over at her unconscious mother. She appeared so frail, so vulnerable. But Salem couldn't leave Ernest, not when his heart was still beating.

He pumped blood for one more minute. He never spoke another word.

A humid fog had settled into the forest. Salem realized that she was sitting in a cloud.

CHAPTER 91

Alcatraz Island

Alcatraz Island, 1.5 miles across the bay from San Francisco, was named for the pelicans that originally colonized it. Most locals referred to it as "the Rock." Humans first used it as a military fortress, housing prisoners there as early as the Civil War. The lonely and impassive concrete cell block that now defined the island was completed in 1912. In 1933, the US Department of Justice acquired the land and turned it into a storage facility for prisoners who caused too much trouble to be housed anywhere else.

The first batch of the worst of the worst arrived on August 11, 1934. Over the years, the legendary prison held the likes of Al Capone, George "Machine Gun" Kelly, James "Whitey" Bulger, and Alvin "Creepy" Karpis.

Agent Clancy Johnson didn't particularly care for criminal name-dropping. He just knew the old prison gave him the willies. It was a haunted house of cinder block windows and industrial cells straight out of a Russian gulag flick.

Alcatraz had officially closed its prison doors in 1963 on orders from then Attorney General Robert F. Kennedy. It cost ten dollars a day to house criminals there, compared to three dollars anywhere else. That, and the prisoners and guards and their families were dumping all their sewage into the bay. It was floating onshore.

The prisoners were moved to Illinois that same year. Clancy figured they hadn't gotten it any easier.

In 1969 a group of Native Americans took over the Rock, calling Indian people from as far away as Minneapolis to occupy the island for nearly two years. They protested all the land and rights the US government had stolen from them over the centuries. It worked—Nixon rescinded the Indian termination policy in 1970 as a direct result of the Alcatraz occupation. Somehow, Clancy suspected Gina Hayes would avoid that page in the history books when she delivered her speech.

Hayes was arriving tomorrow to speak about prison reform, an area where Clancy happened to agree with her wholeheartedly. Sometime during Clancy's tenure with the FBI, prisons had turned into a for-profit business, and that didn't sit well with him. It was simple math: if you made more money the more criminals you had, you were invested in creating more criminals, and there was no more efficient criminal factory than a prison.

You maybe went in stupid—knocked over a convenience store for a pack of smokes, broke a cop's window on a dare—but you came out hard, and you brought that back to your community like an infection. Crimes in the US were dropping, but prison numbers were increasing to the tune of $25,000 a year for each of the 2.5 million incarcerated, billed directly to American taxpayers. And much of it was sliding into the pockets of the prison-owning tycoons, thank you very much.

Clancy wasn't a hippie nor was he a philosopher, but his father had raised a practical man, and he didn't like those numbers.

Hayes and Clancy parted ways from that point on, politically speaking.

Clancy wasn't sure if the Hermitage had pulled strings to assign him to dry-clean the island the evening before Hayes's historic speech and in advance of the Secret Service's sweep tomorrow, or if it was legitimately part of his FBI assignment. He figured the latter because Stone was here, too. Clancy knew for a fact that the Hermitage had arranged his own shift on the island tomorrow, though. He had a job to do for them.

Personally, the island gave Clancy the creeps. It resembled one of those raised pieces in the Game of Life, the green plastic bluffs with a road carved through them, only on Alcatraz, the road ran around the edges, and it was a walking path with a bunch of haunted old buildings sprinkled in the middle. A red handprint marked the door of the prison. Inside, the floor was bomb scarred. Clancy was fine keeping his and Stone's search cursory. Stone was going to town, though, checking every nook and cranny on the weird old prison as if he could locate a gun that someone genuinely wanted hidden.

As if anyone who really wanted Hayes dead would stuff the gun on the island in advance, rather than contract with someone who was not only allowed to bring a gun with him but was required to do so when working.

Clancy stared through a barred sliver of window, watching Stone sprint up the granite steps of the old recreation yard, the shadow of the rickety water tower concealing his partner for a moment. No way could Clancy do that, even on a good day. His bones were the same age as the rest of him—seventy-two. That's when he wondered if he was up for this job. The money sure would be nice. He and Jenny could retire to the Caribbean.

He chuckled, and it turned into a smoker's cough, a habit he'd given up five years earlier but that still rattled around his lungs. Who the hell was he fooling? If he had all the time and money in the world, the first thing he'd do was leave her.

Maybe he'd take up fishing. Buy a hut somewhere, gawk at the tourist girls. Drink beer.

Yeah, he liked the feel of that on his back.

He patted his gun and strolled back into the sunshine.

CHAPTER 92

Virginia

The drive from Beale's vault to Lynchburg General Hospital should have taken an hour. Bel chewed it up in half that. Salem called the police on the way, giving them the coordinates to the vault and the three bodies—Ernest, Ronald, and the assassin. She also called the hospital.

The staff was ready when the rental car screeched up to the emergency room door.

Vida Wiley was rushed into surgery. Salem and Bel waited.

Salem's mom was alive; Bel's was not. Ernest was dead, leaving Mercy a true orphan. There were no words, so the two women simply held each other, the warmth of Bel's body merging with Salem's, shoring her up, grounding her.

"Salem Wiley?"

She and Bel shot to their feet. The doctor wore a blue gown and matching head cover.

"How is she?" Bel asked.

The doctor frowned. "I was a field medic in the first Iraq War, and I've never seen wounds so infected. But there's a good chance she'll pull through. Four broken bones, 173 stitches, severely dehydrated, and a fever of 104, but we think she'll make it. We have her on an antibiotic drip along with other fluids."

"Is she conscious?"

"She goes in and out."

"Can we see her?"

He frowned. "If you don't tax her. We've fixed all the trauma we can identify, but she's not out of the woods yet. She needs rest."

He led them to her room.

It was silent but for the hum and beep of Vida's monitor. She was motionless, blanket pulled to her chest, arms stuffed with needles. Salem ran to her, unsure where to touch her. She was covered in bandages and bruises. Anger and horror wrestled inside Salem.

"Mom?"

Bel went to the other side of the bed and gently brushed Vida's hair back, careful not to touch any flesh. "Hey, Vida," she said softly.

There was no response except the steady beep of the heart monitor. Bel smiled down at the woman. "She came to my Loyola graduation," she told Salem. "You knew that, right? Her and my mom together, like an old married couple."

Fat tears rolled out of her eyes. She swiped at them. "I thought of her as my second mother. Good thing I have a spare, right? You're okay sharing?"

Salem matched Bel's tears. "I'm okay sharing. And you know what else? Someone wise once told me that as long as you and me have each other, we can do anything."

"That *does* sound smart," Bel said, sniffling. "What superintelligent person said that again?"

Salem smiled sadly and leaned over to kiss the one visibly unscathed spot on her mother: her upper ear. When she pulled away, she gasped. "Bel, they cut off part of her lobe."

Bel nodded sadly, as if she'd expected that and more.

"Bel." Vida's voice was a breath more than a sound.

Bel and Salem exchanged a look laden with surprise and joy.

Bel leaned in. "I'm here. So is Salem. You're in the Lynchburg General Hospital in Virginia. You're safe. You don't have to say anything. You need to rest."

Vida's eyes twitched under her lids. Salem was wondering if she'd imagined the sound when Vida's eyes shot open. She jerked, then groaned. Her eyes fell shut. "You're both here. Both the girls."

"We are, Mom. And Bel's right. You need to rest. We'll stay by your side."

A tear leaked past Vida's eyelashes, rolled over her cheek, and was absorbed by a white bandage. "You can't." She cleared her throat, but her voice didn't grow any stronger. "Gracie is dead."

Bel made a sound, a cross between a whimper and a cough. "We know."

Vida blinked her eyes open again. It seemed to take a great effort to keep them that way. "Isabel, it was quick. She was scared, but she wasn't in pain."

Salem reached across her mom and clasped one of Bel's hands. She could read the agony in her friend's face, could see her trying to file it away but having no place to put it.

"Where's her body?"

A sigh rattled through Vida. "Minneapolis, I think. I don't know." She gazed at Salem. "You cut your hair, baby."

Salem touched her short curls. She'd forgotten. "Why didn't you tell us?" Her hand flew to her mouth. That's not what she'd intended to say.

Vida grimaced. "About the Underground? We hoped you'd never have to know. We trained you in case we were wrong."

Salem's emotions were oil and water, betrayal and love. "We had a right to know."

She caught the rest of the words before they left her lips—*Gracie didn't have to die.* If Salem and Bel had been told about this world, about their training, they could have used it to obtain the codes earlier. It hadn't had to happen like this.

Vida was painfully silent for a long moment, her eyes glistening. "Now you do."

Salem realized in that moment, on this critical issue, that she was wiser than her mother. The enormous sadness of that gagged her. She swallowed past it as best she could and held her mom's hand, mourning who they used to be.

"Did you get inside Beale's vault?"

Salem held up the scrolls. They hadn't left her person since Bel'd slammed the rock into the killer's brain stem.

Vida chuckled. It turned into a cough. "That's my girl. You need to fly to San Francisco and take them to Lu. She'll know what to do."

"We're not leaving you," Bel said.

"You are, and you're leaving now. Look at me. Both of you. Look at what's been cut off of me, pounded into me, sliced open on me. This is what they will do to Gina Hayes."

The women locked eyes over Vida.

"I don't know how the Hermitage intends to do it, just when and where: Alcatraz, tomorrow."

Salem felt like she was drowning. "But how can we stop it?"

Vida's eyes fell closed. Her skin had grown shiny and wet-looking. "Get those papers to Lu. You can't trust anyone but her. She has a plan. Go to her."

"Vida? Who gave you this information? Vida?"

Vida didn't answer Bel. Salem glanced at her monitors but couldn't read them. She ran into the hall calling urgently for a nurse. "My mom just passed out."

The nurse jogged into the room and checked the equipment. "She's stable." Her glance was admonishing. "You wore her out."

Bel glared at the nurse until she dropped her gaze. When she did, Bel said to her, "We won't bother her anymore. Give us a moment in here, please."

The nurse reluctantly stepped out of the room. Salem suspected she was looking for someone with the authority to kick them out.

Bel walked around the bed and looked Salem in the eye. "What do you want to do?"

Salem knew what the old version of her would have said: stay by her mom's side until she was well enough to fly back to Minneapolis, and then never leave the house again. "Exactly what my mom said. Take these papers to Lu and save Hayes."

Bel's lip twitched. "I can do it. You stay with Vida."

Salem turned back to her mom, leaning in close to her ear. "Hey, Mom. I know you can hear me. And I know you're in good hands here. If you could talk to me, you'd tell me to stay with Bel, right? Heck, you did with your text. *Follow the trail to the end, no matter what. Stick close to Bel.*"

"Salem." Bel sounded exasperated.

"We're not arguing," Salem said. "You call Lu. Tell her to get us plane tickets out. Have her send someone here to keep an eye on Mom. And then we go. We finish this together." She held up the scrolls.

Bel snorted in disbelief, then laughed, her face puffy from crying. "Why not? My schedule is clear. Why don't we topple a corrupt organization and save the next president of the United States?"

"Exactly," Salem said, kissing her mom's cheek again, lingering for a moment. "Time's wasting."

MONDAY

November 7

CHAPTER 93

San Francisco

The private jet touched down on the San Francisco International Airport's tarmac on schedule.

A car was waiting. The driver stepped out and leaned against the vehicle, arms crossed, fingers freakishly muscular.

The plane taxied to a stop, the wind generated by it ruffling the waiting driver's dark hair.

Within minutes, the jet's clamshell door opened with a pneumatic wheezing and the airstairs were lowered to the ground.

One of the Hermitage's air staff, a flight attendant in a crisp uniform, stepped out and moved to the side of the stairs. His smile was strained, his neck visibly bruised. He looked like he'd been crying.

Jason appeared at the top of the stairs. He stabbed the attendant as he walked past, a quick throat puncture with a replacement blade. He toppled over backward, hitting the tarmac at an awkward angle.

Geppetto laughed.

Jason walked down the steps and slid into the front passenger seat without a word.

Geppetto slid behind the wheel and drove the car to Pier 33. Gina Hayes was scheduled to speak in five hours. A special ferry was waiting to take the assassins to Alcatraz Island.

Jason's face was set as tight as sinew, reflecting his mood. The nature of his unique craniofacial structure had saved his life, the malleability of his bones absorbing rather than shattering beneath the rock's blow, though he had the mother of all headaches. When he didn't call ten minutes after arriving on the scene of the Beale vault, the backup crew had descended. He was revived. The vault was emptied of its treasure. The corpses of the two men Jason had killed were dumped into it. Same with the bodies of the two backwater cops who arrived, presumably sent by Wiley and Odegaard.

He didn't call her Isabel anymore.

The vault, now a tomb, had been resealed, reburied, and their tracks covered as much as possible. The blood remained, but a heavy rain would erase that. One member of the cleanup crew drove the police car several miles away and abandoned it before being driven back to headquarters by his partner. The subterfuge wouldn't last for long, or it would last forever. Jason didn't care either way. The Hermitage possessed the treasure.

They also had the Underground leadership docket, according to Barnaby. It had been downloaded into the Hermitage's computer banks. A new Underground harvest—the final one—would begin soon.

All that remained was to secure and destroy the documents the women had stolen from the vault and then to kill Hayes.

Jason had been disappointed to discover that much of Barnaby's fuss had been about a two-hundred-year-old land treaty. From what Jason knew of American history, he didn't see how Jackson's past indiscretions coming to light would be more than a quick-burning scandal, harmless to the Hermitage without Beale's treasure to finance a lengthy legal battle or Gina Hayes alive to underwrite an investigation.

Nevertheless, like a birthday piñata, all the remaining treats were wrapped in one tight package: Alcatraz. Wiley and Odegaard's plane from Richmond would be landing at SFO in seventeen minutes. They carried the authentic treaty. They would take it to the Golden Lucky, where they would be told to bring it directly to Gina Hayes in person.

Who else *could* they bring it to? FBI? NSA? Local police?

No. There'd be no way to know they weren't simply handing the document over to the Hermitage. The Underground possessed only one escape. It led them to Hayes, now outed as an ancestral Underground member thanks to Wiley's cracking of Beale's Cipher, and the one person with enough power and incentive to use the documents to redistribute much of the Hermitage's wealth back into its rightful hands.

The women would clean up at Golden Lucky and fret over how to sneak onto Alcatraz. The security would be ironclad. They'd find a way in—not so easily as to cause them suspicion but not so hard as to be impossible.

The Hermitage had made sure of it.

And then Jason would tie up every single loose end, all in one place.

Alcatraz was going to be one bloody party.

CHAPTER 94

Alcatraz

"You ready?"

San Francisco's famous fog had unfurled itself like a blanket. Sleet fell, and the air smelled like tidewater. Salem couldn't spot the bay from where they stood, but she could feel it, just on the other side of Pier 33, a big wet maw waiting to pull her down, and she could hear its crashing waves.

They stood a block away from the dungeon-like stone archway marking the pier. Salem knew the building had been a bomb factory in WWII, and that's exactly what it looked like. She did her best to ignore the smell of the sea, and the briny scent of boiling Dungeness crab just up the pier, and the angry honk of sea lions, all of it warning her of the ocean. The three of them did their best to blend in with the masses jostling for a photograph of Senator Hayes.

"No cold feet now!" Lu said, cackling. "You won't believe who I had to blow to get those press passes."

She pointed at the IDs that hung around Salem's and Bel's necks, the photos expertly glued on to match both women's modified appearances. In fact, Bel was no longer even female. Her laminated press pass read John Shaw, and she wore a dark-brown mustache to match her hair along with round, wire-rimmed glasses. With colored contacts and expertly applied eye makeup, Salem passed for Asian, her head covered with a sleek black pageboy wig. Her press pass read Elizabeth Cho.

The documents they'd obtained in Beale's vault were tucked in a leather messenger bag that Salem carried crossways. The knives they'd taken off the killer in Virginia had been mailed along with an anonymous note to Agent Lucan Stone. Lu, who'd been almost as excited to see the locket as she'd been to see the treaty and code, had packed the necklace carefully away. She'd immediately sent a security detail to guard Vida in the hospital.

"For real," Lu said, her laughter melting. "You don't look so good."

"She's afraid of water." Bel was using the gravelly voice she'd practiced. "At least old Salem was. New Salem isn't afraid of anything." She smiled reassuringly.

"I might have nightmares about that mustache." Salem raised an eyebrow, trying for humor. Her stomach felt sour, though, the earth shifty-slidy under her feet. After not leaving Minnesota for twenty-six years, she'd now traveled cross-country three times in a single week. Despite that, she couldn't think of the ocean on the other side of the archway without going jelly from the neck down.

Bel squeezed her shoulder. "You're going to be okay. Look at how much we've survived. Hell, look at how we've *thrived*. My mom and yours did a good job training us."

Bel's proud smile unnerved Salem. "How can you look so happy? Mom and Grace threw us to the wolves."

They'd already had a version of this talk during the airplane ride. Bel's perspective was completely opposite of Salem's. Bel had found her calling and was grateful to their moms for that. "We're part of something important now, Salem. And we're good at it. I get that you're mad at Vida, but you have to get over it. There's no going back and changing it."

Salem dropped her eyes. Strong, street-smart Bel felt like she'd been handed a gift. She couldn't understand Salem's feeling of betrayal. Salem stared in the direction of the water. Hundreds of people stood between it and her, but she could *feel* its pulse.

"No time for fear," Lu said, studying her, her voice grim. "Your dad never let fear get him."

A laugh shocked Salem. She pulled her attention back to Lu. "He killed himself. I'd say that's something like fear."

Lu's eyes grew comically round. "Daniel Wiley didn't kill himself. He was murdered!"

Every lick of moisture in Salem dried up. "I was there. He killed himself."

Lu turned her around, toward the pier, and patted her on the back. "Your mom let you believe that to protect you."

CHAPTER 95

Twelve Years Old
Daniel's Last Hour

It's a perfect summer day. The sun beats its cat-stretch heat on Salem's shoulders, cascading golden down her lean, twelve-year-old body, weaving around her thighs, warming the sand between her toes. Her ringlets are tied up, but the wildest ones break free. They frame her face, each curl dizzy with twists from the aggressive humidity.

Vida is filling in for a colleague, and it is fair and even that Daniel has brought Salem to the beach this day because when she was five years old, Vida brought her to the lake without Daniel.

Salem is wearing her rainbow bikini for the first time, and she gets to wear it without her mother's judging eye. Its colors are electric. She doesn't have much to fill out the top, but running her hands over her sun-warmed tummy, she knows it's flat like it's supposed to be. The stomach flu three days ago helped. The strings of the bikini bottom play along her curved thighs. When her top half catches up with her bottom, she'll really be something in this swimsuit. She realizes she's been alone on the beach for a while. This lake cabin thirty miles north of Minneapolis belongs to the Galvins, friends of her parents. They let the Wileys use it when they aren't. Today is one of those days. Maybe Daniel is inside making lunch?

Salem returns to her book, a thin volume her mother has checked out for her from the library, Helen Fouché Gaines's Cryptanalysis. *The book is sixty years old, the text cramped, but it captivates Salem's hummingbird mind. When she next looks up, the sun has moved enough for her to adjust her towel so she doesn't tan unevenly.*

But there's her dad! He must have been in the cabin. His back is to her.

He's wading into the lake. She calls for him, but he doesn't turn. It's hot, he must be cooling off. She returns to the words, but something on the edge of her gaze catches her attention. It's a person.

Isn't it?

She slides her apple-shaped bookmark between the pages and sets down her paperback, craning her neck. She's sure she heard somebody, or had she seen them? She wants to ask her dad about it, but he's out too far. In fact, she can't even see his head.

Standing, she begins to walk toward the cabin. Maybe Vida got done early and decided to join them. Salem is at the edge of the cabin. She can almost see who's around the corner.

She takes the final steps toward the person, the air molecules straining to hold her back.

She feels their snap like spiderwebs against her skin. Still, she keeps walking.

CHAPTER 96

Alcatraz

Salem scowled. Lu didn't know what she was talking about. Daniel Wiley had definitely killed himself. Lu hadn't been there, and Salem didn't want to go back to the memory, not now, not ever.

"Salem?" Worry lined Bel's eyes. "Time to go."

Salem breathed deeply and nodded. She'd give her left leg for an Ativan right now. "I'm ready."

They threaded the crowd, separating to pass through security. Salem navigated a metal detector, was patted down, emptied her pockets and her purse, and handed over her messenger bag.

A female SFPD police officer held up the scroll of papers. "What are these?"

Salem felt the cold squeeze of fear. This was the first of many junctures at which their plan could go off the rails. "Historical land deeds."

Lu had scanned them back at Golden Lucky, but Salem had been sent with the originals. Without them, and the scientific examination needed to verify their accuracy, the Underground had nothing. "They were written by the same stenographer who wrote some of the documents stored on Alcatraz. I'm hoping to match them up. You know, the signatures."

"This isn't a field trip." The officer looked away from Salem to call over one of her colleagues.

Sweat dripped down Salem's spine. "I'm an amateur historian."

Both officers stared at her before spreading out the papers. They examined them front and back and uncovered nothing. Still, they didn't like it. The female officer was about to call a third officer over when Salem interrupted her.

"It's okay," she said. "I don't need to bring them. I can leave them with you and pick them up after the speech. My boss would fire me if I didn't make it to the island on time." Could they hear her words over the thundercrack of her own heartbeat?

The line behind Salem shifted, the herd antsy.

The female officer glanced from Salem back to the papers and then to the crowd. She made up her mind, re-rolling the documents and handing them to Salem before sliding her messenger bag to her. "Don't give anyone paper cuts." She turned away, not waiting for a response, and began searching the man behind Salem.

Salem nodded, grabbed her bag and the papers, and scurried away. Her relief was so great that she forgot about the ocean, at least for a moment.

But then it came into sight.

The ferry, perched on the bay, riding the lip of the sea's dark, angry mouth.

Salem hadn't been able to conquer her fear of water to save her own father.

Her phobia was too big. She'd been fooling herself. She couldn't do this.

She turned to leave. She felt infinitesimal. Lilliputian. Worthless. Disappearing. There was no tomorrow. Only fear beating like an electric heart. She should have given the documents to Bel. Who was she kidding? She never even should have left Minneapolis. Everything she'd ever done was wrong. All of it. Even being born. She needed to—

"Hey, you're going the wrong direction."

Salem brushed at her face. Agent Lucan Stone stood next to her. She almost said his name, but then she remembered her disguise. He might not even recognize her.

He didn't smile. He took her by the elbow, turned her around, and began leading her up the gangplank.

Her skin prickled. "I'm afraid of water."

"I don't intend to swim. Do you?"

She tried to twist away, but he slid his arm around her waist. She closed her eyes and didn't open them again until they were in the center of the boat, surrounded by the busy chatter of the press and the few lucky civilians who were allowed at the speech. Was the ferry bobbing under her? She could pretend it wasn't.

Stone was staring at her. She blinked, hiding the side of her face with her hand.

"I like the hair," he said. "And thank you for the package."

Of course he recognized her. Her disguise was intended to fool anyone who'd seen her mug shot on the evening news, not someone who actually knew her. "What are you doing here?"

He nodded in the direction of Alcatraz, which she thankfully couldn't see from the center of the ferry. "I've been reassigned to Hayes. Seems there's a connection between the serial killer and her. Anything you want to tell me about?"

Salem shook her head.

"I didn't think so. In a more specific answer to your question, I saw you go through security. You can't enter a room without causing a fuss, can you?" Were his eyes twinkling? "I think I saw Ms. Odegaard as well. Or is she Mr. Odegaard now?"

"We're not going to hurt anyone."

"That's true."

It was an odd reply. Her eyes flew to his face.

He was staring at her, studying her. "How long have you been afraid of water?"

She squeezed her eyes shut, then opened them. "My whole life."

He nodded, glancing over her shoulder. "You won't be able to get to Hayes, not with the security on the island. You have something to give her?"

Salem didn't answer. The ferry was taking off from the pier, a lurch of movement tossing her into Stone. He held her, as solid as his namesake.

"Give it to me," he said. "I'll see that she gets it."

"No!"

He watched her. "You don't trust me."

"Why would I?"

"I gave you thirty-six hours when I could have brought you in."

She squeezed the strap of the messenger bag. "So did the Hermitage. You don't think an organization that could set up a"—she glanced around at the active ears crowding the lower berth—"complex plan like the one for today couldn't have gotten at Bel and me anytime they wanted? No, they waited, using us to retrieve what they couldn't. You might not be working for them, but then again you might. We've done just fine without you, so if you don't mind . . ."

His expression was unreadable.

She turned to go, but there was nowhere to storm off to. Bel must be on this ferry somewhere, but to talk with her would blow her cover. Besides, water was out there. The best Salem could do was make her way to a nearby pole and grip it, the messenger bag pressed between her body and the metal. Fear flapped inside her like a vulture, but she circled her hands around its neck.

Stone didn't bother her again. When the boat heaved to a stop at Alcatraz Island, he was nowhere to be seen. Salem waited until most of the reporters had cleared out before following them off. Technically, she was now on land, but land visibly ringed by water, five-foot swells crashing against it.

It was nearly noon, but a person would have to look at a watch to know because the fog was so dense that it softened sound. The air was chilled, soupy and buoyed by a coldness that emanated from the crumbling gray rocks below. Salem swallowed, tucked her head, and made for the recreation yard on the northwest side of the island. That's where

Hayes was scheduled to speak. The helicopter parked atop the main cell house suggested that she was already on-site.

It was a steep switchback climb to the island's crest. The solid block of the cell house perched to Salem's right. To her left was a craggy rock face slipping straight into the hungry sea.

She kept a steady stream of people between her and the water.

"Salem!"

She turned toward the man's voice. Recognition stopped her in her tracks, confusion overpowering the fear. It wasn't Agent Stone.

"Connor?"

Her booty call lover's face lit up, as broad and handsome as she remembered.

CHAPTER 97

Alcatraz

Salem's unstable world rocked further to the right. The last time she'd seen Connor Sawyer was exactly one week ago, when he'd scared her so badly that she'd peed her pants. He hadn't crossed her mind since Bel had shared her opinion of him back at the Minneapolis airport.

If we get through this, you and me, next time you see that Connor dude, you flush him like the turd he is.

Here the turd stood, stupidly, blondly handsome, embraced by fog, streams of reporters splitting around him as if he were a rock in a river.

"What are you doing here?" Salem asked.

"Bel called me." He stepped closer.

The thickness of the mist carpeted her eyes and ears but heightened her other senses. "What?"

"Bel said you'd be here, that I should come and save you from yourself. She promised she'd take care of everything else."

Salem heard the words, understood each of their meanings individually, but couldn't combine them to make a larger story. They were square thoughts trying to breach the circle of her mind. "Bel would never do that. She'd never betray me."

"She said you'd say that." His voice sounded like he was smiling, but her disorientation had turned his head into a shadowy black thumbprint on top of his neck. "Come here, and I'll tell you what else she said."

He grabbed her wrist, pulled her to his chest. A stranger would think they were hugging. He tipped his mouth to her ear, his lips brushing the tender curve of her lobe. "I liked your hair better long."

She felt the sharpest kiss in the palm of her hand. She swatted at it and glanced down.

He held a glistening needle. "I'm sorry, Lemming. They paid me so much."

He began leading her toward the rocky edge, a rudimentary plastic fence the only barrier between Salem and the bottomless sea. She heard it roar and sing. The water had been hungry for her for years. She knew she should fight, but her brain was separating from its mooring in a way that made her care about nothing. Her bones seemed to be floating free.

A man walking by stopped. "Is she all right?"

"Seasick from the ferry." Connor flashed his best law-school grin. "She just needs to get her bearings. We'll be fine! You don't want to miss the speech."

The man walked away.

Salem tried to open her mouth, to ask for help, but she was too spongy. Connor threw her arm over his neck and his hand around her waist, steering her away from the steepest part of the ledge, checking over his shoulder before ducking under a rope and stumbling down a steep embankment.

They were out of sight of the crowds, on a tiny chunk of the island that hadn't been used in decades, its paths crumbling.

Connor reached a tilting utility shed and led her behind it, the building shielding them from the casual view of anyone who peered over the ledge. The shed blocked the wind, and the smell of brine and damp was overpowering. They stood on a table-size lip that gave way to a steep, craggy pile of rocks and vines dropping sharply into the agitated sea.

"I think I need that messenger bag," Connor said, setting her on a rock abutting the utility shed. He tried to lift it over her head. "Let go of it."

She glanced down. She was indeed holding the bag with both hands. He tried to pry her fingers loose. He couldn't.

"Let it go. You don't want to make a scene, do you?"

Surprisingly, she found that she did.

She loosed one hand from the strap, and with a remote, scientific accuracy, she grabbed Connor's balls and twisted. He fell forward, and still she didn't let go. When the effort of holding his testicles above his body became too much, she dropped him.

She stood. Her legs were shaky, but she was going to get to the speech. She was going to hand the bag to Hayes before the poison rocketing through her veins reached her heart. Her only hope was that she'd pushed the needle away fast enough that she hadn't received a full dose, that she'd bought herself enough life to complete her mission. She began float-walking back toward the main path, stumbling over the loose gravel, tripping on the vining plants. Behind her, Connor charged to his feet.

He lunged at her and pushed her over the side, toward the angry sea. She screamed as she fell, reaching out for any purchase. Her hands found an ancient metal cord screwed into the slippery rock face above an eroding path no wider than her feet. She scrabbled for the cable, its rust and fray piercing the palm of her left hand. Warm blood coursed down her wrist, but she didn't let go. She couldn't. The ocean would have her.

She squeezed past the pain and pulled herself up, arms quivering, until her feet found what was left of the rock path.

Connor Sawyer's head appeared above her. She was just beyond his reach. His head disappeared and was replaced by his legs.

He was dropping himself toward the ledge on which she stood. "Ready or not, here I come," he grunted.

CHAPTER 98

Alcatraz

Jason was putting the final touches on the banquet table.

"Melissa!"

He glanced over his shoulder. The head of catering was staring at him. He pitched his voice high. "Yes?"

"Make sure her chamomile tea is hot," the woman said. "They said she'll want it piping, and she needs it now, before she starts speaking."

Jason nodded. "You got it."

A screech of feedback outside the white catering tent indicated Hayes was just about to begin. Everything was happening exactly on schedule, following to the letter the plan that had been put into place one year earlier. Geppetto would have retrieved his gun from underneath the toilet bowl of the third stall in the men's room, where it had been taped. The gun had never been fired, the bullets specially constructed so they carried no scent. The dogs that had swept the island would not have discovered it.

Clancy Johnson would be in position.

The killers were three deep. If one failed, the next would step up. Gina Hayes's life was no longer hers.

Jason was the first string on the three-man killing team.

He began to prepare Senator Hayes's tea. With specially gloved hands, he dabbed the Polonium-210, a radioactive poison 250,000 times stronger than cyanide, into three of the teacups. It would be a gruesome death drawn out over several days as Hayes was poisoned from the inside out, her organs failing, skin splitting and weeping, her hair shedding in clumps, vomiting when she wasn't shitting her brains out. The poison was a favorite of assassins as it was undetectable, easy to smuggle, untreatable, and didn't begin working until well after the killer had left the scene.

The ensuing chaos, particularly if Gina Hayes was elected president tomorrow, would turn the country, if not the world, upside down.

Chaos was the ripest soil for the Hermitage's seed.

Finally, Jason would be good enough.

CHAPTER 99

Alcatraz

If Connor reached her, he would toss her into the sea. If she let go, she would fall in without his help. She had no choice but to climb parallel to the water away from Connor, following the metal cord, her life a sputtering flame poised over the churning ocean.

She closed her eyes and put one hand over the other, her feet searching for purchase, moving as quickly as she could, which wasn't fast at all. The trauma was comfortable, almost, in its familiarity.

Water. Death.

Shock unlocked shock.

Salem was defenseless as the full memory finally, horrifically, washed over her.

She is onshore, twelve years old and wearing her first bikini, so proud of its rainbow colors, of her flat belly, of the way the shadow of her hips curves on the movie screen of the dirty brown beach.

Her dad has gone into the water. She hears a sound by the cabin. She goes to check. When she looks back at the water, her dad is gone, has been underwater far too long, but she's too scared to save him, to even scream for help.

"No!" She is startled by her own yell. It forces her eyes open.

Connor is maybe five feet behind her. Another twenty feet in the other direction is a doorway cut into the high wall of the Alcatraz recreation yard, from back when there was a stone deck on the other side, before the sea had eaten the rock.

Salem closes her eyes again. The drug Connor injected her with has turned her upside down, stealing her focus and her will. Her attention begins to narrow.

No.

Because it didn't happen that way.

Salem is onshore, twelve years old and wearing her first bikini, so proud of its rainbow colors, of her flat belly, of the way the shadow of her hips curves on the movie screen of the dirty brown beach.

Her dad walks into the water. She hears something and puts down her book to walk to the cabin, thinking it might be Vida.

There's someone in the shadows.

It's the fat-fingered man, the one who picked up the delivery three days earlier. He's come back for Salem. Somehow, she's led him on. That's why he's here, to see her in a swimsuit. Vida was right, she never should have worn one. She feels her blood drain from her.

She is paralyzed by fear. She looks toward the lake. Her dad has disappeared. The water has eaten him. If she goes in, it'll eat her, too. She moans.

The fat-fingered man reaches for her.

She runs toward the lake. Nothing is more important to her than her dad.

She hits an invisible wall, landing on her back. She feels heat slide down her cheek. She can't move.

When she opens her eyes again, the sun has shifted. Her cheek is throbbing. It'll take five stitches to close that wound. Police guess she fainted and split her face when she hit the ground.

She didn't. Someone had sliced her.

She hadn't just watched her dad die. She'd tried to save him.

She had backfilled the details of her father's death because of shock and shame: shame because she'd believed she was the reason the fat-fingered man had come to the lake, because she'd been told she fainted rather than save her dad, that she'd lain on her back while he died.

But that wasn't how it happened.

The realization dropped chains from her neck.

Her eyes shot open again. She tasted salt water on her lips. Connor had closed the distance between them. He was reaching for her, his hand scant inches from hers. Slippery blood ran down her wrists from her death grip on the fraying threads of the wire, but she was faring better than Connor, who kept skidding off the slick rock. Salem's size and her lower center of gravity were an advantage, but barely. She knew she had to move, but whatever Connor had injected her with was turning her legs to mush.

The hungry ocean foamed below, a wet black tongue licking salaciously at sharp sandstone teeth.

Connor gripped her wrist.

His hand was cold. Their eyes met.

She could read his intentions as clearly as if he'd shouted them. He planned to fling her into the ocean.

Salem tightened the grip of her other hand around the frayed cable.

The pain of metal gouging her flesh pierced the poisoned fog clouding her brain and galvanized her to action.

In a move she'd learned in Krav Maga, she twisted her hand under his, slamming the knife edge of her hand into the weak part of his grip. She'd seen Bel perform it successfully on Ernest, twice.

It worked. Her hand was free.

Connor's eyes widened, and they stayed wide because she didn't stop there. She flung out her leg and kicked him with everything she had, her strong, thick thigh powering the heel of her foot as it slammed into his stomach. He grabbed for the cable as he stumbled backward, but his grasping fingers missed and he tumbled over the ledge.

She didn't watch him fall, but she heard the wet *thud* before the ocean swallowed his screams and his body.

There wasn't time to feel or to catch her breath. She had to keep moving. The doorway through the stone was just ahead. She was near enough to see the catering table on the other side of the doorless frame, its top covered by a smooth white tablecloth, everything so normal and just out of reach.

If she could beg one final request from her body, one last hurrah before her system shut down, she could propel herself through that doorway.

She got to her feet and took another step on the crumbling ledge, focusing on the opening ahead and the slippery shelf beneath her feet, poising to jump. She could do this. She *had* to do this.

Her legs threatened to collapse beneath her, but somehow she forced them to flex. Her left foot slid out from under. She fell heavily to one knee, saving herself from going over the narrow lip of rock by her grip on the cable. But when she tried to pull herself back to her feet, her knees wouldn't cooperate. She hadn't the strength to get herself off the ledge.

She was so close, yet she was going to fail.

Movement through the doorway in the rock snagged her eye. A woman was dressed in a white cooking frock and matching cap. One of the caterers, perhaps? She held a glass vial and was dropping liquid into the teacups.

Salem opened her mouth to yell for help. She stopped.

She'd seen those eyes in Massachusetts, outside the First Church and then in the face of the woman wearing the black blazer inside the Hawthorne Hotel lobby. The same snake eyes had gazed at her from the face of the man who'd grabbed her outside the Dolores Mission, and rested in the face of the beautiful man who'd held a knife at her neck at Beale's vault.

They all belonged to the same person.

This person, this creature, could change the shape of his face. And he intended to poison Senator Gina Hayes.

The man glanced up as if he'd heard Salem's realization. His hand shot into the vest of his catering uniform. He pulled out a knife.

Of course. A weapon that would not raise alarms if transported by a caterer.

You could sneak in anywhere in a caterer's outfit.

Anger gave Salem the strength she needed to launch herself to her feet and through the doorway, toward him.

She was inside the catering tent, on firm footing, but still her legs were jelly. The fake caterer strode toward her with deadly intent, knife in hand. But Salem's sudden appearance drew the attention of several men in suits, who were also rushing toward her. Was that Agent Stone?

Time suspended itself.

Through the opening of the tent twenty feet in front of her, Salem spotted Senator Gina Hayes, her back straight and strong. If Salem yelled, she could get the senator's attention. She opened her mouth, but only a croak came out.

On the other side of Hayes, facing Salem's direction, in the very front row, Bel stared up at the senator, her face tight beneath her disguise.

Security ran toward Hayes, intent on pulling her offstage into the safety of the tent. Before they could reach her, a shot screamed out, the sound echoing off the stone, even as Bel leaped in front of Hayes.

More gunshots cried in the sunshine as Bel fell to the ground, her limbs folding in on themselves like a broken doll's.

The last thing Salem saw before she was buried beneath the suits of men was a perfect rose blossoming on Bel's back.

CHAPTER 100

Alcatraz

Clancy Johnson's heart was beating hard enough to shred his wrists. He was backup, the third man. With any luck, he should have been able to walk away from this. Since when does the *third string* get in the big game?

Christ on a cracker. He ran shaking hands through his hair. The smell of gunpowder coated his nostrils. One ear was ringing from the shots.

Hayes was supposed to drink the poison. She takes the tea, she drinks it, she feels like shit, dead in a week.

Bingo.

Except Jason never came out with the tea. In fact, the opposite had happened. The Secret Service went *into* the tent. Not the best way for this to go down, but they still had the number-two guy. Cue Geppetto, whose job was to shoot Hayes between the eyes if, for any reason, she appeared as though she was not going to make her speech.

Messy, but effective. In fact, one of the most popular methods of assassination.

Isabel Odegaard jumping in front of Geppetto's bullet was not part of the plan.

Clancy'd watched her body swallow the hot metal, and goddamn, just like that, he was called in. The goddamned Super Bowl of assassination and they'd called in the third string.

He took aim at Hayes, but it was too late. Odegaard's sacrifice had cost him a clear shot.

He could still take out Geppetto, as ordered. He was surprised how many bullets it took to get the man to lie still.

The Hermitage would not like this.

Ever a practical man, Clancy began to plan how to spin this clusterfuck so he could walk away.

He didn't care anymore about being rich. He just wanted another day aboveground.

CHAPTER 101

3 East 70th Street, New York

Ring.

Carl Barnaby glanced from his computer screen to the phone.

Ring.

His European counterpart was calling.

Surely the man was watching the same live Alcatraz broadcast as Carl. A very much alive Senator Gina Hayes was being helicoptered away along with the body of an unidentified woman who had taken a bullet for the senator. There was one confirmed casualty, the shooter, initial reports suggesting he was taken down by an FBI agent. Another woman was in custody inside the catering tent, her role in the shooting unclear.

A world-class shitshow from all angles.

Ring.

Carl silenced the incoming call and pressed the intercom button. "Abhay?"

The background noise on the other end nearly overpowered Abhay's voice—men yelling, computer keys clacking, paper shredding. "We are watching it, too, sir."

"Initiate Pink Washing. Now."

He stood up from his $200,000 custom-made Parnian desk and strolled to pour three fingers of A.H. Hirsch Reserve bourbon into a Baccarat tumbler. He dropped in a single ice cube. The Hermitage

Foundation's files were all backed up on a remote untrackable server, of course. And the chances of the FBI obtaining a warrant to come in here were slim to none. If they beat those odds, they'd discover nothing on the headquarter computers, no trace of wrongdoing, if they even discovered the comm center two floors below.

The Hermitage would lose nothing but time.

Carl could live with that. He was playing the long game, his brain already working angles to get at Senator Hayes, who would almost certainly be *President* Hayes this time tomorrow. The Hermitage would lose millions in the interim. People might look at what Hayes accomplished and get ideas of their own. Carl had already seen a shift during her campaign, women pushing back against restrictions they'd always accepted as fact.

Yet the Hermitage would survive.

They had for two millennia, in one form or another.

Carl rattled the cube in his glass and chuckled. Survive? Hell, they'd flourish. Making silk purses from sows' ears was Carl's specialty.

It was how he'd made his fortune.

He inhaled the rich caramel of the liquor and took a swallow, letting the golden heat slide down his throat. Reaching for a remote, he clicked on music. Classical. Stravinsky. He closed his eyes and swayed, picturing his grandson. Tomorrow, he'd take the boy to the park.

An irritating reflection pulled him out of his reverie. Red and blue lights flashed outside his expansive window overlooking Central Park. It was a rare but not unheard of sight in this tony neighborhood. When they passed, they always passed quickly.

Not this time.

In fact, they were accumulating, their sirens screaming. The pounding on the door came next.

A greasy unease settled in Carl's stomach. He set down his glass.

When his butler ran into his office moments later, the sweat had begun to pool along Carl's low back, accumulating on a ridge of fat disguised by his well-tailored suits.

Yet his face remained smooth. *Silk purses from sows' ears.*

"Mr. Barnaby . . ."

The butler didn't have time to finish his sentence. The lead FBI agent, at least that's who Carl assumed she was, pushed past him, three of New York's finest at her heels.

"We have a warrant to search the premises, Mr. Barnaby."

"May I ask what you're looking for?" His voice was cool.

She strode forward and flashed the paperwork. "A cell where you held a kidnapped and tortured woman, and approximately $60 million worth of pre–Civil War gold and jewels, if you can believe it."

Was she smirking?

She tucked the warrant back inside her coat, the movement exposing her gun for the smallest moment. "You won't mind that we brought a specialist to run your elevator or a forensics team to sweep the cell, will you? Our victim gave us very clear instructions on where to look and what we should expect to find."

Carl's sweat pool gave way.

Liquid coursed between his cheeks and down his legs.

MONDAY

November 21

CHAPTER 102

San Francisco

Salem's chair was pulled tight to the hospital bed, her hand clasped round Bel's, her head resting on the blanket. She'd been in this position, more or less, for two weeks, stealing sleep, choking down hospital food when the nurses insisted, showering in Bel's bathroom when her own stink became too much.

In this moment, she wasn't so much sleeping as mourning with her eyes closed.

She felt it before she saw it.

Movement.

Her head shot up. "Bellie?"

Bel blinked. She tipped her head to the left, facing a wall of flowers and balloons. She creaked it to the right. More balloons, flowers, and stuffed animals stacked to the ceiling.

"Hey." Bel's voice was hoarse. "Where am I?"

Hot, salty tears coursed down Salem's face. She pushed back Bel's short hair, her hands trembling. "San Francisco General. You, my friend, have just woken up from a coma."

Bel lifted an arm, studied it as if it were a log, dropped it. She did the same with the other, both of them stuck with needles and tubes. She paused. The room was still. She finally spoke. "My legs don't work."

Salem had prepared for this conversation every waking moment for the last two weeks. Now that the time was finally here, all she could do was wrap her arms around Bel and cry with her.

A nurse entered the room, clipboard in hand. Her mouth was open to speak when she saw Bel awake. "Oh my god." She rushed out.

Bel released Salem and let her eyes fall closed. "Tell me what I've missed. What happened to the Hermitage?"

Salem kept a firm grip on Bel's hand. "Carl Barnaby, the CEO, was arrested two weeks ago. You sure you want to hear all this?"

Bel opened her eyes long enough to glare.

It was the most beautiful thing Salem had ever seen.

"The FBI went to Mom's hospital room in Virginia before we got to Alcatraz. She told them that she'd been kept in the Hermitage headquarters. It was enough to obtain a search warrant. The agents who went in located the cell she'd been kept in. It had been scoured clean with bleach, but the agent in charge found a single hair clinging to a wall. DNA testing verified it was Mom's. And thanks to some code-breaking help from Lu's staff, they also discovered a hidden room containing $74 million worth of gold and jewels."

Salem swiped at her hair. "Agent Stone got the treaty to Hayes, who was elected in a landslide the day after Alcatraz. Hayes had the treaty carbon-dated and verified, and fed the story to the media. My favorite headline came from the *New York Times*: '*Hermitage Foundation Built on Trail of Tears.*'

"Between the bad press from the treaty, the evidence of kidnapping, and the stolen treasure, people couldn't distance themselves fast enough from the foundation. Politicians, religious leaders, Fortune 500 CEOs, investors."

Bel's lip quirked. Her color was coming back. "How's your mom?"

Salem swallowed. Vida still wore bandages and bruises, but most of her wounds had healed, at least the visible ones. Salem had hugged her mom tight when she arrived at the San Francisco hospital via a side trip to Minneapolis, a week after Bel had been admitted. Salem was happy her mom was alive, but she was also aware that the distance between them had settled into something permanent.

At the end of the day, it wasn't even due to the sense of betrayal Salem felt because Vida, Daniel, and Gracie had secretly trained her and Bel for this world.

It was because her mother had let her believe that her father had killed himself.

After they'd ended the hug at the San Francisco hospital, Vida had handed Salem a book of Emily Dickinson's poems. "I got it from home."

Home.

Salem wondered what that even meant anymore. She had stared at the book. An envelope was sticking out of it, marking the poem "Tell all the truth but tell it slant." Inside the envelope was a handwritten note from Daniel Wiley.

> Dearest Salem,
>
> I'm writing this note because I fear the Hermitage has discovered my betrayal and will not let me live much longer. Grace and Vida won't stop your training or their work—they can't, there's too much at stake—but our hope is that they can protect you and Isabel from knowing about and subsequently being called into the web. If you're reading this, that means that they couldn't. I love you more than the moon and earth, Bits. Everything I did, I did for you.
>
> You're stronger than you know.
>
> —Dad

Reading the note knocked the wind out of Salem. Everything had been a lie—when her parents had met, how her father had died, what kind of people they were. She cried, mourning the loss of her father all over again, except this time it was his real death. She had to do it at Bel's bedside, not sure if her best friend would ever wake up again.

You'll understand one day, was all her mother had said before leaving to help Lu.

"She'll be okay, I think." Salem wiped away the fresh tears.

Bel tried to get herself on her elbows. "What happened to *you* on the island?"

Salem drew a ragged breath. She'd played the scene out in her mind every day since. "Connor was there. The Hermitage had sent him to give me a sedative, I guess, and then toss me over the side. I got away from him and made my way into the back of the catering tent, where I saw that creep putting poison into teacups."

Salem blinked a few times to clear her vision. "I also saw you get shot."

Bel closed her eyes. "Whose bullet did I take?"

"The fat-fingered man who dislocated your shoulder outside the mission. The same man who forced my dad to take sleeping pills and walk into a lake. His ID was a dead end. Secret Service has knocked a lot of heads, but no one will tell how he got on the island or where he got his gun. His first bullet missed its mark. You took the second one."

Bel's cheek twitched.

"You were in surgery for seven hours." Salem's voice was husky. "The doctors say you're lucky to be alive."

"What happened to him after he got off the second bullet?"

"Agent Clancy Johnson—the Ed Harris guy—shot him. The headlines called him a hero, second only to you in his fast-acting courage. He didn't do any interviews, though. Agent Stone said he took an early retirement."

"You still haven't told me what happened to you," Bel said.

Salem sighed. "I woke up here, under guard. Thanks to Agent Stone, I was reclassified from attempted assassin to victim, which meant I could talk the agents into checking the teacups. They found traces of Polonium-201 in three of them. They didn't catch the man who put it in there."

Bel pulled Salem down into her arms and held her tight. For the first time in two weeks, Salem felt safe.

The doctor walked in minutes later, a huge smile on his face. "Isabel Odegaard, you're something of a miracle."

A rumble like a train sounded outside.

"What is that?" Bel asked, not releasing Salem.

"Your people." The doctor walked to the wall-mounted television set and powered it on, tuning the channel to CNN. The lead story was a crowd of people outside a hospital. *This* hospital. "The world has been praying for the woman who saved the first female president of the United States of America. They've just been informed that you're awake."

The ticker tape banner across the bottom of the screen confirmed his words. The chanting outside turned to a roar that echoed back against itself. Bel let go of Salem's arms but kept a hold of her hand.

The doctor strode over to feel the lymph nodes at Bel's neck. "You two ladies have become a media sensation with all of your skulduggery. You make quite the team."

Salem stroked Bel's beautiful cheek.

Connor's body floated ashore later that evening, nibbles of flesh removed by the sea. Salem still couldn't muster any feeling one way or another about that. She was sure that'd catch up with her.

And she knew she could handle it when it did.

With Bel at her side, she could handle anything the world served up.

EPILOGUE

Washington, DC

"She's amazing, right?" Matthew Clemens smiled in the direction of Gina Hayes, who stood near the entrance of the stage, speaking with two world leaders and Oprah. "Who else do you know who can run the free world in a taupe pantsuit?"

Salem smiled. In all the pomp of the inauguration ceremonies, Matthew seemed like the only real person she'd met. Even Gina Hayes, as welcoming as she'd been, had felt larger than life as she'd walked alongside Bel's wheelchair, escorting Vida, Salem, and Mercy to their prime seats on the inaugural stage.

The weeks after Bel was finally released from the San Francisco hospital had been a whirlwind of rehabilitation. Both Salem and Bel moved into Vida's house, Salem sharing her old bedroom with Mercy and Bel taking the first-floor bedroom, with Vida moving to the second floor.

Even though it was the dead of winter, volunteers traveled from all over Minnesota to build wheelchair ramps for the house, including installing a chair elevator on the stairs in case Bel needed to reach the second level.

Salem's whole world revolved around helping Bel heal. If she slowed down, she'd have to think about the chasm between her and Vida.

Only Bel understood.

Together, they went through Grace's belongings, including, it turned out, the locket they'd discovered on the killer outside Beale's vault. Lu had shipped it to Bel with a note of encouragement and love, as well as a box of fortune cookies. Bel never removed the locket, even to shower. Salem caught her mom staring at it almost as if it scared her, but she didn't ask and her mom didn't tell.

Salem and Bel attended Grace's funeral, side by side. Many of Bel's former colleagues on the Chicago PD, plus most of the Minneapolis PD, and even some Amherst officers attended in solidarity with Bel, their sister, whose record had been cleared in light of her heroics. Salem even thought she caught a glimpse of Agent Stone at the funeral, but when she walked in that direction, he was nowhere to be found.

Bel paid her emotional dues as her mother's coffin was dropped into the ground, weeping all the tears that she'd pushed down to keep herself and Salem alive. Salem cried, too. Everyone did.

They buried Ernest the next day, alongside Grace. Ernest's funeral was much leaner. Only Bel, Vida, Salem, Mercy, and Dr. Keller attended. Mercy clutched the Raggedy Ann doll Salem had bought her, and Salem held the child close, their tears freezing on their faces as the lavender-honey sunset celebrated Ernest's too-short life.

Christmas came and went. Salem didn't have time to think about the future because she needed to get through each day. That's when the invitation to Gina Hayes's inauguration arrived. Salem had fallen into a routine, caring for Bel and tutoring North Minneapolis kids. She'd been happy enough.

Or so she'd thought.

When they'd received the invitation, though, she'd realized she wanted her world to be much larger. The cross-country scavenger hunt had been dark, terrible, soul-crushing. It had also polished some steel in her that she hadn't known she possessed. She was no longer comfortable living in a small cage.

She was thrilled to discover that Bel felt the same way.

Which was how they found themselves in Washington, DC, on the chill morning of January 20.

"I can't ever thank you enough," Gina Hayes was saying to Bel.

Salem glanced out over the crowd of thousands, the front rows dominated by media. The stage itself held about a hundred chairs, all of them filled with famous actors, musicians, senators, representatives, and Supreme Court justices. It was surreal.

Hayes stopped at the seats closest to the podium and indicated that Mercy and Vida should sit in the second row, next to Matthew Clemens, and Salem should sit in the front next to an open spot cleared for Bel's wheelchair. "I wouldn't be standing here today without you, Isabel Odegaard."

Bel smiled and tipped her head.

With the eyes of the world watching, Hayes exchanged a glance with Vida. Something passed between them. Salem guessed the two women had known each other for many years, but she'd resigned herself to maybe never plumbing all her mom's secrets.

"Or you."

Salem started, realizing the president-elect was talking to her, and that Salem's surprised expression was being broadcast on TV screens and computers all across the world.

"You're welcome," she said automatically.

Up close, Hayes was impossibly solid and strong. Salem suddenly wanted to tell her all about Ernest, and even Ronald, to make sure the leader of the free world knew about the courageous men who'd also helped to get her here. Salem wanted Hayes to promise that there would be no more tragic sacrifices.

But Salem couldn't bring those words to her lips.

She did have one question that was burning her up inside, though, something that bullied its way to the surface even though she'd spent the last two months trying to tamp it down.

"Ma'am?" Hayes had already started toward the podium. She had to stop and turn. Salem continued, "Can I ask you something?"

"Of course." Hayes's tone was gracious, but her posture was strained. Billions of people were waiting for her.

"That code we found in Beale's vault with the true Jackson treaty. Did you see it?"

Hayes's eyes flicked over Salem's shoulder. Salem swiveled to see Agent Stone standing behind her, wearing a tuxedo. He was breathtaking. Bel's hand shot out to hold her steady. Stone stood a respectful distance away.

"I saw it." Some of Hayes's warmth was gone.

"What was it?"

Anger-resignation-amusement flitted across her face. "A onetime pad. You can ask your mother all about it." With that, Hayes walked away from them and into history.

Salem took her seat, Matthew behind her and Bel on the other side. Agent Stone followed Hayes to the podium and stood to her left and a few feet back.

"What's a onetime pad?" Bel asked as the pomp continued.

"It's an unbreakable code." Salem pulled her fitted jacket tighter. "Unless you have the key, which is a series of random letters written on one single sheet of paper, which is then ripped off the pad and destroyed after the code has been cracked by the recipient. Hence the name."

Salem turned back to Vida, whose eyes were glossy. "Why should I ask you about it?"

Most of Vida's wounds had healed, but her kidnapping had left her fragile. Still, Salem caught a glimpse of her mom's old mettle under the surface. "That code you found in the vault was a clue to the true history of the Hermitage, which goes back further than Andrew Jackson, over two thousand years."

Salem flashed back to Dickinson's note to them, the one they'd discovered in her grandparents' gravestone. *Mrs. Lucretia Mott was forced to hide the names of the leaders, the treasure of the people, and this: the Truth of the waltz the Dragon and the Underground had been dancing for 2,000 years.*

All along, Salem and Bel had assumed that the Jackson treaty was the lightning bolt that would take down the Hermitage. Maybe it wasn't. Maybe the true lightning bolt had been the code they'd discovered in the vault.

"That's all I know." Vida shaded her eyes against the January sun. "That's all anyone knows or ever will without the key."

Salem nodded thoughtfully and turned to face forward.

"You thinking about it?" Bel asked.

"What?"

"I know you still have the photo of the code that you took while we were in the vault. Are you thinking about trying to crack it?"

Salem shook her head. "If it's a onetime pad, there's no way. Not without the key."

Hayes was introduced. The crowd's roar rolled onto the stage like an army. Hayes waited until it quieted to begin talking. Her speech from the very beginning was compelling, moving, brazen in its honesty.

Salem bent her head toward Bel halfway through, no longer able to contain herself. "Hey, I knew he was easy on the eyes, but has Lucan Stone always been *that* sexy?"

Matthew Clemens cleared his throat in the row behind her. Salem prepared to be scolded. Instead, he leaned forward. "Always. At least as long as I've known him."

Bel nodded. "He's had the hots for you since the beginning, too."

Salem's brow furrowed. "How come I never noticed?"

Bel smiled. "Running for your life will do that."

They settled back into the speech. Hayes thanked Salem and Bel at one point. The audience, including those onstage, stood and applauded. Salem's cheeks grew hot. Then the speech moved on, as they always do. Bel leaned over near the end, about when Salem was finally getting caught up in the speech, and whispered out of the corner of her mouth. "How about when I'm walking again, we go after that one-pad code?"

Salem's smile started small, but it moved to encompass her face, and then her chest, and then everyone around her. Her wholehearted laughter was broadcast across the world. If anyone could accomplish the impossible, it was Bel.

"Deal."

They touched pointer finger to pointer finger and pinkie to pinkie before returning their attention to the inauguration of the president of the United States of America.

Author's Note

The historical events and figures in this novel are accurately portrayed. Specifically, the history of cryptography as presented is established fact, including Charles Babbage's and Alan Turing's contributions to the field, as is the history of the Salem Witch Trials and the origins of the Black Chamber. Same with the accounts of Artemisia Gentileschi, Emily Dickinson, Lucretia Mott, Andrew Jackson, and Thomas J. Beale. I fictionalized their intersection with the characters in this story.

The locations in the book and their history are also accurately described to the best of my ability: Minneapolis, Salem and the First Church (all four), Amherst and the Emily Dickinson Museum, San Francisco's Chinatown, Dolores Park and Dolores Mission in San Francisco, and Alcatraz Island. The Vigenère and Beale Ciphers are also real and a fascinating trip through history, if you have the time.

All other characters and organizations are works of fiction.

Also, for those interested in accessing more of Emily Dickinson's poetry, the body of the complete Dickinson poem in *Salem's Cipher* came from the 1890 edition of *Poems, First Series*, edited by Mabel Loomis Todd and T.W. Higginson.

Acknowledgments

Without the editorial guidance of my agent, Jill Marsal, this would have been a very different book, and not in a good way (not that you'd have known because nobody would have bought it). She's the best in the business, a great editor, able to clone herself so she can respond to emails at all hours of the day, and an all-round fantastic person. Thank you, Jill, for believing in my writing.

Mountains of gratitude to my first editing team of Jessica Morrell, Terri Bischoff, and Nicole Nugent, whose insight and guidance, like water on a gremlin, multiply the good in my writing. Thank you also to Kellie Osborne, who was on my second editing team and is such a gifted proofreader that I'm convinced she's magic. Thanks also to Karin Slaughter, Catriona McPherson, and Chelsea Cain, whose writing I studied to figure out how to balance plot and character. You three make it look easy. (It's not, so my gratitude is counterbalanced by general mistrust and resentment.)

Big, loving gratitude to the SuperFriends for coming to my rescue and telling me that I'm not, in fact, "a miserable fraud of a writer who should give up the dream and teach full-time even though that makes me cry." I might be paraphrasing. In any case, all four of you propped up my sad ego in the spring of 2015, read the first hundred pages of this book, and gave me novel-saving advice. Terri, Catriona, Jessie II, and Linda, I'm lucky to have friends like you. Same with you, Dana Fredsti. You're the best fight writer in the business, and your generous feedback tightened two crucial scenes in this book. Thank you, forever and always!

Tony Van Den Einde, thank you for the moiré idea as well as your research of the Gentileschi in the Uffizi. Johnny Shaw and Matthew Clemens, I'm sorry I'm so bad at coming up with names. Appearing in my books is a casualty of being my friend, I'm afraid. Thanks also to my Squad, Erica Ruth Neubauer, Shannon Baker, Susie Calkins, and Lori Rader-Day, who are simply the best. You too, Christine Hollermann. Cheers to many more research trips for us. And no acknowledgments would be complete without a shout-out to my two favorite people in the world, my beautiful babies, Zoë and Xander, who will always be my best work.

The characters in this book traveled a lot more in 2015 than I did, and so I needed to call on friends for authentic setting descriptions. Thanks to the following for their contributions: Aimee Hix, Jeanne Bielke-Rodenbiker, Heather Ash, Dru Ann Love, Rachel Caitlin Quick, Lisa Alber, Tammy Kaehler, Mary Alderete, Steve Binninger, Douglas Cronk, Missy Davis, Amy Patricia Meade, Corinne Hosfeld Smith, Vallen Queen, Maggie Daniel Caldwell, Kristin Anne, Julie Ann Candoli, Marilyn Buehrer, Dana Fredsti, Sarah Cotter Hogroian, Sharon Dwyer, Jessica Morrell, and Amber Foxx.

Mostly, thanks to you, the reader of this book. Without you, my dream would be a lot lonelier.

About the Author

Photo © 2018 CK Photography

Jess Lourey is the Amazon Charts bestselling author of *The Taken Ones*, *The Quarry Girls*, *Litani*, *Bloodline*, *Unspeakable Things*, *The Catalain Book of Secrets*, the Salem's Cipher thrillers, and the Murder by Month mysteries, among many other works, including short stories, young adult fiction, and nonfiction. Winner of the Anthony, Thriller, and Minnesota Book Awards, Jess is also an Edgar, Agatha, and Lefty Award–nominated author; TEDx presenter; *Psychology Today* blogger; and recipient of The Loft's Excellence in Teaching fellowship. Check out her TEDx Talk for the true story behind her debut novel, *May Day*. She lives in Minneapolis with a rotating batch of foster kittens (and occasional foster puppies, but those goobers are a lot of work). For more information, visit www.jessicalourey.com.